Translator's Acknowledgment

I am deeply indebted to my husband,
William Vennewitz, for his never-failing advice
and assistance in this translation.

LEILA VENNEWITZ

A global catastrophe can serve many purposes.
One of them is to provide an alibi when God asks:
And where were you, Adam?

"I was in the war."

Theodor Haecker,
Tag- und Nachtbücher,
March 31, 1940

I have known many adventures in my time: the
creation of postal routes, Sahara rebellions, South
America ... but war is not really an adventure at all, it
is only a substitute for adventure. ... War is a disease.
Like typhus.

Antoine de Saint-Exupéry,
Pilote de Guerre

AND WHERE WERE YOU, ADAM?

I

First came a face, large, yellow, tragic, moving past their lines; that was the general. The general looked tired. The face with puffy blue shadows under the malaria-yellow eyes, the slack, thin-lipped mouth of a man dogged by bad luck, moved hurriedly past the thousand men. The general started off at the right-hand corner of the dusty hollow square, looked sadly into each face, rounded the corners carelessly, with no dash or precision, and it was there for all to see: his chest bore plenty of medals, it sparkled with silver and gold, but his neck was empty, no decoration hung there. And although they knew that the Knight's Cross around a general's neck didn't mean a lot, it was discouraging to see him without even that much. That skinny yellow neck, unadorned, was a reminder of lost battles, bungled retreats, of rebukes, the unpleasant, scathing rebukes exchanged among senior officers, of sarcastic telephone conversations, transferred chiefs of staff, and a tired, elderly man who seemed without hope as he took off his tunic in the evening and, with his thin legs, his malaria-racked body, sat down on the edge of his bed to drink schnapps. Each of the three times three hundred and thirty-three men into whose faces he looked was aware of a strange feeling: sorrow, pity, fear, and a secret fury. Fury at this war, which had already gone on far too long, far too long for a general's neck to be still without its rightful decoration. The general raised his hand to his shabby cap—at least he saluted smartly—and on reaching the left-hand corner of the hollow square he made a somewhat brisker turn, walked to the middle of the open side, and stood still while the swarm of officers grouped itself around him, casually yet methodically; and it was embarrass-

3

ing to see him standing there, with no decoration around his neck, while the Knight's Crosses of others, lower in rank, could be seen sparkling in the sun.

For a moment it looked as if he were going to say something, but he merely touched his cap again in an abrupt salute and turned so unexpectedly on his heel that the startled swarm of officers stepped back to let him pass. And everyone watched the short, spare figure get into the car, the officers saluted once again, and a swirling white cloud of dust announced that the general was driving west, where the sun was already quite low on the horizon, not far from those flat white roofs over there where the front did not exist.

Then they marched, three times one hundred and eleven men, to another part of the city, southward, past cafés of scruffy elegance, past movie houses and churches, through slums where dogs and chickens lay dozing in doorways, with slatternly, pretty, white-breasted women leaning on windowsills, where from dirty taverns came the monotonous, strangely stirring sound of drinking men singing. Streetcars screeched by at reckless speed—and then they came to a district where all was quiet. Here were villas surrounded by green gardens, army vehicles stood parked in front of stone gateways, and they marched through one of these stone gateways, entered meticulously tended grounds, and once again formed a hollow square, a smaller one this time, three times one hundred and eleven men.

Their packs were set down behind them, in rows, rifles were stacked, and when the men were standing at attention again, tired and hungry, thirsty, fuming and fed up with this damned war, when they were standing at attention again a thin, aristocratic face moved past their lines: that was the colonel, pale, hard-eyed, with tight lips and a long nose. They all took it for granted that the collar under this face should be adorned with the Knight's Cross. But this face was not to their liking either. The colonel took the corners at right angles, with a slow, firm tread, without omitting a single pair of eyes, and when he finally swung into the open side, a few officers in his wake, they all knew he was about to say something, and they all had the same thought, how thirsty they were, how badly they needed something to drink and eat, or to sleep or smoke a cigarette.

"Fellow soldiers!" came the high-pitched, clear voice. "Fellow soldiers, I bid you welcome! I haven't much to say to you, just this: it's up to us to chase those spineless creatures right back to their steppes. Understand?"

The voice paused, and the silence during this pause was embarrassing, almost deathly, and they all saw that by now the sun was red, dark red, and the deathly red reflection seemed to be caught in the Knight's Cross at the colonel's neck, concentrated in those four shining bars of the cross, and they saw for the first time that the cross was surmounted with oakleaves, which they called cabbage.

The colonel wore cabbage at his neck.

"Do you understand?" shouted the taut voice, cracking now.

"Yessir," a few of the men called out, but the voices were hoarse, tired, listless.

"Do you understand, I say!" the voice shouted again, now so strident that it seemed to soar into the sky, swiftly, far too swiftly, like some demented lark trying to pluck a star with its beak.

"Yessir," a few more called out, but not many, and those who did were also tired, hoarse, listless, and nothing in this man's voice could quench their thirst, satisfy their hunger, their craving for a cigarette.

The colonel lashed the air furiously with his cane, they heard something that sounded like "rabble," and he strode rapidly off to the rear, followed by his adjutant, a tall young first lieutenant, who was much too tall, and much too young, for them not to feel sorry for him.

The sun still hung over the horizon, just above the rooftops, a glowing iron egg that seemed to be rolling down over the flat white roofs, and the sky was burned gray, almost white; the sparse leaves hung limply from the trees as they marched on, eastward now at last, through the suburbs, past shacks, over cobbles, past the huts of rag-and-bone men, past a totally incongruous group of modern, dirty apartment blocks, past garbage dumps, through gardens where rotting melons lay on the ground and overripe tomatoes hung from tall stalks, covered with dust, stalks that were much too tall and had an unfamiliar look about them. The maize fields looked odd too, with their thick corncobs being pecked at by flocks of black birds that flew up lethargically at the approach of the men's weary tread, clouds of birds that hovered undecidedly in the air, then settled down to resume their pecking.

Now there were only three times thirty-five men, a weary, dust-coated platoon, with sore feet and sweating faces, led by a first lieutenant whose face plainly showed that he was fed to the teeth. As soon as he took command they knew what kind of man he was. All he had done was look at them and, tired as they were, and thirsty, thirsty, they could read it in his eyes: "It's a lot of shit," said his expression, "just a lot of shit, but we can't do a thing about it." And then came his voice, with studied indifference, contemptuous of all regulation commands: "Let's go."

Next they halted at a grimy school standing among half-withered trees. The foul black puddles, with flies buzzing and darting above them, looked as if they had been standing there for months between rough cobbles and a chalk-scribbled urinal that gave out a nauseating stench, acrid and unmistakable.

"Halt," said the first lieutenant. He went into the schoolhouse, and his walk, elegant and languid, was that of a man who was fed to the teeth.

This time there was no need to form a hollow square, and the captain who walked past them did not even salute; he wore no belt, a straw was stuck between his teeth, and from the look of his plump face with its black eyebrows he appeared to be easygoing. He merely nodded, went "Hm," stopped in front of them, and said: "We haven't got much time, boys. I'll send along the sergeant major and have you assigned to your companies right away." But they had already looked past his round healthy face and seen the ammunition trucks standing ready loaded, and on the ledges of the soiled open windows lay piles of battle packs, neat olive-drab bundles, beside them the belts and the rest of the gear, haversacks, cartridge pouches, spades, gas masks.

When they set off they were only eight times three men, and they marched back through the maize fields as far as the ugly modern apartment blocks, then turned east again until they reached the sparse woods in the midst of which stood a few houses that looked something like an artist's colony: flat-roofed bungalow affairs with picture-windows. There were wicker chairs in the gardens, and when the men halted and about-faced they saw that the sun was behind the roofs now, that its glow filled the whole dome of the sky with a red that was just a shade too pale, like badly painted blood—and behind them, in the east, it was already deep twilight and warm. Soldiers were squatting in the shadow outside the bungalows, there were some rifle-pyramids, ten or so, and they noticed that the men had already buckled on their belts: the steel helmets hooked to their belts shone with a ruddy gleam.

The first lieutenant, coming out now from one of the bungalows, did not walk past them at all. He stopped at once in front of them, and they saw he had only one decoration, a little black one that wasn't really a decoration at all, an insignificant medal stamped out of black tin, a sign that he had shed blood for the Fatherland. The lieutenant's face was tired and sad, and now when he looked at them he looked first at their decorations, then into their faces, and said: "Good," and after a brief pause, with a glance at his watch: "You're tired, I realize that, but it can't be helped—we have to leave in fifteen minutes."

Then he looked at the sergeant major beside him and said: "No point in taking down particulars—just collect the paybooks and put them in with the baggage. Assign the men quickly so they've time for a drink of water. And don't forget to fill up your canteens while you're about it!" he called to the three times eight men.

The sergeant major standing beside him looked irritable and conceited. He had four times as many decorations as the lieutenant, and with a nod he shouted: "Come on now, let's have those paybooks!"

He placed the pile on a wobbly garden table and began sorting them, and while the paybooks were being counted and divided up the men all had the same thought: the journey had been tiring, a bloody bore, but it hadn't been serious. And the general, the colonel, the captain, even the first lieutenant, were all far away, they couldn't do anything to them now. But these fellows here, they owned them, this sergeant major who saluted and clicked his heels the way they all used to four years ago, and that bull of a sergeant who at this point emerged from the rear, threw away his cigarette, and adjusted his belt—these were the fellows who owned them, until they were captured or lay around somewhere wounded—or dead.

Of the thousand men only one was left, and he stood facing the sergeant major, looking helplessly around because there was no one beside, behind, or in front of him; and when he looked at the sergeant major again he realized he was thirsty, very thirsty, and that of those fifteen minutes at least eight had already gone by.

The sergeant major had picked up his paybook from the table and opened it; he looked at the first page, raised his eyes, and asked: "Feinhals?"

"Yessir."

"And you're an architect—you can draw?"

"Yessir."

"Headquarters platoon, we can use him, sir," said the sergeant major, turning to the first lieutenant.

"Good," said the first lieutenant, looking over toward the city, and Feinhals followed his gaze, and now he could see what was evidently fascinating the officer: the sun was lying on the ground, at the end of a street, between two houses; it looked very odd, just lying there on the ground like a flattened, shining apple between two dirty Rumanian houses at the edge of town, an apple growing dimmer by the second, almost as if lying in its own shadow.

"Good," repeated the first lieutenant, and Feinhals didn't know whether he really meant the sun or was just saying the word mechanically. It occurred to Feinhals that he had been on the move for four years now, and four years ago the post card had said he was being called up for a few weeks' maneuvers. But suddenly the war had started.

"Go and get yourself a drink," the sergeant major told Feinhals. Feinhals ran over to join the others and found the water supply right away: a rusted iron pipe with a leaky garden faucet among some scrawny pine trees, and the water ran out in a stream no thicker than half the size of a little finger, but even worse was the fact that about ten men were standing there, shoving, cursing, and pushing away each other's mess bowls.

The sight of the trickling water drove Feinhals almost frantic. He grabbed the mess bowl from his haversack, forced his way through the others, and suddenly felt a surge of boundless strength. He squeezed his mess bowl in between the others, between all those shifting metal apertures, no longer knowing which was his; his eyes followed his arm, saw that his was the one with the darker enamel; he thrust it forward, and felt something that made him tremble: it was getting heavy. He was past knowing which was more wonderful: to drink, or to feel his mess bowl getting heavier. Suddenly, feeling his hands lose their strength, he jerked it back, his very veins trembling with weakness, and while behind him voices shouted: "Fall in—let's go!" he sat down, held the mess bowl between his knees because he lacked the strength to lift it, and bent over it like a dog over its bowl, his shaking fingers pressing it gently down so that the lower edge dipped and the water level touched his lips, and when he actually felt his upper lip getting wet and he began to sip, the word danced before his eyes in a kaleidoscope of colors: "Water, terwa, aterw," with insane clarity he saw it written in his mind's eye: water. Strength flowed back into his hands, he could lift the bowl and drink.

Someone jerked him upright and gave him a shove, and he saw the company lined up, headed by the first lieutenant, who was shouting, "Let's go, let's go!" and he swung his rifle over his shoul-

der and slipped into the space up front indicated by a wave of the
sergeant major's hand.

Off they marched, into the darkness, and he moved without
wanting to: what he really wanted was to drop, but he marched
on, without wanting to, the weight of his body forcing him to
straighten his knees, and when he straightened his knees his sore
feet propelled themselves forward, carrying along great slabs of
pain that were much too big for his feet; his feet were too small
for this pain; and when he propelled his feet forward the whole
bulk of his backside, shoulders, arms, and head started moving
again, forcing him to straighten his knees, and when he straightened his knees his sore feet propelled themselves forward. . . .

Three hours later he was lying exhausted somewhere on sparse
steppe grass, his eyes following a vague shape that was crawling
away in the gray darkness; the shape had brought him two greasy
pieces of paper, some bread, a roll of lemon drops, and six cigarettes, and it had said:

"D'you know the password?"

"No."

"Victory. That's the password: victory."

And he repeated softly: "Victory. That's the password: victory,"
and the word tasted like tepid water on his tongue.

He peeled the paper off the roll and stuck a lemon drop in his
mouth; when he felt the thin, acid, synthetic flavor in his mouth,
the saliva came pouring out of his glands, and he washed down
the first wave of this sweet-tasting bitterness—and at that moment
he heard the shells: they had been rumbling around for hours over
some distant line, and now they were flying across it, sputtering,
hissing, rattling like badly nailed crates, and bursting behind them.
The second lot landed not far ahead of them: fountains of sand
showed up like disintegrating mushrooms against the bright darkness of the eastern sky, and he noticed that it was dark now behind him and a bit lighter in front. The third lot he never heard:
right in amongst them, sledge hammers seemed to be smashing up
plywood sheets, crashing, splintering, close, dangerous. Dust and

powder fumes were drifting along near the ground, and when he had thrown himself over and lay pressed against the earth, his head thrust into a hollow in the mound he had heaped up, he heard the command being passed along: "Get set to advance!" Coming from the right, the whisper hissed past them like a burning fuse, quiet and dangerous, and as he was about to adjust his battle pack, to tighten it, there was a crash right next to him, and it felt as if someone had knocked away his hand and was tugging violently at his upper arm. His whole left arm was bathed in moist warmth, and he raised his face from the ground and shouted: "I've been hit!" but didn't even hear himself shouting, all he heard was a quiet voice saying: "Horse Droppings."

Far, far away, as if separated from him by thick panes of glass, very close and yet far away: "Horse Droppings," said the voice; quiet, well-bred, far away, subdued: "Horse Droppings, Captain Bauer speaking, yessir." Not a sound, then came the voice: "I can hear you, Colonel." Pause, not a sound, only a kind of bubbling in the distance, a gentle hissing and sputtering as if something were boiling over. Then he realized he had closed his eyes, so he opened them: he saw the captain's head, and now he could also hear the voice more distinctly; the head was framed in a dark, dirty window opening, and the captain's face was tired, unshaven and ill-tempered, his eyes were screwed tight, and he said three times in succession, with barely a pause between each: "Yes, Colonel"—"Yes, Colonel"—"Yes, Colonel."

Then the captain put on his steel helmet, and his broad, good-natured face and dark head looked quite ridiculous now as he said to someone beside him: "Hell—there's a breakthrough at Horse Droppings 3, Sharpshooter 4, I'll have to go forward." Another voice shouted into the building: "Dispatch rider, report to the captain," and it carried on like an echo, reverberating around inside the building and getting fainter and fainter: "Dispatch rider, report to the captain—dispatch rider, report to the captain!"

Next he heard the rattle of a motor and followed the dry rasping sound as it came closer; he saw the motorcycle slowly turn a corner, slackening speed until it stopped in front of him, throbbing, covered with dust, and the driver, his face tired and apathetic, remained seated on the pulsing machine and shouted toward the window: "Motorcycle for the captain reporting!" And the captain came out, walking slowly, legs wide apart, a cigar in his mouth, the steel helmet giving him the look of a sinister squat mushroom. He climbed without enthusiasm into the sidecar, said "Let's go," and the machine bounced and rattled off, at high speed, veiled in dust, in the direction of the seething confusion up front.

Feinhals wondered if he had ever been so happy in his life. He felt almost no pain; his left arm, lying beside him like a tight bundle, stiff and bloody, damp and unfamiliar, felt faintly uncomfortable, that was all. Everything else was all right; he could raise each leg separately, wriggle his feet in his boots, lift his head, and he could smoke as he lay there, facing him was the sun as it hung a hand's breadth above the gray cloud of dust in the east. All noise was somehow remote and subdued, his head felt as if wrapped in a layer of cotton wool, and it occurred to him that he had had nothing to eat for almost twenty-four hours except an acid, synthetic lemon drop and nothing to drink except a little water, rusty and tepid and tasting of sand.

When he felt himself being lifted up and carried away, he closed his eyes again, but he could see it all, it was so familiar, it had all happened to him somewhere else: they carried him past the exhaust fumes of a throbbing vehicle into the hot, gasoline-reeking interior, the stretcher scraped against the metal rails, and then the engine started up and the noise outside retreated farther and farther, almost imperceptibly, just as the evening before it had come imperceptibly closer. A few isolated shells burst in the suburbs, regularly, quietly, and just as he felt himself dropping off to sleep he thought: How nice, it was all over so quickly this time, so quickly.... All it had meant was a little thirst, sore feet, and a little fear.

When the ambulance stopped with a jerk he awoke from his

half-sleep. Doors were flung open, once again the stretchers scraped against the metal rails, and he was carried into a cool white corridor where it was very quiet; the stretchers stood in rows like lounge chairs on a narrow deck, and next to him he saw a head of thick black hair, lying quietly, and on the stretcher beyond that a bald head, moving restlessly from side to side, and up at the end, on the first stretcher, a white head, heavily bandaged, completely covered, ugly and much too narrow, and from this bundle of gauze came a voice, piercing, shrill, clear, harsh as it rose to the ceiling, helpless yet insolent, the voice of the colonel, and the voice cried: "Champagne!"

"Piss," said the bald head calmly, "drink your own piss." Someone behind laughed, quietly and cautiously.

"Champagne," cried the voice in fury, "chilled champagne!"

"Shut up," said the bald head calmly, "why don't you shut up?"

"Champagne," whimpered the voice, "I want some champagne"; and the white head sank back, it was lying flat now, and from between thick layers of gauze rose a thin pointed nose, and the voice became even shriller and shouted: "A girl—get me a girl. . . ."

"Do it to yourself," retorted the bald head.

At last the white head was carried through a door, and there was silence.

In the silence they could hear only the isolated shells bursting in distant parts of the city, muffled far-off explosions thrumming softly away at the edge of the war. And when the white head of the colonel, now lying silently on one side, was carried out and the bald head was carried in, the sound of a car could be heard approaching outside: the muted sound of a whining engine came closer, quickly and almost threateningly, and now it was so close it seemed about to ram the cool white building: then suddenly silence fell, outside a voice shouted something, and when they turned their heads, startled out of their peaceful, dozing weariness, they saw the general walking slowly past the stretchers and wordlessly placing packs of cigarettes on the men's laps. The silence became more and more oppressive the nearer the little man's footsteps approached from behind, and at last Feinhals saw the general's face quite close: yellow, large and sad, with snow-white eyebrows, dark traces of dust around the thin mouth, and written in this face was the message that this battle, too, had been lost.

II

He heard a voice saying "Bressen—Bressen, look at me," and he knew this was the voice of Kleewitz, the divisional medical officer, who must have been sent here to find out when he would be going back. But he wouldn't be going back, he never wanted to be reminded again of that regiment—and he didn't look at Kleewitz. He looked fixedly at the picture hanging way over to the right, almost in the dark corner: a flock of sheep, painted gray and green, and in the middle of them a shepherd in a blue cloak playing a flute.

He thought about things no one else on earth would have dreamed of, things he liked thinking about, repulsive though they were. He wasn't sure whether he heard Kleewitz' voice; he did hear it, of course, but he didn't want to admit it, and he looked at the shepherd playing his flute—instead of turning his head and saying: "Kleewitz, how nice of you to come."

Next he heard the shuffle of papers, and he assumed they were studying his medical history. He looked at the back of the shepherd's neck and recalled how for a time he had been a nodder at a hotel, in a very high-class restaurant. At noon, when the local businessmen came for lunch, he would walk through the restaurant, very erect, and bow, and it was funny how quickly and accurately he had grasped the required nuances: whether he gave a short bow or a deep one, whether he merely nodded and, if so, how he nodded, and sometimes he would just move his head very briefly, more of an opening and closing of his eyes really, that gave the impression he was moving his head. He found status-differences so easy to recognize—like army ranks, that hierarchy of braided and flat, starred and unstarred, shoulder loops, all the way down to the great mass of people with their more or less undecorated shoulders.

In this restaurant the scale of bowing was relatively simple: it was all a matter of bankroll, of the size of the bill. He wasn't even especially obliging, he almost never smiled, and his face—despite his efforts to look as impassive as possible—his face never lost that expression of severity and vigilance. A feeling crept over everyone he looked at, not so much of being honored as of being guilty; all felt themselves observed, inspected, and he soon discovered that there were certain people who became confused, so confused that they unthinkingly applied their knives to their potatoes the moment his glance rested on them and who nervously fingered their wallets as soon as he had passed. The only thing that surprised him was that they kept coming back, even this kind. Back they came and submitted to being nodded at, to that uncomfortable scrutiny that goes with a high-class restaurant. His thin, aristocratic face and a knack of wearing clothes well brought him in quite a decent income; besides, he ate there for nothing. But while he tried to assume a certain air of haughtiness, he was in fact often quite nervous. There were days when he could feel the sweat gathering and breaking out all over his body so that he could hardly breathe. And the owner was a coarse fellow, good-natured, vain about his success but awkward in manner; late at night, when the place was gradually emptying and he could think about going home, the owner would sometimes dig his stubby fingers into the cigar box and, despite his protests, stuff three or four cigars into the top pocket of Bressen's jacket. "Go on," the owner would mumble with his diffident smile, "take them—they're good cigars." And he would take them. He smoked them in the evening with Velten, with whom he shared a small furnished apartment, and Velten never failed to be surprised at the quality of the cigars. "Bressen," Velten would say, "I must say, Bressen, you smoke an excellent weed." He would make no comment and no pretense at refusing when Velten brought home an especially good bottle. Velten traveled for a wine merchant, and when business was good he would take home a bottle of champagne.

"Champagne," he said out loud to himself, "chilled champagne."

"That's all he ever says," said the ward medical officer standing beside him.

"Are you referring to the colonel?" asked Kleewitz coldly.

"That's right, Colonel Bressen. The only thing the colonel ever says: Champagne—chilled champagne. And sometimes he talks about women—girls."

He had loathed having to take his meals at the restaurant. In a grubby back room off a worn tablecloth, served by the ungracious cook who paid absolutely no attention to his fondness for desserts —and in his nose, throat, and mouth that sickening stale reek of cooking, greasy and disgusting—and that constant coming and going of the owner, the way he would plump himself down beside him for a few seconds, cigar in mouth, pour himself a schnapps, and sit there silently knocking back the stuff.

Later on he had given lessons in social etiquette. The town he lived in was very suitable for this kind of instruction, containing as it did a great many rich people who didn't even know that fish was eaten differently from meat, who had literally eaten with their fingers all their lives, and who now had cars, villas, and women— people who could no longer bear to be the kind of people they really were. He taught them how to perform adequately on the slippery ice of social obligations; he went to their homes, discussed menus, taught them how to handle servants, and stayed for dinner —he had to teach them every gesture, watch them like a hawk, correct them, and he tried to show them how to open a bottle of champagne without assistance.

"Champagne," he said out loud to himself, "chilled champagne."

"Oh for God's sake," cried Kleewitz, "Bressen, look at me!" But he had no intention of looking at Kleewitz; he never wanted to be reminded of it again, the regiment that had disintegrated in his hands like dry tinder; Horse Droppings, Sharpshooter, Sugarloaf—under the command of his staff known as Hunting Lodge—all finished! And shortly after that he heard Kleewitz leave.

He was glad to be able to detach his gaze at last from the flock of sheep and the stupid shepherd; it was hanging a bit too far over to the right and he was getting a crick in his neck. The second picture hung almost directly opposite him, and he was compelled to look at it, although that one didn't appeal to him either: it showed Crown Prince Michael talking to a Rumanian peasant, flanked by Marshal Antonescu and the Queen. The stance of the Rumanian peasant was alarming. He was standing with his feet too close and too firmly together, and he seemed about to tip forward and throw the gift in his hands at the young King's feet: Bressen couldn't quite make out what the gift was—salt or bread or a hunk of goat cheese—but the young King was smiling at the peasant. Bressen had long ceased to see these things; he was thankful to have found a spot to stare at without worrying about getting a crick in his neck.

What had amazed him so during those etiquette lessons—what he hadn't known and had long tried to ignore—was that such things could actually be learned, this little performance: how to handle a knife and fork correctly. It often shocked him to see these fellows and their womenfolk treating him after three months with formal courtesy, as if he were a competent instructor of limited scope, and smile as they handed him a check. There were some, of course, who never made it—their fingers were too clumsy, they were incapable of cutting the rind off a piece of cheese without picking up the whole slice, or of holding a wineglass properly by the stem—and then there was a third category who never learned but who couldn't have cared less—as well as those he never met but heard about, who considered it a waste of time to consult him.

His sole consolation during this period was the opportunity for an occasional affair with their wives—there was no risk attached to these little adventures, which didn't disappoint him although they seemed to put the women off him. He had many affairs during this time—with all kinds of women—but not a single one had ever come to him or gone out with him a second time, although he usually ordered champagne.

"Champagne," he said out loud to himself, "chilled champagne."

He said it when he was alone too—it felt better that way—and for a moment he thought about the war, this war, just for an instant, until he heard two more people entering the room. He went on staring at that indefinable hunk that the Rumanian peasant was holding out to young King Michael—and for a moment he caught a glimpse, between himself and the picture, of the pink hand of the senior medical officer as the latter leaned over and took the chart down from its hook.

"Champagne," said Bressen in a loud voice, "champagne and a girl."

"Colonel Bressen," said the senior medical officer, urgently but softly. "Colonel Bressen!" There was a brief silence, and the senior medical officer said to the person beside him: "Mark his tag 'Home Hospitalization' and transfer him to Vienna—needless to say the division will be very sorry to have to get along without Colonel Bressen, but. . . ."

"Right, sir," said the ward medical officer. Bressen heard nothing more, although they must be standing beside him because he had not heard the door. Then came the rustling of those damned papers again, they must be rereading his medical history. Not a word was said.

Later on certain people had recalled that there were things he really could teach and which there was some point in teaching: the new army regulations, already familiar to him because he received the new issues regularly. He was put in charge of training the Stahlhelm and Youth Groups in his area, and he clearly remembered this honor having coincided with that period in his life when he had discovered an inordinate craving for sweet things and a decline in his interest in affairs with women. His notion of keeping a horse had proved a good one, although it meant scrimping a bit, for now on maneuver days he could ride out onto the heath early in the morning, hold discussions with subordinates, go through the drill plan—and best of all he could get to know the men in a way that was hardly possible while they were on duty: veterans and strangely clear-headed yet naive young men who now and again had gone so far as to risk openly contradicting him. What saddened him was a certain amount of official secrecy that prevented him from riding back to town at the head of the troops —but while on duty it was almost like the old days: he was thoroughly familiar with combat duty at battalion level, and he had no cause to find fault with the new regulations, which had made good use of wartime experience without aiming at anything in the way of an actual revolution in methods. The things he had always encouraged and considered of prime importance were: route marches, standing at attention, about-turns executed with maximum precision—and those were red-letter days when he felt sufficiently strong and confident to risk something that even in peacetime and with well-disciplined troops had been risky: battalion maneuvers.

But the secrecy was soon dropped, before long there were daily maneuvers, and it didn't feel very different when one day he was made a real major again, in command of a real battalion.

For a moment he was not sure whether he was actually turning or whether this turning was already one of those things beyond the edge of his consciousness, but turning he was, and he was aware that he was turning, and it was depressing to find that so far nothing had occurred beyond the edge of his consciousness: he was being turned. They had lifted him up and swung him carefully out of his bed onto a stretcher. At first his head fell back, for a moment he was staring at the ceiling, but then a pillow was pushed under his head and his gaze fell precisely on the third picture hanging in his room. This was a picture he had never seen, it hung near the door, and at first he was glad to be able to look at it since otherwise he would have had to look straight at the two doctors, between whom the picture was now hanging. The senior medical officer seemed to have left the room. The ward medical officer was talking to another, younger medical officer he had never seen before; he saw the short, plump ward M.O. read some passages from his medical history to his colleague in a low voice and explain something to him. Bressen couldn't understand what they were saying, not because he couldn't hear—it bothered him very much that so far he had not been able to close his ears—no, it was just that they were too far away and whispering. From the corridor he could hear everything: people calling out, cries of the wounded, and the throbbing hum of motors outside. He saw the back of the stretcher-bearer standing in front of him, and now the one standing behind him said: "Let's go."

"The bags," said the front stretcher-bearer. "Major," he called across to the ward M.O., "someone'll have to carry out those bags."

"Get hold of a few fellows."

The two stretcher-bearers went out into the corridor.

Without moving his head Bressen carefully studied the third picture between the two doctors' heads: this picture was incredible, he couldn't understand how it had ever got here. He didn't know whether they were in a school or a convent, but as for there being Catholics in Rumania, he had never heard of such a thing. In Germany there were some, he had heard about those—but in Rumania! And now here was a picture of the Virgin Mary. It annoyed him to be forced to look at this picture, but he had no option, he was forced to stare at her, that woman in the sky-blue cloak whose face he found disconcertingly grave; she stood poised on a globe, looking up to Heaven, which consisted of snow-white clouds, and around her hands was twisted a string of brown wooden beads. He gently shook his head and thought: What a repulsive picture, and suddenly he noticed the two doctors watching him. They looked at him, then at the picture, followed his gaze and slowly returned to him. It wasn't easy to stare between those two heads—those four eyes that were looking into his—at the picture which he found so repulsive. He couldn't think of anything to take his mind off it; he tried to let his thoughts slip back to those years which a moment ago had been so easy to recall, years when he felt that the things which had once been his world were slowly becoming a world again: the association with staff officers, barracks gossip, adjutants, orderlies. He found himself unable to think about them. He was hemmed in by those eight inches left free by the two heads, and in those eight inches hung the picture—but it was a relief to see this space become larger because now they were approaching him, separating, and standing one on either side of him.

Now he couldn't see them at all, just their white smocks at the periphery of his vision. He heard exactly what they were saying.

"So you don't think it has anything to do with this injury?"

"Definitely not," said the ward M.O.; he opened the medical history again, papers rustled. "Definitely not. It's only a trifling scalp wound—very minor. Healed in five days. Nothing—not a trace of the usual symptoms of concussion, not a thing. I can only assume it was shock—or. . . ." He broke off.

"What were you going to say?"

"I'm not going to stick my neck out."

"Go on—tell me."

It was annoying that both the doctors should remain silent, they seemed to be exchanging some kind of signals—then the younger one burst out laughing. Bressen hadn't heard a word spoken. Then both doctors laughed. He was glad when the two soldiers came in accompanied by a third with his arm in a sling.

"Feinhals," the ward medical officer told him, "take the brief case out to the ambulance. The heavy bags will be sent on later," he called to the stretcher-bearers.

"Are you serious?" asked the other doctor.

"Absolutely."

Bressen felt himself being lifted up and carried off; the picture of the Virgin slipped away to his left, the wall came closer, then the window frame outside in the corridor, again he was swung—he looked into the long corridor, one more swing, and he closed his eyes: outside the sun was dazzlingly bright. He was relieved when the ambulance door closed behind him.

III

There were a great many sergeants in the German Army—with enough stars to decorate the sky of some thick-witted underworld —and a great many sergeants called Schneider, and of these quite a number who had been christened Alois, but at this particular time only one of these sergeants called Alois Schneider was stationed in the Hungarian village of Szokarhely; Szokarhely was a compact little place, half village, half resort. It was summer.

Schneider's office was a narrow room papered in yellow; on the door outside hung a pink cardboard sign on which was printed in black Indian ink: Discharges, Sgt. Schneider.

The desk was so placed that Schneider sat with his back to the window, and when he had nothing to do he would get up, turn around, and look out onto the narrow dusty road leading on the left to the village, and on the right, between maize fields and apricot orchards, out into the puszta.

Schneider had almost nothing to do. Only a few seriously wounded men still remained in the hospital; all those fit to be moved had been loaded into ambulances and taken away—and the rest, the walking wounded, had been discharged, loaded onto trucks, and taken to the redeployment center at the front. Schneider could look out of the window for hours on end: outside the air was close, muggy, and the best remedy for this climate was pale-yellow apricot schnapps mixed with soda water. The schnapps was mildly tart, as well as cheap, pure, and good, and it was very pleasant to sit by the window, look out at the sky or onto the road, and get drunk; intoxication was a long time coming, Schneider had to fight hard for it; it was necessary—even in the morning—to consume a considerable quantity of schnapps in order to reach a state in which boredom and futility became bearable. Schneider had a system: in the first glass he took only a dash of schnapps, in the second a bit more, the third was 50:50, the fourth he drank neat, the fifth 50:50 again, the sixth was as strong as the second, and the seventh as weak as the first. He drank only seven glasses—by about ten-thirty he was through with this ritual and had reached a state he called raging soberness, a cold fire consumed him, and he was armed to cope with the boredom and futility of the day. The first discharge cases usually turned up shortly before eleven, most of them around eleven-fifteen, and that still gave him almost an hour to look out onto the road, where from time to time a cart, drawn by lean horses and churning up a lot of dust, would race past on its way to the village—or he could catch flies, conduct ingenious dialogues with imaginary superiors—sarcastic, terse—or maybe sort out the rubber stamps on his desk, straighten the papers.

About this time—around ten-thirty—Schmitz was standing in the room containing the two patients on whom he had operated that morning: on the left, Lieutenant Moll, aged twenty-one, looking like an old woman, his peaked face seemed to be grinning under the anesthetic. Clouds of flies swarmed over the bandages on his hands, squatted drowsily on the blood-soaked gauze around his head. Schmitz fanned them away—it was hopeless, he shook his head and drew the white sheet as far as he could over the sleeping man's head. He began pulling on the clean white smock he wore on his rounds, buttoned it slowly, and looked at the other patient, Captain Bauer, who seemed to be gradually coming out of the anesthetic, mumbling indistinctly, his eyes closed; he tried to move but couldn't, he was strapped down, even his head had been firmly tied to the bars at the head of the bed—only his lips moved, and now and again it looked for a moment as if he were about to open his eyelids—and he would start mumbling again.

Schmitz dug his hands into the pockets of his smock and waited
—the room was shadowy, the air fetid, there was a slight smell of
cowdung, and even with closed doors and windows there were
swarms of flies; at one time cattle had been kept in the basement
beneath.

The captain's sporadic, inarticulate mumbling appeared to be
taking shape; now he was opening his mouth at regular intervals
and seemed to be uttering one single word, which Schmitz could
not understand—an oddly fascinating mixture of E and O and
throaty sounds—then all of a sudden the captain opened his eyes.
"Bauer," cried Schmitz, but he knew it was no use. He stepped
closer and waved his hands in front of the captain's eyes—there
was no reflex. Schmitz held his hand close to the captain's eyes, so
close that he could feel the man's eyebrows on his palm: nothing
—the captain merely went on repeating his incomprehensible
word at regular intervals. He was looking inside himself, and no
one knew what was inside. Suddenly he uttered the word very distinctly, sharply articulated as if he had learned it by heart—then
again. Schmitz held his ear close to the captain's mouth: "Byelyogorshe," said the captain. Schmitz listened intently, he had never
heard the word and had no idea what it meant, but he liked the
sound of it, it was beautiful, he thought—mysterious and beautiful. Outside all was quiet—he could hear the captain's breathing,
he looked into his eyes and with bated breath waited each time for
the word: "Byelyogorshe." Schmitz looked at his watch, following
the seconds hand—how slowly that tiny finger seemed to crawl
across the watch face—fifty seconds: "Byelyogorshe." It seemed to
take forever for the next fifty seconds to pass. Outside, trucks were
driving into the courtyard. Someone called out in the corridor,
Schmitz remembered that the senior M.O. had sent a message asking him to do his rounds for him, another truck drove into the
yard. "Byelyogorshe," said the captain; Schmitz waited once more
—the door opened, a sergeant appeared, Schmitz signaled impatiently to him to keep quiet, stared at the little seconds hand and
sighed as it touched the thirty: "Byelyogorshe," said the captain.

"What is it?" Schmitz asked the sergeant.

"Time to do the rounds," said the sergeant.

"I'm coming," said Schmitz. He pulled his sleeve down over his watch when the seconds hand came to twenty and the captain's lips had just closed—he stared at the man's mouth, waited, and drew back his sleeve when the lips began to move. "Byely-ogorshe": the seconds hand stood exactly at ten.

Schmitz walked slowly out of the room.

That day there were no discharge cases. Schneider waited until eleven-fifteen, then went out to get some cigarettes. In the corridor he stopped by the window. Outside, the senior M.O.'s car was being washed. Thursday, Schneider thought. Thursday was the day for washing the senior M.O.'s car.

The building was in the form of a square open toward the rear, toward the railway. In the north wing was Surgery, in the center Administration and X-rays, in the south wing kitchen and staff quarters, and at the far end a suite of six rooms occupied by the administrator. This complex had once housed an agricultural college. At the rear, in the large grounds running straight across the open side, were shower rooms, stables, and model plantations, neatly defined beds containing all kinds of plants. The grounds and orchards went all the way down to the railway, and sometimes the administrator's wife could be seen riding there with her small son, a six-year-old straddling a pony and yelling. The administrator's wife was young and pretty, and whenever she had been playing with her son at the end of the grounds she would call in at the administration office and complain about the unexploded shell lying down there by the cesspool, in her view extremely dangerous. She was invariably assured that something would be done about it, but nothing ever was.

Schneider stood by the window watching the senior M.O.'s driver painstakingly performing his duties; although he had been driving and looking after this car for two years, he was obeying the rules and had spread the lube chart out on a crate, had put on his fatigues, and stood surrounded by pails and oilcans. The senior M.O.'s car was upholstered in red leather, and very low-slung. Thursday, thought Schneider, Thursday again. In the calendar of routines, Thursday was the day for washing the senior M.O.'s car. He greeted the fair-haired nurse hurrying past him and walked a few steps to the canteen door, but the door was locked.

Two trucks drove into the yard and parked well away from the M.O.'s car. Schneider continued to look out of the window: at that moment the girl who brought the fruit drove into the yard. She held the reins herself, seated on an upturned crate, and drove her little cart carefully between the vehicles toward the kitchen. Her name was Szarka, and every Wednesday she brought fruit and vegetables from one of the nearby villages. People came with fruit and vegetables every day, the paymaster had a number of suppliers, but on Wednesdays only Szarka came. Schneider was quite sure about this: many a time he had interrupted his work on a Wednesday about ten-thirty, gone over to the window, and stood there waiting until the dust cloud stirred up by her little cart at the side of the avenue leading to the station came in sight, and he always waited until she came closer, until he could make out the little horse through the dust cloud, then the cartwheels, and finally the girl with the pretty oval face and the smile around her mouth. Schneider lighted his last cigarette and sat down on the windowsill. Today I'm going to speak to her, he thought, and at the same instant he thought of how every Wednesday he thought: today I'm going to speak to her, and that he never had. But today he would for sure. There was something about Szarka that he had felt only in the women here, in these girls from the puszta, girls who were always shown in movies as hot-blooded, capering ninnies: Szarka was cool, cool and of an almost impalpable tenderness; she behaved tenderly toward her horse, toward the fruit in her baskets: apricots and tomatoes, plums and pears, cucumbers and paprikas. Her gaily painted little cart slipped in between the greasy oilcans and crates, stopped at the kitchen, and she tapped her whip on the window.

Generally at this hour of the day all was quiet indoors. The M.O. was making his rounds, spreading a mood of anxious solemnity, everything was tidy, and an indefinable tension could be felt in the corridors. But today there was a restless hubbub, everywhere doors were being banged, people were calling out. Schneider was somehow aware of this at the edge of his consciousness; he smoked his last cigarette and watched Szarka negotiating with the mess sergeant. Normally she negotiated with the paymaster, who tried to pinch her behind—but Pratzki, the mess sergeant, was a slightly built, practical fellow, a bit high-strung, who was an excellent cook and reputed to have no use for women. Szarka seemed to be urging him, gesticulating, mostly the gesture for paying, but the cook merely shrugged his shoulders and pointed to the main building, to the very spot where Schneider was sitting. The girl turned and looked almost straight at Schneider; he jumped off the windowsill and heard his name being called in the corridor: "Schneider, Schneider!" There was a moment's silence, and again someone shouted: "Sergeant Schneider!" Schneider gave one more glance outside: Szarka took her little horse by the bridle and led it toward the main building; the M.O.'s driver was standing in a large puddle folding up his lube chart. Schneider walked slowly toward the office, thinking of many things before he reached it: that he must speak to the girl today, whatever happened, that the M.O.'s car couldn't be washed on a Wednesday—and that it was out of the question for Szarka to come on a Thursday.

He was met by the retinue accompanying the medical officer on his rounds. It emerged from the big ward, now almost empty; white smocks, a few nurses, the ward sergeant, the orderlies, a mute procession led not by the senior M.O. but by Schmitz, a noncommissioned medical officer, a man who was seldom heard to speak. Schmitz was short and plump and nondescript-looking, but his eyes were cool and gray, and sometimes, when he lowered the lids for an instant, he seemed about to say something, but he never did. The retinue dispersed as Schneider reached the office; he saw Schmitz approaching, held open the door for him, and the two men walked into the room together.

The sergeant major had his ear to the receiver. His broad face wore a look of annoyance. He was just saying: "No, sir," then the senior M.O.'s voice was audible through the receiver, the sergeant major looked at Schneider and the noncommissioned M.O., gestured to the latter to take a seat, and smiled as he looked at Schneider. Then he said: "Yes, sir; very well, sir," and replaced the receiver.

"What's up?" asked Schmitz. "I take it we're getting out of here." He opened the newspaper lying in front of him, flapped it shut again immediately, and looked over the shoulder of Feinhals, who was sitting beside him. Schmitz regarded the sergeant major coolly. He had seen that Feinhals was preparing a map of the surrounding area. "Szokarhely Base" was printed across the top.

"Yes," said the sergeant major, "we've orders to redeploy." He was trying to remain calm, but there was a nasty glint in his eyes as he looked at Schneider. And his hands were trembling. He glanced at the crates, painted army-gray, stacked along the walls; with their lids open they could be used as lockers or desks. He still did not offer Schneider a chair.

"Give me a cigarette, Feinhals, till I can get some more," said Schneider. Feinhals got up, opened the blue package, and held it out to Schneider. Schmitz took one too. Schneider stood leaning against the wall, smoking.

"I know," he said into the silence. "I'll be with the rear unit. It used to be the advance unit."

The sergeant major flushed. The sound of a typewriter came from the next room. The telephone rang, the sergeant major lifted the receiver, gave his name, and said: "Very well, sir—I'll have them sent over for signature."

He replaced the receiver. "Feinhals," he said, "go over and see if the order of the day is ready." Schmitz and Schneider exchanged glances. Schmitz looked at the desk and opened the newspaper again. "High Treason Trial Begins," he read. He flipped the paper shut again immediately.

Feinhals returned with the clerk from the next room. The clerk was a pale, fair-haired noncom with fingers stained from smoking.

"Otten," Schneider called out to him, "will you be opening up the canteen again?"

"Just a moment, if you don't mind," said the sergeant major, furious. "I've got more important things to do right now." He drummed on the desk with his fingers while the clerk sorted the sets of paper. He turned the typed sheets face down and pulled out the carbons. There were three sets, each consisting of two typed pages and four carbon copies. The typed sheets appeared to contain nothing but names. Schneider thought about the girl. Probably she was with the paymaster now, getting her money. He stepped closer to the window to get a better view of the gate.

"Don't forget," he said to Otten, "to leave us some cigarettes."

"Shut up!" shouted the sergeant major.

He handed the papers to Feinhals, saying: "Take these over to the senior M.O. for signature." Feinhals clipped them together and left the room.

The sergeant major turned to Schmitz and Schneider, but Schneider was looking out of the window, it was almost noon, and the road was empty; opposite was a large field where a market was held on Wednesdays: the littered stalls stood abandoned in the sunshine. So it *is* Wednesday, he thought, turning toward the sergeant major, who had a carbon copy of the order of the day in his hand. Feinhals had returned and was standing by the door.

". . . will remain here," the sergeant major was saying. "Feinhals has a sketch map of the place. This time everything's to be done in battle order. A formality, as you know, Schneider," he added. "You'd better round up a few men and have the weapons brought in from the infectious ward. The other wards have already been notified."

"Weapons?" asked Schneider. "Is that a formality too?"

The sergeant major flushed again. Schmitz took another cigarette from Feinhals' package. "I'd like to see the list of wounded
—will the senior M.O. be leading the advance unit?"

"Yes," said the sergeant major, "he's the one that drew up the
list."

"I'd like to see it," said Schmitz.

Once more the sergeant major flushed. Then he reached into
the drawer and handed Schmitz the list. Schmitz read it through
carefully, saying each name quietly over to himself; there was silence in the room, no one said anything, they were all looking at
the man reading the list. Outside in the corridor there was a commotion. They all jumped as Schmitz suddenly cried out: "Lieutenant Moll and Captain Bauer, for Christ's sake!" He flung the list
onto the desk and looked at the sergeant major. "Any medical student knows that no patient is fit to travel an hour and a half after
a serious operation." He picked up the list from the desk and
rapped the paper with his fingers. "I might just as well put a bullet through their heads as load them into an ambulance." He
looked at Schneider, then at Feinhals, then at the sergeant major
and Otten. "They must have known yesterday that we were clearing out today—why wasn't the operation postponed, eh?"

"Orders only arrived this morning, an hour ago," said the sergeant major.

"Orders! Orders!" exclaimed Schmitz. He threw the list onto
the desk, saying to Schneider: "Come on, let's get out of here."
When they were outside he said: "You weren't listening just then
—I'm in charge of the rear unit—we'll talk about it later." He
walked rapidly toward the senior M.O.'s office, and Schneider
strolled away to his room.

He paused at each window on the way, looking out to make
sure Szarka's cart was still standing in front of the gate. By now
the courtyard was jammed with trucks and ambulances, and in the
middle stood the M.O.'s car. They had already begun loading, and
Schneider noticed that outside the kitchen the baskets of fruit

were also being loaded, and the M.O.'s driver was lugging a gray metal trunk across the yard.

The corridors were crowded. In his room Schneider walked quickly to the locker, poured the rest of the apricot schnapps into a glass and added some soda water, and as he drank it he could hear the first motor starting up outside. Glass in hand, he went out into the corridor and stood by the window: he had heard right away that the first motor to start up was the M.O.'s; it was a good motor, Schneider knew nothing about such things, but he could tell by the sound that it was a good motor. Just then the M.O. crossed the courtyard, he wasn't carrying any baggage, and his field cap was slightly askew. He looked pretty much as usual; only his face, otherwise rather distinguished, pale, with faint pinkish overtones, was scarlet. The M.O. was a good-looking man, tall and spare, an excellent horseman who mounted his horse every morning at six, whip in hand, and rode off into the puszta at a steady canter, a dwindling figure vanishing into that flat landscape that seemed to consist only of horizon. But now his face was scarlet, and only once had Schneider seen the M.O.'s face scarlet, and that was when Schmitz had carried out with success an operation that the M.O. had not wanted to tackle. Now Schmitz was walking beside the M.O.; Schmitz was quite calm, whereas the M.O. was waving his arms ... but now Schneider had seen the girl coming toward him along the corridor. She seemed to be confused by all the commotion and looking for someone who was not involved in the general exodus. She said something in Hungarian which he did not understand, then he pointed to his room and beckoned her over. Outside, the first vehicle, the M.O.'s, was moving off, and the column slowly followed. ...

Evidently the girl took him for a deputy of the paymaster's. She did not sit down on the chair he offered, and when he perched on the edge of the desk she continued to stand facing him, trying to make him understand what she wanted and gesturing vigorously as she spoke. It was a relief to be able to look at her without having to listen to her, for it was hopeless to try and understand what she was saying. But he let her talk just so that he could look at her: she seemed rather thin, perhaps she was too young, very young, much younger than he had thought—her breasts were small, the beauty of her small face was perfect, and he waited almost breathlessly for the moments when her long eyelashes lay on the brown cheeks—very brief moments in which her small mouth remained closed, round and red, the lips slightly too narrow. He studied her very carefully and had to admit that he was a bit disappointed—but she was charming, and all of a sudden he raised his hands defensively and shook his head. She stopped speaking at once, looking at him suspiciously; he said softly: "I'd like to kiss you, do you understand?" By this time he no longer knew whether he really did want to kiss her, and it embarrassed him to see her blush, to see the color slowly spreading over that dark skin, and he realized she hadn't understood a single word but knew what he meant. She took a step back as he slowly approached her, and he could see from the scared look in her eyes and from the thin neck with its wildly pulsing vein that she was three months too young. He stopped, shook his head, and said in a low voice: "Forgive me—forget it—understand?" But the look in her eyes became more scared than ever, and he was afraid she was going to scream. This time she seemed to understand even less—with a sigh he stepped up to her, took hold of her small hands, and as he lifted them to his mouth he saw they were dirty, they smelled of earth and leather, leeks and onions, and he brushed them with his lips and tried to smile. She looked at him in growing bewilderment, until he patted her on the shoulder, saying: "Come along, we'll go and see you get your money." Not until he held up his hand and made the unmistakable gesture of paying did she give a little smile and follow him out into the corridor.

In the corridor they ran into Schmitz and Otten.

"Where are you going?" asked Schmitz.

"To see the paymaster," said Schneider. "The girl wants her money."

"The paymaster's gone," said Schmitz, "he left yesterday evening, for Szolnok; from there he's going to join up with the advance unit." He lowered his lids for a moment, then looked at the men. No one said a word. The girl glanced from one to the other. "Otten," said Schmitz, "round up the rear unit, I need a few men for unloading, no one seemed to think of leaving any food for us."

"And the girl?" asked Schneider.

Schmitz shrugged his shoulders. "I can't give her any money."

"Should she come back tomorrow morning?"

Schmitz looked at the girl. She smiled at him.

"No," he said, "it had better be this afternoon."

Otten ran along the corridor, shouting: "Rear unit fall in!"

Schmitz went out into the courtyard and stood beside the truck, while Schneider accompanied the girl to her cart. He tried to explain to her that she should come back in the afternoon, but she kept vigorously shaking her head until he realized she was not going to leave without her money. He continued to stand beside her, watched her climb onto the cart, turn her crate up, and take out a brown-paper parcel. Then she hung the feedbag over the horse's nose and unwrapped the parcel: part of a loaf of bread, a large flat meat patty, and a leek. Her wine was in a squat green bottle. She was smiling at him now, and suddenly, in the midst of chewing, she said "Nagyvárad," and struck the air several times with her fist, horizontally away from her body, making a solemn face as she did so. Schneider imagined she was demonstrating a fist fight which someone had lost, or maybe—he thought—she was trying to show that she felt she had been cheated. He didn't know what Nagyvárad meant. Hungarian was a very difficult language, it didn't even have a word for tobacco.

The girl shook her head. "Nagyvárad, Nagyvárad," she repeated vehemently several times, striking the air again with her fist, horizontally away from her chest. She shook her head and laughed, chewing hard, and took a quick gulp of wine. "Oh!" she went, "Nagyvárad—Russ," again the boxing gesture, this time prolonged and in a wide arc: "Russ—Russ"; she pointed to the southeast and imitated the noise of tanks approaching: "Bru-bru-bru...."

Suddenly Schneider nodded, and she laughed out loud, but broke off in the middle and assumed a very grave expression. Schneider realized that Nagyvárad must be a town, and the boxing gesture was now quite clear. He looked across to the men standing by the truck and unloading. Schmitz was standing up front beside the driver and signing something. Schneider called out to him: "When you have a moment, sir, would you mind coming over here?" Schmitz nodded.

The girl had finished her meal. She carefully wrapped up the bread and the remains of the leek and stuck the cork back in the bottle.

"Would you like some water for the horse?" asked Schneider. She looked at him questioningly.

"Water," he said, "for the horse." He leaned slightly forward and tried to imitate a horse drinking.

"Oh," she cried, "oh, yo!" Her eyes held a strange look, of curiosity somehow, curiosity and tenderness.

Across the yard the truck moved off, and Schmitz walked over.

Their eyes followed the truck; outside another column stood waiting for the entrance to become free.

"What is it?" asked Schmitz.

"She's talking about a breakthrough near a town beginning with Nagy."

Schmitz nodded: "Nagyvárad," he said, "I know."

"You know?"

"I heard it last night over the radio."

"Is it far from here?"

Schmitz looked thoughtfully at the long column of trucks driving into the yard. "Far," he said with a sigh, "far doesn't mean a thing in this war—must be about sixty miles. Maybe we should give the girl her money in cigarettes—right now."

Schneider looked at Schmitz and felt himself blushing. "Hold on a minute," he said, "I'd like her to stay for a bit."

"Suit yourself," said Schmitz, walking slowly off toward the south wing.

As he entered the patients' room the captain said in a low, hollow tone: "Byelyogorshe." Schmitz knew it was pointless to look
at his watch; that rhythm was more precise than any watch could
ever be, and while he sat on the edge of the bed, the medical history in his hand, almost lulled to sleep by that ever-recurring word,
he tried to figure out how such a rhythm could come about—what
mechanism, what clockwork, in that appallingly patched-up,
sliced-up skull, was releasing that monotonous litany? And what
happened in those fifty seconds when the man said nothing,
merely breathed? Schmitz knew almost nothing about him: born
March 1895 in Wuppertal; rank: captain; service: army; civilian
occupation: businessman; religion: Lutheran; residence, troop unit,
wounds, illnesses, type of injury. Nor was there anything particu-
larly striking about this man's life: his school record was not good,
he had been a very mediocre student, somewhat unreliable; he
had only had to repeat a year once, and on graduating he had even
had a B in geography, English, and Phys. Ed. He had had no love
for the war; without wanting to, he had been made a lieutenant in
1915. He drank a bit, but not excessively—and later, when he was
married, he could never bring himself to deceive his wife, however
simple and enticing it might sometimes have been to arrange an
affair. He just couldn't bring himself to do it.

Schmitz knew that everything in the medical history was vir-
tually irrelevant as long as he didn't know why the man said "Byelyogorshe" and what it meant to him—and Schmitz knew that he
would never know, yet he would have happily sat there forever,
waiting for that word.

Outside it was very quiet—he listened tensely and expectantly
to the silence into which from time to time that word dropped.
But the silence was stronger, oppressively strong, and slowly, almost reluctantly, Schmitz got up and went out of the room.

After Schmitz had left them, the girl looked at Schneider and
seemed embarrassed. She made a hurried gesture of drinking. "Oh,
of course," he said, "the water." He went toward the building to
get some water. At the entrance he had to jump back: an elegant

red car drove past him, quietly, but a little too fast and, carefully avoiding the parked ambulances, swung toward the rear where the administrator had his quarters.

On coming back with the pail of water Schneider had to jump aside again. Horns were sounding, the column was getting under way. In the first truck sat the sergeant major, the others followed slowly. The sergeant major did not look at Schneider. Schneider let the long line of trucks pass and stepped into the courtyard, now oppressively empty and quiet. He set the pail down in front of the horse and looked at the girl; she pointed to Schmitz, just then emerging from the south wing. Schmitz walked past them out through the entrance, and they slowly followed. They stood side by side watching the column move off in the direction of the station. "The two from the infectious ward actually did bring along some weapons," Schmitz said quietly.

"Ah yes," exclaimed Schneider, "I'd forgotten about that."

Schmitz shook his head. "We won't be needing them—on the contrary. Come on, let's go." He paused beside the girl: "I think we'd better give her the cigarettes now, eh? Just in case?"

Schneider nodded. "Didn't they leave us a truck? How are we supposed to get away?"

"One truck's supposed to be coming back," said Schmitz. "The M.O. promised me."

The two men exchanged glances.

"There come some refugees," said Schmitz, pointing toward the village: a weary group was approaching. The refugees trudged slowly past without looking at them. They were tired and sad and did not look at either the soldiers or the girl.

"They've come a long way," said Schmitz. "Look how tired the horses are. It's useless to run away; at that speed they'll never escape the war."

A car horn blew behind them, sharp and impatient, insolent. They moved slowly apart, Schneider toward the girl. The administrator's car was pushing its way out; it was forced to stop, almost hitting a refugee cart. They could see the occupants quite dis-

tinctly, they were sitting right in front of their noses, it was like
being in the front row at the movies, painfully close to the screen.
In front, at the wheel, sat the administrator, his sharp, rather weak
profile motionless; beside him on the seat was a pile of suitcases
and blankets, firmly fastened with ropes so they would not topple
over on him during the drive. Behind him sat his wife, her beautiful profile as motionless as his; both seemed bent on looking neither right nor left. She was holding the baby on her lap, their six-
year-old boy was beside her: he was the only one looking out; his
lively face was pressed to the glass, and he smiled at the soldiers. It
was two minutes before the car could go on—the horses were
tired, and somewhere further along the trek had stalled. They
could see the man at the wheel grow tense: he was sweating, he
blinked rapidly, and his wife whispered something to him from
the back seat. There was scarcely a sound, only the refugees calling
out wearily along the trek, and a child crying; but suddenly from
the courtyard behind them came shouts, hoarse yells, and they
looked back. At that instant a stone struck the car, but it only
smacked into the folded tent; the second stone knocked a dent in
the saucepan tied to the top as if for a family outing. The man
who was yelling and running up to them was the janitor; he occupied two rooms in the bathhouse at the far end of the grounds.
He was quite close now, standing right in the entrance, but he had
run out of stones. As he bent down, cursing, the snag in the trek
sorted itself out, and the car, hooting imperiously, got under way.
A flowerpot swished through the air but landed only where a second ago the car had been standing, on the swept pavement of blue
chips. The clay pot shattered, the fragments rolled apart, forming
an oddly symmetrical circle around the lump of soil, which first
seemed to retain its shape but then suddenly crumbled apart, releasing the roots of a geranium whose blossoms, red and innocent,
remained upright in the center.

The janitor stood between the soldiers. He was not cursing now,
he was weeping, the tears clearly visible on his grimy cheeks, and
his posture was both touching and horrifying: leaning forward,

fists clenched, his grubby old jacket flapping about his hollow chest. He jumped when a woman's voice screamed behind him in the courtyard, then he turned and walked slowly back, weeping. Szarka followed him, drawing away when Schneider put out his hand toward her. She took hold of her horse, led it outside, climbed onto the cart, and picked up the reins.

"I'll go and get the cigarettes," cried Schmitz, "don't let her leave—I'll be right back." Schneider held the horse firmly by the bridle, the girl brought the whip down on his hand; it hurt, but he hung on. He looked back and was surprised to see Schmitz running. He wouldn't have thought Schmitz would ever run. The girl raised her whip again, but instead of bringing it down on his hand she placed it beside her on the seat, and Schneider was amazed to see her suddenly smile: it was the smile he had often seen on her, tender and cool, and he went up to the cart and carefully lifted her down from her upturned crate. She called out something to the horse, and when Schneider put his arms around her he saw that she was still a bit nervous, but she did not resist, she just looked uneasily about her. It was dark in the entrance; Schneider kissed her carefully on the cheeks, on the nose, and pushed back her smooth black hair to kiss the nape of her neck. He was startled to hear Schmitz throw the cigarettes into the cart. The girl's head shot up, her eyes went to the red packages. Schmitz did not look at Schneider but turned on his heel and went back into the courtyard. The girl was blushing, she looked at Schneider but deliberately past his eyes, and all at once she called out to the horse, a crisp, short word, and jerked the reins. Schneider moved aside. He waited until she was fifty paces away, then called her name into the silence—she hesitated, did not turn around, raised the whip over her head in a farewell gesture, and drove on. Schneider walked slowly back into the courtyard.

The seven men of the rear unit were sitting over a meal outside what had been the kitchen; there was a pail of soup on the table in the courtyard, and beside it thick slices of bread and meat.

Schneider heard muffled blows coming from inside the building. He raised his eyebrows at the men.

"The janitor's breaking down the door to the administrator's quarters," said Feinhals, adding a moment later: "At least he might have left the door open; there's no point in destroying it."

Schmitz entered the building with four soldiers to collect all the material for loading. Schneider stayed behind with Feinhals and Otten.

"I've been given a nice job," said Otten.

Feinhals was drinking red schnapps out of an enamel mug; he passed a few packages of cigarettes to Schneider. "Thanks," said Schneider.

"I've been given the job," said Otten, "of throwing the machine gun and the machine pistol and the rest of the junk into the cesspool, down there where the dud shell's lying. You can give me a hand, Feinhals."

"Okay," said Feinhals. With his soup spoon he was slowly drawing patterns on the table from a soup puddle that ran broad and brown from the center to the edge.

"Let's go then," said Otten.

Shortly after this Schneider fell asleep, bent over the lid of his mess bowl. His cigarette went on burning. It was lying at the edge of the table; the fine ash ate its way slowly out of the cigarette paper, the burning tip crept on, burning a narrow black trail in the table as far as the edge of the cigarette, and four minutes later only a slender gray stick of ash was left, stuck to the table. This little gray stick lay there a long time, almost an hour, until Schneider woke up and brushed it off with his arm without ever having seen it. He woke up just as the truck was driving into the yard. Almost simultaneously with the sound of the truck they heard the first tanks. Schneider leaped to his feet—the others, who were standing around smoking, were on the point of laughing, but stopped short of it: that distant rumble spoke for itself.

"How about that," said Schmitz, "the truck really did turn up.

Feinhals, go up into the attic, maybe you can see something from there."

Feinhals walked over to the south wing. The janitor was leaning on a windowsill in the administrator's quarters, watching the men. His wife could be heard moving about inside, there was a faint tinkle, she appeared to be counting glasses.

"Let's load the stuff," said Schmitz. The driver gestured impatiently; he looked very tired. "Balls," he said, "climb in and leave the crap behind." He picked up a package from the table, ripped it open, and lit a cigarette.

"Start loading," said Schmitz. "We've got to wait anyway till Feinhals gets back."

The driver shrugged his shoulders, sat down at the table, and ladled some soup from the pail into Schneider's mess bowl.

The rest of the men loaded the truck with everything that had been left behind in the building: a few beds, an officer's barrack box, his name printed on it in black paint: Lt. Greck, a stove, and a pile of soldiers' packs, knapsacks, kit bags, and a few rifles; then a pile of underwear: bundled shirts, underpants, socks, and some fur-lined vests.

Feinhals called down from the attic: "I can't see a thing. There's a row of poplars in the village blocking my view. Can you hear them? I can, quite clearly."

"Yes," called Schmitz, "we can hear them. Come on down."

"Okay," said Feinhals. His head vanished from the skylight.

"Someone ought to go down to the railway embankment," said Schmitz, "he'd be sure to see them from there."

"It's no use," said the truck driver, "they're not in sight yet."

"How can you tell?"

"By listening. I can hear they're not in sight yet. Besides, they're coming from two directions."

He pointed toward the southwest, and his gesture seemed to conjure up the rumble over there too: he was right, they could hear it now.

"Hell," said Schmitz. "What do we do now?"

"Get going," said the driver. He stepped aside and, shaking his head, looked on as the others finished off the job of loading the table onto the truck, as well as the bench he had been sitting on.

Feinhals came out of the building. "One of the patients is yelling," he said.

"I'll go," said Schmitz. "You fellows get going."

They stood there, hesitating. Then they slowly followed him, all except the driver. Schmitz turned around, saying quietly: "Get going, I tell you, I have to stay behind anyway, with the patients." Again they hesitated, then promptly followed him again.

"Damn it all," Schmitz called back to them, "get going, I tell you. You need to get a head start on this damned plain."

This time they halted and did not follow. Only Schneider walked slowly after him as he disappeared into the building. The rest moved slowly toward the truck. Feinhals hesitated a moment. It was a brief pause, then he entered the building and came face to face with Schneider.

"D'you need something?" Schneider asked. "Everything's already on the truck."

"Unload some bread, and some margarine—and cigarettes." The door to the sickroom opened. Feinhals looked in and exclaimed: "My God, the captain."

"D'you know him?" asked Schmitz.

"Yes," said Feinhals, "I once spent half a day in his battalion."

"Where?"

"I don't know what the place was called."

"Get out of here, you two," cried Schmitz, "and quit fooling around."

Feinhals said: "Be seeing you," and left.

"What made you stay behind?" asked Schmitz, but he did not seem to expect a reply, and Schneider gave none. They both stood listening to the noise of the departing truck, the motor sounding hollow as the truck drove through the entrance; then it was outside on the road to the station—and even beyond the station they could still hear it, until it gradually became very faint.

The rumbling of the tanks had stopped. They heard firing.

"Heavy flak," said Schmitz. "We really should go down to the embankment."

"I'll go," said Schneider. Inside the room the captain said "Bye-lyogorshe." He said it almost without emphasis, yet with a certain pleasure. His face was dark, with a dense black growth of beard, his head was firmly bandaged. Schneider looked at Schmitz. "Hopeless," he said. "If he gets better, comes through this, well. . . ." He shrugged his shoulders.

"Byelyogorshe," said the captain. Then he started to cry. He cried soundlessly, without the least alteration in his expression, but even through his tears he said: "Byelyogorshe."

"There's a court-martial proceeding against him," said Schmitz. "He was thrown off a motorbike and wasn't wearing a steel helmet. He was a captain."

"I'll just run down to the embankment," said Schneider, "maybe I can see something from there. If any more troops come back I'll join them . . . so. . . ."

Schmitz nodded.

"Byelyogorshe," said the captain.

When Schneider came out into the courtyard he saw that at the far end the janitor had run up a flag in the administrator's quarters, a pathetic red rag with a clumsy yellow sickle and white hammer stitched to it. Now the rumbling in the southeast was also becoming more distinct again. The firing seemed to have ceased. He walked slowly past the planted beds, only stopping when he reached the cesspool. Beside the cesspool lay the dud shell. It had been lying there for months. Months ago, S.S. units that had been dug in along the railway tracks had been fighting Hungarian rebels holed up in the school, but it had been only a very brief skirmish: the traces of firing had almost disappeared from the façade. Only the dud had remained where it was, a rusty piece of iron, the length of an arm and tapering to a round point, scarcely noticeable. It looked almost like a piece of rotting wood. In the high grass it was hardly visible, but the administrator's wife had made numerous protests against its existence, and reports had been submitted that never received a reply.

Schneider's pace slackened a little while he had to pass the dud. In the grass he saw the footprints of Otten and Feinhals, who had thrown the machine gun into the cesspool, but the surface of the cesspool was smooth again, a green, greasy smoothness. Schneider continued on past the beds, through the tree farm, across the meadow, and climbed up onto the railway embankment. Those four or five feet seemed to raise him to an immense height above the ground. He looked beyond the village out onto the broad plain to the left of the tracks and saw nothing. But the sound had become more distinct. He listened carefully for any firing. Nothing. The rumbling came from exactly the same direction as the tracks. Schneider sat down and waited. The village was absolutely silent; it lay there as if dead, with its trees, the little houses, the square church tower. It looked very small because to the left of the embankment there was not a single house. Schneider began to smoke.

Indoors Schmitz was sitting beside the man who said "Byelyogorshe." Over and over again. His tears had dried up. The man stared straight ahead with his dark eyes and repeated "Byelyogorshe," like a beautiful melody, Schmitz thought—anyway, he could have listened forever to this one word. The other patient was asleep.

The man who kept saying "Byelyogorshe" was called Bauer, Captain Bauer. He had previously been a textile agent, and before that a student, but before he became a student he had been a lieutenant, for almost four years, and later, as a textile agent, things had not been easy for him. It all depended on whether people had money, and people hardly ever did have money. At least, not the people who might have bought his sweaters. Expensive sweaters always sold well, so did cheap ones, but his particular line, the medium-priced range, were always very hard to sell. . . . He hadn't managed to pick up an agency for cheap sweaters, or for expensive ones—those were the good agencies, and good agencies went to the people who didn't need them. Fifteen years he had spent as an agent for those slow-selling sweaters; the first twelve years had been a loathsome, never-ending, horrible struggle, chasing from store to store, from building to building, the kind of life that wore a man down. It had put years on his wife. When he first met her she had been twenty-three and he twenty-six—he was still a student, fond of a drink, while she was a slender, fair-haired girl who couldn't drink any wine at all. But she had never uttered a cross word to him, a quiet woman who had held her tongue even when he sacrificed his university career to sell sweaters. He had often been surprised himself at his own stamina—to have been selling those sweaters for twelve years!—and at his wife's calm acceptance of everything. Then for three years things had gone a bit better, and suddenly, after fifteen years, the whole situation had changed: he acquired the agency for both the expensive and the cheap sweaters and kept the agency for the medium-priced range. Business had been booming, and now others were doing the legwork for him. He could spend all his time at home, telephoning and signing, he had a warehouseman, a bookkeeper, and a stenographer. Now he had money, but now his wife—who was never really well and had had five miscarriages in quick succession—had cancer. It had finally been confirmed. And besides, these halcyon days had lasted only four months—until the war broke out.

"Byelyogorshe," said the captain.

Schmitz looked at him; he would have liked to know what the man was thinking about. He felt an ungovernable curiosity to know the whole man, that large and rather hollow face, deathly pale under its stubble, those staring eyes that seemed to say "Byelyogorshe"—for now his mouth barely moved. Then the man started crying again, his tears running soundlessly down his cheeks. He was no hero, and it had been pretty rough to have the lieutenant-colonel shout into the phone telling him to find out what his bunch were doing, that something was wrong at Horse Droppings, and to have to drive up to the front line with that steel helmet on his head, knowing what a fool he looked in it. He was no hero, he had never said he was, in fact he knew he wasn't. And when he

AND WHERE WERE YOU, ADAM?

was close to the front line he had taken off the steel helmet because he didn't want to look like a fool when he got to the front and had to start shouting. He held the steel helmet in his hand and thought: What the hell, why not take a chance, and the closer he got to that stupid mess up front the less scared he was. Hell, they all knew there wasn't a thing he could do, that anyone could do, because they had too few guns and no tanks. So why start shouting like an idiot? Every officer knew that too many tanks and too many guns had been ordered back to cover staff quarters. Shit, he thought, unaware that he was being brave. And then he was thrown off the machine and his whole skull was ripped open, and the only thing left inside him was the word "Byelyogorshe." That was all. It seemed to be enough to keep him talking for the whole of the rest of his life, it was a world for him, a world that no one knew or ever would know.

He had no idea, of course, that a court-martial had been instituted against him on grounds of self-mutilation because he had removed his steel helmet while under fire and, what was more, while on a motorcycle. He had no idea of this—and he never would have. The drawing up of the paper bearing his name and file number, and all the other documents, had been so much wasted effort —he would never find out about them, they would never reach him now. He merely said, every fifty seconds: "Byelyogorshe."

Schmitz never took his eyes off him. He would willingly have gone out of his mind himself to know what was going on inside this man's mind. And at the same time he envied him.

He jumped when Schneider opened the door. "What is it?" asked Schmitz. "They're coming," said Schneider. "They're here. No more of our troops managed to get through."

Schmitz had heard nothing. Now he heard them. They were there. To the left they were already in the village. Now he understood what the driver had meant: "I can hear they're not in sight yet." Now you could hear they were in sight—clearly in sight.

"The flag," said Schmitz, "we should have hung out the flag with the red cross—it would have been worth a try."

"We still can."

"Here it is," said Schmitz. He pulled it out from under his pack on the table. Schneider took it.

"Coming?" he asked.

They left. Schneider stuck his head out of the window and pulled it back in again immediately. His face was white.

"They're right there," he said, "by the embankment."

"I'll go and meet them," said Schmitz.

Schneider shook his head. He raised the flag high above his head and went out through the door. He swung round to the right and made straight for the embankment. It was very quiet, even the tanks were quiet as they stood parked at the edge of the village. The school was the last building before the station. It was in that direction that their gun barrels were pointing, but Schneider didn't see them. He didn't see the tanks at all, he saw nothing. He felt ridiculous, holding the flag like that in front of himself as if he were in a parade, and he could feel that his blood was fear. Just plain fear. He walked stiffly, straight ahead, almost like a puppet, holding the flag in front of himself. He walked slowly until he stumbled. That woke him up. He had stumbled over a wire connecting the vinestocks in a model plantation. Now he saw everything. There were two tanks, they were parked behind the embankment, and the one in front was slowly veering its turret to aim at him. Then, when he had passed the trees, he saw there were more. They were standing behind and beside one another in formation across the field, and the red stars painted on them seemed repulsive and very alien to him. He had never seen them before. Next came the cesspool. Now he had only to pass the beds, cross the tree farm, climb up the embankment—but at the cesspool he hesitated; he was suddenly scared again, worse than before. Before he hadn't realized; he had thought his blood was turning to ice, he hadn't realized it was fear—now his blood was like fire, and he saw nothing but red—nothing else—gigantic red stars that struck terror into him. Just then he stepped on the dud, and the dud exploded.

At first nothing happened. In the silence the explosion was staggeringly loud. The Russians knew only that the shell had not come from them, and that the man with the flag had suddenly vanished in a cloud of dust. Shortly after that they started pounding away at the building in a frenzy. They swung all their gun barrels around, redeployed themselves for firing, fired first into the south wing, then into the central building and the north wing, where the janitor's tiny flag hung limply from the window. It fell into the dirt that crumbled down from the building—and finally they fired again into the south wing, this time long and furiously; they had not fired their guns for a long time, and they sawed through the thin façade until the building toppled forward. It was not until later that they noticed there had not been a single shot from the other side.

IV

Only two big patches of color were left: one green, a cucumber-vendor's great mound, the other pinkish-yellow, apricots. In the middle of the market square stood the swingboats. They were there permanently. Their colors had faded, their blue and red as dingy and dirty as the colors of a venerable old ship anchored in the harbor and patiently waiting to be scrapped. The swingboats hung down stiffly, not one was moving, and smoke curled up from the chimney of the caravan parked alongside them.

The patches of color were slowly breaking up: the dark and light greens of the intertwined mosaic of cucumbers dwindled rapidly; Greck could see from a long way off that two people were busy breaking it up. The apricots took longer, much longer: a woman, all by herself, was picking the apricots up one by one and carefully placing them in baskets. Cucumbers were evidently not as fragile as apricots. Greck slowed his pace. Deny it, he thought, simply deny everything. That's the only thing to do if they find out. The only thing. Life was worth a denial, after all. But they wouldn't find out, he was sure of that. It did surprise him, though, to find that there were so many Jews still around here.

The paving between the low trees and little houses was uneven, but he did not notice it. He was pretty scared, and he had the feeling: the faster I get away from there, the less chance there is of attracting attention, and most likely I won't have to deny anything. But I must hurry. He was walking faster again now, hurrying along. He had almost reached the square; the cart with the cucumbers was already passing him, and beyond it there was still that woman painstakingly packing away her apricots. Her pile had not yet been reduced by half.

Greck saw the swingboats. Never in his life had he gone for a ride on a swingboat. Such pleasures had not been for him; they were forbidden in his family, first because he was never really well, and then because that was no way to behave, in public, swinging through the air like some silly monkey. And he had never done anything that was forbidden—today had been the first time, and right off something so terrible, almost the worst thing you could do, something that automatically cost you your life.

Greck could feel the panic in his throat, and he lurched quickly, reeling in the sunshine, across the empty square toward the swing-boats. Smoke was puffing more vigorously now from the caravan's chimney. They must have put some more coal on, he thought: no, wood. He didn't know what they put on stoves in Hungary. And he didn't care. He knocked on the caravan door: a man appeared, naked to the waist, he was blond, unshaven, and big-boned, his face had something almost Dutch about it; only the nose was strikingly narrow, and he had very dark eyes.

"What is it?" he asked in German. Greck could feel the sweat trickling into his mouth; he licked his lips, wiped the palm of his hand across his face, and said: "The swings, I'd like to go for a ride."

The man in the caravan door screwed up his eyes, then nodded. He ran his tongue over his teeth; behind him appeared his wife, she was in her petticoat, sweat was dripping down her face, and the dark-red shoulder straps were sweat-stained. In one hand she was holding a wooden spoon, in the other arm a child. The child was dirty. The woman was very dark, somber, Greck thought. There was definitely something sinister about these people. Perhaps they were suspicious of him. Greck no longer wanted a ride on the swingboats, but the man, whose tongue had finally settled down, said: "Well, if you really want to—in this heat—at midday."

He came down the steps; Greck moved aside and followed him the few paces to the swingboats.

"How much?" he asked feebly. They'll think I'm nuts, he thought. The sweat was driving him crazy. He wiped his sleeve across his face and climbed the wooden steps to the iron framework. The man released a brake, one of the swingboats in the middle swayed gently to and fro.

"I guess," said the man, "you'd better not go too high, or I'll have to stay here and watch. It's the law."

Greck found his German repulsive. It was an odd mixture of softness and impudence, as if he were uttering an entirely foreign language with German words.

"I won't," Greck said. "You can go . . . how much?"

The man shrugged his shoulders. "Give me one pengö," he said. Greck gave him his last pengö and carefully climbed in.

The little boat was wider than he had thought. He felt quite safe and began to use the technique he had so often been able to watch but not use. He held on to the iron stanchions, unclasped his fingers to wipe off the sweat, then straightened his knee, bent it, straightened it, and was amazed to feel the swingboat move. It was very simple, all you had to do was make sure the bending of your knee did not interfere with the rhythmic movement set up by the swing: you had to increase the rhythm by throwing your weight back, with straight legs, as the boat swung forward, and by letting yourself fall forward as the boat swung back. Greck saw that the man was still standing beside him, and he shouted: "What's the matter? You don't have to stay." The man shook his head, and Greck ceased to pay attention to him. All of a sudden he knew he had been missing something vital in his life: riding a swingboat. It was glorious. The sweat dried on his forehead, and the gentle coolness of the rocking motion even dried the sweat on his body: the air blew through him, fresh and exquisite, with every swing, and furthermore: the world was changed. One minute it consisted merely of a few dirty planks with broad grooves running along them, and on the downward swing he had the whole sky to himself. "Watch out!" cried the man down below, "hold tight!" Greck could feel the man putting on the brake: a gentle jolt that severely hampered his swinging.

"Leave me alone!" he shouted. But the man shook his head. Greck quickly swung himself up again. This was the glorious part: to stand parallel to the earth as the little boat swung back—to see those dirty planks that signified the world—and then, plunging forward again, to kick your feet into the sky, to see it overhead as if you were lying in a meadow, only this way you were closer to the sky, infinitely closer. Everything in between was insignificant. On his left the woman was carefully packing away her apricots; her pile never seemed to get any less. On the right stood that fat blond fellow who had to obey the law and slow him down; a few chickens waddled across his field of vision, over there was a road. His cap flew off his head.

Deny it, he thought, as he calmed down, simply deny it; they won't believe it if I deny it. I don't do things like that. No one would believe I could do a thing like that. I've got a good reputation. I know they don't think much of me because I've got chronic indigestion, but they like me in their way, and no one would believe I could do a thing like that. He was both proud and timid, and it was a glorious feeling to find he had the courage to go on this swingboat. He would write to his mother about it. No, better not. Mama didn't understand about things like that. Whatever life may bring: Always behave with dignity! was her motto. She would never understand how her son, an attorney, Lieutenant Greck, could take a ride in a swingboat, in the middle of a

broiling hot day in a dirty Hungarian market square, in full view
of anyone—anyone at all—who happened to be passing by. No, no
—he could picture her shaking her head, a woman without humor;
he knew that and it was no use trying to fight it. And that other
thing: oh God! Although he didn't want to, he couldn't help
thinking about it, how he had undressed in the Jewish tailor's back
room: a stuffy little hole with scraps of patching material lying
around, half-finished suits with buckram tacked onto them, and a
repulsively large bowl of cucumber salad with drowning flies float-
ing around in it—he could feel fluid rising into his mouth, and he
knew he was turning pale, disgusting fluid in his mouth—but he
could still see himself, taking off his pants and revealing his second
pair, taking the money, and the toothless old man's grin following
him as he hurried out of the shop.

Suddenly the world began to spin round him. "Stop!" he yelled,
"stop!" The man down below jammed on the brake, he felt it, the
hard rhythmic jolting. Then the swing came to a standstill; he
knew he looked ridiculous and pathetic, and he carefully stepped
out, walked behind the framework, and spat: his stomach had settled down but he still had that disgusting taste in his mouth. He
felt giddy, sat down on a step, and closed his eyes; the rhythm of
the ride was still in his eyes, he could feel his eyeballs twitching,
he had to spit again. It took quite a while for the movement of
his eyeballs to calm down.

He rose and picked up his cap from the ground. The man was
standing beside him, looked at him impassively; then his wife appeared, Greck was surprised to see how small she was. A tiny
swarthy little thing with a gaunt face. She was holding a mug. The
blond fellow took the mug from her and held it out to Greck:
"Drink," he said without emotion. Greck shook his head. "Drink,"
said the man, "it will do you good."

Greck took the mug; the stuff tasted very bitter, but it helped.
The couple smiled, they smiled mechanically because they were
used to smiling at this kind of thing, not because they cared for
him or pitied him.

"Thanks very much," he said. He felt in his pocket for coins, there were none left, only that terrible great hundred-pengö bill, and he shrugged his shoulders helplessly. He could feel himself flushing. "Okay," said the man, "that's okay." "Heil Hitler," said Greck. The man merely nodded.

Greck did not look back. The sweat was beginning to flow again. It seemed to come boiling out of his pores. Across the square was a tavern. He longed for a wash.

Inside the tavern the air was oddly chilly yet stuffy. The room was almost empty. Greck noticed that the man standing behind the bar looked first at his medals. The man's gaze was cool, not unfriendly, but cool. In the corner to the left sat a young couple with dirty dishes on the table in front of them and a carafe of wine, there was a beer bottle on the table too. Greck sat down in the corner to the right so he could look out on the street. He felt a sense of relief. His watch showed one o'clock, and he didn't have to be back until six. The man came out from behind the bar and walked slowly over to him. Greck wondered what he should drink. He really didn't want anything. Just a wash. He wasn't one for alcohol; besides, it didn't agree with him. Not for nothing had his mother warned him against it, just as she had against riding swingboats. Once again the innkeeper, now facing him, looked first at the left side of his chest.

"Afternoon," said the man. "What can I get you?"

"Some coffee," said Greck, "d'you have any coffee?" The man nodded. The nod said everything: it said that the glance to the left side of Greck's chest and the word coffee had told everything. "And a schnapps," said Greck. But it seemed to be too late.

"What kind?" asked the man.

"Apricot," said Greck.

The fellow went off. He was fat. His pants made fat rolls across his backside, and he was wearing slippers. Sloppy—like everything else here, thought Greck. He looked across at the young lovers. Swarms of flies were perched on the dirty plates with remains of food, chop bones, little mounds of vegetables, and wilted lettuce in earthenware bowls. Disgusting, thought Greck.

A soldier came in, looked nervously around, saluted Greck across the room, and walked over to the bar. The soldier had no medals at all. And yet there was a warmth in the innkeeper's eyes that annoyed Greck. Maybe, he thought, because I'm an officer they expect me to have more medals, splendid gold and silver affairs, these knuckleheads here in Hungary. Maybe I look as though I ought to be wearing medals: I'm tall and slim, blond. Hell, he thought, what a revolting business. He looked out of the window.

The woman with the apricots was almost through now, and all of a sudden he knew what he really wanted to eat: some fruit. Oh, that would do him good! His mother had always given him plenty of fruit when it was in season and cheap, and it had done him a lot of good. Fruit was cheap here, and he had money, and wanted to eat some fruit. He hesitated at the thought of the money; his thoughts hesitated. Sweat broke out heavily again. Nothing would happen, and if something did: deny it, deny it, just deny everything. Nobody was going to believe some dirty Jew that he, Greck, had sold him his pants. Nobody would believe it if he denied it, and even if they identified the pants as his he could say they had been stolen or something. But nobody was going to go to all that trouble. And anyway, why should they find out in his particular case? The affair had opened his eyes in a flash: everyone sold something, damn it all. Everyone. He knew now what happened to the gasoline that the tanks were short of, what became of the warm winter clothing—and they were his own pants, after all, that he had sold, the ones that had been made for him, at his own expense, at Grunk's, the tailor in Coelsde.

Where were all those pengös supposed to come from? Nobody's pay was enough for the kind of extravagances that cocky little lieutenant managed to afford, the one who shared his room and ate cream pastries in the afternoon and drank real whisky in the evening, had all the women he wanted and turned up his nose at anything but a particular brand of cigarette that by this time cost a lot of money.

What the hell, he thought, I've been a fool, I've been a fool all along. Always respectable and law-abiding, while everyone else—everyone else has been having himself a good time. What the hell.

The innkeeper brought the coffee and apricot schnapps. "Anything to eat?" he asked.

"No thanks," said Greck.

The coffee smelled unfamiliar. He tried it: it was mild, with an odd mildness. Some quite pleasant substitute. The schnapps was sharp and burning but felt good. He sipped it slowly, drop by drop. That was it: he must take alcohol like medicine, that was it.

The apricot patch outside on the square had gone. Greck jumped up and ran to the door. "Just a minute," he called to the innkeeper.

The old woman was slowly driving her cart across the square; now she was level with the swingboats, and she speeded up her horse to a comfortable trot. Greck stopped her as she turned into the street. She pulled in the reins. He looked at her face: a broad-boned, elderly woman with handsome features, her face suntanned and sturdy. Greck went up to the cart.

"Fruit," he said, "give me some apricots, please." She looked at him with a smile. Somehow her smile had no warmth. Then she glanced at her baskets and asked: "Bag?" Greck shook his head. Her voice was warm and deep. He watched while she climbed around her seat onto the cart; her legs were surprisingly sturdy. Noticeably so. Greck's mouth watered at the sight of the fruit: it was magnificent. He thought of home. Apricots, he thought, those times when Mama had been able to get apricots! And here, here they got taken back from market. Cucumbers too. He took an apricot from the cart and ate it: it was tart yet at the same time sweet, already a shade too soft and warm, but he enjoyed it. "Very good," he said.

The woman smiled at him again. She took some loose pieces of paper and deftly made a kind of bag into which she very carefully laid the apricots. The way she looked at him struck him as odd. "Enough?" she asked. He nodded. She folded over the ends of paper, tucked them in, and handed him the package. He took his hundred-pengö bill out of his pocket. "Here," he said. Her eyes opened wide, and she said: "Oh, oh," then shook her head. But she took the bill, and for an instant she held on to his hand, clasping it up by the wrist although there was no need to, up by the wrist, for the merest second; then she took the bill, stuck it between her lips, and rummaged around under her skirt to pull out her purse. "No," cried Greck, "no, no, put it away." He looked anxiously around. That great red bill was horribly conspicuous. The street was busy, even a streetcar was passing. "Put it away," he cried, "put it away!" He tore it out of her mouth. She bit her lip, whether with anger or amusement he couldn't tell.

Furious, he dug out a second apricot, sank his teeth into it, and waited. The sweat was standing in thick beads on his forehead. He was having a hard time holding the apricots together in the loose bag. It seemed to him that the old woman was deliberately taking her time—he even considered running away, but she would probably set up a terrible hue and cry and everyone would come running. The Hungarians were allies, not enemies. He sighed and waited. Across the street a soldier emerged from the tavern, not the one who had just gone in. This one had medals on his chest: three—as well as insignia on his sleeve. He saluted Greck, and Greck nodded in response. Again a streetcar passed, on the other side this time, people walked by, many people, and behind him, behind that dilapidated board fence, the swingboat calliope softly began to drone. The old woman smoothed out one bill after another until it looked as though her purse held no more. Then came the coins. Patiently she stacked up little nickel piles beside her on the seat. Then she carefully took the bill from him and handed him first the bills, then the nickel piles. "Ninety-eight," she said. He turned to go, but she suddenly laid her hand on his forearm: her hand was broad and warm and quite dry, and her face came closer. "Girl?" she asked in a whisper, smiling at him. "Pretty girl, eh?"

"No, no," he said hastily, "thanks all the same."

She darted her hand under her skirt, drew out a scrap of paper, and quickly passed it to him. "There," she said. "There." He added it to the bills, she gave a flick to the reins, and he walked back across the street carefully carrying his loose package.

The table in front of the young couple had still not been cleared. He couldn't understand these people: flies clustered in hordes on the plates, the rims of the glasses, and this young man was gesturing animatedly as he spoke in a low insistent voice to the girl. The innkeeper came toward Greck. "Can I have a wash?" asked Greck. The innkeeper stared at him. "A wash," said Greck impatiently. "A wash, for God's sake." Infuriated at the man's obtuseness, he rubbed his hands together. The innkeeper gave a sudden nod, turned, and beckoned Greck to follow him.

Greck followed, paused to let the innkeeper hold back the dark-green curtain for him—the fellow's expression seemed to have changed. It looked as if he were asking something. They walked along a short narrow passage, and the innkeeper opened a door. "Here you are," he said. Greck went in. The cleanliness of the washroom surprised him. The washbasins were neatly cemented to the wall, the doors were painted white. Beside the washbasin hung a towel. The innkeeper brought a cake of green army soap. "Here you are," he repeated. Greck felt at a loss. The innkeeper left. Greck sniffed the towel, it seemed clean. Then he quickly removed his tunic, washed his neck and face all over, and ran water over his arms. He hesitated a moment, then put on his tunic again and slowly washed his hands. The soldier he had seen before came in, the one with no medals. Greck stepped aside so the soldier could get to the urinal. He buttoned his tunic, picked up the soap, and left. At the bar he gave the innkeeper the soap, said "Thanks," and sat down again.

The innkeeper's expression was stony. Greck wondered what was keeping the soldier. The young couple in the corner had gone. The table had still not been cleared, a jumble of dirty dishes. Greck drank the rest of his cold coffee and sipped the apricot schnapps. Then he began to eat his fruit.

He felt an insane craving for this juicy, fleshy stuff and ate six apricots in quick succession—and suddenly he felt nauseated: the apricots were too warm. He took another sip of schnapps, the schnapps was also too warm. The innkeeper stood behind the bar, smoking and somnolent. Another soldier came in. The innkeeper seemed to know him, and the two men whispered together. The soldier drank beer; he had one medal, the Cross of Merit. The soldier who had just been to the toilet came back, paid at the bar, and left. At the door he saluted. Greck returned the salute, and then the soldier who had just arrived went to the toilet. Outside the swingboat calliope was droning away. The sound, wild yet sluggish, filled Greck with melancholy. He would never forget that ride. Too bad it had turned his stomach. Outside, things had begun to liven up a bit: across the square there was an ice-cream parlor, people were crowding in front of it. The tobacco shop next-door to it was empty. The soiled green curtain in the corner was pushed aside, and out came a girl. At once the innkeeper's eyes went to Greck. The girl looked at him too. He could only just make her out; she seemed to be wearing a red dress, in that dense, greenish light the color looked nondescript, and the only thing he could see clearly was her heavily made-up face, very white, the mouth painted startlingly red. He could not see the expression on her face, he thought she was smiling a little, but he could be wrong; he could hardly see her. She was holding some money, holding the bill out straight, like a child, the way she would have held a flower or a stick. The innkeeper gave her a bottle of wine and some cigarettes, without switching his gaze from Greck. He did not look at the girl at all, not a word passed between them.

Greck took the crumpled bills from his pocket and picked out the scrap of paper the old woman had given him. He placed it on the table and put the money back in his pocket. He was acutely conscious of the innkeeper's gaze and looked up. There was no doubt about it now, the girl was smiling at him; there she stood, holding the green bottle, her fingers curved around a few loose cigarettes, little white sticks that matched her face. All he was aware of in the darkness were her startling white face, the dark mouth, and the piercingly white cigarettes in her hand. She gave a brief smile, then moved aside the curtain and left.

The innkeeper was now gazing fixedly at Greck. His expression was stony, with something menacing about it. Greck was scared of him. That's how murderers look, he thought, and he would have welcomed the chance to leave quickly. Outside the calliope was droning away, the streetcar squealed past, and sadness filled him, an alien and solemn sadness. The repulsive apricots, soft and warm, lay in front of him on the table, and flies were sticking to his cup. He did not wave them away. All at once he got up and called: "The bill, please," raising his voice to give himself courage. The innkeeper hurried over. Greck took some money from his pocket. He watched the flies now slowly gathering on the apricots, black sticky dots on that repulsive pink; the thought of having eaten them almost turned his stomach.

"Three pengös," said the innkeeper. Greck handed him the money. The innkeeper glanced at the schnapps glass, still half full, then at Greck's chest, at the scrap of paper lying on the table, and he picked it up at the very instant Greck reached for it. The innkeeper grinned, his big fat pale face looked repulsive. The innkeeper read the address on the paper: it was his own. He grinned, more hideously than ever. Sweat broke out over Greck's body again.

"Do you still need this paper?" asked the innkeeper.

"No," said Greck. "Good-by." It occurred to him he had to say Heil Hitler, and in the doorway he added "Heil Hitler!" The innkeeper did not respond. Turning round, Greck saw the man toss the remains of the schnapps onto the floor. The apricots shone warm and pink, like rose-pink wounds in a dark body. . . .

Greck was glad to be out on the street, and he hurried off. He was ashamed to go back to the hospital before his leave was up, the cocky little lieutenant would laugh at him. But what he really wanted was to go back right now and lie down on his bed. He felt like having a decent meal, but when he actually thought of food he remembered the apricots, repulsively pink, and his nausea increased. He thought of the woman he had gone to at noon, straight from the hospital. Her mechanical kisses on his neck suddenly hurt, and he knew why he had found the apricots so repulsive: they were the same color as her underwear, she had sweated a bit, and her body had been warm. It was a stupid idea to go to a woman in the middle of the day in this heat. But he had been following the advice of his father, who had told him he must be sure and have a woman at least once a month. This woman hadn't been bad, a sturdy little person who would probably have been delightful in the evening. She had taken the last of his money off him and known right away what he was up to as soon as she saw he was wearing two pairs of pants. She had laughed and given him the name of the Jewish tailor where he could sell them.

He slowed down. He felt sick to his stomach. He knew it: he should have had a proper meal. Now it was too late, he wouldn't be able to eat a thing. Everything disgusted him: the woman, the dirty Jew, even the swingboats, though that had been a novelty, but they disgusted him too, and the fruit, the innkeeper, the soldier—the lot. He had liked the girl. He had liked her very much. But it wouldn't do to have a woman twice in one day. She had looked very lovely, standing there in the dark in that green corner with her white face, but close up she was sure to be sweaty and smelly too. These girls probably couldn't help being sweaty, they didn't have the money to smell nice in the middle of the day in this heat.

He was passing a restaurant. Chairs stood on the street among tubs of stiff green plants. He sat down in a corner and ordered some soda water. "With ice," he called after the waiter. The waiter nodded. A couple at the next table were talking Rumanian.

Greck was now thirty-three and had been suffering from chronic indigestion ever since he was sixteen. Fortunately his father was a doctor, not a good doctor but the only one in the small town, and they were reasonably well off. But his mother was thrifty. In the summer they used to go to health resorts, or south to the Alps, and often to the coast, and during the winter, when they stayed home, they ate poorly. The only time they ate well was when guests came, but they had few guests. In their small town the center for all social gatherings was the inn, and he was not allowed to go with his parents to the inn. When guests came wine was served, but by the time he reached the age when he could have drunk wine he was already suffering from chronic indigestion. They had always eaten a lot of potato salad. He didn't know exactly how often it had actually been, whether three or four times a week, but some days he had the feeling that as a boy he had eaten nothing but potato salad. A doctor once told him, years later, that his symptoms almost bordered on those of malnutrition, and that potato salad was poison to his system.

Word soon got around his home town that he was sick, and indeed you could see he was, and the girls more or less ignored him. His father wasn't that well off, not enough to compensate for his ill health. In school he didn't shine either. On finishing high school, in 1931, he was allowed to choose a graduation gift, and he chose a trip. He soon got off the train, in Hagen, took a room in a hotel, and spent the evening feverishly roaming the town, but he couldn't find a prostitute in Hagen and left the next day for Frankfurt, where he stayed a week. At the end of a week he had run out of money and took the train home. On the train he thought he would die. At home he was received with shocked surprise; he had had enough money for a three-week trip. His father looked at him, his mother wept, and there was a terrible scene with his old man, who forced him to take off his clothes and be examined. It was a Saturday afternoon, he had never forgotten it; outside all was quiet in those clean streets, so medieval and idyllic, warm and deep, the bells rang for a long, long time, and he stood

facing his father and had to submit to having his body tapped by
the old man's fingers. In the surgery. He hated that fat face and
the breath that always smelled slightly of beer, and he made up
his mind to commit suicide. His father's hands kept tapping his
body, that gray head of thick hair moving for a long time below
his chest. "You're crazy," said his father on finally raising his head,
and he grinned softly. "You're crazy. A woman once or twice a
month is plenty for you." He knew his old man was right.

That evening he sat with Mama drinking weak tea. She didn't
say a word, but all at once she began to cry. He laid aside the
newspaper and went to his room.

Two weeks later he went to Marburg, to the university. He followed his father's advice to the letter, much as he hated him.
After five years he graduated in law. In 1937 he did his first tour of
military duty, in 1938 his second, and in 1939, after he'd spent two
years in the district attorney's office, the war broke out, and he was
sent to the front as a second lieutenant. He disliked the war. The
war made new demands on him. It was no longer enough to be a
qualified attorney, to have a good position with chances of promo-
tion. Now they all looked at his chest when he came home. His
chest was but meagerly decorated. In her letters Mama told him
to take care of himself and at the same time made hints that felt
like pinpricks.

"The Beckers' boy Hugo has been home on leave. He has the
Iron Cross, First Class. Not bad for a boy who never got through
high school, who couldn't even make out as a butcher's appren-
tice. I hear they're even going to make him an officer. Sounds incredible to me. Wesendonk has been badly wounded, they say he's
going to lose his leg." Even that was something, to lose a leg.

He told the waiter to bring him some more soda water. The
soda water made him feel better. It was ice-cold. He longed to be
able to wipe out everything he had done, that silly business with
the Jew, and that stupid idea of buying a bit of fruit on a busy
street with a hundred-pengö bill. The thought of that scene made
him sweat again. Suddenly he felt his stomach beginning to rebel.

He kept his seat and looked around for the toilet. Everyone in the restaurant was sitting quietly chatting. Not a soul moved. He looked anxiously around until his eyes fell on a green curtain beside the counter; he got slowly to his feet and walked stiffly toward the green curtain. On the way he had to salute, a captain was sitting there with a woman; his salute was brief and smart, and he was glad to reach the green curtain.

By four o'clock he was already back at the hospital. The cocky little lieutenant was sitting there with his bags packed. He was wearing his black tank uniform, numerous decorations shone on his chest. Greck knew exactly which ones they were. There were five of them. The lieutenant was drinking wine and eating slices of bread and meat. He called to Greck as he entered: "Your barrack box has arrived."

"Good," said Greck. He walked over to his bed and dragged the box by the handle over to the window.

"By the way," said the lieutenant, "they had to leave your battalion commander behind at Szokarhely. Schmitz stayed with him. He wasn't fit to be moved, that captain of yours."

"Too bad," said Greck. He began to open his box. "I'd leave it shut if I were you," said the lieutenant, "we have to move on, the lot of us, you too."

"Me too?"

"That's right," the lieutenant laughed, then his childlike face became solemn: "They're soon going to be organizing stomach-commandos."

Greck could feel his stomach protesting again. He breathed heavily at the sight of the meat lying there right in front of his eyes in all its clarity. Those gritty specks of fat in the canned meat looked to him like fly eggs. He walked rapidly to the window to get some air. Outside, a cart was driving by loaded with apricots. Greck vomited—he felt an incredible sense of relief.

"Bon appétit!" cried the little lieutenant.

V

Feinhals had gone into town to buy pins, cardboard, and Indian ink, but all he had managed to get was the cardboard, deep-pink cardboard, the kind the sergeant major liked for making placards. On his way back from town it started to rain. The rain was warm. Feinhals tried to push the thick roll under his tunic, but the roll was too long and too thick, and when he noticed the wrapping paper beginning to get wet at the edges and the pink of the cardboard coming through, he walked faster. At a street corner he had to wait. Tanks were clumsily rounding the curve, slowly swinging first their gun barrels and then their rear ends as they continued on toward the southeast. People stood quietly watching the tanks. Feinhals walked on. The rain was coming down solidly now, dripping from the trees, and when he turned into the street leading to his clearing station there were already large puddles on the black ground.

On the door hung the big white sign on which he had printed in pale red pencil: "Hospital Clearing Station—Szentgyörgy." Soon a better sign would hang there, sturdy, deep pink, printed in script with Indian ink. Plain for all to see. At this hour there was no one about. Feinhals rang the bell, inside the porter pressed the switch for the latch; he nodded to the porter as he passed his little cubicle, and entered the corridor. In the corridor a machine pistol and a rifle were hanging on coathooks. Beside each door was a little glass peephole with a thermometer hanging behind it. Everything was clean, and it was very peaceful, and Feinhals walked very quietly. Behind the first door he could hear the sergeant major on the telephone. In the corridor hung photographs of schoolmistresses and a large colored view of Szentgyörgy.

Feinhals turned to the right, went out through a door, and was in the schoolyard. The schoolyard was surrounded by big trees, and beyond its walls clustered tall buildings. Feinhals looked at a window on the fourth floor: the window was open. He walked quickly back into the building and up the stairs.

On the landings hung the photographs of former graduating classes. A whole row of big brown and gilt frames surrounding waist-length photos of girls: thick oval pieces of cardboard, each with a picture of a girl. The first frame showed the class of '18. 1918 seemed to have been the first graduating year. The girls were wearing stiff white blouses and smiling sadly. Feinhals had looked at them often, every day for almost a week. Surrounded by the girls' pictures was one of a very dark, severe-looking lady wearing pince-nez; she must be the headmistress. From 1918 to 1932 it was the same lady—in those fourteen years she did not seem to have changed. It was always the same photo, most likely she always took the same one to the photographer and had him stick it in the center. Feinhals paused in front of the class of '28. Here his eyes were drawn to a girl because of her figure: her name was Maria Kartök, she wore her hair in bangs low on her forehead, almost to her eyebrows, and her face was confident and pretty. Feinhals smiled. He had now reached the second landing and walked on up to the class of '32. He had also graduated in 1932. He looked at ecah girl in turn, they must have been nineteen at the time, his own age then, and now they were thirty-two: in this class there was another girl wearing bangs, only half-way down her forehead, and her face was confident and of a certain severe tenderness. Her name was Ilona Kartök and she was very like her sister, only she seemed slighter and less vain. The stiff blouse suited her well, and she was the only girl in the frame who was not smiling. Feinhals stood there for a few seconds, smiled again, and continued slowly on up to the fourth floor. He was sweating but had no free hand to take off his cap, so he walked on.

At one end of the landing a statue of the Virgin Mary stood in a niche in the wall. It was made of plaster, a vase of fresh flowers had been placed in front of it; that morning there had been tulips in the vase, now there were yellow and red roses, tight, barely opened buds. Feinhals halted and looked along the corridor. Seen as a whole, that corridor full of girls' pictures looked monotonous: all those girls looked like butterflies, innumerable butterflies with slightly darker heads, preserved and collected in large frames. It seemed to be always the same ones, only the large dark center one changed from time to time. It changed in 1932, in 1940, and in 1944. Way up on the left, at the end of the third landing, hung the year of '44, girls in stiff white blouses, smiling and unhappy, and in the middle a dark elderly lady who was also smiling and also seemed unhappy. As he passed, Feinhals glanced at the year of '42; there was a Kartök in that one too, called Szorna, but there was nothing striking about her: she wore her hair like all the others, her face was round and touching. When he got to the top, to the corridor that was as silent as the rest of the house, he heard trucks driving up outside. He threw his stuff on the windowsill, opened a window, and looked out. The sergeant major was standing down on the street facing a column of trucks, their motors still running. Soldiers with bandages jumped down onto the road, and at the rear, from a large red furniture van, came a whole group of soldiers with their packs. The street quickly filled up. The sergeant major shouted: "Here—over here—everyone into the corridor—and wait there." A straggling gray procession moved slowly in through the doors. Across the street windows were flung open, heads looked out, and people gathered at the corner.

Some of the women were crying.

Feinhals shut the window. The building was still quiet—the first sounds were just rising faintly from the corridor below; he walked slowly to the end of the corridor where he kicked once at a door, and a woman's voice inside said: "Yes?" He felt himself blushing as he pressed down the latch with his elbow. He did not see her right away; the room was full of stuffed animals, wide shelves held rolled maps and neatly galvanized glass-topped cases displaying rock specimens, and on the wall hung a colored print of embroidery samples and a numbered series of illustrations showing all the stages of infant care.

"Hallo there," cried Feinhals.

"Yes?" she called. He went toward the window where a narrow aisle opened up between cupboards and map stands. She was sitting at a little table. Her face was rounder than downstairs in the picture, the severity seemed to have grown softer and the tenderness more pronounced. She was shy yet amused when he said "Good afternoon," and she nodded to him. He threw the big paper roll on the windowsill, then the parcel he had been carrying in his left hand, tossed his cap down beside them and wiped the sweat off his face.

"I need your help, Ilona," he said. "I'd appreciate it if you could let me have some Indian ink."

She stood up, closing the book lying in front of her.

"Indian ink," she said. "Indian ink, I don't know what that is."

"I thought you were a teacher!"

She laughed.

"Indian ink," he said, "is a kind of drawing ink. Well then— d'you know what a lettering-pen is?"

"I can imagine," she said with a smile. "A pen for writing fancy lettering—yes, I know what that is."

"D'you think you could lend me one?"

"I believe so." She gestured toward the cupboard behind him, but he saw that she would never come out from the corner behind the table.

He had discovered her three days earlier in this room and had spent hours with her every day, but she had never come close: she seemed scared of him. She was very devout, very innocent and intelligent, he had already had long talks with her, and he could feel that she was drawn to him—but she had never come close—close enough for him to suddenly put his arms around her and kiss her. He had had long talks with her, hung around her for hours, and a few times they had discussed religion, but he would have liked to kiss her; only she never came close.

He frowned and shrugged his shoulders. "Just one word," he said hoarsely. "You've only to say one word, and I'll never come into your room again."

Her expression became serious. She lowered her lids, pursed her lips, looked up again: "I don't know," she said softly, "whether I'd like that—besides, it wouldn't make any difference, would it?"

"No," he said. She nodded.

He walked back to the aisle leading to the door and said: "I don't understand how anyone can become a teacher in a school they've gone to for nine years."

"Why not?" she said. "I always liked school, and I still do."

"Isn't there any school now?"

"Oh yes—we've combined with another one."

"And it's your job to stay here and keep an eye on things, I know—very smart of your headmistress to leave the prettiest teacher behind in the building," he saw her blush, "as well as the most reliable, I know. . . ." He glanced round at the teaching aids. "D'you have a map of Europe in here?"

"Of course," she said.

"And some pins?" She looked at him in surprise and nodded.

"Be a nice girl," he said, "and let me have the map of Europe and a few pins." He unbuttoned his left pocket, fished out a small wax-paper envelope, and shook the contents carefully into his hand: little red cardboard flags; he picked one up and showed it to her. "Come on," he cried, "we're going to play General Staff, it's a great game." He saw her hesitate. "Come on," he cried, "I promise I won't touch you."

She came slowly out and walked over to the rack that held the maps. He looked down into the yard as she passed him, then turned around and helped her set up the stand she was dragging out from somewhere. She fastened in the map, undid the cord, and slowly cranked up the stand. He stood beside her holding the little red flags. "Good God," he muttered, "are we like animals, that all you girls are so scared of us?"

"Yes," she said in a low voice, looking at him; he could tell she was still scared. "Like wolves," she said, breathing hard. "Wolves that are liable to start talking about love any minute. Disturbing kind of people. Please," she said very softly, "don't do that."

"Don't do what?"

"Talk about love," she said very softly.

"Not for the present, I promise." He was peering at the map and did not notice the sidelong smile she gave him.

"The pins, please," he said without turning his head. He stood impatiently facing the map, staring at the brightly colored, irregular shapes, and passed his hand over them. The main front from East Prussia's eastern corner ran down almost dead straight as far as Nagyvárad, except in the middle, near Lvov, where there was a bulge, but no one had any exact information.

He glanced impatiently across at her; she was rummaging in a big drawer of a heavy walnut closet: towels, sheets, diapers, a large naked doll—then she hurried back holding out a big tin full of pins. His fingers groped around in it, hastily picking out the ones with red or blue heads. She watched closely as he inserted the pins in the little cardboard flags and carefully stuck them into the map.

They looked at each other; outside in the corridor there was noise, doors banging, boots tramping, the voices of the sergeant major and soldiers.

"What's happening?" she asked in alarm.

"Nothing," he said calmly, "the first patients have arrived."

He planted a flag down at the bottom where there was a large dot: Nagyvárad—ran his hand gently across Yugoslavia and carefully stuck a flag on Belgrade, then farther along on Rome, and was surprised to see how close Paris was to the German frontier. With his left hand resting on Paris, he slowly ran his right hand all the way across to Stalingrad. The distance between Stalingrad and Nagyvárad was greater than between Paris and Nagyvárad. He shrugged his shoulders and carefully stuck little flags in the spaces between the marked points.

"Oh," she cried—he turned to her, she looked tense, excited, her face seemed to have narrowed, it was smooth and brown, and on those pretty cheeks the down was visible almost up to her dark eyes. She still wore bangs, but shorter than downstairs in the picture. She was breathing hard. "Isn't it a great game?" he asked softly.

"Yes," she said, "terrible—it's all so—you say it—so—like a relief map."

"Three-dimensional, you mean," he said.

"That's it!" she cried. "It's all three-dimensional—it's like looking into a room."

The noise in the corridor had died down, the doors seemed to be closed, but Feinhals suddenly heard his name quite clearly. "Feinhals," shouted the sergeant major, "Where the hell are you?"

Ilona looked at him with raised eyebrows.

"Are they calling you?"

"Yes."

"You'd better go," she said in a low voice. "Please, I don't want them to find you here."

"How long will you be here?"

"Till seven."

"Wait for me—I'll be back."

She nodded, her cheeks fiery red, and stood facing him until he stepped aside to let her into her corner.

"There's some cake in that parcel on the windowsill," he said. "It's for you." He opened the door, looked out, and hurried into the corridor.

He walked slowly downstairs, although he could hear the sergeant major calling "Feinhals" on the third-floor corridor. He smiled at Szorna as he passed the class of '42, but the light was already fading, and he could not make out Ilona's face; the big frame hung in the middle of the wall, and the shadows were closing in. And at the bottom of the stairs stood the sergeant major, who shouted: "For Christ's sake, where the hell have you been? I've been looking for you for an hour."

"I had to go into town, remember? I bought some cardboard for the placards."

"I know, I know, but you've been back half an hour. Let's go."

He took Feinhals by the arm and walked down to the lower floor with him. The sound of singing came from the rooms, and the Russian nurses were hurrying along the corridor with trays.

The sergeant major had been very easy on Feinhals ever since the latter had returned from Szokarhely; he was easy on everyone and at the same time very much on edge since being given the job of organizing a hospital clearing station. The sergeant major was worried about things Feinhals could not know about. During the last few weeks something had happened in this army of which Feinhals could not be aware and the consequences of which he could not judge. But the sergeant major lived on these things, by them and them only, and the fact that they were no longer working worried him very much. Until recently, the possibility of a transfer or an unwelcome posting had been relatively remote; every order was circumvented before it even got to the unit. The authority that drew up the order was the first to circumvent it, and confidential phone calls informed the units to which the order was transmitted of the means of circumventing it—and as orders and regulations became more and more threatening, so the means of bypassing them became more and more simple, and in fact no one acted on them except to secure the removal of undesirable people. As a last resort: a medical examination or a phone call—and things went back to normal.

But all this had changed: phone calls were no good now because the people you had been used to talking to no longer existed, or existed someplace where they couldn't be reached—and the ones you did talk to now didn't know you and had no incentive to help you because they knew you in turn wouldn't be able to help them. The threads were confused or tangled, and the only thing left to do was to save your own skin from one day to the next. Until now the war had taken place over the telephone, but now the war had begun to dominate the telephone. Authorities, code names, superior officers changed every day, and it might happen that you were assigned to a division which the next day consisted only of a general, three staff officers, and a few clerks. . . .

On reaching the bottom the sergeant major let go of Feinhals' arm and opened the door himself. Otten was sitting at the table smoking. The table had a distinct black scorch-mark from a cigarette. Otten was reading a newspaper.

"Well, it's about time," he said, laying aside the paper.

The sergeant major looked at Feinhals, Feinhals looked at Otten.

"I can't do a thing about it," said the sergeant major with a shrug. "I have to transfer all those under forty who aren't on the permanent staff or who no longer qualify as patients. Honestly—I can't do a thing about it. You'll have to go."

"Where to?" asked Feinhals.

"To the redeployment center at the front—and what's more, 'forthwith,'" said Otten. He passed the marching orders to Feinhals. Feinhals read them through.

"'Forthwith,'" said Feinhals. "'Forthwith'—nothing sensible ever happened 'forthwith.'" The marching orders still in his hand, he said: "Do we both have to appear on the same marching orders—I mean, together . . . ?"

The sergeant major gave him a close look: "What d'you mean? Now don't go making a fool of yourself," he said in a low voice.

"What's the time?" asked Feinhals.

"Just on seven," said Otten. He stood up, he had already buckled on his belt and placed his pack on the table.

The sergeant major sat down at the table, pulled open the drawer, and looked at Otten. "Suit yourselves," he said. "Once you fellows are on your way it's no longer up to me." He shrugged his shoulders.

"Okay then, I'll make out one for each of you."

"I'll get my stuff," said Feinhals.

When he saw Ilona upstairs he stopped in the corridor and watched her shut the door, then rattle the latch and nod. She had on her hat and coat and was carrying the parcel of cake. She was wearing a green coat and a brown beret, and he thought she looked even prettier than in her red sleeveless jacket. She was short, a shade too buxom maybe, but when he saw her face, the line of her neck, he felt something he had never felt before at the sight of a woman: he loved her and wanted to possess her. She gave the latch one more rattle, to make sure the door was really locked, and then walked slowly along the corridor. He watched her tensely and noticed that she smiled yet was startled to find him suddenly in front of her.

"I thought you were going to wait for me," he said.

"I'd forgotten I had to leave in a hurry. I was going to leave a message downstairs that I'd be back in an hour."

"Did you really mean to come back?"

"Yes," she said. She looked at him and smiled.

"I'll come with you," he said. "Wait for me. I'll only be a minute."

"You can't come with me. Don't." She shook her head wearily. "I promise I'll be back."

"Where are you going?"

She was silent, glanced around, but the corridor was empty; it was dinnertime, and subdued noises came from the rooms. Then she looked at him again. "To the ghetto," she said. "I have to go to the ghetto with my mother." She looked at him expectantly, but he merely asked: "What are you going to do there?"

"It's being evacuated today. Our relatives are there. We're taking some things to them. The cake too." She looked at the parcel she was carrying, and held it out to him. "You don't mind my giving it away, do you?"

"Your relatives," he said, taking her arm. "Come on—let's go." He walked down the stairs beside her, grasping her arm.

"Your relatives are Jews? Your mother?"

She nodded. "And me," she said, "all of us." She stopped. "Just a moment." She freed her arm, took the flowers out of the vase in front of the Virgin Mary's statue, and carefully removed the faded ones. "Will you promise to put fresh water in the vase? I won't be here tomorrow. I have to be at school. Promise—and maybe some flowers too?"

"I can't. I have to leave tonight. Otherwise. . . . "

"Otherwise you would?"

He nodded. "I'd do anything to please you."

"Only to please me?" she said.

He smiled. "I don't know—I'd do it anyway, I think, but it would never have occurred to me to do it. Just a minute!" he exclaimed.

They had reached the third-floor corridor. He ran along it to his room and quickly stuffed a few oddments into his bag. Then he put on his belt and ran out. She had walked slowly on ahead, and he caught up with her in front of the photos of the class of '32. She looked thoughtful.

"What is it?" he asked.

"Nothing," she said softly. "I would so much like to be sentimental—I can't. This picture doesn't move me, it means absolutely nothing to me. Let's go."

She promised to wait for him by the entrance, and he ran quickly into the office to pick up his marching orders. Otten had already left. The sergeant major grasped Feinhals by the sleeve. "Don't go making a fool of yourself," he said, "and good luck."

"Thanks," said Feinhals and hurried out of the building.

She was waiting for him at the street corner. He took her arm and walked slowly beside her into town. It had stopped raining, but the air was still moist, with a sweet smell, and they walked along very quiet side streets that ran almost parallel to the main streets but were very quiet, past small houses with little low trees in front of them.

"How come you don't live in the ghetto?" he asked.

"Because of my father. He was an officer in the last war and got a lot of medals and lost both legs. But yesterday he sent his medals back to the garrison commander, and his artificial legs—a big brown-paper parcel. Please, let me go on alone now," she urged.

"Why?"

"I want to walk home alone."

"I'll go with you."

"It's no use. You'll be seen, someone from my family will see you . . . ," she looked at him, "and then they won't let me come any more."

"You'll be back?"

"Yes," she said quietly. "For sure. I promise."

"Give me a kiss," he said.

She blushed and stood still. The street was empty and silent. Over the wall beside them hung branches of faded pink hawthorn.

"Why should we kiss?" she asked in a low voice; she looked at him sadly, and he was afraid she was going to cry. "I'm scared of love."

"Why?" he asked softly.

"Because there's no such thing—or only for a few moments."

"We won't have much more than a few moments," he said softly. He set his bag down on the ground, took the parcel from her, and put his arms around her. He kissed her on the neck, behind the ears, and felt her mouth on his cheek. "Don't go away," he whispered in her ear, "don't go away. It's not right to go away when there's a war on. Stay here." She shook her head. "I can't," she said, "my mother gets scared to death if I'm late." She kissed him once more on the cheek and was surprised to find she didn't mind—she liked it very much. "Here," she said. She turned his head as it rested against her shoulder and kissed him on the corner of the mouth. She now felt really glad that she would soon be with him again.

She kissed him once more on the corner of the mouth and looked at him for a moment: she used to think it must be wonderful to have a husband and children; she had always thought of both of them at the same time, but now she wasn't thinking of children—no, she hadn't been thinking of children when she kissed him and realized she would see him again soon. It made her sad, yet the thought pleased her. "There!" she whispered, "I really must go. . . ."

He looked over her shoulder along the street; it was empty and silent, and the noise from the next street seemed very remote. The

little trees had been carefully pollarded. Ilona's hand was groping
for his neck, and he could tell that this hand was very small, firm,
and slender. "Stay here," he said, "or let me go with you. Never
mind what happens. It won't work out—you don't know what war
is—you don't know the people who make it. It's not right to sepa-
rate even for a minute unless you have to."

"I have to," she said. "Try to understand."

"Then let me go with you."

"No, no," she pleaded. "I can't do that to my father, don't you
understand?"

"I understand," he said, kissing her neck. "I understand everything, much too much. But I love you, and I want you to stay.
Please stay."

She freed herself, looked at him, and said: "Don't ask me to.
Please."

"I won't," he said softly. "Off you go. Where shall I wait?"

"Walk on a bit with me, I'll show you a little café where you
can wait."

He tried to walk slowly, but she pulled him along, and he was
surprised when they suddenly crossed a busy street. She pointed to
a little narrow building, saying: "Wait there for me."

"Will you be back?"

"Yes," she said with a smile, "I promise—as soon as I can. I
love you."

She threw her arms around his neck and kissed him on the
mouth. Then she hurried off; he didn't want to watch her go so he
walked toward the little café.

As he entered he felt very miserable, very empty, as if he had
missed something. He knew there was no point in waiting, yet at
the same time he knew he had to wait. He must give God this
chance of making everything turn out as it should, as it might
have, although there was no doubt in his mind that everything
had already turned out differently: she wouldn't be back. Something would happen to prevent her coming back—perhaps it was
asking too much to love a Jewish girl while this war was on and to

hope she would come back. He didn't even know her address, and he must go through the motions of hope by waiting for her here, although he had no hope. He might have run after her, maybe, and forced her to stay—but you couldn't force people, you could only kill people, that was the only thing you could force on them. You couldn't force anyone to live, or to love, it was useless; the only thing that had any real power over them was death. And now he had to wait, although he knew it was useless. Moreover, he knew he would wait for longer than an hour, longer than tonight, because this was the only thing that linked them together: this little café her finger had pointed out, and the only certainty was that she had not lied. She would come, right away and very quickly, as quickly as she could, if she had the power to decide. . . .

From the clock over the counter he saw it was twenty to eight. He didn't feel like anything to eat or drink so he ordered some soda water when the proprietress came over, and when he saw she was disappointed he ordered a carafe of wine. Near the door sat a Hungarian soldier with his girl, and in the middle a fat fellow with a sallow face and a pitch-black cigar in his mouth. He quickly finished the carafe of wine so as to reassure the proprietress, and ordered another. The woman gave him a friendly smile; she was middle-aged, thin and blonde.

There were moments when he even thought she would come. Then he imagined where he would go with her: they would take a room somewhere, and before they went through the bedroom door he would tell her she was his wife. The room was dark, the bed in it old and brown and wide, and there was a religious picture hanging on the wall, there was a chest of drawers with a blue china basin containing lukewarm water, and the window looked out onto an orchard. That room existed, he knew it did, he had only to go into town and look for it and he would find it, that room, wherever it was he would find it, that very room, in a cheap hotel, in an inn, in a pension, that room existed, the room which for one moment had been destined to receive them tonight—but they

would never enter that room: with painful clarity he saw the
soiled rug beside the bed and the little window opening onto the
orchard, the brown paint had peeled off the window frame; it was
a lovely room with its big, brown, wide bed they had almost lain
in together. But now that room would stay empty.

All the same, there were moments when he believed it wasn't
decided yet. If she hadn't been Jewish—it was very hard to love a
Jewish girl while this war was on, but he did love her, he loved her
very much, enough to want to sleep with her and talk to her, for
hours and very often and over and over again—and he knew there
weren't many women you could sleep with and talk to for hours.
With her it would have been possible—a lot of things would have
been possible with her.

He ordered another carafe of wine. He had not yet opened the
bottle of soda water. The fellow with the pitch-black cigar left,
and now he was alone in the café with the middle-aged blonde
proprietress, who had a skinny neck, and the Hungarian soldier
with his girl. He drank some wine and tried to think of something
else. He thought about his home—but he had hardly ever been
there. Since leaving school he had hardly been home at all; besides, at home he was scared—the little town lay between railroad
and river, in a great loop, as it were; the roads leading to it and
through it were treeless, asphalted, and in summer there was only
the musty, airless shade of the fruit trees. It didn't cool off even in
the evening. He had usually gone home in the fall and helped
with the harvest because he enjoyed that: those great orchards full
of fruit, great trucks full, so many trucks full of pears and apples
and plums being driven along the Rhine to the cities; home was
beautiful in the fall, and he got along well with his mother and
dad, and it made no difference to him when his sister got married
to some fruit grower or other—but home was beautiful in the fall.
In winter the little place lay once again flat and deserted between
river and railroad in the cold, and the heavy, cloying smell from
the jam factory would drift in thick clouds across the plain and

take your breath away. No, he was always glad to get away again. His job was building houses and schools, factories and apartment houses for a large firm, and army barracks. . . .

But there was no point in trying to think about these things. Now he had to think of having forgotten to ask Ilona for her address—just in case. But he could get it from the building superintendent at the school, or from her headmistress, and there was no reason, after all, why he couldn't make inquiries, look for her, talk to her, perhaps go and see her. But all that belonged to those pointless things you had to do to give God a chance, you just had to do them, and sometimes it turned out that there was some point to them after all. The moment you admitted there might be some point to them, that they might come off—the moment you had to admit that, you were lost. And you had to keep on doing them. Search and wait—that was all there was to hope for, and that was terrible. He didn't know what they did with the Hungarian Jews. He had heard there had been a dispute over this between the Hungarian and German governments, but you could never tell what the Germans would do. And he had forgotten to ask Ilona for her address. The most important thing to do in wartime, exchange addresses, was the one thing they had forgotten, and for her it was still more important to have an address. But this was all pointless: she would never come back.

He preferred thinking about the room they would have shared together. . . .

He saw it was close on nine: the hour had long since passed. The clock hand moved very slowly while you were looking at it, but as soon as you took your eyes off it, even for a moment, it seemed to jump. It was nine o'clock, and he had been waiting here for almost an hour and a half; he had to go on waiting, or he could hurry over to the school and ask the building superintendent for her address, and go there. He ordered another carafe of wine and saw that the proprietress was satisfied.

At five after nine the military police checked the café, an officer with a corporal, and at first they merely glanced inside and turned to leave—he saw them very distinctly because he had begun to stare at the door. There was something wonderful about staring at the door: the door was hope, but all he saw was this officer in his steel helmet and the corporal behind him, just looking in and then turning to leave, until the officer caught sight of him and walked slowly over to him. He knew the game was up: these people had the only effective means, they had death at their beck and call, death obeyed them instantly. And to be dead meant not to be able to do anything in this world any more, and he still had plans for doing something in this world: he wanted to wait for Ilona, to look for her and to love her—even though he knew it was point-less, he wanted to, because there was just a chance it might come off. These men in their steel helmets held death in the palm of their hand, death was in their little pistols, their unsmiling faces, and even if these two men didn't want to call upon death, there were thousands standing behind them who were only too glad to give death a chance, with gallows and machine pistols—death was at their beck and call. The officer looked at him, said nothing, just held out his hand. The officer was tired, couldn't have cared less, really; he did his job mechanically, probably it bored him, but he did it, and he did it consistently and seriously. Feinhals handed over his paybook and marching orders. The corporal made a sign to Feinhals to stand up. With a shrug Feinhals stood up. He no-ticed the proprietress was trembling and that the Hungarian sol-dier looked alarmed.

"Come along," said the officer quietly.

"I haven't paid yet," said Feinhals.

"Pay at the counter."

Feinhals buckled on his belt, picked up his bag, and walked be-tween the two men to the counter. The proprietress took the money, and the corporal went ahead and opened the door. Fein-hals went out. He knew they couldn't do anything to him; still, he might have been scared, yet he wasn't. Outside it was dark, lights were showing in stores and restaurants, and everything looked very nice and summery. On the street outside the café stood a large red

furniture van: the door at the back had been opened, part of it
had been let down and rested on the rough paving like a ramp.
People were standing about on the street and watching uneasily:
in front of the opening stood a guard holding a machine pistol.

"Get in," said the officer. Feinhals climbed up the ramp into
the van; in the darkness he saw a lot of heads, weapons—but no
one inside said a word. When he was all the way in he noticed the
van was full.

VI

The red furniture van drove slowly through the town; it was securely locked, the padded doors bolted, and on its sides was
painted in black lettering: "Göros Bros., Budapest. Forwarding
Agents." The van did not stop again. Through the opening in the
roof a man's head looked out, carefully noting the surroundings,
from time to time bending down apparently to call out something.
The man saw lighted cafés, ice-cream parlors, people in summer
clothes, but suddenly his eye was caught by a green furniture van
that was trying vainly to overtake them on the wide boulevard. The
driver of the green van was a man in army uniform, beside
him sat a second man in army uniform holding a machine pistol
on his knees, but the opening in the roof of the green van had
been secured with barbed wire. The driver of the green van
honked impatiently behind the red van as the latter lumbered
through the town. Not until they reached a major intersection and
the street widened and opened out could the green van overtake; it
nipped quickly past, and the man looking out of the opening noticed that the green van turned into a wide street evidently going
north whereas the red van drove south, almost due south. The face
of the man in the opening grew more and more serious. He was
short and slight, and his face had a wizened look, and when the
red van had driven on a bit farther he bent his head and shouted

down into the van: "I'm pretty sure we're driving out of town, the houses aren't so close together now." From below came a muffled murmur in reply, and the red van was driving faster now, faster than one would have given it credit for. The road was empty and dark, and between the close branches of the trees the air hung moist and heavy and sweet, and the man in the roof opening bent down and shouted: "No more houses, highway now—going south."

The howls from below grew louder, but the van drove even faster. The man in the opening was tired, he had a long train trip behind him, and he was standing on the shoulders of two men of different heights, which made him even more tired, and he was ready to quit, but he was the shortest and slightest of the men in the van, and they had picked him to see what was going on outside.

Now came a long stretch where he saw nothing. A very long stretch, it seemed to him—and when the men down below pulled at his leg and wanted to know what was going on he said nothing was going on, all he could see was the trees bordering the highway and the dark fields. Then he saw two soldiers with a motorcycle standing by the roadside, the soldiers were shining their flashlight back and forth across a map. They glanced up as the big furniture van passed. Then the man in the opening saw nothing again for a while, until they passed a stationary tank column. One tank seemed to have broken down, someone was lying on his stomach underneath it and someone else was shining a carbide lamp over it. Farmhouses slid past them very quickly, dark farmhouses, and a truck column overtook them on the left, driving very fast; soldiers were sitting on the trucks. From behind the trucks came a small gray car flying a commandant's pennant. The commandant's car was driving even faster than the trucks. Some soldiers, infantrymen, were sitting hunched up beside a barn, some were lying on the ground smoking. Next they went through a village, and shortly after the village the man in the opening heard firing for the first time: it was a heavy battery located to the right of the road; great barrels pointed steep and black into the dark blue sky. Bloody fire flashed from the gun muzzles, casting a soft ruddy sheen on the wall of a barn. The man recoiled, he had never hear firing before, and he was scared. He was a sick man, a very sick man, with some chronic stomach ailment, his name was Sergeant Finck, and he was the commissary at a big hospital near Linz, on the Danube, and he had had misgivings ever since the head of the hospital had sent him to Hungary to pick up some genuine Tokay wine, Tokay and liqueurs and as much champagne as he could lay hands on. Imagine going to Hungary for champagne. Still: he, Finck, was the only man at the hospital who could be trusted to tell a genuine Tokay from a phony one, and after all: in Tokay there must be some genuine Tokay wine. The old man, Colonel Ginzler, was very partial to genuine Tokay, but it was probably mostly because of his drinking pal and skat companion, that Colonel Bressen whom you involuntarily called von Bressen because he looked so distinguished with his narrow unsmiling face and the unusual decoration around his neck. Finck owned an inn back home, and he knew people, and he knew the old man was just showing off, sending him off like that to pick up fifty bottles of genuine Tokay— some bet or other which that colonel had probably goaded him into.

Finck had been to Tokay, where he had picked up fifty bottles of Tokay wine, and genuine at that, much to his surprise—he was an innkeeper, an innkeeper in a wine town, he had his own vineyards too, and he knew his wines. And he didn't trust the Tokay he had bought as genuine in Tokay, a suitcase and a wicker basket full. He had managed to bring along the suitcase, it was down there in the van, but he hadn't been able to bring the wicker basket. There had been no time at Szentgyörgy, they had been herded straight from the train into the furniture van; it had been no good protesting, saying he was ill, the whole platform had been cordoned off, it was no good even trying, they were marched straight into the furniture van parked outside the station. Some of the men started to mutiny and shout, but the guards seemed to be deaf and dumb.

Finck was nervous about his Tokay—the old man was touchy about wine and even touchier about what he called his honor. He was pretty certain to have given that colonel his word or some such thing that he would drink Tokay with him on Sunday. Most likely he had even named the hour. But now it was Thursday, probably Friday morning—it must be getting on for midnight at least—and now they were driving south, quite fast, and there wasn't the faintest chance of being able to deliver the wine on Sunday. Finck was scared, scared of the old man and scared of the colonel. He didn't like that colonel. He knew something about him that he never had and never could tell anyone, because no one would believe it, something disgusting that Finck wouldn't have thought possible. Finck had seen it for himself, quite distinctly—and he knew how important it was for him that the colonel shouldn't know he had seen it. He had to go along to the colonel's room several times a day, with something to eat or drink or some books. And the colonel was someone you handled with great care. One evening he had gone into the colonel's room without knocking, and there in the semidarkness he had seen it, that ghastly expression on the elderly white face—it took Finck's appetite away for the rest of that evening. When a young fellow was caught doing something like that back home they poured cold water over him right away, and it worked. . . .

Down below, the men were pulling at his leg again, and he shouted down to them that he had seen cannon, cannon firing, and the yelling down below grew louder. The flashes from the gun muzzles they had driven past were fading away behind them, and the sound of the shells being fired, which at first had seemed horribly close, now seemed as far away as the sound of the shells landing, while the van was steadily approaching the area where the shells were landing. They drove past more tanks, stationary columns, then came more guns, these seemed to be smaller, they were standing next to a draw well, and the flames from their muzzles lit up the sinister gallows-outline of the well in sharp flashes. Again there was nothing for a while, until they passed some more columns, then nothing again—and then Finck heard the firing of machine guns. The van was heading straight for the area toward which the machine guns were firing.

And suddenly they stopped in a village. Finck clambered down inside and got out with the others. In the village all was confusion; there were trucks standing around all over the place, people yelling, soldiers running across the road, and the firing of the machine guns grew louder and louder. Feinhals walked behind the little sergeant who had been standing in the roof opening and was now carrying his heavy suitcase; he was so short and walked so doubled up that the butt of his rifle dragged along the ground. Feinhals fastened his bag to the carrying strap and took a stride forward to catch up with the little sergeant. "I'll give you a hand," he said. "What have you got in there anyway?"

"Wine," said the little man, gasping. "Wine for our hospital administrator."

"Leave it here, for God's sake," said Feinhals. "How can you lug a suitcase full of wine up to the front?"

The little man shook his head obstinately. He was so exhausted he could hardly walk, his knees were wobbling, and he shook his head sadly and nodded his thanks as Feinhals reached for the handle. The suitcase seemed fantastically heavy to Feinhals.

The machine gun on the right had stopped firing, the tanks were firing into the village now. From behind them came the crash of splitting timbers, and a gentle reflection from a fire threw a soft light over the muddy, rutted road.

"Throw the thing away, man," said Feinhals, "you must be out of your mind."

The sergeant did not answer; he seemed to grip the handle even tighter. Behind them another house started burning.

Suddenly the second lieutenant walking ahead of them halted and called out: "Get close to the house!" They ran right up to the wall of the house in front of which they had stopped. The little sergeant lurched against it and sat down on his suitcase. Now the machine gun on the left had also stopped firing. The officer went indoors and came out at once with a first lieutenant. Feinhals recognized him. They had to line up, and Feinhals knew the first lieutenant was trying to make out their decorations in the reddish twilight: on his own chest he now had one more, a proper one now, at least the ribbon for it, adorning his chest in black-white-and-red. Thank God, thought Feinhals, he has that medal at least. The first lieutenant looked at them for a moment, smiling, then said: "Very nice," smiled again, and repeated: "Very nice, eh?" to the second lieutenant standing behind him. But the second lieutenant said nothing. They could see him distinctly now. He was short and pale, no longer very young, it seemed, and his face was grimy and unsmiling. He didn't have a single medal on his chest.

"Brecht," the first lieutenant told him, "take two men as reinforcement. And some bazookas. We'll send the others to Undolf —four, I guess. I'll keep the rest here."

"Two," said Brecht. "Yes sir, two men, and some bazookas."

"Right," said the first lieutenant. "You know where to find those things?"

"Yes sir."

"Report back in half an hour, please."

"Yes sir," said the second lieutenant.

Feinhals and Finck were the first in line, and the second lieutenant tapped them on the chest, saying: "Come along," then turned on his heel and marched off. They had to hurry to keep up with him. The little sergeant snatched up his suitcase, Feinhals helped him, and they hurried off as fast as they could behind the little second lieutenant. Beyond the house they turned to the right into a narrow lane that seemed to lead out into the country between hedges and meadows. Ahead of them all was quiet, but behind them that tank was still firing regularly into the village, and the small battery, the last one they had driven past, was still firing to the right, roughly in the direction in which they were heading.

Feinhals suddenly dropped to the ground and shouted to the others: "Watch out!" There was a tinkle as they let go of the suitcase, and the second lieutenant up front also dropped to the ground. From up ahead, from the direction in which they had been marching, grenade launchers were firing into the village, they were firing in rapid succession now, there seemed to be a great many of them; splinters whizzed through the air, smacked against house walls, bigger fragments droned past them not far away.

"Get up," shouted the second lieutenant. "Carry on."

"Hold it!" cried Feinhals. He had heard that brittle clack again, a delicate, almost cheerful sound, and he was scared. There was a great crash as the grenade struck Finck's suitcase—the lid of the suitcase flew off with a fierce hiss and hit a tree twenty yards away, broken glass tore through the air like a swarm of demented birds, Feinhals could feel the wine splashing onto the back of his neck, he ducked in alarm: he hadn't heard these being fired, but there was an explosion ahead of them on the field above a low earth bank. A haystack standing out black against the reddish background fell apart and started to smolder; it began to glow in the middle like tinder, then blazed up as it burst into flames.

The second lieutenant came crawling back down the hollow. "What the hell's going on here?" he whispered to Feinhals.

"He had wine in the suitcase," whispered Feinhals. "Hey there," he called softly across to Finck—a dark lump lying crouched beside the suitcase. Nothing stirred. "Hell," said the second lieutenant under his breath, "surely he's not. . . ."

Feinhals crawled the two paces over to Finck, bumped his head against Finck's foot, propped himself up on his elbows, and pulled himself closer. The light from the burning haystack did not reach this hollow, it was dark in this shallow depression while the field at the side of the lane was already bathed in reddish light. "Hey there," said Feinhals quietly. He smelled the strong sweet fumes from a wine puddle, drew back his hands because he had thrust them into broken glass and, beginning with the shoes, groped carefully up the man's legs, surprised to find how short this sergeant was; his legs were short, his body skinny. "Hey there," he called softly, "hey there, pal," but Finck did not answer. The second lieutenant had crawled over and said: "What's up?" Feinhals groped farther along until he touched blood—that wasn't wine— he drew back his hand and said quietly: "I think he's dead. A big wound in the back, soaked with blood; d'you have a flashlight?"

"Perhaps we could. . . ."

"Or lift him up there onto the field. . . ."

"Wine," said the second lieutenant, "a suitcase full of wine . . . what did he want that for. . . ."

"For a commissariat, I think."

Finck was not heavy. They carried him, walking doubled up, across the path, rolled him over the grass bank until he was lying flat, dark and flat in the light. His back was black with blood. Feinhals turned him over carefully—he saw the face for the first time; it was frail, very frail, thin, still slightly damp with sweat, the thick black hair clinging to the forehead.

"My God," said Feinhals.

"What is it?"

"He got one right in the chest. A splinter as big as your fist."

"In the chest?"

"That's right—he must have been kneeling over his suitcase."

"Contrary to regulations," said the second lieutenant, but his own joke seemed to turn sour on him. "Get his paybook and identity disk. . . ."

Feinhals carefully unbuttoned the blood-soaked tunic, felt for the neck until his fingers closed on a bloodied piece of metal. He found the paybook right away too, it was in the left-hand breast pocket and seemed clean.

"Hell," the second lieutenant said behind him, "the suitcase is heavy—it still is." He had dragged it across the path and was also pulling Finck's rifle along by its strap. "Did you get the things?"

"Yes," said Feinhals.

"Let's get out of here." The second lieutenant dragged the suitcase along by one corner until the hollow came to an end and the ground was flat again, then he whispered to Feinhals: "Get behind that wall on the left," and crawled ahead. "Push the suitcase after me." Feinhals pushed the suitcase after him and crawled slowly up the little rise. Behind the wall, which ran at right angles to their path, they could stand upright, and now they looked at each other. The glow from the burning haystack was bright enough for them to see one another distinctly, and they stared at each other for a moment. "What's your name?" asked the officer.

"Feinhals."

"Mine's Brecht," said the second lieutenant. He smiled awkwardly. "I must admit I've got a hell of a thirst." He bent down over the suitcase, drew it onto the strip of thick grass, and carefully tipped out the contents. There was a gentle clinking and burbling. "Look at that," he said, picking up a small, undamaged bottle. "Tokay." The label was smeared with blood and wet with wine. Feinhals watched the officer carefully push aside the broken glass —five or six bottles seemed to be still intact. Brecht got out his pocketknife and opened one. He drank. "Marvelous," he said as he put down the bottle. "Want some?"

"Thanks," said Feinhals. He took the bottle and drank a mouthful; he found it too sweet, handed the bottle back, and repeated, "Thanks."

The grenade launchers were firing again into the village, farther away now, and suddenly a machine gun fired quite close in front of them. "Thank God," said Brecht. "I was beginning to think those had gone too."

He finished the bottle and let it roll down into the hollow. "We have to get past this wall on the left."

The haystack was in full blaze now, but at the very bottom only a glow was left. Sparks showered.

"You look pretty sensible," said the officer.

Feinhals was silent.

"What I mean is," said Brecht as he started to open the second bottle, "what I mean is, sensible enough to know that this war's a load of shit."

Feinhals was silent.

"By that I mean," went on Brecht, "that when you win a war it isn't a load of shit, and this war—so it seems to me—is a very, very bad war."

"Yes," said Feinhals. "It's a very, very bad war." The heavy firing of the machine gun at such close quarters was getting on his nerves.

"Where's the machine gun?" he asked quietly.

"Over there where this wall comes to an end—it's a farm—we're in front of it now—the machine gun's behind it. . . ."

The machine gun fired a few more short sharp rounds, then stopped. Next a Russian machine gun fired, then they heard rifle shots, and again the German and Russian machine guns fired together. And suddenly there was silence.

"Shit," said Brecht.

The haystack began to collapse, the flames were no longer beating so high, there was a gentle crackling, and darkness fell lower. The second lieutenant held out a bottle to Feinhals. Feinhals shook his head. "No thanks, it's too sweet for me," he said.

"Have you been with the infantry long?" asked Brecht.

"Yes," said Feinhals, "four years."

"My God," said Brecht. "The stupid thing is that I don't know much about the infantry—practically speaking, that is, and I'd be a fool to say I did. I've had two years' training as a night fighter— just finished it—and my training cost the government a few nice single-family homes, all so that I can get blown to pieces in the infantry and lay down my life to get to Valhalla. What a load of shit, eh?" He took another drink. Feinhals was silent.

"What does one do, actually, when the enemy is superior?" the second lieutenant persevered. "Two days ago we were fifteen miles away, and we kept hearing we weren't going to budge. But we did budge. I know the rules too well, the rules say: The German soldier does not yield, he would rather be killed—something like that, but I'm not blind and I'm not deaf. I ask you," he said solemnly, "what do we do?"

"Clear out, I guess," said Feinhals.

"Great," said the second lieutenant. "Clear out. Great—clear out," he laughed softly. "There's something missing in our fine Prussian regulations: there's no provision for retreat in our training, that's why we have to be so smart when we do retreat. I believe our regulations are the only ones that say nothing about retreat, only 'delaying tactics,' and these jokers aren't going to let themselves be delayed any longer. Let's go," he said. He stuffed two bottles into his pockets. "Off to this lovely war again. My God," he added, "the poor bugger lugged that wine all the way here—the poor bugger...."

Feinhals followed slowly. As they turned the corner of the wall they heard men running toward them. The footsteps were clearly audible, close now. The second lieutenant jumped back behind the wall, tucked his machine pistol under his arm, and whispered to Feinhals: "Here's your chance to earn eighteen pfennigs' worth of tin for your chest." But Feinhals noticed he was trembling. "Hell," whispered the second lieutenant, "this is serious, this is war."

The footsteps came closer, the men were no longer running.

"Don't worry," said Feinhals quietly, "those aren't Russians."

Brecht was silent.

"I wonder why they were running—and making all that racket...."

Brecht was silent.

"They're your men," said Feinhals. The footsteps sounded quite close now.

Although they could tell from the silhouettes that the men wearing steel helmets and rounding the corner were Germans, the second lieutenant called softly: "Halt, password." The men were startled; Feinhals saw them hesitate and flinch. "Shit," said one of them. "The password's shit."

"Tannenberg," said another voice.

"What the hell are you doing here?" said Brecht. "Get in behind that wall. One of you stand at the corner and listen."

Feinhals was surprised to see how many there were. He tried to count them in the dark, there seemed to be six or seven. They sat down on the grassy strip. "That's wine," said the second lieutenant; he groped for the bottles and passed them across. "Split it up between you."

"Prinz," he said, "Corporal Prinz, what's going on?"

Prinz was the one standing at the corner. Feinhals saw his medals glinting in the dark as he turned.

"Lieutenant," said Prinz, "this is just nonsense. They've already overtaken us left and right, and surely you're not trying to tell me that here of all places, right next to this dirty farm, here of all places where our machine gun happens to be standing, the front is supposed to be held. Lieutenant, the front is several hundred miles wide and has been slipping for quite a while now—and I don't believe these hundred and fifty yards have been destined to produce a Knight's Cross—it's time we cleared out; if we don't we'll be caught in the middle, and not a bloody soul's going to give a damn. . . ."

"The front's got to be held somewhere—are you all there?"

"Yes," said Prinz, "we're all here—and I don't think a front can be held by convalescents and men just back from sick leave. Incidentally, young Genzki's been wounded—he got a bullet through his arm—Genzki," he called softly, "where are you?"

A slight figure detached itself from the wall.

"All right," said the second lieutenant, "you can go back. Feinhals, you go with him, the first-aid post is right where your bus stopped. Report to the old man that I've moved the machine gun back thirty yards—and bring some bazookas back with you—send another man along with them, Prinz."

"Wecke," said Prinz, "you go. Did you come with the furniture van too?" he asked Feinhals.

"Yes."

"So did we."

"Go on," said the second lieutenant, "get a move on; hand in the paybook to the old man. . . ."

"Someone killed?" asked Prinz.

"Yes," said the second lieutenant impatiently. "Go on, get a move on."

Feinhals walked slowly to the village with the two men. Now several tanks were firing into it from the south and east. Ahead of them, where the main road entered the village to the left, they heard deafening explosions, men yelling, and they stood still for a moment and exchanged glances.

"Great," said the short fellow with the wounded arm.

They hurried on, but when they emerged from the hollow a voice called: "Password?"

"Tannenberg," they growled.

"Brecht? Combat unit Brecht?"

"Yes," called Feinhals.

"Go back! Everyone back into the village, assemble on the main road!"

"Run back to the others," Wecke told Feinhals, "you go. . . ."

Feinhals ran down the hollow, up the other side, and called from half-way up: "Hey, Lieutenant Brecht!"

"What is it?"

"We've all got to go back—back to the village, assemble on the main road. . . ."

They all walked slowly back together.

The red furniture van had almost filled up again. Feinhals slowly climbed the ramp, sat down just inside, leaned back, and tried to sleep. The deafening explosions seemed somewhat ridiculous to him—now he could hear that it was German tanks trying to keep the road open. They were banging away much too much, there was altogether more banging in this war than necessary, but no doubt it was all part of this war. Everyone was in now except for a major handing out decorations and the few men to whom he was handing them. A corporal, a sergeant, and three privates were standing facing the little gray-haired major who, his head bare, was hurriedly presenting the crosses and documents. From time to time he would call: "First Lieutenant Greck—First Lieutenant Greck!" Finally he shouted: "Brecht, where's Lieutenant Brecht?" From the depths of the van Brecht called: "Here, sir!" moved slowly forward, touched his hand to his cap and, standing on the ramp, reported: "Second Lieutenant Brecht, Major."

"Where's your company commander?" asked the major. Although not furious, the major did look annoyed. The soldiers he had decorated walked slowly up the ramp and squeezed past Brecht into the van.

And the major stood all by himself on the village street holding an Iron Cross First Class, and Brecht, his face expressing complete blankness, said: "No idea, Major. A few minutes ago Lieutenant Greck ordered me to lead the company to the assembly point, he had to . . . ," Brecht stopped and wavered: "Lieutenant Greck was suffering from severe indigestion. . . ."

"Greck!" shouted the major in the direction of the village. "Greck!" He turned away, shaking his head, and said to Brecht: "Your company fought very well indeed—but we have to get out. . . ."

A second German tank banged away from the street in front of them toward the right, and the small battery behind seemed to have veered round; it was firing in the same direction as the tanks. In the village many houses were burning now—and the church, which stood in the center of the village and was taller than any of the houses, was filled with a ruddy glow. The motor of the furniture van began to throb. The major stood irresolutely at the roadside and shouted to the van driver: "Get started. . . ."

Feinhals opened the paybook and read: "Finck, Gustav, sergeant; civilian occupation: innkeeper; place of residence: Heidesheim. . . ."

Heidesheim, thought Feinhals, with a shock. Heidesheim was two miles from his home, and he knew the inn with the sign, painted brown, "Finck's Wineshop & Hotel, estab. 1710." He had often driven past but never gone in—then the door was slammed in his face, and the red furniture van drove off.

Again and again Greck tried to stand up and run to the end of the village where they were waiting for him, but he couldn't. As soon as he straightened himself, a griping pain like a corkscrew in his stomach forced him to double up, and he felt the urge to defecate—he was squatting beside the low wall surrounding the cesspool, his stool came in driblets, barely a tablespoonful at a time, while the pressure in his racked abdomen was enormous; he could not sit properly, the only bearable position was squatting, completely doubled up, and getting some slight relief when the stool left his bowels in small quantities—at such moment his hopes would rise, hopes that the cramps might be over, but they were only over for that moment. This griping pain was so paralyzing that he couldn't walk, he couldn't even have crawled slowly; the only way he could have propelled himself would have been to tip forward and drag himself painfully along by his hands, but even then he wouldn't have got there in time. It was another three hundred yards to the departure point, and now and again through the noise of the firing he would hear Major Krenz calling his name —but by this time he hardly cared: he had stomach cramps, intense, violent stomach cramps. He held onto the wall, his naked bottom shivering, and in his bowels that grinding pain would form and re-form, like some slowly accumulating explosive that surely must be devastating in effect but, when it did come, was always minimal, kept accumulating, kept promising to bring final release while never releasing more than a tiny morsel of stool. . . .

Tears ran down his face: he no longer thought of anything connected with the war, although all around him shells were bursting and he could distinctly hear the trucks driving away from the village. Even the tanks withdrew onto the highway and moved off, firing, toward the town; he could hear it all, very graphically, and in his mind's eye he had a clear picture of the village being surrounded. But the pain in his stomach was bigger, closer, more important, monstrous, and he thought about this pain that wouldn't let up, that paralyzed him—and in a frenzied, grinning procession all the doctors he had ever consulted for his agonizing condition passed in front of him, headed by his repulsive father; they surrounded him, those useless creatures who had never had the guts to tell him straight out that his illness was due simply to constant malnutrition in his youth.

A shell landed in the cesspool, a wave splashed over him, soaking him with that disgusting liquid; he could taste it on his lips, and he sobbed more bitterly than ever, until he noticed that the farmhouse was in the tanks' direct line of fire. Shells were whining right past his ears, over his head, incredibly hard round balls that caused a great rush of air. Glass tinkled behind him, timbers shattered, and inside the house a woman screamed, chunks of plaster and splinters of wood flew all around him. He tipped forward, ducked behind the wall surrounding the cesspool, and carefully buttoned his pants. Although his bowels were still convulsively releasing tiny amounts of that terrible pain, he crawled slowly down the steep little stone path to get away from the immediate vicinity of the farmhouse. His pants were done up. But he could crawl no farther, the pain was paralyzing him, he lay where he was—and for a few seconds his whole life spun round him—a kaleidoscope of unspeakably monotonous pain and humiliation. Only his tears seemed important and real to him as they flowed freely down his face into the muck, that muck he had tasted on his lips—straw, excrement, mud, and hay. He was still sobbing when a shell hit the center beam of a barn roof, and the great wooden structure with its bales of pressed straw collapsed and buried him.

VII

The green furniture van had an excellent engine. The two men up front in the cab, who took turns driving, did not talk much, but

when they did they spoke almost exclusively about the engine.
"Isn't she a beaut," they would say from time to time, shaking
their heads in amazement and listening spellbound to that powerful, dark, regular throbbing with never a false or disquieting note
to it. The night was warm and dark, and the road, as they drove
steadily northward, was sometimes choked with army vehicles or
horse-drawn carts, and every now and again they had to jam on the
brakes because they suddenly came face to face with marching columns and almost drove into that strange formless mass of dark figures whose faces were lit up by their headlights. The roads were
narrow, too narrow to allow furniture vans, tanks, and marching
columns to pass, but the farther north they drove the emptier became the road, and for a long time there was nothing to stop them
driving the green van as fast as it would go; the cones of their
headlights lit up trees and houses, sometimes, in a curve, shooting
into a field and making the tall maize or tomato plants stand out
sharp and clear. Finally the road became quite empty, the men
were yawning now, and they stopped somewhere in a village on a
side road for a rest; they opened their packs, gulped the hot, very
strong coffee from their canteens, opened flat round cans of chocolate, and calmly made themselves sandwiches, opening their cans
of butter, sniffing the contents, and spreading the butter thickly
on the bread before covering it with slabs of sausage, the sausage
red and ingrained with peppercorns. The men took their time over
their meal. Their gray, tired faces revived, and one—the man now
sitting on the left and the first to finish—lit a cigarette and drew a
letter from his pocket; he unfolded it and took a snapshot out of
the folds: it showed a charming little girl playing with a rabbit in
a meadow. Holding the picture out to the man beside him, he
said: "How d'you like that—cute, eh? My kid," he laughed, "a
home-leave kid." The other man went on chewing as he answered,
stared at the picture and mumbled: "Cute—home-leave kid, eh?
How old is she?"

"Three."

"Haven't you got a picture of your wife?"

"Sure." The man on the left took out his wallet—but suddenly paused, saying:

"Listen to that, they must have gone nuts...." From the interior of the green van came a deep, angry mumbling and the shrill screams of a woman.

"Go and make them shut up," said the man behind the wheel. The other man opened the cab door and looked out onto the village street—it was warm and dark outside, and the houses were unlighted, there was a smell of manure, a very strong smell of cowdung, and in one of the houses a dog barked. The man got out, cursing under his breath at the deep soft mud of the village street, and walked slowly around the van. From outside the mumbling was only faintly audible, more like a gentle buzzing inside a box, but now two dogs were barking in the village, then three, and suddenly a light went on in a window somewhere, and a man's silhouette became visible. The driver—his name was Schröder—couldn't be bothered to open the heavy padded doors at the rear, it didn't seem worth the effort, so he took his machine pistol and banged the steel butt a few times against the side of the van: there was silence at once. Then Schröder jumped up onto the tire to see if the barbed wire was still securely in place over the closed opening in the roof. The barbed wire was still securely in place.

He climbed back into the cab: Plorin had finished his meal, he was drinking coffee now and smoking, and the picture of the three-year-old girl with the rabbit was lying in front of him. "Cute kid all right," he said, raising his head for a moment. "You're not saying anything—don't you have a picture of your wife?"

"Sure." Schröder took out his wallet again, opened it, and removed a well-thumbed snapshot: it was of a woman, short, grown a little stout, wearing a fur coat. The woman was smiling inanely, her face was rather haggard and tired, and the black shoes with the heels that were much too high looked as though they hurt. Her thick hair, heavy and brownish, had been permed. "Good-looking girl," said Plorin. "Let's get going."

"Right," said Schröder, "start her up." He gave another glance outside: by this time a lot of dogs were barking in the village, and a lot of windows showed lights, and people were calling out to each other in the darkness.

"Let's go," he said, slamming the door. "Start her up."

Plorin turned the key in the ignition, the motor started at once; Plorin let it idle for a few seconds, then pressed down the gas pedal, and the green furniture van maneuvered itself slowly onto the highway. "She's a beaut all right," said Plorin, "a real beaut."

The noise of the engine filled the whole cab, their ears were full of the steady hum, but after a short distance that deep murmur from the inside of the van became audible again. "Let's have a song," Plorin said to Schröder.

Schröder sang. He sang lustily, lifting up his voice, not very beautifully and not altogether accurately, but with real feeling. The emotional parts he sang with special fervor, and in some parts his voice was so emotional it sounded as if he were about to cry, but he did not cry. One song he seemed especially fond of was "Heidemarie," it was clearly his favorite. For a whole hour he sang at the top of his voice, and after an hour the two men changed places, and now Plorin sang.

"Good thing the old man can't hear us singing," said Plorin with a laugh. Schröder laughed too, and Plorin resumed his singing. He sang almost the same songs as Schröder, but he seemed to like "Gray Columns on the March" best, this was the one he sang most often; he sang it slowly, he sang it fast, and the especially moving parts, the ones stressing the misery and nobility of a hero's life, he sang very slowly and dramatically and sometimes several times in a row. Schröder, now at the wheel, stared fixedly at the road, driving the van at top speed, and softly whistled an accompaniment. They heard nothing more now from the inside of the green van.

It was getting chilly up front; they wrapped blankets around their legs, and from time to time, as they drove, they gulped coffee from their flasks. They had stopped singing, but inside the green van it was silent. Everything was silent, for that matter; outside everything was asleep, the highway was empty and wet—it must have been raining here—and the villages they drove through looked dead. They were caught briefly by the headlights in the darkness, a house of two, sometimes a church on the main road—for an instant they would leap up out of the darkness and then were left behind.

About four in the morning they stopped for a second breather. They were both tired by this time, their faces gray and drawn and grimy, and they hardly spoke; the hour's drive still ahead of them seemed endless. They made only a brief halt by the roadside, wiped their faces with schnapps, listlessly ate up their sandwiches, and swilled down the rest of the coffee. They finished the chocolate from their flat cans and lighted cigarettes. Somewhat refreshed they drove on, and Schröder, now at the wheel again, whistled softly to himself, while Plorin, wrapped in a blanket, slept. Not a sound came from the inside of the green van.

A light rain started to fall, and dawn was breaking as they turned off the main road, wound their way through the narrow streets of a village out into the open country, and began driving slowly through a forest. Ground mist was rising, and when the van emerged from the forest there was a meadow, with army huts on it, then another little forest and a meadow, and the van stopped and impatiently sounded its horn in front of a big gate consisting of beams and barbed wire. The gate was flanked by a black-white-and-red sentrybox and a tall watchtower on which a man in a steel helmet was standing beside a machine gun. The gate was opened by the sentry, the sentry grinned as he looked into the cab, and the green van drove slowly into the fenced enclosure.

The driver nudged his neighbor: "We're here," he said. They opened the cab doors and got out with their packs.

Birds were twittering in the forest, the sun came up in the east and shone on the green trees. Soft mist covered everything.

Schröder and Plorin walked wearily toward a hut behind the watchtower. As they climbed the few steps to the door, they saw a whole column of trucks parked on the camp road ready to leave. It was quiet in the camp, nothing moved but the smoke that came pouring out of the crematorium chimney.

The S.S. lieutenant was sitting crouched over a table and had fallen asleep. As he woke up with a start, the two men gave him a tired grin, saying: "Here we are."

He got up, stretched, and said with a yawn: "That's good." He sleepily lit a cigarette, ran his fingers through his hair, put on a cap, straightened his belt, and glanced into the mirror as he flicked the grains of sleep from the corners of his eyes. "How many are there?" he asked.

"Sixty-seven," said Schröder, tossing a sheaf of papers onto the table.

"Is that the lot?"

"Yes—that's the lot," said Schröder. "What's new?"

"We're clearing out—tonight."

"Is that definite?"

"Yes—it's getting too hot around here."

"Where to?"

"Toward 'Greater Germany—Subdivision Austria'!"

The S.S. lieutenant laughed. "Go and get some sleep," he said. "It's going to be another tough night; we're off tonight at seven sharp."

"And the camp?" asked Plorin.

The S.S. Lieutenant took off his cap, carefully combed his hair, and with his right hand arranged his forelock. He was a handsome fellow, brown-haired and slim. He sighed.

"The camp," he said, "there's no more camp now—by tonight there'll be no more camp—it's empty."

"Empty?" asked Plorin; he had sat down and was slowly rubbing his sleeve along his machine pistol, which had got damp.

"Empty," repeated the S.S. lieutenant; he grinned faintly, shrugged his shoulders. "The camp's empty, I tell you—isn't that enough?"

"Have they been taken away?" asked Schröder, already at the door.

"Damn it all," said the S.S. lieutenant, "leave me alone, can't you; I said empty, not taken away—except for the choir." He grinned. "We all know the old man's crazy about his choir. Mark my words, he'll be taking that along again. . . ."

"Hm," said each of the two men, and then again: "Hm . . ." and Schröder added: "The old man's completely nuts about his singing." All three laughed.

"Okay then, we'll be off now," said Plorin. "I'll leave the van where it is, I'm all in."

"Never mind the van," said the S.S. lieutenant. "Willi can drive it away."

"Okay then—we're off. . . ." The two drivers left.

The S.S. lieutenant nodded, walked to the window, and looked out at the green furniture van parked on the camp road, just where the waiting column began. The camp was quite silent. It was another hour before the green van was opened, when S.S. Captain Filskeit arrived at the camp. Filskeit had black hair, he was of medium height, and his pale and intelligent face radiated an aura of chastity. He was strict, a stickler for order, and would tolerate no deviation. His actions were governed solely by regulations. When the sentry saluted he nodded, blanced at the green furniture van, and stepped into the guardroom. The S.S. lieutenant saluted.

"How many?" asked Filskeit.

"Sixty-seven, sir."

"Good," said Filskeit, "I'll expect them in an hour for choir practice." He nodded casually, left the guardroom, and walked across the camp ground. The camp was square, a quadrangle consisting of four times four huts with a small gap on the south side for the gate. At the corners were watchtowers. In the center were the cookhouse, the latrine hut, and in one corner of the camp next to the southeast watchtower was the bath hut, next to the bath hut the crematorium. The camp was completely silent except for one of the sentries—the one on the northeast watchtower—who was singing something softly to himself; apart from that the silence was unbroken. Wispy blue smoke was rising from the cook-house, and from the crematorium came dense black smoke, fortu-nately drifting south; the crematorium had been belching dense clouds of smoke for a long time—Filskeit gave a quick look round, nodded, and went to his office, which was next to the kitchen. He threw his cap on the table and nodded in satisfaction: everything was in order. He might have smiled at the thought, but Filskeit never smiled. To him life was very serious, his army career even more so, but the most serious thing of all was art.

S.S. Captain Filskeit loved art, music. Some people found his pale, intelligent face handsome, but the angular, oversized chin dragged down the finer part of his face and gave his intelligent features an expression of brutality that was as shocking as it was surprising.

Filskeit had once studied music, but he loved music too much to be able to summon that grain of realism that the professional must have, so he went to work for a bank and remained a passion-ate amateur of music. His hobby was choral singing.

He was a hard-working and ambitious individual, very reliable, and he soon advanced to the post of department head in the bank. But his real passion was music, choral singing. At first all-male choirs.

At one time, in the distant past, he had been choirmaster of the Concordia Choral Society, he had been twenty-eight, but that was fifteen years ago—and, although a layman, he had been elected choirmaster. It would have been impossible to find a professional musician who would have furthered the society's aims more pas-sionately or more meticulously. It was fascinating to watch his pale, faintly twitching face and his slender hands as he conducted. The members were afraid of him because he was so meticulous, no wrong note escaped his hearing, he flew into a rage whenever someone was guilty of sloppiness, and there had come a time when these decent, worthy singers had enough of his strictness, his tireless energy, and chose another choirmaster. At the same time he had been conductor of the church choir in his parish, although the liturgy did not appeal to him. But in those days he had seized every opportunity of getting his hands on a choir. The parish priest was popularly known as "the saint," a gentle, rather foolish man who could sometimes look very severe: white-haired and old, he knew nothing about music. But he invariably attended choir practice, and sometimes he would smile gently, and Filskeit hated that smile: it was the smile of love, a compassionate, poignant love. And sometimes the priest's face would take on a look of severity, and Filskeit could feel his aversion to the liturgy mounting simultaneously with his hatred of that smile. That smile of "the saint" seemed to say: futile—futile—but I love you. He did not want to be loved, and his hatred of those anthems and that priest's smile steadily increased, and when the Concordia dismissed him he left the church choir. He would often think of that smile, that elusive severity, and that "Jewish" look of love, as he called it, which seemed to him both down-to-earth and loving, and his breast was devoured by hate and torment. . . .

His successor was a schoolteacher who enjoyed his beer and a good cigar and liked listening to dirty stories. Filskeit had loathed all these things: he neither smoked nor drank, and he was not interested in women.

Not long after, attracted by the idea of racism, corresponding as it did to his secret ideals, he joined the Hitler Youth, where he rapidly advanced to the position of regional choirmaster, organized choirs, including "speaking choirs," and discovered his real love: mixed choral singing. At home—he had an austerely furnished barrack-like room in a Düsseldorf suburb—he devoted his time to choral literature and to every work on racism that he could get hold of. The result of this long and intensive study was an article of his own, which he entitled "The Interrelationship of Choir and Race." He submitted it to a state music academy which returned it to him, with the addition of some sarcastic marginal notes. It was not until later that Filskeit found out that the head of this academy was a Jew called Neumann.

In 1933 he gave up banking for good in order to devote himself entirely to his musical assignments within the Party. His article was approved by a music school and, after some condensing, printed in a professional journal. He held the rank of unit leader in the Hitler Youth but his duties also embraced the S.A. and the S.S., his specialty being speaking choirs, male choirs, and mixed choral singing. His qualities of leadership were undisputed. When war broke out he resisted being classified as indispensable, applied several times for admission to the S.S. Death's Head units, and was rejected twice because he had black hair, was too short, and patently belonged to the stocky, "pyknic" type. No one knew that he often stood for hours in despair in front of the mirror at home and saw what it was impossible not to see: he was not a member of that race which he so ardently admired and to which Lohengrin had belonged.

But the third time he applied, the Death's Head units accepted him because of the excellent references he submitted from all the Party organizations.

During the early war years he suffered greatly as a result of his musical reputation: instead of being sent to the front, he was assigned to training courses, later becoming a course director and then a director of a course for course directors; he directed the choral training of whole S.S. armies, and one of his supreme achievements was a choir of legionaries which, while representing thirteen different countries and eighteen different languages, sang a chorus from "Tannhäuser" in perfect vocal harmony. Later he was awarded the Cross of Merit First Class, one of the rarest military decorations; but not until he volunteered for the twentieth time for military service was he assigned to a military training course and finally got to the front: in 1943 he was given a small concentration camp in Germany, and at last, in 1944, was made commandant of a ghetto in Hungary. Later, when that ghetto had to be evacuated because the Russians were getting close, he was given this little camp in the north.

It was a matter of pride with him to carry out all orders to the letter. He had quickly discovered the enormous latent fund of musical talent among the prisoners: he was surprised to find this among Jews, and he applied the selective principle by ordering each new arrival to undergo a singing test and by recording each one's vocal capacity on an index card, with marks ranging from zero to ten. Very few were given ten—those were assigned immediately to the camp choir, and those who got zero had little prospect of remaining alive for more than two days. When required to supply batches of prisoners for removal, he chose them in such a way as to retain a nucleus of good male and female voices so that his choir always remained complete. This choir, which he conducted with a strictness harking back to the days of the Concordia Choral Society, was his pride and joy. With this choir he could have beaten any competition, but unfortunately the only audience it ever had were the dying prisoners and the guard personnel.

But orders were even more sacred to him than music, and he had recently received a number of orders that had weakened his choir: the ghettos and camps in Hungary were being evacuated, and because the large camps to which he had formerly sent Jews no longer existed, and his small camp had no railway connection, he had to kill them all in his camp, but even now there were still sufficient work-parties—for cookhouse and crematorium and bath hut—to preserve at least the very best of the voices.

Filskeit did not like killing. He had never killed anyone himself, and that was one of his frustrations: he was incapable of it. He realized that it was necessary, and admired the orders which he saw were strictly carried out; the important thing, after all, was not whether one liked carrying out orders but to realize their necessity, to respect them, and to see that they were carried out. . . .

Filskeit went to the window and looked out: two trucks had driven up behind the green furniture van, the drivers had just got down and were walking wearily up the steps to the guardroom.

S.S. Lieutenant Blauert came through the gate with five men and opened the big heavy padded doors of the furniture van: the people inside screamed—the daylight hurt their eyes—their screams were long and piercing, and the ones who jumped down staggered to where Blauert pointed.

The first was a dark-haired young woman wearing a green coat; she was dirty, and her dress seemed to be torn; she was anxiously trying to keep her coat closed with her hands, and a girl of twelve or thirteen was clinging to her arm. Neither had any baggage.

The people who staggered out of the van lined up on the assembly square, and Filskeit counted them under his breath as he watched the roll call proceed: there were sixty-one men, women, and children, varying greatly in dress, behavior, and age. Nothing more emerged from the green van—six had apparently died. The green van moved slowly off and halted by the crematorium. Filskeit nodded in satisfaction: six corpses were unloaded and hauled off into the building.

The baggage of the van's occupants was stacked up in front of the guardroom. The two trucks were also unloaded: Filskeit counted the rows of five as they slowly filled up: twenty-nine rows of five. S.S. Lieutenant Blauert shouted through the megaphone: "Attention everyone! You are at present in a transit camp. You will not remain here long. You will proceed one by one to the prisoners' registration section, then to the office of the Camp Commandant, to whom you will submit for a personal test—this will be followed by a bath and delousing, after which there will be hot coffee for all. Anyone offering the slightest resistance will be instantly shot." He pointed to the watchtowers, whose machine guns had now been swiveled round to aim at the assembly square, and to the five men standing behind him with cocked machine pistols.

Filskeit paced impatiently up and down behind his window. He had noticed a few fair-haired Jews. There were many fair-haired Jews in Hungary. He liked them even less than the dark ones, although there were specimens among them that might have embellished any illustrated work on the Nordic race.

He watched the first woman, the one in the green coat and the torn dress, enter the registration hut, and he sat down, placing his cocked pistol beside him on the table. In a few minutes she would be here to sing for him.

For ten hours Ilona had been waiting for fear. But fear did not come. In these ten hours she had had to experience and submit to many things: disgust and horror, hunger and thirst, gasping for air, and despair when the light struck her, and a strangely cool kind of happiness when, for minutes or quarters of an hour, she managed to be alone—but she had waited in vain for fear. Fear did not come. This world in which she had been living for ten hours was spectral, as spectral as reality—as spectral as the things she had heard about. But hearing about them had frightened her more than now finding herself in the midst of them. She had very few desires left: one of these desires was to be alone so that she could really pray.

She had pictured her life quite differently. Up to now its course had been orderly, satisfying, according to plan, pretty well exactly as she had pictured it—even when her plans had turned out to be mistaken—but this was something she had not expected. She had counted on being spared this.

If all went well she would be dead in half an hour. She was lucky, she was the first. She knew very well what kind of bath huts those were that that creature had spoken of, she knew she had to face ten minutes of death-throes, but even this, because it still seemed so remote, did not frighten her. In the van, too, she had had to endure many things that touched her personally but did not penetrate. Someone had tried to rape her, a fellow whose sexual craving she had smelled in the dark and whom she now tried in vain to identify. Someone else had shielded her from him, an elderly man who had whispered to her later that he had been arrested because of a pair of pants, because of one pair of pants that he had bought from an officer; but now she couldn't recognize that man either. The other fellow had felt for her breasts in the dark, torn her dress, and kissed the nape of her neck—but luckily the other man had come between them. Even the cake had been knocked out of her hand, the little parcel, the only thing she had taken with her—it had fallen to the floor, and in the dark, groping around on the floor, she had managed to get hold of only a few broken pieces ingrained with grit and icing. She had eaten them with Maria—some of the cake had been squashed in her coat pocket—but hours later, when she drew small sticky lumps out of her pocket, they tasted wonderful; she gave some to the child and ate some herself, and it tasted wonderful, this squashed gritty cake which she scraped to the last crumb from her pocket. Some people had committed suicide, they bled to death almost without a sound, emitting odd gasps and groans in the corner, until those next to them slipped in the flowing blood and screamed hysterically. But they stopped screaming when the guard banged on the side of the van—it had sounded ominous and terrible, that banging, it couldn't have been done by a human being, they had long ceased to be among human beings. . . .

She was also waiting in vain for remorse; it had been senseless to leave that soldier, whom she liked very much, whose name she did not even know, absolutely senseless. Her parents' apartment was already empty, the only person she found there was her sister's confused and terrified child, young Maria, who had come home from school and found the apartment empty. Her parents and grandparents had already gone—neighbors told her they had been picked up at midday. And it had been senseless for her and Maria to run to the ghetto to look for her parents and grandparents: as always, they reached the ghetto by way of the back room of a hairdresser's and ran through the empty streets, arriving just in time to be shoved into that furniture van which had been standing there, waiting to leave, and in which they hoped to find their relatives. They found neither parents nor grandparents, they were not in that van. Ilona was amazed that none of the neighbors had thought of hurrying over to the school to warn her, but even Maria had not thought of it. Still, it would probably have made no difference if someone had warned her. . . . In the van someone had stuck a lighted cigarette between her lips, later she found out it had been the man who was picked up because of the pants. It was the first cigarette she had ever smoked, and she found it very refreshing and very soothing. She did not know her benefactor's name, none of them revealed their identity, neither that panting, lecherous fellow nor her benefactor, and when a match flared up all the faces looked alike: terrible faces full of fear and hatred.

But there had also been long stretches when she could pray: at the convent she had learned by heart all the prayers, all the litanies, and long sections of the liturgy for high holidays, and she was glad now that she knew them. Praying filled her with a cool serenity. She did not pray to be given something, or to be spared something, not for a quick painless death or for her life, she simply prayed, and she was glad when she could lean against the padded rear door and that at least her back was alone—at first she had stood the other way around, with her back to the press of bodies, and when she became tired and started to droop, tipping over backward, her body must have aroused that raging lust in the man she fell against, a lust that frightened but did not offend her—almost the opposite, she had a feeling of being somehow part of him, of this stranger. . . .

She was glad to be standing free, at least with her back alone against the padding intended for the protection of good furniture. She held Maria close to her body and was glad the child was asleep. She tried to pray as devoutly as she always did but found she couldn't, all she could manage was a cool rational meditation. She had pictured her life quite differently: she had passed her teacher-training finals at twenty-three, then she had entered the convent—her relatives were disappointed but approved her decision. She had spent a whole year at the convent, it had been a very happy time, and if she had actually become a nun she would now be a teaching sister in Argentina, in some very beautiful con-

vent no doubt; but she had not become a nun, because the desire
to marry and have children was so strong in her that even after a
year it had not been subdued—and she had gone back into the
world. She became a very successful teacher, and she enjoyed it,
she loved her two subjects of German and Music and was fond of
the children, she could hardly imagine anything more beautiful than a children's choir; she was very successful with her children's choir which she organized at school, and the choral works
sung by the children, those Latin choral works which they re-
hearsed for feast days, had a truly angelic neutrality—it was a free
and inward joy from which the children sang, sang words they did
not understand and which were beautiful. Life seemed beautiful to
her—for long periods, almost always. What troubled her was this
desire for tenderness and children, it troubled her because she
found nobody; there were many men who became interested in
her, some even confessed their love, and she let some of them kiss
her, but she was waiting for something she could not have de-
scribed, she did not call it love—there were many kinds of love—
she would have preferred to call it surprise, and she had believed
she was experiencing this sense of surprise when the soldier whose
name she did not know stood beside her facing the map and stuck
in the little flags. She knew he was in love with her, the last two
days he had been spending hours chatting with her, and she found
him very nice, although his uniform worried and alarmed her a little, but suddenly, in those few minutes while she stood next to
him and he seemed to have forgotten her, his grave, poignant face,
and his hands as they explored the map of Europe, had surprised
her, she had a sense of joy and could have sung. He was the first
man whose kiss she had ever returned. . . .

She walked slowly up the steps to the hut, pulling Maria along;
she glanced up astonished when the guard jabbed the muzzle of
his machine pistol into her side and shouted: "Faster—faster." She
walked faster. Inside sat three clerks at tables, big stacks of index
cards lay in front of them, the cards as big as cigar-box lids. She
was pushed toward the first table, Maria toward the second, and

toward the third table came an old man, in rags and unshaven, who gave her a fleeting smile, she smiled back; that must be her benefactor.

She gave her name, her occupation, her date of bith, and her religion, and was surprised when the clerk asked her age. "Twenty-three," she said.

Another half-hour, she thought. Maybe she would still have a chance to be alone for a bit after all. She was astonished at the casual atmosphere in this place given over to the administration of death. Everything was done mechanically, somewhat irritably, impatiently: these people were doing their job with the same lack of enthusiasm they would have brought to any other clerical work, they were merely doing their duty, a duty which they found tiresome but which they did. No one did anything to her; she was still waiting for fear, the fear she had been dreading. She had been very scared when she left the convent, very scared as she walked to the streetcar carrying her suitcase, clasping her money in her moist fingers: the world had seemed alien and ugly, this world to which she had longed to return so as to have a husband and children—a series of joys which she could not find in the convent and which now, walking to the streetcar, she no longer hoped to find, but she was very ashamed, ashamed of this fear. . . .

As she walked over to the second hut, she scanned the rows of waiting people for familiar faces but found none; she went up the steps, when she hesitated at the door the guard waved her impatiently inside, and she went in, pulling Maria along: that seemed to be the wrong thing to do, and she had her second encounter with brutality when the guard wrenched the child from her and, when the child struggled, pulled her by the hair. She heard Maria scream, and walked into the room holding her registration card. There was only one man in the room, and he was in the uniform of an officer; he was wearing a very impressive, narrow silver decoration in the shape of a cross on his chest. His face looked pale and haggard, and when he raised his head to look at her she was shocked at his massive chin, which almost disfigured him. He mutely held out his hand, she gave him the card and waited: still no fear. The man read the card, looked at her, and said quietly: "Sing something."

She hesitated. "Go on," he said impatiently, "sing something— never mind what. . . ."

She looked at him and opened her mouth. She sang the All Saints' Litany in a version which she had recently discovered and set aside to practice with the children. While she sang, she watched the man very intently, and suddenly she knew what fear was when he stood up and looked at her.

She continued to sing while the face in front of her became contorted like some horrible growth in a state of convulsion. She sang beautifully, and she did not know she was smiling, despite the slowly mounting fear now caught in her throat and waiting to be spewed out. . . .

As soon as she started to sing, silence fell, outside as well. Filskeit stared at her: she was beautiful—a woman—he had never had a woman—his life had been spent in stifling chastity—much of it, when he was alone, in front of the mirror, in which he vainly sought beauty and nobility and racial perfection—here it was: beauty and nobility and racial perfection, combined with something that completely paralyzed him: faith. He did not realize he was letting her sing on, even beyond the antiphony—perhaps he was dreaming—and in her gaze, although he saw she was trembling—in her gaze was something almost like love—or was it scorn—Fili, Redemptor mundi, Deus, she sang—he had never heard a woman sing like that.

Spiritus Sancte, Deus—her voice was powerful, warm, and of incredible clarity. He must be dreaming—now she would sing: Sancta Trinitas, unus Deus—he still remembered it—and she sang it:

Sancta Trinitas—Catholic Jews? he thought—I must be going mad. He ran to the window and flung it open: outside they were all standing there, listening, not a soul moved. Filskeit could feel himself twitching, he tried to shout, but from his throat came only a hoarse toneless rasp, and from outside came that breathless hush while the woman went on singing:

Sancta Dei Genitrix ... with trembling fingers he picked up his pistol, turned around, and fired blindly at the woman, who slumped to the floor and began to scream—now he had found his voice again, once hers had stopped singing. "Wipe them out!" he screamed. "Wipe out the whole bloody lot—and the choir too— bring out the choir—bring it outside—" he emptied the entire magazine into the woman, who was lying on the floor and in her agony spewing out her fear. . . .

Outside the slaughter began.

VIII

The widow Suchan had been watching the war for the past three years. It had all begun with the arrival of German soldiers and army vehicles, and cavalry—they had crossed the bridge that dusty autumn and headed toward the passes leading over onto the Polish side. It had had the genuine look of war, grimy soldiers, weary officers and horses, motorcycles chasing back and forth, a whole afternoon of war, with a few intermissions: a fine spectacle, you might say—the soldiers had marched across the bridge, with the trucks driving up ahead and motorcycles fore and aft, and the widow Suchan had never seen them again.

After that things had quieted down a bit, except for a German army truck turning up now and again; it would drive across the bridge and disappear into the forest, and she could hear the sound of its engine for a long time in the silence as it drove up the mountain on the other side, laboriously wheezing, groaning, with a few intermissions—for a long time—until it had evidently disappeared over the ridge. She pictured the trucks driving past her native village, where she had spent her childhood, the summers on the pastures and the winters at the spinning wheel—very high up, all by herself in summertime on those barren stony meadows. She had often leaned over the ridge for hours to see if anything was moving up or down the road. But in those days there were no cars here yet; occasionally there would be a cart, usually it was gypsies or Jews going across to the Polish side. It was not until much later, long after she had left, that the railroad had been built crossing the bridge near Szarny and running along the very same valley she used to look down on from those upland pastures. She had not been up there for a long time, almost ten years, and she listened for the trucks as long as she could—and she could still hear them even after they had vanished over the ridge and were driving along the mountain road, and maybe now it was her nephew's boys who were looking down at the German army vehicles toiling along.

But they did not come often. The truck came regularly every two months, and betweentimes there were not many vehicles—occasionally one carrying soldiers who stopped in for a beer before having to drive up into the mountains, and in the evening it would come down carrying the other soldiers who stopped in for a beer before driving down into the plain. But there were not many soldiers up there, the truck came only three times altogether, for, six months after the war had passed by her on its way into the mountains, the bridge leading behind her house across the river was blown up. It happened at night, and she would never forget the blast and the shriek she let out, the neighbors calling from across the street, and the steady screaming of her daughter Maria, who was then twenty-eight and getting more and more peculiar. The windowpanes were smashed, the cows lowed in the stable, and the dog barked the whole night through, and when daylight came they saw what had happened: the bridge had gone, the concrete piers were still standing, catwalk, roadway, railings, had all been neatly blown away, and the rusty girders lay down below in the river, sticking out here and there. That very morning a German officer had arrived with five soldiers; they searched all of Berczaba, first her house, every room, the stables, and even Maria's bed, with Maria still in it—she had been lying there whimpering in her room since the blast during the night. Next they went through the Temanns' house across the street: every room, every bale of hay and straw in the barn; and even Brachy's house was searched although no one had lived in it for three years and it was slowly falling to pieces. The Brachys had gone to work in Bratislava, and so far no one had turned up who wanted to buy the house and farm.

The Germans had been furious, but they hadn't found a thing, and they had hauled out the boat from her shed and rowed across the river to Tzenkoshik, the little village that lay just where the road started to climb: you could see the church spire beyond the forest from her attic window. But in Tzenkoshik they hadn't found a thing either, or in Tesarzy—although, of course, they probably didn't know that the two Svortchik boys had disappeared after the bridge was blown up.

To her mind it was ridiculous to blow up the bridge: the German truck crossed it only about every two months, and betweentimes, very occasionally, a car would turn up carrying soldiers, and the bridge served no one but the farmers who owned pastureland and forests on the other side. It certainly couldn't matter to the Germans if once every two months they had to make half an hour's detour as far as Szarny, only three miles away, where the railway bridge crossed the river.

It took a few days for her to grasp what the destruction of the bridge meant to her. At first a lot of inquisitive people had shown up, they would have a schnapps or a beer at her place and want to be told the whole story, but then Berczaba became quiet, very quiet; the farmers and hired hands who had to go into the forest or up to the pastures on the other side stopped coming, so did the people who used to drive to Tzenkoshik on Sundays, the couples out for a stroll in the woods, and even the soldiers, and the only thing she sold in two weeks was a beer to Temann from across the street, that skinflint who made his own schnapps. It was very depressing to think that in future all she was going to sell was a glass of beer to that stingy Temann, for everyone knew how stingy he was.

But this very quiet period lasted only three weeks. One day a gray, high-speed little army car arrived with three officers who inspected the ruined bridge, paced up and down the bank for half an hour, field glasses in hand, stared out over the countryside, first from the Temanns', then went up into her attic and stared out over the countryside from up there, and drove off, without having so much as a single schnapps at her place.

And two days later a slow cloud of dust moved from Tesarzy toward Berczaba—it was some tired soldiers, seven of them plus a corporal, who tried to explain that they were to live, sleep, and eat at her place. At first she was scared, but then she realized what a good thing it was for her, and she hurried upstairs to Maria, who was still in bed.

The soldiers seemed in no hurry, they waited patiently—men, no longer young, who filled their pipes, drank beer, unloaded their packs, and made themselves comfortable. They waited patiently until she had emptied out three little rooms upstairs: the hired hand's room, empty for the past three years because she could no longer afford hired help; the little room which her husband had once said was for visitors or guests, but there were never any visitors, and guests never came; and her bedroom, the one she had shared with her husband. She herself moved in with Maria, into the latter's room. Later, when she came downstairs, the corporal began to explain that the village council would have to pay her a lot of kronen for this, and that she was to cook for the soldiers and would be paid for this too.

The soldiers were the best customers she had ever had: those eight men consumed more in a month than all the people together who used to cross the bridge separately. The soldiers appeared to have plenty of money and any amount of time. Their duties seemed ridiculous to her: two of them always had to cover a certain route together—along the riverbank, then across in the boat, back again, along another stretch of riverbank—they were relieved every two hours; and up in the attic sat one man who scanned the countryside through his field glasses and was relieved every three hours. They made themselves comfortable up there in the attic, they had widened the dormer window by removing a few tiles, covering it with a sheet of metal at night, and there they sat all day long in an old armchair, with cushions on it, that stood perched on a table. There one of the men would sit all day long, staring up into the mountains, into the forest, at the riverbank, sometimes also back toward Tesarzy, and the others loafed around and were bored. She was horrified when she found out how much the soldiers got paid for this, and their families at home got paid too. One of them was a schoolteacher, and he worked out for her exactly how much his wife got, but it was so much that she couldn't believe it. It was too much, what that schoolteacher's wife got paid for her husband to lounge around here, eat goulash, vegetables, and potatoes, drink coffee, eat bread and sausage—they even got tobacco every day—and when he wasn't eating he was lounging around in her bar leisurely drinking his beer and reading, he read all the time, he seemed to have a whole pack full of books, and when he wasn't eating or reading he was lounging up there in the attic with his field glasses, of no use to anyone, staring at the forests and meadows or watching the farmers in the fields. This soldier was very nice to her, his name was Becker, but she didn't care for him because all he did was read, just drink beer and read and lounge around the place.

But that was all a long time ago. Those first soldiers hadn't stayed long, four months, then others had come who had stayed for six months, then others again for almost a year, and then they were relieved regularly every six months, and some would come back who had been there before, and they all did the same thing, for three years: loaf around, drink beer, play cards, and lounge about up there in the attic or over in the meadow, and stroll uselessly around in the forest with their rifles on their backs. She was paid a lot of money for housing the soldiers and cooking for them.

Others came too; the bar had become a living room for the soldiers.

The sergeant who had been quartered with her for the past four months was called Peter, she didn't know his surname; he was heavy-set, walked like a farmer, even had a mustache, and the sight of him often reminded her of her husband, Wenzel Suchan, who had not returned from another war: soldiers had crossed the bridge then too, covered with dust, on foot and on horseback, with mud-caked baggage trains, soldiers who never came back—it was years before they came back, and she couldn't tell whether they were the same ones who had gone up the other side so long ago. She had been young, twenty-two, a pretty woman, when Wenzel Suchan brought her down from the mountain and made her his wife: she felt very rich, very lucky, to be the wife of an innkeeper who kept a hired hand to work in the fields, and a horse, and she loved the twenty-six-year-old Wenzel Suchan with his deliberate walk and his mustache. Wenzel had been a corporal with a rifle brigade in Bratislava, and shortly after the unfamiliar, dusty soldiers had made their way through the forest up the hill, past her native village, Wenzel Suchan had gone to Bratislava again, as a corporal with a rifle brigade, and they had sent him south to a country called Rumania, to the mountains; from there he had written her three post cards saying he was fine, and on the last post card he told her he had been made a sergeant. After that she heard nothing for four weeks, then she got a letter from Vienna saying he had been killed.

Soon after that Maria was born, Maria who was now pregnant by that sergeant called Peter who looked like Wenzel Suchan. In her memory Wenzel lived on as a young man, twenty-six years old, and this sergeant who was called Peter and was forty-five—seven years younger than herself—seemed very old to her. Many a night she had lain awake waiting for Maria, and Maria had not come until dawn, slipping barefoot into the room and getting quickly into bed just before the cocks began to crow—many a night she had waited and prayed, and she had put many more flowers before the Virgin Mary's picture downstairs than she used to, but Maria had become pregnant, and the sergeant came to see her, embarrassed, awkward as a peasant, and explained that he would marry Maria when the war was over.

Well, there was nothing she could do about it, and she continued to put lots of flowers before the Virgin Mary's picture downstairs in the passageway, and waited. Things became quiet in Berczaba, much quieter it seemed to her, although nothing had changed: the soldiers lounged around in the bar, wrote letters, played cards, drank schnapps and beer, and some of them had started up a trade in things that were not obtainable here: pocketknives, razor blades, scissors—wonderful scissors—and socks. They took money for them, or exchanged the money for butter and eggs because they had more leisure than money to spend on drinks during this leisure. Now there was another one who read all day and even had a whole case of books driven over by truck from Tesarzy station. He was a professor, he also spent half the day in the attic staring through his field glasses at the mountains, into the forest, at the riverbank, and sometimes back toward Tesarzy, or watching the farmers at work in the fields, and he also told her his wife received money, large sums of money, so and so many thousand kronen a month—and she didn't believe him either, it was too much, a crazy sum, he must be lying, his wife couldn't be paid all that for her husband to sit around here reading books and writing, half the day and often half the night, and then a few hours a day sitting up there in the attic with the field glasses. One of the men used to sketch: in fine weather he would sit outdoors by the river, sketching the mountains there was such a fine view of from here, the river, the remains of the bridge, and he sketched her too a few times, and she admired the pictures very much and hung one of them in the bar.

They had been stationed here for three years now, these soldiers, always eight men, doing nothing. They strolled along the river, crossed over in her boat, strolled through the woods as far as Tzenkoshik, came back, crossed the river again, walked past along the bank, then part-way down to Tesarzy, and were relieved. They ate well, slept a lot, and had plenty of money, and she often thought that maybe Wenzel Suchan had been taken away, all those years ago, to do nothing in another country—Wenzel, whom she badly needed, who could work and liked to work. They had most likely taken him away to do nothing in that country called Rumania, to wait around doing nothing until he was killed by a bullet. But these soldiers under her roof didn't get hit by bullets: as long as they had been here they had only fired their rifles a few times, each time there was great excitement, and each time it had turned out to be a mistake—usually they had shot at game that was moving in the forest and hadn't halted when challenged, but even that didn't happen very often, only four or five times in these three years, and once they had shot at a woman who had come down the river at night from Tzenkoshik and then run through the forest to get a doctor in Tesarzy for her child, they had shot at this woman too, but luckily they hadn't hit her, and afterward they had helped her into the boat and even rowed her across—and the professor, who hadn't gone to bed yet and was sitting in the bar reading and writing, the professor had gone with her to Tesarzy. But in these three years they hadn't found a single partisan—everybody knew there were none left here now that the Svortchik boys had gone; even in Szarny, where the big railway bridge was, no partisans were ever seen. . . .

Although she was making money from the war, it was bitter for her to imagine that Wenzel Suchan had probably done nothing in that country called Rumania, that he hadn't been able to do anything. Most likely that's what war meant, men doing nothing and going to other countries so no one could see them at it—anyway, she found it both disgusting and ridiculous to watch these men doing nothing for three years but steal time, and getting well paid to shoot once a year, at night, by mistake, at game or some poor woman who was trying to get the doctor for her child; disgusting and ridiculous for these men to have to loaf around while she had so much to do she didn't know which way to turn. She had to cook, look after the cows and pigs and chickens, and many of the soldiers even paid her to clean their boots, darn their socks, and wash their underclothes; she had so much to do that she had to take on a hired hand again, a man from Tesarzy, for Maria had been doing nothing ever since she got pregnant. She treated this sergeant as if he were her husband: slept in his room, got him his breakfast, kept his clothes clean, and sometimes scolded him.

But one day, after almost exactly three years, a very high-ranking officer turned up, with red stripes down his pants and a gold-braided collar—she heard later that he was a real general—this high-ranking officer arrived with a few others in a very fast car from Tesarzy; his face was all yellow, he looked sad, and in front of her house he bawled out Sergeant Peter because Peter hadn't been wearing his belt and pistol when he came out to report—and the officer stood there, furious, and waited. She saw him stamping his foot, his face seemed to shrink and get even yellower, and he barked at another officer standing beside him and saluting with a trembling hand, a gray-haired, tired-looking man of over sixty whom she knew because sometimes he would ride down from Tesarzy on his bicycle and chat in a very nice friendly way with the sergeant and the soldiers in the bar—and then later, wheeling his bicycle and accompanied by the professor, walk slowly back to Tesarzy. At last Peter came out wearing his belt and pistol and walked with the men to the river. They crossed over in the boat, walked through the forest, returned, and stood for a long time beside the bridge—then they went up into the attic, and finally the officers drove off again, and Peter stood outside the house with two soldiers; they raised their arms in salute and stayed that way for a long time, until the car was almost back in Tesarzy. Then Peter went into the house again, furious, threw his cap onto the table, and the only thing he said to Maria was: "Looks like they're going to rebuild the bridge."

And two days later another vehicle, a truck, came dashing up from Tesarzy, and out of this truck jumped seven young soldiers and a young officer who strode into the house and spent half an hour with the sergeant in his room. Maria tried to join in this conversation, walking right into the room, but the young officer waved her out, and she went in again, and again the young officer impatiently waved her out; she stayed at the top of the stairs, crying, and had to look on while the old soldiers collected their packs and the young ones moved into their rooms. She waited for half an hour, crying, flew into a rage when the professor patted her on the shoulder, and clung shrieking and sobbing to Peter when he finally came out of the room carrying his pack and with a very red face tried to calm her down, to comfort her—she clung to him until he had climbed into the truck; then, still weeping she stood on the steps and watched the truck dash off toward Tesarzy. She knew he would never be back, although he had promised her he would. . . .

Feinhals arrived in Berczaba two days before the rebuilding of the bridge began. The tiny hamlet consisted of a tavern and two houses, one of which was abandoned and falling into decay, and when he got out with the others the whole place was enveloped in the bitter smoke from the potato fires smoldering in the fields. It was quiet and peaceful, nowhere any sign of war. . . .

It was only during the return trip in the red furniture van that he was found to have a splinter in his leg, a glass splinter, as the operation revealed, a minute fragment of a bottle of Tokay, and there had been an odd and embarrassing negotiation because he might have been in line for the silver medal for wounds except that the senior medical officer did not award silver medals for wounds caused by glass splinters, and for a few days the suspicion of self-mutilation hung over him, until Lieutenant Brecht, whom he named as a witness, sent in his report. The wound healed quickly, although he drank a lot of schnapps, and after a month he was sent to some redeployment center that packed him off to Berczaba. He waited downstairs in the tavern until the room Gress had chosen for them became free. He drank some wine, thought about Ilona, and heard the noise in the house made by the men getting ready to leave: the old soldiers were hunting for their be-

longings, the landlady stood behind the counter dourly taking in
the scene, a middle-aged woman, quite pretty, still quite pretty,
and in the passageway beyond her another woman was bawling her
head off.

Then he heard the woman wailing and sobbing more lustily
than ever, and heard the truck take off for the village they had just
come from. Gress appeared and took him up to his room. The
room was low, the plaster flaking off in places, black beams sup-
ported the ceiling, and it smelled stuffy; the air outside was close,
and the window gave onto a garden: a grassy plot with old fruit
trees, flowerbeds along the sides, stables, and at the end, outside a
shed, a boat on blocks, its paint peeling off. It was quiet outside.
To the left across the hedge he could see the bridge, rusty iron girders stuck out of the water, and the concrete piers were overgrown
with moss. The little river seemed to be some forty or fifty yards
wide.

So now he was sharing a room with Gress. He had met him yesterday at the redeployment center and decided not to say one
word more than necessary to him: Gress had four decorations on
his chest, and he liked telling tales—never stopped, in fact—about
the Polish, Rumanian, French, and Russian girls he claimed to
have left behind, all with broken hearts. Feinhals didn't feel like
listening, it was a nuisance as well as a bore, embarrassing too, and
Gress seemed to be one of those men who believed people would
listen to them because they had decorations on their chest, more
decorations than most.

Feinhals himself had only one decoration, a single medal, and
he was a born listener because he never said anything, or hardly
ever, and asked for no explanations. He was glad to learn that he
and Gress were to take turns manning the observation post: this
would mean he would be rid of him during the daytime at
least.... He lay down on the bed the minute Gress announced his
intention of breaking the heart of a Slovak girl, any Slovak girl.

He was tired, and every night when he lay down to sleep somewhere he hoped to dream about Ilona, but he never did. He would

recapture every word he had exchanged with her, think about her very hard, but when he fell asleep she did not come. Often he felt, before falling asleep, that he needed only to turn over to feel her arm, but she was not there beside him, she was a long way away, and it was useless to turn over. He was a long time falling asleep because he was thinking so hard about her and imagining the room that had been intended to receive them—and when he did drop off he slept badly, and in the morning he had forgotten what he had dreamed about. He had not dreamed about Ilona.

He prayed in bed at night too, and thought about the talks he used to have with her before they had to leave—she had invariably blushed, and she seemed embarrassed by his presence in the room, among stuffed animals, rock specimens, maps, and health charts. But maybe it had only embarrassed her to talk about religion—she had always gone fiery red—it seemed to distress her to state her beliefs, and she stated her belief in faith, hope, and charity, and was shocked when he said he couldn't go to church because the faces and sermons of most priests were more than he could stand. "We have to pray to console God," she had said. . . .

He never thought she would let herself be kissed, but he had kissed her, and she him, and he knew she would have gone with him to that room he now saw so often in his mind's eye: none too clean, water still standing in the bluish wash basin, the wide brown bed and the view into the neglected orchard where windfalls lay decaying under the trees. He always pictured himself lying in bed with her and talking, but he never dreamed about it. . . .

Next morning the regular routine began. He sat perched up there in the armchair on the wobbly table, in the fusty attic of this house, looking with the field glasses out through the dormer window into the mountains, into the forest, scanning the riverbank and sometimes back toward the hamlet they had driven over from in the truck: he couldn't find any partisans—maybe the farmers in the fields were partisans, only you couldn't tell this with field glasses. It was so quiet that it hurt, and he felt as though he had been perched up here for years, and he raised the field glasses, adjusted the screw, and looked out across the forest, past the yellow church spire, into the mountains. The air was very clear, and way up there among craggy rocks he could see a herd of goats; the animals were scattered like tiny, white, hard-edged cloudlets, very white against that gray, soft-green background, and he could feel himself capturing the silence through the field glasses, and the loneliness too: the animals moved very slowly, very seldom—as if they were being pulled along on short strings. With the field glasses he could see them as he would have done with the naked eye at two or three miles; they seemed very far away, infinitely far away, silent and lonely, those animals—he could not see the goatherd; it was a shock to put down the glasses and find he could no longer see them, not a trace of them, although he gazed intently beyond the church spire up at the mountain. Not even their whiteness was visible, they must be a long way off, and he picked up the glasses again and looked at the white goats, whose loneliness he could feel—but the sound of commands being given down in the garden startled him, and he lowered the glasses, looked first without them into the garden and watched the men drilling. Lieutenant Mück himself was in command. Feinhals lifted the glasses to his eyes, adjusted the lenses, and studied Mück closely; he had known him only two days, but he had already seen that Mück took matters seriously, his fine, dark profile was like a mask, deadly serious, the hands on his back did not move, and the muscles of the thin neck twitched. Mück did not look well, his complexion was pasty, almost gray, the lips were bloodless and barely moved when they uttered "Left turn," "Right turn," and "About turn." At the moment Feinhals could see only Mück's profile, that deadly serious, rigid half of his face, the lips that barely moved, the sorrowful left eye that seemed to be looking not at the drilling soldiers but far away, somewhere—maybe back into the past. Then he looked at Gress: his face was swollen, he looked in some way upset.

When—again without the glasses—he looked down into the garden where the soldiers were doing "left turns," "right turns," and "about turns" on that lush, wonderful expanse of grass, he saw a woman hanging out the washing on a line strung between the stables. It must be the daughter who had been crying and carrying on in the passageway yesterday. She looked grave, somber—so somber that she was not pretty but beautiful, a fine-drawn, very dark face with tightly pressed lips. She did not even glance at the four soldiers and the lieutenant.

When he went up to the attic next morning, just before eight, he felt as if he had been there for months, years almost. The silence and loneliness seemed quite natural: the gentle mooing of the cows in the stable and the smell of the potato fires still hanging in the air, a few fires were still smoldering, and when he adjusted the glasses, aiming them at a point far off in the distance in line with the tip of the yellow church spire, all he captured in the lenses was loneliness. Up there it was empty—a gray, soft-green surface dotted with black rocks. . . .

Mück had gone with the four soldiers to the riverbank to practice sighting. The sound of his brief, sad commands came softly across, too faint to disturb the silence—they enhanced it almost; and downstairs in the kitchen the young woman was singing a halting Slovak folk song. The old woman had gone into the field with the hired hand to dig potatoes. Across the street in the other farmhouse it was quiet too. Although he scanned the mountains for quite a time his eyes saw nothing but silent, lonely expanses, steep rocks, except to the right where a train's white vapor came puffing out of the forest and quickly drifted apart—through the field glasses the vapor looked like dust settling over the treetops; there was not a sound to be heard except for Mück's brief commands at the riverbank and the young woman's haunting song from downstairs. . . .

Then they returned from the riverbank, and he could hear them singing. It was sad to hear those four men singing, a pathetic, ragged, very thin quartet singing "Gray Columns on the March." He could also hear Mück's "left, right—left, right"; Mück seemed to be desperately battling the loneliness, but it was no use. The silence was stronger than his commands, stronger than the singing.

As they halted outside the house he heard the first truck arriving from the hamlet they had left the day before yesterday. He quickly trained his glasses on the road: a cloud of dust was rapidly approaching, he could make out the cab and something large and bulky showing above the roof. . . .

"What's up?" they called to him from the street.

"A truck," he said, keeping the lenses on the approaching vehicle, and at that moment he heard the young woman come out of the house. She spoke to the soldiers and called something up to him. He could not make out what she was saying, but he called down: "The driver's a civilian, there's a Brownshirt sitting next to him, seems to be someone from the Party; on the back of the truck there's a cement mixer!"

"A cement mixer?" they called up.

"Yes!" he said.

Now those down below could also make out the cab of the truck, and the man in brown, and the cement mixer, and they could see another truck approaching from the village, a smaller cloud of dust, then another and another, a whole column heading from the village toward the remains of the bridge. By the time the first truck halted just before the approach to the bridge, the second truck was already so close that they could make out the cab and the load of that one too: hut prefabs. But now they all ran up to the first truck, including Maria, all except the lieutenant, as the truck door opened and a man in brown jumped out. The man was bareheaded, suntanned, with a frank, attractive face. "Heil Hitler, boys," he shouted, "is this Berczaba?"

"Yes," said the soldiers. They took their hands uncertainly out of their pockets. The man had a major's shoulder loops on his brown tunic. They did not know how to address him.

He called into the cab: "We're here, switch off the motor!" Looking beyond the soldiers at the lieutenant, he paused for a moment, advanced a few steps. The lieutenant also advanced a few steps, then the man stopped and waited, and Lieutenant Mück walked the rest of the way quite fast until he stood facing the man in brown. First Mück's hand went to his cap, then his arm went up for the Heil Hitler salute, and he said: "Mück!" and the man in brown also raised his arm, then held his hand out to Mück, shook hands, and said: "I'm Deussen—in charge of construction —we're going to rebuild the bridge here."

The lieutenant looked at the soldiers, the soldiers looked at Maria, Maria ran into the house, and Deussen bounced jauntily away to direct the approaching vehicles.

Deussen went about everything with great determination, great vigor, but with something obliging and friendly in his manner. He asked the widow Suchan to show him the kitchen, smiled, pursed his lips, said nothing, went across to the abandoned house, inspected it very thoroughly, and when he emerged he was smiling, and within minutes two trucks loaded with prefabs were on their way back to Tesarzy. He set up his own quarters at the Temanns', appeared shortly thereafter leaning on the windowsill smoking and watching the unloading of the trucks. There was another young man in brown with the trucks, wearing a sergeant's shoulder patches. Now and again Deussen would call something out to him from the window. Meanwhile all the trucks had arrived, ten of them, and the place was a hive of workmen, iron girders, beams, sacks of cement, and an hour later a little motorboat came down the river from Szarny. A third man in brown got out of the boat, and two pretty, suntanned Slovak women who were greeted gaily by the workmen.

Feinhals watched it all very closely. First the big kitchen stove was carried into the dilapidated house, then the following were unloaded: complete iron railings, rivets, screws, creosoted beams, survey instruments, and kitchen supplies. By eleven the Slovak women were already peeling potatoes, and by noon all the stuff had been unloaded, even a shed for the cement had been assembled, and three more trucks arrived from the village to strew gravel on the approach to the bridge. When he went downstairs for lunch, Gress having relieved him, he saw that a sign had been nailed over the bar entrance saying "Canteen."

For the next few days he continued to watch the building activities very closely and was astonished at the precision with which everything had been planned: nothing was done needlessly, no material lay farther away than necessary from the point at which it was to be used. Feinhals had been on many construction sites in his time, and in charge of several construction jobs, but he was astonished to see how neatly and deftly this one was carried out. After only three days the bridge piers had been carefully filled with concrete, and while they were still pouring the last pier the erection of the heavy iron girders was already under way on the first one. By the fourth day a catwalk across the bridge had already been completed, and after a week he saw trucks driving up on the other side of the river carrying bridge sections, heavy vehicles that Deussen used simultaneously as ramp and base for erecting the final girder sections. Now that the catwalk was finished everything went much faster, and Feinhals spent less time looking up to the mountains or into the forest. He observed the building of the bridge very closely, and even when he had to drill with the other men he usually watched the workmen: he loved this work.

In the evenings, when dusk was falling and the attic observation post was not manned, he would sit in the garden listening to a young Russian called Stalin—Stalin Gadlenko—playing the balalaika. Indoors there was singing, drinking, even dancing, although dancing was prohibited, but Deussen seemed to close his eyes to all that. He was in very good spirits: he had been given two weeks to build the bridge, and if the work continued at this rate he would be through in twelve days. He saved a lot of gas because he could buy all the cooking supplies from Temann and the widow Suchan without sending a truck out all over the countryside, and he saw to it that the workmen were issued cigarettes, were well fed, and felt at ease; he knew this was better than exerting authority which, although it induced fear, actually inhibited the work.

He had already built a number of bridges—most of which had meanwhile been blown up again, but for a time at least they had served their purpose, and he had never had any trouble meeting his deadlines.

The widow Suchan was pleased: the bridge would be there again, it would still be there even when the war was over, and if it was there the soldiers would probably stay and people from the villages would start coming back too. The workmen also seemed content. Every third day a snappy little light-brown car would drive down from Tesarzy and screech to a halt outside the tavern, and from the car would emerge a man in brown who looked old and tired and wore a captain's shoulder loops, and the workmen were rounded up and paid; they were paid plenty, enough to be able to buy socks from the soldiers, and shirts, and to spend the evening drinking and dancing with the pretty Slovak women who worked in the kitchen.

On the tenth day Feinhals saw that the bridge was finished: the railing was in place, the framework for the roadway completed, and he watched cement and girders being loaded and driven away, as well as the shed that had housed the cement. Half the workmen went back too, and one of the kitchen women, and Berczaba quieted down somewhat. All that was left now were fifteen workmen, Deussen and the young man in brown with the sergeant's shoulder patches, and one woman in the kitchen, at whom Feinhals looked very often. She spent the whole morning sitting by the window peeling potatoes, singing to herself, and she would pound the meat and clean the vegetables and was very pretty: when she smiled he felt a pang, and through the field glasses he could plainly see her mouth on the other side of the street, and her fine dark eyebrows and white teeth. She always sang softly to herself—and that evening he went into the bar and danced with her. He danced a lot with her, and he saw her dark eyes close up, felt her firm white arms under his hands, and was rather disappointed to find that she smelled of cooking—it was close and smoky in the bar—she was the only woman, except Maria, who sat at the counter and didn't dance. That night he dreamed about this Slovak woman whose name he didn't know, he had a very vivid dream about her, although after getting into bed he had again thought for a long time and very hard about Ilona.

Next day he didn't look across at her through his field glasses, although he could hear her singing, softly humming; he looked up to the mountains and was pleased to be able to pick out a herd of goats again, now they were to the right of the church spire, white specks moving jerkily against a gray, soft-green background.

Suddenly he put down the field glasses: he had heard a shot, the echo of a distant explosion coming down from the mountains. There it was again, very distinct, not loud, very far away. The workmen on the bridge paused, the Slovak woman broke off her singing, and Lieutenant Mück came running up to the attic in a state of agitation, wrenched the field glasses out of his hands, and looked up to the mountains. He looked up to the mountains for a very long time, but there were no more explosions, and Mück handed the glasses back to him, murmuring: "Keep watching now —keep watching," and ran back into the yard where he was supervising the men cleaning their weapons.

That afternoon seemed quieter than previous ones, although the sounds remained the same: the workmen on the bridge sawing creosoted beams, joining and screwing them together, the voice of the old woman scolding her daughter downstairs in the kitchen and getting no reply, and the gentle humming of the Slovak woman sitting by the open window as she prepared supper for the workmen: big yellow potatoes were frying in the pan, and an earthenware bowl of tomatoes shone in the dusk. Feinhals trained his glasses on the mountains, on the forest, scanned the riverbank; all was quiet on the other side, nothing moved. The two sentries had disappeared into the forest, and he aimed the glasses at the workmen on the bridge: they were already half-way through their work, the black, solid beams of the roadway were gradually meeting, and when he swung the glasses around he could look down on the road at all the remaining material being loaded, tools and girders, beds, chairs, and the kitchen stove, and soon after that the truck with eight workmen aboard drove off toward Tesarzy. The Slovak woman leaned on the windowsill and waved them good-by, the place seemed quieter, even the motorboat went off up the river in the late afternoon, and in the roadway over the bridge there was only one bit missing—three or four beams. There was a gap of about six feet when the men knocked off work. Feinhals saw them leave their tools lying on the bridge. The truck returned from Tesarzy, stopped outside the kitchen, and unloaded a small basket of fruit and a few bottles, and shortly before Feinhals was relieved there came again the echo of muffled explosions from above: it resounded from the mountains like stage thunder, artificially multiplied, reverberating, dying away, three times—four times—then there was silence. And again Lieutenant Mück came running upstairs and looked through the field glasses, his face twitching. Swinging them from left to right he scanned the rocks, the ridges, put down the glasses with a shake of his head, wrote a message on a piece of paper, and within a few minutes Gress was pedaling off to Tesarzy on Deussen's bicycle.

After Gress had left, Feinhals distinctly heard sounds of a machine-gun duel from the mountains: the hard, hollow rasp of a Russian machine gun contrasting with the high-pitched, nervous barking of a German one that grated like a frenzied hornet—the shots came so fast they seemed to skid. The skirmish was brief, only a few rounds were exchanged; then hand grenades burst, three or four, and again the noise was multiplied. Over and over again, until they died away, they sent their echo down into the plain. Somehow it seemed ridiculous to Feinhals: the war, wherever it showed up, was associated with completely unnecessary noise. This time Mück didn't come upstairs, he stood on the bridge and stared at the mountains; one more isolated shot came from above, from a rifle apparently, the echo sounding as thin as the noise of a rolling stone; then all was quiet until dusk fell. Feinhals replaced the sheet of metal on the roof and slowly went downstairs.

Gress was not back yet, and down in the bar Mück was anxiously holding forth about increased alertness for the night. There he stood, his face deadly serious, his fingers fumbling nervously with his two decorations; he had hung his loaded machine pistol around his neck and his steel helmet from his belt.

Before Gress got back, a gray car arrived from Tesarzy and out of it got a stout, red-faced captain and a spare, stern-looking first lieutenant, both of whom walked across the bridge with Mück. Feinhals stood in front of the house and watched them. It looked as though the three figures had disappeared for good, but they soon came back; the car turned. Across the street Deussen was looking out of the window, and on the ground floor of the workmen's quarters the men were sitting in the semidarkness around a rough table, tomatoes and potatoes on their plates. In the corner of the room stood the Slovak woman, one hand on hip, in the other a cigarette—the flourish of her arm as she brought the cigarette to her lips seemed to Feinhals a shade too elaborate. Then, as the motor of the gray car started up, she came closer, leaned on the windowsill, smoking her cigarette, and smiled at Feinhals. He looked intently at her face, forgetting to salute the two departing officers—the woman was wearing a dark bodice, and the white of her breast shone heartshaped below her brown face. Mück walked past Feinhals on his way into the house and said: "Bring the machine gun over here." Feinhals now saw that where the officers' car had been parked a black, slender machine gun was lying on the road beside some ammunition cases. He slowly crossed the road and brought back the machine gun, then crossed over a second time and brought back the ammunition cases. The Slovak woman was still leaning on the windowsill, she flicked off the glowing end of her cigarette and stuck the rest into her apron pocket. She was still looking at Feinhals but no longer smiling—she looked sad, her mouth was a poignant pale red. Then all at once she pursed her lips a little, turned, and began to clear the table. The workmen came out of the house and walked toward the bridge.

They were still working on it when Feinhals walked across the bridge half an hour later with the machine gun. They were putting the last beam in place in the dark. Deussen himself screwed in the very last rivet. He had one of the men hold a carbide lamp for him, and to Feinhals it looked as though he were holding the spanner like the handle of a barrel organ, as though he were boring into a great dark box that produced no sound. Feinhals put down the machine gun, said "Just a moment" to Gress, and went back once more. He had heard the motor being started up in the truck standing outside the workmen's quarters, he walked back to the ramp and watched the rest of the household objects being loaded. There was not much left: a stove, a few chairs, a basket of potatoes, crockery, and the workmen's own things. The workmen walked back from the bridge and all got in the truck. They were carrying bottles of schnapps and drinking from them. The last person to get in was the Slovak woman. She was wearing a red kerchief around her head and had very little to carry: a bundle wrapped up in a blue cloth. Feinhals hesitated a moment as he watched her get in the truck, then walked quickly back. Deussen was the last to come off the bridge: he was holding the spanner and went slowly into Temann's house.

They spent half the night crouching there with the brand-new machine gun behind the little wall that bordered the ramp, listening into the night. The silence was unbroken—now and again the patrol emerged from the forest; they would exchange a few desultory words and then go on crouching there mutely, their eyes fixed on the narrow road leading into the forest. But nothing came. Up in the mountains the silence was unbroken too. Just before midnight, when they were relieved, they went indoors and fell asleep at once. It was almost morning when they heard a noise and got up. Gress waited to put on his boots, but Feinhals stood barefoot at the window and looked across to the other side: a crowd of people were standing over there, arguing with the lieutenant, who evidently did not want to let them cross the bridge. They had apparently come down from the mountains and from the village whose church spire was visible beyond the forest, a long file of people

with carts and bundles that seemed to extend even beyond the
point where the forest began. Their shrill voices were full of fear,
and Feinhals saw the widow Suchan, in slippers, throw a coat over
her shoulders and walk across the bridge. She stopped beside the
lieutenant and talked for a long time to the crowd, then started to
argue with the lieutenant. Deussen arrived too; he walked slowly
across, cigarette between his lips, and also spoke to the lieutenant,
then to the landlady, then to the crowd—until at last the file of
refugees on the other side started to move in the direction of
Szarny. There were many carts piled high with children and crates,
chickens in baskets, a long file that could proceed only at a snail's
pace; Deussen returned with the landlady and, shaking his head,
tried to explain something to her.

Feinhals dressed slowly and lay down again on the bed. He tried
to sleep, but Gress was fussing about as he shaved and whistling
softly to himself, and a few minutes later they heard two vehicles
approaching. At first it sounded as though they were driving side
by side, then one seemed to overtake the other; one was hardly audible yet as the other drove up to the door. Feinhals got up and
went downstairs: it was the brown car that had sometimes brought
the captain with the workmen's pay. He was standing across the
street outside Temann's house, and just then Deussen walked toward the bridge with a man in brown who was also wearing a major's shoulder loops. But now the second car arrived too. This car
was gray and caked with dirt and mud-splashed, and there seemed
to be something wrong with it; it drew up in front of the tavern,
and a cheery little lieutenant jumped out and called to Feinhals:
"Start packing, it's getting sticky here. Where's the old man?"
Feinhals noticed that the little lieutenant was wearing a sapper's
shoulder patches. He pointed toward the bridge, saying: "Over
there."

"Thanks," said the lieutenant. He called to the soldier in the
car: "Get everything ready," and ran quickly toward the bridge.
Feinhals followed. The man in the brown uniform with the major's shoulder loops inspected the bridge minutely, had Deussen

show him everything, nodded appreciatively, even shook his head appreciatively, and walked slowly back with Deussen. Deussen emerged at once from Temann's house with his pack, spanner in hand, and the brown car drove quickly off.

Mück returned with the two machine-gunners, the sapper lieutenant, and an artillery noncom without a weapon, dirty and harassed in appearance: sweat was running down the man's face, he had no pack either, not even a cap, and kept pointing excitedly into the forest, and beyond the forest up into the mountains. Now Feinhals could hear: vehicles were coming slowly down the road. The little sapper lieutenant ran over to his car shouting: "Hurry, hurry!" The soldier came running up with gray metal boxes, brown cardboard packages, and a bundle of wires. The lieutenant looked at his watch: "Seven," he said, "we've got ten minutes." He glanced at Mück: "It's to be blown up at exactly ten past. The counterattack's been called off."

Feinhals slowly mounted the stairs, collected his things in his room, picked up his rifle, placed everything outside the door of the house, and walked back inside. The two women, still not dressed, ran distractedly along the passages, snatching random objects from the rooms and screaming at one another. Feinhals looked at the Virgin Mary: the flowers had wilted—he carefully picked out the wilted stalks, rearranged the remaining fresh flowers, and looked at his watch. It was eight minutes past, and across on the other side the sound of the approaching vehicles could be heard more clearly now, they must have already passed the village and be in the forest. Outside everyone stood ready to leave. Lieutenant Mück had a message pad in his hand and was taking down the particulars of the harassed artillery noncom, who was sitting exhausted on the bench.

"Schniewind," said the noncom, "Arthur Schniewind . . . we're with 912." Mück nodded and slipped the message pad into his leather satchel. At that moment the little sapper lieutenant came running back with the soldier, shouting: "Take cover—take cover!" They all threw themselves onto the road, as close as they could to the house, the front of which stood at an angle to the bridge ramp. The sapper lieutenant looked at his watch—then the bridge blew up. There was not much of a crash, nothing whizzed through the air; there was a rending sound, then an explosion like a few hand grenades, and they heard the heavy roadway smacking into the water. They waited another moment or two until the little lieutenant said: "That's it." They stood up and looked at the bridge: the concrete piers were still standing, the catwalk and roadway had been neatly blown away, only across on the other side one section of the railing still hung in the air.

The approaching vehicles sounded quite close by now, then suddenly there was silence: they must have stopped in the forest.

The little sapper lieutenant had got into his car and, cranking down a window, called out to Mück: "What are you waiting for? You've no orders to wait here."

He saluted briefly and drove off in his dirty little car.

"Fall in!" shouted Lieutenant Mück. They lined up on the road, Mück stood there and looked at the two houses, but in the two houses nothing stirred. All they could hear was a woman weeping, but it sounded like the old woman.

"Forward march!" shouted Mück, "forward march, march at ease." He strode ahead: deadly serious and sad—he seemed to be gazing somewhere far away—or back into the past, somewhere.

IX

Feinhals was surprised at the size of Finck's premises. All he had seen from the front was this narrow old building with the sign saying "Finck's Wineshop & Hotel, estab. 1710," some rather dilapidated-looking steps leading into the bar, a window on the left, two on the right of the door, and next to the farthest window on the right the entrance to the courtyard, which was like every other winegrower's entrance: a sagging gateway, painted green, just wide enough for a cart to drive through.

But now, on opening the front door, he found himself looking through the passage into a large, neatly paved courtyard, its four sides formed by sturdy buildings. Around the second floor ran a balcony enclosed by a wooden railing, and through another gateway a second courtyard was visible, with sheds in it, and on the right a single-story building, obviously a reception hall. He took it all in carefully, listened, and paused suddenly at the sight of the two American sentries: they were guarding the second gateway, walking past each other like caged animals who have discovered a certain rhythm that enables them to pass; one was wearing glasses and his lips moved continuously, the other was smoking a cigarette; they had pushed their steel helmets to the back of their heads and looked pretty tired.

Feinhals tried the latch of the left-hand door, onto which someone had stuck a piece of paper marked "Private," then the latch of the right-hand door, which bore a sign saying "Bar." Both doors were locked. He stood there waiting while he watched the sentries steadily pacing up and down. In the silence there was only the occasional shot to be heard; the opposing sides seemed to be exchanging shells like balls not meant to be taken seriously, just a token that the war was still on; they rose like alarm signals that burst somewhere, exploded, and announced in the silence: "War, this is war. Look out: war!" Their echo was only faintly audible. But after listening for a few minutes to this harmless noise, Feinhals realized he had been mistaken: the shells were coming from the American side only, none from the German side. It was not an exchange of fire, it was a purely one-sided discharge of explosions occurring at regular intervals and producing a multiple, slightly menacing echo on the other side of the little river.

Feinhals stepped forward, slowly, into the dark corner of the passage where it led on the left into the cellar and on the right to a little door with a cardboard notice nailed to it saying "Kitchen."

He knocked at the kitchen door, heard a faint "Come in—please," and pressed down the latch. Four faces looked at him, and he was shocked by the resemblance of two of the faces to that lifeless, exhausted face that he had seen, dimly lit by the ruddy reflection from the fire, on that far-off grassy slope outside a Hungarian village. The old man by the window smoking a pipe resembled that face very much; he was thin and old, with a tired wisdom in his eyes. The second face whose resemblance startled him was that of a boy of about six, playing with a toy wagon as he squatted on the floor and raised his eyes to him: the child also was thin, he also looked old, tired, and wise; his dark eyes looked at Feinhals, then the boy lowered his incurious gaze and listlessly pushed the wagon across the floor.

The two women sat at the table peeling potatoes. One was old, but her healthy face was broad and brown, and it was clear that she had been a handsome woman. The one beside her looked faded and aging, although she was obviously younger than she appeared: she looked tired and dispirited, the movements of her hands were apathetic. Wisps of blonde hair fell over her pale forehead whereas the older woman wore her hair combed tightly back.

"Good morning," said Feinhals.

"Good morning," they replied.

Feinhals closed the door behind him and hesitated, he cleared his throat and could feel the sweat breaking out on him, a fine sweat that made his shirt cling to his armpits and back. The younger of the two women sitting at the table looked at him, and he noticed she had the same delicate white hands as the boy, who was squatting on the floor and calmly guiding his wagon around some chipped tiles. In the small room there was a stale smell of innumerable meals. Frying pans and saucepans hung all around the walls.

The two women glanced at the man by the window who was looking out into the courtyard. He pointed to a chair, saying: "Please sit down."

Feinhals sat down beside the older woman and said: "My name's Feinhals—I'm from Weidesheim—I'm trying to get home."

Both the women looked up, the old man showed more interest. "Feinhals," he said, "from Weidesheim—Jacob Feinhals' son?"

"Yes—how are things in Weidesheim?"

The old man shrugged his shoulders, puffed out a cloud of smoke, and said: "Not too bad—they're waiting for the Americans to occupy the place, but they haven't done so yet. They've been here for three weeks, but they won't go the mile and a half to Weidesheim; the Germans aren't there either, it's a no-man's-land, nobody's interested in it, the location's not good. . . ."

"You can hear the Germans firing into it sometimes," the young woman said, "but not very often."

"That's right, you can hear them," said the old man; he looked keenly at Feinhals.

"Where have you come from now?"

"From the other side—I waited over there for three weeks, for the Americans to come."

"Directly across from here?"

"No—farther south—near Grinzheim."

"Grinzheim, eh? That's where you crossed over?"

"Yes—last night."

"And changed into civilian clothes?"

Feinhals shook his head. "No," he said, "I was wearing civilians over there—they're discharging a good many soldiers now."

The old man laughed softly and looked at the young woman. "D'you hear that, Trude," he said, "they're discharging a good many soldiers now—oh, what can one do but laugh. . . ."

The women had finished peeling potatoes; the young woman picked up the bowl, went to the sink in the corner, and shook the potatoes into a sieve. She turned on the water and began listlessly washing the potatoes.

The older woman touched Feinhals' arm. He turned toward her. "Are they discharging very many?" she asked.

"Yes, they are," said Feinhals. "Some units are discharging everyone—on condition that they assemble in the Ruhr. But I didn't go to the Ruhr."

The woman at the sink began to cry. She cried soundlessly, barely moving her thin shoulders.

"Or cry," said the old man by the window, "laugh or cry." He looked at Feinhals. "Her husband was killed—my son." He pointed his pipe at the woman standing at the sink, crying as she slowly and carefully washed the potatoes. "In Hungary," said the old man, "last fall."

"He was supposed to be discharged last sumer," said the old woman sitting next to Feinhals. "They were just about to several times; he was a sick man, very sick, but I suppose they didn't want to let him go. He was running the canteen." She shook her head, and her eyes went to the younger woman at the sink. The younger woman shook the washed potatoes carefully into a clean saucepan and filled it with water. She was still crying, very quietly, almost without a sound, and she placed the pan on the stove and went over to the corner to get her handkerchief from the pocket of a smock.

Feinhals knew his expression must have changed. He had not often thought of Finck, only now and again and for brief moments, but now it all came back to him so vividly that the scene was clearer in his mind's eye than when he had seen it in reality: that incredibly heavy suitcase the shell had suddenly exploded into, the way the suitcase lid had whirled up and how the wine had splashed in the dark onto the path and the back of his neck, how the broken glass had tinkled—and how small and skinny the man had felt as his hand had groped along the body until it reached the great bloody wound and he had drawn back his hand. . . .

He watched the child playing on the floor. With his thin white fingers he calmly pulled the wagon around the chipped tiles—little pieces of kindling lay there being loaded, unloaded, loaded, unloaded. The boy looked very frail and had the same listless move-

ments as his mother, now seated at the table holding her handkerchief to her face. Feinhals looked around the room in distress and
wondered whether he ought to tell them, but he lowered his head
again and decided to tell them later. He would tell the old man
about it. Right now he didn't want to talk about it: in any case, it
didn't seem to occur to them to wonder how Finck had got from
his field hospital all the way to Hungary. The old woman touched
his arm again. "What is it?" she asked quietly. "Are you hungry?
Don't you feel well?"

"No, I'm all right," said Feinhals, "thanks very much." With
her penetrating gaze still on him he repeated, "No, I'm all right
really, thanks just the same."

"How about a glass of wine," asked the old man from the window, "or a schnapps?"

"Yes," said Feinhals, "a schnapps would be fine."

"Trude," said the old man, "get the gentleman a schnapps."

The young woman stood up and went into the next room.
"We're rather cramped," the old woman told Feinhals, "all we
have is this kitchen and the bar, but we hear they're moving on
soon; they've got a lot of tanks here, and the prisoners are going to
be taken away."

"Do you have prisoners here in the house?"

"Yes," said the old man, "there are some over there in the hall,
they're all high-ranking officers being interrogated here. As soon as
they've been interrogated they get taken away. One of them's even
a general. Look, over there!"

Feinhals went to the window, and the old man pointed past
the sentries and through the gateway into the second courtyard, to
the windows of the hall that were covered with barbed wire.

"There," said the old man, "another of them's being taken off
for interrogation."

Feinhals recognized the general at once: he looked better, more
relaxed, and he was wearing the Knight's Cross at his neck now,
he even seemed to be smiling gently as he walked quietly and doc-
ilely ahead of the two sentries, who had the barrels of their ma-

chine pistols trained on him. Almost all the yellow had left the general's face, and he no longer looked tired either; his face was harmonious, quiet, cultivated, and humane, that very gentle smile made his face beautiful. He passed through the gateway, walked calmly across the yard, and preceded the two sentries up the steps.

"That was the general," said Finck. "They've got colonels in there too, and majors, all staff officers, close to thirty of them."

The young woman returned from the bar carrying glasses and the bottle of schnapps. She placed one glass on the windowsill in front of Finck and the other on the table in front of Feinhals' place. Feinhals remained standing at the window. From there he could see out across the second courtyard as far as the street leading past the rear of the building. Two sentries with machine pistols were standing there too, and across the street from where the sentries stood Feinhals now recognized the window of the coffin shop, and he knew this was the street where the high school was. The coffin was still in the window: polished black with silver fittings and a black cloth with silver tassels. Maybe it was the same coffin that had been there thirteen years ago, when he had gone to high school.

"Prost," said the old man, raising his glass.

Feinhals went quickly to the table, picked up his glass, said "Thanks" to the young woman and "Prost" to the old man, and drank. The schnapps was good. "When d'you imagine would be a good time for me to try and get home?"

"You have to be sure and get through at a place where there are no Americans—by the Kerpel would be best—do you know the Kerpel?"

"Yes," said Feinhals. "Aren't there any there?"

"No, none. People often come across to get bread—at night— women, they all come through the Kerpel. . . ."

"During the day they do sometimes fire into it," said the young woman.

"Yes," said the old man, "during the day they do sometimes fire into it. . . ."

"Thanks," said Feinhals, "thanks very much," and finished his schnapps.

The old man stood up. "I'm driving up the hill," he said. "You'd better come along. From up there you have a good view of everything, even your father's house. . . ."

"Right," said Feinhals, "I'll come along."

He looked at the women seated at the table cleaning vegetables, carefully removing the leaves from two cabbages, inspecting the leaves, shredding them, and throwing them into a sieve.

The child looked up, suddenly abandoning the wagon, and asked: "May I come too?"

"Yes," said Finck, "come along." He put his pipe down on the windowsill.

"Now it's the next one's turn," he called. "Look."

Feinhals hurried to the window: the colonel was dragging his feet now, his gaunt face looked ill, and his collar, with the decorations dangling from it, was much too big for him. He hardly raised his knees, his arms hung limp. "A disgrace," muttered Finck, "a disgrace." He took his hat from the peg and put it on.

"Good-by," said Feinhals.

"Good-by," said the women.

"We'll be back for dinner," said Finck.

Private Berchem did not like the war. He had been a waiter and bartender in a nightclub, and until the end of 1944 he had managed to avoid being called up, and during the war he had learned a lot of things in this nightclub, things that had been confirmed for him once and for all in nearly fifteen hundred war-nights. He had always known that most men can't take as much alcohol as they think, and that most men spend a great part of their lives persuading themselves that they are real devils when it comes to drinking, and that they also try to convince the women they bring along of the same thing. But there were very few men who really knew how to drink, whom it was a pleasure to watch drinking. And even in wartime there were still precious few of those around.

And most people made the mistake of assuming that a piece of shiny metal on the chest or at the neck could change the man who wore it. They seemed to believe that a stupid fellow could become intelligent and a weakling strong if at some prominent spot on his uniform he were hung with a decoration, which he may very possibly have earned. But Berchem had realized this wasn't so: if it *was* possible to change a man by way of a decoration, then it could only be for the worse. But most of these men he had seen only one night, and he hadn't known them before, and all he knew was that most of them couldn't take alcohol, although they all thought they could and told convincing tales of how much they had drunk at one session at such and such a time and at such and such a place. It wasn't a pretty sight when they got drunk, and this nightclub, where he had spent fifteen hundred war-nights as a waiter, was not very closely checked for black-market goods: after all, there had to be some place where heroes could get something to drink and smoke and eat, and his boss was twenty-eight, as fit as a fiddle, and even by December 1944 he still hadn't joined up. Nor was the boss bothered by the bombs, although they were gradually destroying the whole town; the boss had a villa out in the country, among trees, it even had an air-raid shelter, and sometimes he got a kick out of inviting a few heroes, the ones who were the best company, to a private drinking party, and he would load them into his car and entertain them in his villa outside the town.

Throughout fifteen hundred war-nights Berchem had kept a careful eye on what went on, and he had often had to listen too, although he found that boring. He didn't know how many assaults and encirclements he was familiar with from hearsay. For a time he had considered writing it all down, but there were too many assaults, too many encirclements, and there were too many heroes who wore no decorations and felt obliged to tell you that actually they deserved them because—he had listened to so many of these because-stories, and he was fed up with the war. But some told the truth when they were drunk—and he also heard the truth from many heores and barmaids from France and Poland, Hungary and Rumania. He had always got along well with barmaids. Most of them could handle their liquor, and he had a soft spot for women you could have a drink with.

But now he was lying in a barn in a place called Auelberg, with a pair of field glasses, an exercise book and a few pencils, and a wristwatch, and it was his job to write down everything he observed in a place called Weidesheim a hundred and fifty yards away on the other side of the little river. There was not much to see in Weidesheim: half the front of the place consisted of the wall of the jam factory, and the jam factory had closed down. Sometimes people crossed the street once in a while; they would go off in the direction of Heidesheim and were soon out of sight in the narrow lanes. People climbed up to their vineyards and their orchards, and he could see them working up there, beyond Weidesheim, but he did not have to write anything down in his exercise book that happened beyond Weidesheim. The cannon for which he was acting as observer here got only seven shells a day, and these shells had to be fired somehow or other, otherwise the cannon wouldn't get any at all, and the seven shells weren't enough for a duel with the Americans who were occupying Heidesheim—it was useless, in fact forbidden, to fire at the Americans because they returned every shot with a hundred of their own, they were very touchy. So no purpose was achieved by Berchem entering in his little book: "10.30 American vehicle from Heidesheim stopped at house next to entrance to jam factory. Car parked in front of jam factory. Returned 11.15." This car came every day and parked for nearly an hour a hundred and fifty yards away from him, but it was useless for him to enter it in his book: this car was never fired at. Every day an American soldier would get out of the car, remain in the house almost always for an hour, and then drive off again.

Berchem's first gunnery officer had been a lieutenant called Gracht, and he was said to be a clergyman. Berchem had not had much to do with clergymen, but he found this one very nice.

Gracht had always directed his seven shells into the mouth of the river, which was to the left of Heidesheim, a sandy, swampy little delta, known to the local inhabitants as the Kerpel, where only reeds grew. His shells certainly wouldn't harm anyone there, and Berchem had thereupon begun to enter in his little book, several times a day: "Noticeable activity at river mouth." The lieutenant had made no comment and continued to direct his seven shells into the swamp. But two days ago the command up there had changed; now it was a sergeant major called Schniewind who took his seven shells very seriously. Schniewind also did not fire at the American car that was always parked outside the jam factory, what he had his eye on was the white flags: obviously the inhabitants of Weidesheim were still counting daily on the Americans occupying their village, but the Americans did not occupy the village. Its position was very unfavorable, in a loop, very exposed, whereas Heidesheim was hardly exposed at all, and the Americans were clearly not planning to advance. At other points they had already marched a hundred and twenty miles into Germany, they had almost reached the center of the country, but here in Heidesheim they had been stationary for the last three weeks, and for every shell that struck Heidesheim they had returned more than a hundred, but nobody was firing at Heidesheim now: the seven shells were intended for Weidesheim and its environs, and Sergeant Major Schniewind had decided to punish the people of Weidesheim for their lack of patriotic feeling. A white flag was something he could not stomach.

Nevertheless, that day Berchem entered in his little book as usual: "9 a.m. noticeable activity at river mouth." And he made the same entry at 10.15—and again at 11.45 he wrote: "American vehicle from H. to W. jam factory." At noon he left his post for a few minutes to go and pick up his lunch. As he was about to climb down the ladder, Schniewind called to him from below: "Hold on up there for a moment." Berchem crawled back to the barn window and picked up the field glasses. Schniewind took the glasses from him, threw himself on his stomach in the prescribed combat-ready position, and squinted through the lenses. Berchem looked sidelong at him: Schniewind was one of those people who couldn't take alcohol but persuade themselves and manage to convince others that they could take a great deal. There was something not quite genuine about the keenness with which he lay there on his stomach staring at the desolate, lifeless village of Weidesheim, and Berchem noticed that the star on his shoulder patch was still quite new, like the piece of braid encircling his shoulder patch with a perfect horseshoe. Schniewind passed the field glasses back to Berchem, saying: "The bastards, those goddamn bastards with their white flags—give me your book." Berchem handed it to him. Schniewind leafed through it. "What a load of crap," he said. "I can't think what you fellows imagine is going on in that swampy river mouth of yours, there's nothing but frogs there—give me those." He snatched the field glasses from Berchem and trained them on the river mouth. Berchem noticed a slight trace of saliva around Schniewind's mouth and a very fine thread of saliva hanging down. "Nothing," muttered Schniewind, "not a single solitary thing in that river mouth—nothing's moving—what crap." He ripped a page from the exercise book, took a pencil stub from his pocket and, still looking out of the window, wrote something on the paper. "Bastards," he muttered, "those bastards." Whereupon he turned away, without saluting, and climbed down the ladder. Berchem followed him one minute later to go and pick up his lunch.

From up here, looking down from the vineyard, there was a good view over the whole area, and Feinhals realized why Weidesheim had not been occupied by either Germans or Americans: it wasn't worth it. Fifteen houses, and a jam factory that had closed down. The railway station was at Heidesheim, and across the river Auelberg station was occupied by Germans: Weidesheim lay in a dead loop. Between Weidesheim and the hills, in a hollow, lay Heidesheim, and he could see solid rows of parked tanks on every open space of any size: in the schoolyard, alongside the church, in the market square, and on the big parking lot by the Hotel zum Stern—wherever you looked, tanks and vehicles that were not even camouflaged. In the valley the trees were already in blossom, slopes and meadows were covered with blossoming tree-tops, white, pink, and blue-white, and the air was mild: it was spring. From up here he could see the Finck premises lying like a fissure, the two square courtyards between the narrow streets; he could even make out the four sentries, and in the yard of the coffin shop he saw a man working at a big creamy-yellow box, slightly slanting, that was evidently to be a coffin—the freshly planed wood stood out clearly, shining pinkish yellow, and the carpenter's wife was sitting on a bench in the sun, near her husband, cleaning vegetables.

The streets were busy with women shoppers and soldiers, and just then a crowd of schoolchildren came out of the school building at the end of the village. But in Weidesheim the silence was complete. The houses looked as if they were hiding among the great treetops, but he knew every house in the place and saw at first glance that the Berg and Hoppenrath houses were damaged but that his father's was undamaged; there it stood, broad and yellow beside the main road with its comfortable façade, and the white flag hanging from his parents' bedroom on the second floor was extra large, larger than the white flags he could see hanging from the windows of other houses. The linden trees were already green. But not a soul was in sight, and the white flags hung stiff and dead in the windless air. The big courtyard of the jam factory was empty too, rusty pails lay around untidily in heaps, the sheds had been locked. Suddenly he saw an American car approaching from Heidesheim station and driving quite fast through meadows and orchards toward Weidesheim. Now and again the car would vanish beneath the white treetops, then reappear, finally emerging onto the main street of Weidesheim and pulling up at the entrance to the jam factory.

"For God's sake," Feinhals said quietly to Finck, pointing to the car. "What's that?"

Finck was sitting beside him on the bench outside the toolshed and calmly shook his head. "Nothing," he said, "nothing of any importance; that's Fräulein Merzbach's lover, he drives over every day."

"An American?"

"Of course," said Finck. "She's scared to come to him over here because sometimes the Germans fire into the village—so he goes to her."

Feinhals smiled. He knew Fräulein Merzbach well: she was a few years younger than himself, and at the time he left home she had been fourteen, a skinny, restless teenager who played the piano much too much and badly—he could recall many a Sunday afternoon when she had been playing downstairs in the living room of the manager's apartment while he sat reading in the garden next door, and when her playing stopped her thin pale face would appear at the window, and she would look out into the gardens, sad and discontented. Then for a few minutes it would be quiet, until she went back to the piano to continue her playing. She must be twenty-seven now, and somehow he was pleased that she had a lover.

He thought about how he would soon be down there, at home, right next-door to the Merzbachs, and that at noon tomorrow he would probably see this American. Maybe he could speak to him, and maybe there would be a chance of getting hold of some papers through him—he was sure to be an officer. It wasn't likely Fräulein Merzbach would have a private for a lover.

He also thought about his little apartment in town, which he knew no longer existed. The people there had written him that the house was no longer standing, and he tried to imagine it, but he couldn't imagine it, although he had seen many houses that no longer existed. But that his apartment should no longer exist was something he couldn't imagine. He hadn't even gone there when he was granted leave to check the damage, he couldn't see why he should go there just to see that there was nothing left. The last time he had been there, in 1943, the house had still been standing;

he had nailed cardboard across the broken windows and had gone to the nightclub a few doors away—there he had sat for three hours, until his train left, and he had chatted for a while with the waiter, who was very nice, a quiet, matter-of-fact type, still young, who had sold him the cigarettes for forty pfennigs and a bottle of French cognac for sixty-five marks. That was cheap, and the waiter had even told him his name—he had forgotten it now—and had recommended a woman whose attraction lay in her apparently genuine German respectability. Her name was Grete, and everyone called her Ma, and the waiter had said she was a very nice person to have a drink with and a chat. He had spent three hours chatting with Grete, who really did seem to be respectable; she told him about her old home in Schleswig-Holstein and tried to cheer him up about the war. It had really been very nice at that nightclub, although after midnight a few drunk officers and men had insisted on doing the goose step.

He was glad to be going home and to be able to stay there now. He would stay a long time, doing nothing until he could see what was what. There would certainly be plenty of work after the war, but he didn't intend to work much. He didn't feel like it—he didn't want to do anything, maybe help a bit with the harvest, without getting involved, like the summer vacationers who don't mind putting their hand to a pitchfork once in a while. Maybe later on he would start rebuilding a few houses in the neighborhood, if he could get the contracts. His gaze swept over Heidesheim: much of it had been destroyed, a whole row of houses next to the station, as well as the station itself. A freight train was still standing there, its engine shot to pieces beside the tracks; lumber was being loaded from one freight car onto an American truck, and the fresh planks stood out as clearly as the coffin in the carpenter's garden that had been lighter and brighter than the blossoms on the trees, its creamy yellow shining brightly up at him. . . .

He wondered which way to go. Finck had explained that American sentries were posted along the railroad tracks, where they had dug themselves in, and they didn't bother individuals going out to work in the fields. But, if he wanted to make quite sure, he could crawl through the canal in which the silted-up river was caught for a few hundred yards; you could duck as you went through it, and many people who for some reason or other wanted to get to the other side had used it—and at the end of the canal was the dense underbrush of the Kerpel reaching all the way to the gardens of Weidesheim. Once he was in the gardens nobody could see him, and there he knew every step of the way. Or he might carry a hoe or a spade on his shoulder. Finck assured him that many people came across every day from Weidesheim to work in the vineyards and orchards.

All he wanted was peace and quiet: to lie at home in bed, to know that no one could bother him, to think about Ilona, perhaps to dream about her. Later on he would start working, sooner or later—but first he wanted to sleep as long as he liked and be spoiled by his mother; she would be very happy if he came to stay for a long time. And most likely there would be tobacco or cigarettes at home, and at last he would have a chance to catch up on his reading. Fräulein Merzbach could almost certainly play the piano better by this time. He realized how happy he had been in those days, when he could sit in the garden reading and having to listen to Fräulein Merzbach play the piano badly; he had been happy, although he hadn't known it at the time. Now he knew it —once he had dreamed of building houses such as nobody had ever built, but later he had built houses that were almost exactly the same as the ones other people built. He had become a very mediocre architect, and he knew it, but still it was nice to understand one's craft and build simple, good houses that sometimes turned out to be quite pleasing when they were finished. The important thing was not to take oneself too seriously—that was all. The way home seemed very long now, although it couldn't be much more than half an hour; he felt very tired and lazy, and he would have liked to drive the rest of the way very quickly by car, drive home, get into bed, and go to sleep. It seemed such an effort to have to walk the route he soon must walk: right through the

American front line. There might be trouble, and he didn't want any more trouble, he was tired, and it all seemed such an effort.

He removed his cap and folded his hands when the noonday bell struck—Finck and the little boy did the same; and the carpenter down there in the yard, working away at the coffin, put down his tool, and his wife laid aside the vegetable basket and stood with folded hands in the yard. People no longer seemed ashamed of praying in public, and he found it somehow repugnant, in himself too: at one time he used to pray—Ilona had prayed too, a very devout, intelligent woman, who was even beautiful, and so intelligent that she couldn't be confounded in her faith even by the priests. Now as he prayed he caught himself praying for something, as a matter of habit almost, although there was nothing he wanted: Ilona was dead, what was there to pray for? But he prayed for her return—from somewhere or other, for his safe homecoming, although this was now almost accomplished. He suspected all these people of praying for something, for the fulfilment of some wish or other, but Ilona had told him: "We have to pray to console God . . . ," she had read that somewhere and found it worth remembering, and as he stood there with folded hands he made up his mind that he would only pray properly when he could cease to pray for anything. When that happened he would go to church too, although he found it hard to bear the faces of most priests and their sermons, but he would do it to console God—maybe to console God for the faces and sermons of the priests. He smiled, unclasped his hands, and put on his cap. . . .

"Look," said Finck, "now they're being taken away." He pointed down toward Heidesheim, and Feinhals saw that a truck was standing outside the coffinmaker's house, a truck that was slowly filling up with officers from Finck's little reception hall: even from up here their decorations stood out clearly. Then the truck disappeared rapidly along the tree-lined road toward the west, to where the war was over. . . .

"People are saying they'll be advancing soon," said Finck. "D'you see all the tanks?"

"I hope they take Weidesheim pretty soon," said Feinhals.

Finck nodded. "It won't be long now—will you come over and see us?"

"Yes," said Feinhals, "I'll come and see you often."

"I'd like that very much," said Finck. "Have some tobacco?"

"Thanks," said Feinhals; he filled a pipe, Finck held out a match, and for a while they gazed down onto the blossoming plain, Finck's hand resting on his grandson's head.

"I'll be off now," said Feinhals suddenly. "I must go, I want to get home...."

"Go ahead," said Finck, "it's quite all right, there's no danger."

Feinhals shook hands with him. "Thank you very much," he said and looked at him. "Thank you very much—I hope I can come over and see you soon." He shook hands with the boy too, and the child looked at him thoughtfully and a bit suspiciously out of his dark, narrow-lidded eyes.

"You'd better take along the hoe," said Finck.

"Thanks, I will," said Feinhals, taking the hoe from Finck.

For a while as he walked down the hill it seemed as if he were heading straight for the coffin being made down there in the yard, he was walking straight for it, he watched the yellow shining box grow bigger and more distinct, as if through the lenses of field glasses, until he swung to the right past the village; there he was swallowed up by the stream of schoolchildren just leaving the school, he stayed among a group of children as far as the town gate and was alone as he quietly crossed the road to the underpass. He didn't want to crawl through the canal, it was too much of an effort. And to walk through the trackless, marshy Kerpel was also too much of an effort—and besides it would just make him conspicuous if he entered the village first from the right and then from the left. He took the direct path that led across meadows and orchards and was completely calm when a hundred yards ahead he saw someone walking along carrying a hoe.

The Americans had posted only a couple of sentries at the underpass. The two men had taken off their steel helmets and were smoking as they stared with bored expressions at the blossoming gardens between Heidesheim and Weidesheim; they paid no attention to Feinhals, they had been here for three weeks now, and for the last two weeks nothing had been fired at Heidesheim. Feinhals walked calmly past them, nodded, they casually nodded back.

Only ten more minutes now: straight through the gardens, then around to the left between the Heusers and the Hoppenraths, down the main road a bit, and he would be home. He might meet someone he knew on the way, but he met no one; it was perfectly quiet except for the distant sounds of rumbling trucks, but at this hour no one seemed to think of firing. Right now there were not even the regular sounds of shells exploding that had seemed like warning signals.

He thought with a certain bitterness of Ilona: somehow he felt she had shirked things, she was dead, and to die was perhaps the easiest—she should have been with him now, and he felt she might have been with him. But she seemed to have known that it was better not to become very old and build one's life on a love that was real only for a few moments while there was another, everlasting love. She seemed to have known many things, more than he did, and he felt cheated because he would soon be home, where he would live, read, not work too hard if he could avoid it, and pray, to console God, not to ask Him for something He couldn't give, because He loved you: money or success, or something that helped you to muddle along through life—most people muddled along through life somehow, he would have to too, for he wouldn't be building houses that could only be built by him—any mediocre architect could build them. . . .

He smiled as he passed the Hoppenraths' garden: they still hadn't sprayed their trees with that white stuff his father claimed was indispensable. He was always having rows with old Hoppenrath about it, but old Hoppenrath still hadn't got that white stuff on his trees. It wasn't far now to his parents' house—on the left was the Heusers' house, on the right the Hoppenraths', and he had only to walk through this narrow lane, then to the left down the main road a bit. The Heusers had the white stuff on their trees. He smiled. He distinctly heard the shell being fired from the other side, and he threw himself to the ground—instantly—and tried to go on smiling, but he couldn't help flinching when the shell landed in the Hoppenraths' garden. It burst in a treetop, and a gentle dense rain of white blossoms fell onto the grass. The second shell seemed to land farther along, more toward the Bäumers' house, almost directly opposite his father's, the third and fourth landed at the same level but more to the left, they sounded as if they were of medium caliber. He got slowly to his feet as the fifth also fell over there—and then there was nothing more. He listened for a while, heard no more firing, and quickly walked on—dogs were barking all over the village, and he could hear the chickens and ducks frantically flapping their wings in Heuser's barn—from some barns came the muffled lowing of cows too, and he thought: pointless, how pointless. But maybe they were firing at the American car, which he hadn't heard driving back yet; no, as he turned the corner of the main road he saw the car had already left—the street was quite empty—and the muffled lowing of the cows and the barking of the dogs accompanied him for the few steps he still had to take.

The white flag hanging from his father's house was the only one in the whole street, and he now saw that it was very large—it must be one of his mother's huge tablecloths, the kind she took out of the closet on special occasions. He smiled again, but suddenly threw himself to the ground and knew it was too late. Pointless, he thought, how utterly pointless. The sixth shell struck the gable of his parents' house—stones fell, plaster crumbled onto the street, and he heard his mother scream down in the basement. He crawled quickly toward the house, heard the seventh shell being fired, and screamed even before it landed, he screamed very loud, for several seconds, and suddenly he knew that dying was not that easy—he screamed at the top of his voice until the shell struck him, and he rolled in death onto the threshold of the house. The flagpole had snapped, and the white cloth fell over him.

THE TRAIN
WAS ON TIME

As they walked through the dark underpass they could hear the train rumbling up to the platform overhead, and the resounding voice came smoothly over the loudspeaker: "The troop-train now arriving from Paris will depart for Przemysl via. . . ."

Then they had climbed the steps to the platform and were standing by the leave-train from which beaming soldiers were emerging, weighed down with huge packages. The platform quickly emptied, it was the usual scene. At some of the windows stood girls or women or a very silent, grim-faced father . . . and the resounding voice was telling people to hurry. The train was on time.

"Why don't you get on?" the chaplain asked the soldier anxiously.

"Get on?" asked the soldier, amazed. "Why, I might want to hurl myself under the wheels, I might want to desert . . . eh? What's the hurry? I might go crazy, I've a perfect right to, I've a perfect right to go crazy. I don't want to die, that's what's so horrible—that I don't want to die." His voice was cold and hard, as if the words were pouring from his lips like ice. "Don't say any more! I'll get on all right, there's always a spot somewhere . . . yes . . . yes, don't mind me, pray for me!" He grasped his pack, boarded the train through the nearest door, let down the window from inside, and leaned out, while overhead the resounding voice hung like a cloud of mucus: "The train is now leaving. . . ."

"I don't want to die!" he shouted. "I don't want to die, but the terrible thing is that I'm going to die . . . soon!" The black figure on that cold gray platform retreated farther and farther into the

159

distance . . . farther and farther, until the station was swallowed up by night.

Now and again what appears to be a casually spoken word will suddenly acquire a cabalistic significance. It becomes charged and strangely swift, races ahead of the speaker, is destined to throw open a chamber in the uncertain confines of the future and to return to him with the deadly accuracy of a boomerang. Out of the smalltalk of unreflecting speech, usually from among those halting, colorless goodbyes exchanged beside trains on their way to death, it falls back on the speaker like a leaden wave, and he becomes aware of the force, both frightening and intoxicating, of the workings of fate. To lovers and soldiers, to men marked for death and to those filled with the cosmic force of life, this power is sometimes given, without warning; a sudden revelation is conferred on them, a bounty and a burden . . . and the word sinks, sinks down inside them.

As Andreas was slowly groping his way back into the center of the car, the word *soon* entered him like a bullet, painlessly and almost imperceptibly penetrating flesh, tissue, cells, nerves, until at some point it caught, like a barbed hook, exploded, and ripped open a savage wound, making blood pour out . . . life, pain. . . .

Soon, he thought, and felt himself turning pale. At the same time he did all the usual things, almost unconsciously. He struck a match, lighting up the heaps of sitting, stretched out, sleeping soldiers who lay around, across, under, and on top of their luggage. The smell of stale tobacco smoke was mixed with the smell of stale sweat and that strangely gritty dirt which clings to all soldiers in the mass. The flame of the dying matchstick flared up with a final hiss, and in that last glow he saw, over by the narrowing corridor, a small empty space. He carefully picked his way toward it, his bundle tucked under one arm, his cap in his hand.

Soon, he thought, and the shock of fear lay deep, deep. Fear and absolute certainty. Never again, he thought, never again will I see this station, never again the face of my friend, the man I abused right up to the last moment . . . never again. Soon! He reached the empty space, set his pack carefully on the floor in order not to wake the sleeping men around him, and sat down on it so he could lean back against a compartment door. Then he tried to arrange his legs as comfortably as possible; he stretched the left one carefully past the face of one sleeping soldier, and placed the right one across a piece of luggage that was shielding the back of another. In the compartment behind him a match flared up, and someone began to smoke silently in the dark. By turning slightly to one side he could see the glowing tip of the cigarette, and sometimes, when the unknown man drew on it, the reflection spread over an unfamiliar soldier's face, gray and tired, with bitter creases in it, starkly and terribly sober.

Soon, he thought. The rattle of the train, it was all so familiar. The smell, the desire to smoke, the feeling he had to smoke. The last thing he wanted to do was sleep. The somber outlines of the city moved past the window. Somewhere in the distance searchlights were raking the sky, like long spectral fingers parting the blue cloak of the night ... from far away came the firing of antiaircraft guns ... and those darkened, mute, somber houses. When would this Soon be? The blood flowed out of his heart, flowed back into his heart, circling, circling, life was circling, and all this pulse beat said was: Soon! He could no longer say, no longer even think: "I don't want to die." As often as he tried to form the sentence he thought: I'm going to die ... soon.

Behind him a second gray face now showed up in the glow of a cigarette, and he could hear a subdued, weary murmuring. The two unknown men were talking.

"Dresden," said one voice.

"Dortmund," the other.

The murmuring continued, became more animated. Then another voice swore, and the murmuring subsided again; it petered out, and again there was only one cigarette behind him. It was the second cigarette, and finally this one went out too, and again there was this gray darkness behind and beside him, and facing him the black night with the countless houses, all mute, all black. Only in the distance those silent, uncannily long, spectral fingers of the searchlights, still groping across the sky. It seemed as if the faces belonging to those fingers must be grinning, eerily grinning, cynically grinning like the faces of usurers and swindlers. "We'll get you," said the thin-lipped, gaping mouths belonging to those fingers. "We'll get you, we'll grope all night long." Maybe they were looking for a bedbug, a tiny bug in the cloak of the night, those fingers, and they would find the bug....

Soon. Soon. Soon. Soon. When is Soon? What a terrible word: Soon. Soon can mean in one second, Soon can mean in one year. Soon is a terrible word. This Soon compresses the future, shrinks it, offers no certainty, no certainty whatever, it stands for absolute uncertainty. Soon is nothing and Soon is a lot. Soon is everything. Soon is death....

Soon I shall be dead. I shall die, soon. You have said so yourself, and someone inside you and someone outside you has told you that this Soon will be fufilled. One thing is sure, this Soon will be in wartime. That's a certainty, that's a fact.

How much longer will the war go on?

It can last for another year before everything finally collapses in the East, and if the Americans in the West don't attack, or the British, then it will go on for another two years before the Russians reach the Atlantic. They will attack, though. But all in all it will last another year at the very least, the war won't be over before the end of 1944. The way this whole apparatus is built up, it's too obedient, too cowardly, too docile. So I may still have anything from one second to one year. How many seconds are there in a year? Soon I'm going to die, before the war is over. I shan't ever know peacetime again. No more peacetime. There'll be no more of anything, no music...no flowers...no poetry...no more human joy; soon I'm going to die.

This Soon is like a thunderclap. This little word is like the spark that sets off the thunderstorm, and suddenly, for the thousandth part of a second, the whole world is bright beneath this word.

The smell of bodies is the same as ever. The smell of dirt and dust and boot polish. Funny, wherever there are soldiers there's dirt. The spectral fingers had found the bug. . . .

He lit a fresh cigarette. I'll try and picture the future, he thought. Maybe it's an illusion, this Soon, maybe I'm overtired, maybe it's tension or nerves. He tried to imagine what he would do when the war was over. He would . . . he would . . . but there was a wall he couldn't get over, a totally black wall. He couldn't imagine anything. Of course he could force himself to complete the sentence in his mind: I'll go to university . . . I'll take a room somewhere . . . with books . . . cigarettes . . . go to university . . . music . . . poetry . . . flowers. But even as he forced himself to complete the sentence in his mind he knew it wouldn't happen. None of it would happen. Those aren't dreams, those are pale, colorless thoughts devoid of weight, blood, all human substance. The future has no face now, it is cut off somewhere; and the more he thought about it the more he realized how close he was to this Soon. Soon I'm going to die, that's a certainty that lies between one year and one second. There are no more dreams. . . .

Soon. Maybe two months. He tried to imagine it in terms of time, to discover whether the wall rose this side of the next two months, that wall he would not be going beyond. Two months, that meant the end of November. But he can't grasp it in terms of time. Two months: an image that has no power. He might just as well say: three months or four months or six, the image evokes no echo. January, he thought. But the wall isn't there at all. A strange, unquiet hope awakens: May, he thought with a sudden leap ahead. Nothing. The wall is silent. There's no wall anywhere. There's nothing. This Soon . . . this Soon is only a frightening bogey. November, he thought. Nothing! A fierce, terrible joy springs to life. January: January of next year, a year and a half away—a year and a half of life! Nothing! No wall!

He sighed with relief and went on thinking, his thoughts now racing across time as over light, very low hurdles. January, May, December! Nothing! And suddenly he was aware that he was groping in a void. The place where the wall rose up couldn't be grasped in terms of time. Time was irrelevant. Time had ceased to exist. And yet hope still remained. He had leaped so splendidly over the months. Years. . . .

Soon I'm going to die, and he felt like a swimmer who knows he is near the shore and finds himself suddenly flung back into the tide by the surf. Soon! That's where the wall is, the wall beyond which he will cease to exist, will cease to be on this earth.

Krakow, he thought suddenly, and his heart missed a beat as if an artery had twisted itself into a knot, blocking off the blood. He is on the right track—Krakow! Nothing! Farther. Przemysl! Nothing! Lvov! Nothing! Then he starts racing: Cernauti, Jassy, Kishinev, Nikopol! But at the last name he already senses that this is only make-believe, make-believe like the thought: I'll go to university. Never again, never again will he see Nikopol! Back to Jassy. No, he won't see Jassy again either. He won't see Cernauti again. Lvov! Lvov he'll see again, Lvov he'll reach alive! I'm mad, he thought, I'm out of my mind, this means I'll die between Lvov and Cernauti! What a crazy idea . . . he forced himself to switch off his thoughts and started smoking again and staring into the face of the night. I'm hysterical, I'm crazy, I've been smoking too much, talking, talking for nights on end, days on end, with no sleep, no food, just smoking, it's enough to make anyone lose their mind. . . .

I must have something to eat, he thought, something to drink. Food and drink keep body and soul together. This damn smoking all the time! He started fumbling with his pack, but while he peered toward his feet in the dark, trying to find the buckle, and then began rummaging around in his pack where sandwiches and underwear, tobacco, cigarettes, and a bottle of schnapps all lay in a heap, he became aware of a leaden, implacable fatigue that clogged his veins . . . he fell asleep . . . his hands on the open pack, one leg—the left—next to a face he had never seen, one leg—the right—across someone's luggage, and with his tired and by now dirty hands resting on his pack he fell asleep, his head on his chest. . . .

He was awakened by someone treading on his fingers. A stab of pain, he opened his eyes; someone had passed by in a hurry, bumped him in the back and trodden on his hands. He saw it was daylight and heard another resounding voice hospitably announcing a station name, and he realized it was Dortmund. The man who had spent the night behind him smoking and murmuring was getting out, cursing as he barged along the corridor; for that unknown gray face, this was home. Dortmund. The man next to him, the one whose luggage his right leg had been resting on, was awake and sat up on the cold floor of the corridor, rubbing his eyes. The man on the left, whose face his left foot was resting against, was still asleep. Dortmund. Girls carrying steaming pots of coffee were hurrying up and down the platform. The same as ever. Women were standing around weeping; girls being kissed, fathers . . . it was all so familiar: he must be crazy.

But, to tell the truth, all he knew was that the instant he opened his eyes he knew that Soon was still there. Deep within him the little barb had drawn blood, it had caught and would never let go now. This Soon had grabbed him like a hook, and he was going to squirm on it, squirm until he was between Lvov and Cernauti. . . .

Like lightning, in the millionth part of a second it took him to wake up, came the hope that this Soon would have disappeared, like the night, a bogey in the wake of endless talking and endless smoking. But it was still there, implacably there. . . .

He sat up, his eye fell on his pack, still half open, and he stuffed back a shirt that had slipped out. The man on his right had let down a window and was holding out a mug into which a thin, tired girl was pouring coffee. The smell of the coffee was horrible, thin steam that made him feel queasy; it was the smell of barracks, of army cookhouses, a smell that had spread all over Europe . . . and that was meant to spread all over the world. And yet (so deep are the roots of habit) and yet he also held out his mug for the girl to fill; the gray coffee that was as gray as a uniform. He could smell the stale exhalation from the girl; she must have slept in her clothes, gone from train to train during the night, lugging coffee, lugging coffee. . . .

She smelled penetratingly of that vile coffee. Perhaps she slept right up close to the coffeepot as it stood on a stove to keep hot, slept until the next train arrived. Her skin was gray and rough like dirty milk, and wisps of her scanty, pale-black hair crept out from under a little cap, but her eyes were soft and sad, and when she bent over to fill his mug he saw the charming nape of her neck. What a pretty girl, he thought: everyone will think she's ugly, and she's pretty, she's beautiful . . . she has delicate little fingers too . . . I could spend hours watching her pour my coffee; if only the mug had a hole, if only she would pour and pour, I would see her soft eyes and that charming nape, and if only that resounding voice would shut up. Everything bad comes from those resounding voices; those resounding voices started the war, and those resounding voices regulate the worst war of all, the war at railway stations.

To hell with all resounding voices!

The man in the red cap was waiting obediently for the resounding voice that had to say its piece, then the train got under way, lighter by a few heroes, richer by a few heroes. It was daylight but still early: seven o'clock. Never again, never ever again will I pass through Dortmund. How strange, a city like Dortmund; I've passed through it often and have never been in the town itself. Never ever will I know what Dortmund is like, and never ever again will I see this girl with the coffeepot. Never again; soon I'm going to die, between Lvov and Cernauti. My life is now nothing but a specific number of miles, a section of railway line. But that's odd, there's no front between Lvov and Cernauti, and not many partisans either, or has there been some glorious great cave-in along the front overnight? Is the war suddenly, quite suddenly, over? Will peace come before this Soon? Some kind of disaster? Maybe the divine beast is dead, assassinated at last, or the Russians have launched an attack on all fronts and swept everything before them as far as between Lvov and Cernauti, and capitulation. . . .

There was no escape, the sleeping men had woken up, they were beginning to eat, drink, chat. . . .

He leaned against the open window and let the chill morning wind beat against his face. I'll get drunk, he thought, I'll knock back a whole bottle, then I won't know a thing, then I'll be safe at least as far as Breslau. He bent down, hurriedly opened his pack, but an invisible hand restrained him from grasping the bottle. He took out a sandwich and quietly and slowly began to chew. How terrible, to have to eat just before one's death. Soon I'm going to die, yet I still have to eat. Slices of bread and sausage, air-raid sandwiches packed for him by his friend the chaplain, a whole package of sandwiches with plenty of sausage in them, and the terrible thing was that they tasted so good.

He leaned against the open window, quietly eating and chewing, from time to time reaching down into his open pack for another sandwich. Between mouthfuls he sipped the lukewarm coffee.

It was terrible to look into the drab houses where the slaves were getting ready to march off to their factories. House after house, house after house, and everywhere lived people who suffered, who laughed, people who ate and drank and begat new human beings, people who tomorrow might be dead; the place was teeming with human life. Old women and children, men, and soldiers too. Soldiers were standing at windows, one here, one there, and each man knew when he would be on the train again, traveling back to hell. . . .

"Hey there, mate," said a husky voice behind him, "want to join us in a little game?" He swung round: "Yes!" he said without thinking, at the same time catching sight of a deck of cards in a soldier's hand: the soldier, who was grinning at him, needed a shave. I said Yes, he thought, so he nodded and followed the soldier. The corridor was deserted except for two men who had taken themselves off with their luggage to the vestibule, where one of them, a tall fellow with blond hair and slack features, was sitting on the floor, grinning.

"Find anybody?"

"Yes," said the unshaven soldier in his husky voice.

Soon I'm going to die, thought Andreas, squatting down on his pack, which he had brought along. Each time he put down the pack his steel helmet rattled, and now the sight of the steel helmet reminded him that he had forgotten his rifle. My rifle, he thought, it's standing propped up in Paul's closet behind his raincoat. He smiled. "That's right, mate," said the blond fellow. "Forget your troubles and join the game."

The two men had made themselves very snug. They were sitting by a door, but the door was barricaded, the handle tightly secured with wire, and luggage had been stacked up in front of it. The unshaven soldier took a pair of pliers out of his pocket—he was wearing regular blue work pants—he took out the pliers, fished out a roll of wire from somewhere under the luggage, and began to wind fresh wire still more tightly around the door handle.

"That's right, mate," said the blond fellow. "They can kiss our arses till we get to Przemysl. You're going that far, aren't you? I see you are," he said when Andreas nodded.

Andreas soon realized they were drunk; the unshaven soldier had a whole battery of bottles in his carton, and he passed the bottles around. First they played blackjack. The train rattled, daylight grew stronger, and they stopped at stations with resounding voices and stations without resounding voices. It filled up and emptied, filled up and emptied, and all the time the three men stayed in their corner playing cards.

Sometimes, at a station, someone outside would rattle furiously at the locked door and swear, but they would only laugh and go on with their game and throw the empty bottles out of the window. Andreas didn't think about the game at all, these games of chance were so wonderfully simple there was no need to think, your mind could be somewhere else. . . .

Paul would be up by now, if he had slept at all. Maybe there had been another air-raid alarm, and he hadn't had any sleep. If he had slept, then it could only have been for a few hours. He must have got home at four. Now it was almost ten. So he had slept till eight, then got up, washed, read mass, prayed for me. He prayed for me to be happy because I had denied human happiness.

"Pass!" he said. Marvelous—you just said "Pass!" and had time to think. . . .

Then he would have gone home and smoked cigarette butts in his pipe, had a bite to eat, some air-raid sandwiches, and gone off again. Some place or other. Maybe to a girl having an illegitimate baby by a soldier, maybe to a mother, or maybe to the black market to buy a few cigarettes.

"Flush," he said.

He had won again. The money in his pocket made quite a packet now.

"You're a lucky bastard," said the soldier who needed a shave. "Drink up, my friends!" He passed the bottle around again, he was sweating, and beneath the mask of coarse joviality his face was very sad and preoccupied. He shuffled the cards . . . a good thing I don't have to shuffle them. I need one more minute to think about Paul, to concentrate on Paul, tired and pale; now he's walking through the ruins and praying, all the time. I gave him hell, you should never give anyone hell, not even a sergeant. . . .

"Three of a kind," he said, "and a pair." He had won again.

The other men laughed, they didn't care about the money, all they wanted was to kill time. What a laborious, frightful business it was, this killing time, over and over again that little seconds-hand racing invisibly beyond the horizon, over and over again you threw a heavy dark sack over it, in the certain knowledge that the little hand went racing on, relentlessly on and on. . . .

"Nordhausen!" proclaimed a resounding voice. "Nordhausen!" The voice announced the name of the station just as he was shuffling the cards. "Troop-train now departing for Przemysl via . . ." and then it said: "All aboard and close the doors!" How normal it all was. He slowly dealt the cards. It was already close on eleven. They were still drinking schnapps, the schnapps was good. He made a few complimentary remarks about the schnapps to the soldier who needed a shave. The train had filled up again. They had very little room now, and quite a few of the men were looking at them. It had become uncomfortable, and it was impossible to avoid overhearing the men's chatter.

"Pass," he said. The blond fellow and the unshaven soldier were sparring good-naturedly for the kitty. They knew they were both bluffing, but they both laughed, the point was to see who could bluff best.

"Practically speaking," said a North German voice behind him, "practically speaking we've already won the war!"

"Hm," came another voice.

"As if the Führer could lose a war!" said a third voice. "It's crazy to say such a thing anyway: winning a war! Anyone who talks about winning a war must already be considering the possibility of losing one. Once we start a war, that war is won."

"The Crimea's already cut off," said a fourth voice. "The Russians have closed it off at Perekop."

"That's where I'm being sent," said a faint voice, "to the Crimea. . . ."

"Only by plane, though," came the confident voice of the war-winner. "It's great by plane. . . ."

"The Tommies won't risk it."

The silence of those who said nothing was terrible. It was the silence of those who don't forget, of those who know they are done for.

The blond fellow had shuffled, and the unshaven soldier opened with fifty marks.

Andreas saw he was holding a royal flush.

"And fifty," he said, laughing.

"I'm in," said the unshaven soldier.

"Raise twenty."

"I'm in."

Needless to say, the unshaven soldier lost.

"Two hundred and forty marks," said a voice behind them, accompanied, as the sound of the voice indicated, by a shake of the head. It had been quiet for a minute while they had been battling for the kitty. Then the chatter started up again.

"Have a drink," said the unshaven soldier.

"This door business is crazy, I tell you!"

"What door?"

"They've barricaded the door, those bastards, those scabs!"

"Shut up!"

A station without a resounding voice. God bless stations without resounding voices. The buzzing chatter of the other men went on, they had forgotten about the door and the two hundred and forty marks, and Andreas gradually began to realize he was a bit drunk.

"Shouldn't we have a break?" he said. "I'd like a bite to eat."

"No!" shouted the unshaven soldier, "not on your life, we'll carry on till we get to Przemysl! No"—his voice was filled with a terrible fear. The blond fellow yawned and began muttering. "No," shouted the unshaven soldier. . . .

They went on playing.

"The 42 MG is all we need to win the war. The others have nothing like it. . . ."

"The Führer knows what he's doing!"

But the silence of those who said nothing, nothing at all, was terrible. It was the silence of those who knew they were all done for.

At times the train got so full they could hardly hold their cards. All three were drunk by now, but very clear in the head. Then the train would empty again, there were loud voices, resounding and unresounding. Railway stations. The day wore on to afternoon. From time to time they would pause for a snack, then go on playing, go on drinking. The schnapps was excellent.

"Well, it's French, after all," said the soldier who needed a shave. He seemed to need one more than ever now. His face was pallid under the black stubble. His eyes were red, he hardly ever won, but he appeared to have a vast supply of money. Now the blond fellow was winning often. They were playing chemin-de-fer, the train being empty again, then they played rummy, and suddenly the cards fell from the unshaven soldier's hand, he slumped forward and began to snore horribly. The blond fellow straightened him, gently arranging him so that he could sleep propped up. They put something over his feet, and Andreas returned his winnings to the man's pocket.

How gently and tenderly the blond fellow treats his friend! I'd never have expected it of that slob.

I wonder what Paul's doing now?

They got to their feet and stretched, shook crumbs and dirt from their laps, and cigarette ash, and flung the last empty bottle out of the window.

They were traveling through an empty countryside, left and right glorious gardens, gentle hills, smiling clouds—an autumn afternoon. . . . Soon, soon I'm going to die. Between Lvov and Cernauti. During the card game he had tried to pray, but he kept having to think about it; he had tried again to form sentences in the future and realized they had no force. He had tried again to grasp it in terms of time—it was make-believe, idle make-believe! But he had only to think of the word Przemysl to know he was on the right track. Lvov! His heart missed a beat. Cernauti! Nothing . . . it must be somewhere in between . . . he couldn't visualize it, he had no mental picture of the map. "D'you have a map?" he asked the blond fellow, who was looking out of the window.

"No," he said amiably, "but he does!" He pointed to the soldier who needed a shave. "He has a map. How restless he is. He's got something on his mind. That's a fellow with something terrible on his mind, I tell you. . . ."

Andreas said nothing and looked over the man's shoulder through the window. "Radebeul!" said a resounding Saxon voice. A decent voice, a good voice, a German voice, a voice that might just as well be saying: The next ten thousand into the slaughterhouse, please. . . .

It was wonderful outside, still almost like summer, September weather. Soon I'm going to die, I'll never see that tree again, that russet tree over there by the green house. I'll never see that girl wheeling her bike again, the girl in the yellow dress with the black hair. These things the train's racing past, I'll never see any of them again. . . .

The blond fellow was asleep now too, he had sat down on the floor beside his pal, and in sleep they had sunk against one another; the snores of one were harsh and loud, of the other soft and whistling. The corridor was deserted except for now and again someone going to the john, and occasionally someone would say: "There's room inside, you know, mate." But it was much nicer in the corridor, in the corridor you were more alone, and now that both the others were asleep he was quite alone, and it had been a terrific idea to secure the door with wire.

Everything the train's leaving behind I'm leaving behind too, once and for all, he thought. I'll never see any more of this again, never again this segment of sky full of soft gray-blue clouds, never again this little fly, a very young one, perched on the window frame and flying off now, off to somewhere in Radebeul; that little fly will stay in Radebeul, I guess . . . stay behind under this segment of sky, that little fly will never keep me company between Lvov and Cernauti. The fly is on its way to Radebeul, maybe it's flying into some kitchen heavy with the odor of potatoes boiled in their jackets and the acrid smell of cheap vinegar, where they're making potato salad for some soldier who's now free to suffer for three weeks through the alleged joys of home leave . . . that's all I'll ever see, he thought, for at that moment the train swung in a great loop and was coming into Dresden.

At Dresden the platform was very full, and at Dresden many men got out. The window faced a whole cluster of soldiers headed by a stout, red-faced young lieutenant. The soldiers were all dressed up in brand-new uniforms, the lieutenant was also in his brand-new hand-me-downs for the doomed; even the decorations on his chest were as new as freshly cast lead soldiers, they looked like complete fakes. The lieutenant grasped the door handle and rattled it.

"Open up there!" he shouted at Andreas.

"The door's closed, it won't open," Andreas shouted back.

"Don't shout at me, open up, open up at once!"

Andreas shut his mouth and glowered at the lieutenant. I'm soon going to die, he thought, and he's shouting at me. His gaze went beyond the lieutenant; the soldiers standing with the lieutenant grinned behind his back. At least the faces of these men were not new, they had old, gray, knowing faces, only their uniforms were new, and even their decorations seemed old and worn. Only the lieutenant was new from top to toe, he even had a brand-new face. His cheeks became redder still, and his blue eyes went a bit red too. Now he lowered his voice, and it was so soft, with such a soft threat in it, that Andreas had to laugh. "Are you going to open the door?" he asked. Rage was exploding from his shiny buttons. "Look at me at least!" he roared at Andreas. But Andreas did not look at him. I'm going to die soon, he thought; all these people standing around on the platform, I'll never see any of them again, not one. And he wouldn't smell that smell again either, that smell of dust and railway smoke, here at his window saturated with the smell of the lieutenant's brand-new uniform that smelled of synthetic wool.

"I'll have you arrested," roared the lieutenant. "I'll report you to the military police!"

Luckily the blond fellow had woken up. He came to the window, sleepy-eyed, stood impeccably at attention, and said to the lieutenant:

"Regret to report, sir, that the door was sealed off on the station side on account of its being defective: to prevent accidents." He delivered this in the regulation manner, briskly and submissively, it was marvelous the way he spoke, like a clock striking twelve. The lieutenant let out one more furious sigh. "Why didn't you say so?" he yelled at Andreas.

"Regret to report further, sir, that my companion is deaf, stone deaf," the blond fellow rattled off. "Head wound." The soldiers behind the lieutenant laughed, and the lieutenant turned beet-red, swung round, and went off to look for space somewhere else. The bevy of men followed him. "Stupid bastard," muttered the blond fellow after him.

I could get out here, thought Andreas as he watched the lively bustle on the platform. I could get out here, go off someplace, any place, on and on, till they caught me and put me up against a wall, and I wouldn't die between Lvov and Cernauti, I would be shot in some little village in Saxony or die like a dog in a concentration camp. But I'm standing here by the window and I feel as if I were made of lead. I can't move, I feel paralyzed, this train is part of me and I'm part of the train, this train that has to carry me to my appointed end, and the strange part about it is that I have absolutely no desire to get out here and stroll along the banks of the Elbe under those nice trees. I long for Poland, I long for that horizon as intensely, as fiercely and ardently, as only a lover can long for his beloved. If only the train would move, if only it would get going! Why is it standing here, why is it standing so long in this godforsaken Saxony, why has the resounding voice been silent for so long? I'm bursting with impatience, I'm not scared, that's the strange thing, I'm not scared, just indescribably curious and restless. Anl yet I don't want to die. I want to live, theoretically life is beautiful, theoretically life is glorious, and I don't want to get out, it's funny to think I could get out. I need only walk along the corridor, leave my useless pack behind and clear out, anywhere, stroll under trees with their fall coloring, and I go on standing here as if I were made of lead; I want to stay on this train, I have a terrible longing for the gray drabness of Poland and for that unknown stretch between Lvov and Cernauti where I have to die.

Shortly after Dresden the unshaven soldier woke too. His face was ashen under the stubble, and his eyes sadder than ever. Without a word he opened a can and began eating the meat inside, spearing lumps of it onto his fork; with it he ate some bread. His hands were dirty, and from time to time scraps of meat would fall to the floor, the floor where he would be sleeping again tonight, with its litter of cigarette butts and that accumulation of impersonal grime which every soldier seems to attract like a magnet. The blond fellow was eating too.

Andreas stood at the window and saw nothing; it was light outside and the sunshine still mild, but he saw nothing. His thoughts were seething as the train sped by the pleasant garden suburbs around Dresden. He waited impatiently for his unshaven friend to finish his meal so that he could ask him for the map. He had no idea what it was like between Lvov and Cernauti. Nikopol he could imagine, even Lvov and Przemysl ... Odessa and Nikolayev ... and Kerch, but Cernauti was only a name; it made him think of Jews and onions, of gray streets with flat-roofed houses, wide streets, and traces of administration buildings of the old Austrian Empire, neglected gardens around crumbling Imperial façades that might now be sheltering hospitals or first-aid posts; and those boulevards of Eastern Europe with their brooding charm, their squat trees, cropped to prevent the flat-roofed houses from being crushed by treetops. No treetops. ...

That's what Cernauti would be like, but what came first, what came between Lvov and Cernauti, was something he couldn't picture at all. It must be Galicia, Lvov being the capital of Galicia. And somewhere there was Volhynia—all dark, somber names smelling of pogroms and vast gloomy estates where brooding women dreamed of adultery since they had begun to find their blubber-necked husbands repulsive. ...

Galicia, a dark word, a terrible word, and yet a splendid word. It sounded something like a knife cutting very quietly ... Galicia. ...

Lvov is all right, Lvov he can visualize. Splendid and gloomy and without lightness, those cities, with bloody pasts and untamed back streets, silent and untamed.

The soldier who needed a shave threw his can out of the window, returned the loaf, from which he had been biting off mouthfuls, to his pack, and lit a cigarette. His face was sad, sad, full of remorse somehow, as if he were ashamed of the orgy of cards and boozing; he joined Andreas at the window, leaning his elbows on it, and Andreas sensed that he wanted to talk.

"Look at that, a factory," he said, "a chair factory."

"Yes," said Andreas. He saw nothing, nor did he want to see anything, only the map. "Might I," he made a great effort, "might I have a look at the map?"

"What map?" Andreas felt a deep stab of fear and knew he turned pale. Supposing this fellow didn't have any map?

"The map of Poland," he stammered, "the map of where we're going."

"Oh, that one," said the man. He bent down at once, fumbled in his pack, and handed him the folded map.

It was horrible to have the man leaning over the map with him. Andreas could smell the canned meat on his breath, which was still not quite free of the odor of digested, partially acidulated schnapps. He could smell the sweat and grime and was too wrought up to see anything; then he saw the man's finger, a thick, red, dirty, yet very good-natured finger, and the man said: "That's where I have to go." Andreas read the name of the place: "Kolomyya." Strange, now that he looked closer he could see that Lvov was not far at all from this Kolomyya ... he went back ... Stanislav, Lvov ... Lvov ... Stanislav, Kolomyya, Cernauti. Strange, he thought; Stanislav, Kolomyya ... these names evoked no definite echo. That voice inside him, that wakeful, sensitive voice, oscillated and trembled like a compass needle which cannot settle. Kolomyya, shall I get as far as Kolomyya? Nothing definite ... a strange wavering of the ever-vibrating needle ... Stanislav? The same quivering. Nikopol! he thought suddenly. Nothing.

"Yes," said the man, "that's where my unit is. Repair depot. I'm lucky." But it sounded as if he really meant: I'm having a terrible time.

Funny, thought Andreas. I had imagined there would be a plain in that area, a green patch with a few black dots, but the map is whitish-yellow there. Foothills of the Carpathians, he thought suddenly, and in his mind's eye he instantly saw his school, all of it, the corridors and the bust of Cicero and the narrow playground squeezed in between tenements, and in summertime the women leaning out of the windows in their bras, and the janitor's room downstairs where you could get a mug of cocoa, and the big store-room, dry as a bone, where they used to go for a quick smoke during recess. Foothills of the Carpathians. . . .

Now the man's finger was lying farther to the southeast. "Kherson," he said, "that's where we were last, and now we're moving farther back, probably as far as Lvov or right into the Hungarian Carpathians. The front's collapsing in Nikopol—I guess you heard that on the news, eh? They're wading through the mud, a retreat through mud! Must be a madhouse, all the vehicles get stuck, and when three happen to get stuck one behind the other everything on the road behind them has had it, there's no going back and no going forward, and they blow up the lot . . . they blow up the lot, and everyone has to foot-slog it, the generals too, I hope. But I bet they get flown out. . . . They ought to go on foot, on foot like the Führer's beloved infantry. Are you with the infantry?"

"Yes," said Andreas. He had not taken in much. His gaze was resting almost tenderly on this section of the map, it was yellow-ish-white with only four black dots, one big fat one: Lvov, and one slightly smaller: Cernauti, and two very little ones: Kolomyya and Stanislav.

"Let me keep the map," he said huskily, "let me keep it," without looking at the other man. He could not bear to part with the map, and he trembled at the thought that the man might say no. Many people are like that, an object suddenly becomes valuable to them because someone else would like to have it. An object that the very next moment they might throw away becomes precious and valuable and they wouldn't dream of selling it, just because someone else would like to own it and use it.

Many people are like that, but the unshaven soldier wasn't.

"Sure," he said, surprised, "it's not worth anything. Twenty pfennigs. Besides, it's an old one. Where're you heading for anyway?"

"Nikopol," said Andreas, and again he was aware of that appalling void as he uttered the word, he felt as if he had cheated his companion. He dared not look at him.

"Well, by the time you get down there Nikopol will be gone, maybe Kishinev . . . that's as far as you'll get."

"Think so?" Andreas asked. Kishinev didn't mean anything to him either.

"Sure. Maybe even Kolomyya," laughed the man. "How long will it take you to get down there? Let's see. Tomorrow morning Breslau. Tomorrow night Przemysl. Thursday, Friday night, maybe sooner. Then: Lvov. Let's see, Saturday evening I'll be in Kolomyya; you'll need a few days longer, another week if you're smart, in a week they'll have left Nikopol, in a week Nikopol will be gone for good as far as we're concerned."

Saturday, Andreas thought. Saturday feels quite safe, no emptiness there. Saturday I'll still be alive. He hadn't dared think that close. Now he understood why his heart had been silent when he thought in months, let alone years. That had been a leap, far far beyond the goal, a shot in the void that had no echo, into the no-man's-land that no longer existed for him. It's quite close, the end is staggeringly close. Saturday. A fierce, exquisite, painful vibration. Saturday I'll still be alive, all of Saturday. Three more days. But by Saturday evening this fellow plans to be in Kolomyya, so I should be in Cernauti by late Saturday night, and it isn't going to be in Cernauti but between Lvov and Cernauti, and not Saturday. Sunday: he thought suddenly. Nothing . . . not much . . . a gentle, very, very sad and uncertain feeling. On Sunday morning I'm going to die between Lvov and Cernauti.

Now for the first time he looked at his unshaven friend. He was shocked by his face, chalk-white under the black stubble. And there was fear in the eyes. Yet he's going to a repair depot and not to the front, thought Andreas. Why this fear, why this sorrow? This was more than just a hangover. Now he looked the man straight in the eye, and he was even more shocked by that yawning abyss of despair. This was more than just fear and emptiness, something ghastly was draining him, and he knew why the man had to drink, had to drink, to pour something, anything, into that abyss. . . .

"The funny part is," the man burst out hoarsely, "the funny part is that I'm on leave. Till next Wednesday, a whole week. But I just cleared out. My wife is . . . my wife," he was choking on something terrible between a sob and rage. "My wife, you see," he said, "has got someone else. Yes," he laughed abruptly, "that's right, she's got someone else, my friend. Funny thing, you go all over Europe, sleep with a French girl here and a Rumanian whore there, and in Kiev you chase the Russian girls; and when you go on leave and stop over in some place like Warsaw or Krakow, you can't resist the pretty Polish girls either. It's impossible . . . and . . . and . . . and—" again he choked down that horrible mass of something between a sob and rage as if it were offal— "and then you get home, no warning of course, after fifteen months, and there's a guy lying on your sofa, a man, a Russian, that's right, a Russian's lying on your sofa, the phonograph's playing a tango, and your wife's sitting at the table wearing red pajamas and mixing something . . . yes that's how it was, exactly. God knows I sent home enough schnapps and liqueurs . . . from France, Hungary, Russia. The guy's so scared he half swallows his cigarette, and your wife screams like an animal . . . I tell you, like an animal!" A shudder passed over his massive shoulders. "Like an animal, I tell you, that's all I know." Andreas looked back in alarm, just one brief glance. But the blond fellow couldn't hear anything. He was calmly sitting there, quite calmly, almost comfortably, and spreading scarlet jam from an immaculate glass jar onto white bread. He spread the jam neatly and calmly, taking bites like a civil servant, almost like a chief inspector. Maybe the blond fellow was an inspector. The unshaven soldier was silent, and something made him shiver. Nobody could have heard what he said. The train had torn away his words . . . they had flown away, flown off inaudibly with the rush of air . . . maybe they had flown back to Dresden . . . to Radebeul . . . where the little fly was perched somewhere and the girl in the yellow dress was leaning against her bicycle . . . still leaning . . . still leaning. . . .

"Yes," said the unshaven soldier, speaking rapidly, almost impersonally, as if he wanted to reel off a tape he had begun. "I cleared out, simply cleared out. On the way there I had put on my work pants, I wanted to save my new black Panzer ones with the creases in them for my leave. I had been looking forward to seeing my wife . . . God, I was looking forward to it . . . not only to . . . not only to that. No, no!" He shouted: "It's something quite different, the thing you look forward to. It's at home, it's your wife, see? What you do with the other women is nothing, you've forgotten it after an hour . . . and now, now a Russian's sitting there, a tall guy, I could see that much, and the way he was lying there and smoking . . . nowhere else in the world can a man lounge around and smoke that way. Besides, I could tell by his nose he was a Russian . . . you can always tell by their noses. . . ."

I must pray more, Andreas thought, I've hardly prayed since I left home. His companion fell silent again, looking out into the gentle countryside with the sunlight lying over it like a golden shimmer. The blond fellow was still sitting there, he drank some coffee from a flask; now he was eating white bread and butter, the butter was in a brand-new container; he was eating very methodically, very neatly. I must pray more, Andreas thought, and just as he was about to begin the unshaven soldier started up again. "Yes, I cleared out. By the next train, and took the whole lot back with me. Booze and meat and money, all that money I'd taken along, everything was for her, don't you see? Why else would I have lugged all that stuff along? Just for her. What I need now is a drink . . . where can a fellow get some booze now, I've been racking my brains; these people are daft here, they don't have any black market here. . . ."

"I've got some schnapps," said Andreas, "d'you want some?"

"Schnapps . . . God, man, schnapps!"

Andreas smiled. "I'll let you have the schnapps in exchange for

the map, okay?" His companion hugged him. His face was almost
happy. Andreas bent over his pack and dug out a bottle of
schnapps. For a moment he thought: I'll ration him, I won't give
him the second bottle till he needs it or till he wakes up from the
stupor he's going to drink himself into. But then he rummaged in
the pack again and brought out the second bottle.

"There you are," he said, "you drink it, I don't want any!"

Soon I'm going to die, he was thinking ... soon, soon, and this
Soon was no longer quite so blurred, he had already groped his way
up to this Soon, circled it and sniffed it, and already he knew that
he was going to die during the night of Saturday to Sunday, between Lvov and Cernauti ... in Galicia. Down there was Eastern
Galicia, where he would be quite close to Bucovina and Volhynia.
Those names were like unfamiliar drinks. Bucovina—that sounded
like a sturdy plum schnapps, and Volhynia—that sounded like a
very thick, swampy beer, like the beer he had once drunk in Budapest, a real soupy beer.

He glanced back once more through the glass pane and saw the
unshaven soldier lifting the bottle to his mouth, and the blond fellow shake his head when the other man offered it to him. Then he
looked out again but saw nothing ... only that Polish horizon,
away in the distance beyond an endless plain, that intoxicating,
wide horizon that he would see when the hour came. . . .

It's a good thing I'm not alone, he thought. Nobody could go
through this alone, and he was glad he had agreed to join in the
game and had met these two fellows. That one who needed a
shave—he had liked him from the start, and the blond fellow,
well, he didn't seem as effete as he looked. Or maybe he really was
effete, but he was a human being. It is not good for man to be
alone. It would be terribly difficult to be alone with the others
now filling up the corridor again, those fellows nattering about
nothing but leave and heroism, promotions and decorations, food
and tobacco and women, women, all those women who had been
madly in love with every man jack of them. . . . No girl will cry
over me, he thought, how strange. How sad. If only somewhere a

girl would think of me! Even if she were unhappy. God is with those who are unhappy. Unhappiness is life, pain is life. It would be nice if somewhere a girl were thinking of me and crying over me . . . I would pull her after me . . . I would drag her along behind me by her tears, she shouldn't wait for me for ever and ever. There's no such girl. A strange thought. No girl I've kissed. It's just possible, though not probable, that there is one girl who still thinks of me; but she can't be thinking of me. For a tenth of a second our eyes held each other's, maybe even less than a tenth of a second, and I can't forget her eyes. For three and a half years I've had to think about them and haven't been able to forget them. Only a tenth of a second or less, and I don't know her name, I don't know a thing about her, her eyes are all I know, very gentle, almost pale, sad eyes the color of sand dark with rain; unhappy eyes, much that was animal in them and all that was human, and never, never forgotten, not for a single day in three and a half years, and I don't know her name, I don't know where she lives. Three and a half years! I don't know whether she was tall or short, I didn't even see her hands. If I had at least seen her hands! Only her face, and not even that clearly; dark hair, maybe black, maybe brown, a slender, long face, not pretty, not smooth, but the eyes, almost slanting, like dark sand, full of sorrow, and those eyes belong to me, only to me, and those eyes rested on me and smiled for a tenth of a second. . . . There was just a wall and beyond that a house, and on the wall rested two elbows, and between those elbows rested that face, rested those eyes in some French hamlet near Amiens; beneath the scorching summer sky burned gray by the heat. And there was a country road ahead of me running uphill between scrawny trees, and on the right was a wall running alongside, and behind us lay Amiens steaming as if in a cauldron; smoke hung over the town, and the murky smoke of battle smoldering like a thunderstorm; on the left motorbikes drove by with hysterical officers, tanks rumbled past on their broad tracks and showered us with dust, and somewhere up front cannon were roaring. The road going uphill suddenly made me feel giddy, it tilted before my eyes, and the wall charging madly up the hill beside the road suddenly tipped over, it simply tipped over, and I fell over with the wall, as if my life were the life of the wall. The whole world turned upside down, and all I saw of it was a plane crashing, but the plane didn't crash from above downward, from sky to ground, it crashed from ground to sky, and now I saw that the sky was the ground, I was lying on the gray-blue pitilessly hot surface of the sky. Then someone tipped brandy over my face, rubbed me, tipped some brandy down my throat, and I could raise my eyes and above me I saw the wall, that wall, that wall made of bricks with gaps in between, and on that wall rested two pointed elbows, and between the elbows I saw those eyes for a tenth of a second. Just at that moment the lieutenant shouted: "Keep going! Keep going! Get up!" And someone grabbed me by the collar and thrust me into the road, and the road pulled me away, and once again I was crammed into the column and couldn't turn around, couldn't even turn around. . . .

Is it such a disgrace, then, to long to know what forehead belonged to those eyes, what mouth and what breast and what hands? Would it have been asking too much to be allowed to know what heart belonged to them, a girl's heart perhaps; to be allowed to kiss that mouth belonging to those eyes, just once, before I got thrust into the next hamlet where all of a sudden they knocked my leg out from under me? It was summer, and the harvest stood golden in the fields, thin blades, some of them scorched black, that had been eaten up by the summer, and I hated nothing so much as to die a hero's death in a field of corn, it reminded me too much of a poem, and I didn't care to die like in a poem, to die a hero's death like a propaganda picture for this dirty war . . . and even so it was like some patriotic poem, to be lying in a field of corn, bleeding and wounded and cursing, and perhaps to have to die there, five minutes away from those eyes.

But only the bone was broken. I was a hero, wounded on the fields of France, not far from Amiens, not far from the wall that charged madly up the hill, and a mere five minutes from that face, of which I had been allowed to see only the eyes. . . .

For only a tenth of a second was I allowed to see my only love, who was perhaps no more than an apparition, and now I must die, between Lvov and Cernauti, facing the wide Polish horizon.

And didn't I promise them, those eyes, to pray for them every day, every day, and today is almost over? It's already getting dark, and yesterday I gave her only a passing thought while I was playing cards, the girl whose name I don't know and whose mouth I never kissed. . . .

It shocked Andreas to find he was suddenly hungry. It was Thursday evening, and on Sunday he was going to die, and he was hungry, he was so hungry his head ached, he was so hungry he was exhausted. It was very quiet in the corridor, and not so crowded now. He sat down beside the unshaven soldier, who promptly made room for him, and all three men were silent. Even the blond fellow was silent: he had a mouth organ between his lips and was playing it on the closed side. It was a little mouth organ, and he slid the closed side gently back and forth across his lips, and you could tell from his expression that he was hearing the tunes in his head. The unshaven soldier was drinking, drinking systematically and silently at regular intervals, and his eyes were beginning to glisten. Andreas finished the last package of air-raid sandwiches. They had got a bit dry, but his hunger welcomed them eagerly, and they tasted marvelous; he ate six whole sandwiches and asked the blond fellow for the flask of coffee. The sandwiches were really delicious, they tasted wonderful, and afterward he felt disgracefully relaxed, shockingly content. He was very glad the other two weren't talking, and the regular rattle of the train, of which they could feel the least movement, was rather soothing. Now I'll pray, he thought, I'll say all the prayers I know by heart, and a few more as well. First he said the Credo, then a Paternoster and Ave Maria, de Profundis . . . ut pupillam oculi—Come Holy Ghost; then the Credo again because it was so wonderfully complete;

then the Good Friday intercession, because it was so wonderfully all-embracing, it even included the unbelieving Jews. That made him think of Cernauti, and he said a special prayer for the Jews of Cernauti and for the Jews of Lvov, and no doubt there were Jews in Stanislav too, and in Kolomyya ... then another Paternoster, and then a prayer of his own; it was a great place to pray, sitting beside those two silent men, one soundlessly and intently playing the wrong side of his mouth organ, the other steadily drinking schnapps. . . .

Outside it had got dark, and he prayed a long time for the eyes, a terribly long time, much longer than for all the others. And for the unshaven soldier too, and the blond fellow, and for the one who had said yesterday: Practically speaking, practically speaking we've already won the war, especially for him.

"Breslau," said the unshaven soldier suddenly, and his voice had a strangely heavy, almost metallic sound, as if he were beginning to get a bit drunk again. "Breslau, we must soon be getting into Breslau. . . ."

Andreas now recited the poem to himself: "Once there was a belfryman, in Breslau Town of old. . . ." To his mind it was a magnificent poem, and he greatly regretted not knowing quite all of it by heart. No, he thought, I'm not going to die right away. I shall die on Sunday morning or during the night, between Lvov and Cernauti, facing that immense Polish horizon.

After that he said the poem "Archibald Douglas" over to himself, thought about the sorrowful eyes, and fell asleep with a smile. . . .

Waking up was always terrible. The night before someone had stepped on his fingers, and tonight he had a terrible dream: he was sitting somewhere on a wet, very cold plain and had no legs, no legs at all, he was sitting on the stumps of his thighs, and the sky over this plain was black and lowering, and this sky was slowly sinking onto the plain, getting closer and closer, closer and closer, the sky was sinking very slowly, and he couldn't run away, and he couldn't scream because he knew it was no use screaming. The futility of it paralyzed him. Where would there be a soul hereabouts to hear his screams? Yet he couldn't let himself be crushed by that descending sky. He didn't even know whether the plain was grass, wet grass, or just earth or only mud . . . he couldn't move, he refused to hop forward on his hands like a lame bird, and where to anyway? The horizon was endless, endless, wherever he looked, and the sky was sinking, and then suddenly something very cold and wet splashed onto his head, and for a millionth of a second he thought the black sky was only rain and that it would open now, that was what he thought in the millionth of a second, and he tried to scream . . . but he awoke and instantly saw that the unshaven soldier was standing over him, the bottle raised to his mouth, and knew that a drop from the bottle had splashed onto his forehead. . . .

It all came back to him right away. Sunday morning . . . now it was Friday. Two more days. It all came back. The blond fellow was asleep, the unshaven soldier was drinking in fierce gulps, and it was cold in the compartment; there was a draft under the door, and the prayers had expired, and the thought of the eyes no longer aroused that poignant bliss, just sorrow and loneliness. It all came back, and in the morning everything looked different, everything was glamorless and everything was futile, and it would be wonderful, too wonderful for words, if in the morning this Soon could expire too, this Soon that had now become quite definite, quite certain. But this Soon was there, it was always there right away, as if it had been waiting to pounce; ever since he had uttered the word it had lain on him like second sight. For two days now it had been as close to him, as inseparably linked to him, as his soul, his heart. This Soon was just as strong and sure in the morning. Sunday morning. . . .

The unshaven soldier had also noticed that Andreas was awake. He was still standing over him, drinking from the bottle. In the dim gray light it was frightening, that bulky outline, leaning forward as if to pounce, the bottle at his lips, and the glittering eyes, and the strange, menacing gurgle from the bottle.

"Where are we?" Andreas asked in a hoarse whisper. He was scared, it was cold and still almost totally dark.

"Not far from Przemysl now," said the man. "Want a drink?"

"Yes." The schnapps tasted good. It ran into him like sharp fire, driving his blood around as fire under a kettle brings water to the boil. The schnapps tasted good, it warned him. He handed the bottle back.

"Go on, have another drink," said the man roughly. "I got myself some more in Krakow."

"No."

The man sat down beside him, and it felt good to know there was someone there who wasn't asleep, when you were awake and utterly miserable. Everyone was asleep, the blond fellow was snoring again, soft whistling sounds coming from his corner, and the others, the terribly silent and the terribly talkative, they were all asleep. The air in the corridor was foul—sour and grimy, full of sweat and steam.

Suddenly he realized they were already in Poland. His heart stood still for a moment, missed another beat as if the artery had suddenly knotted, blocking off the blood. Never again will I be in Germany, Germany's gone. The train left Germany while I was asleep. Somewhere there was a line, an invisible line across a field or right through the middle of a village, and that was the border, and the train passed callously over it, and I was no longer in Germany, and no one woke me so I could have one more look out into the night and at least see a piece of the night that hung over Germany. Of course no one knows I shan't see it again, no one knows I'm going to die, no one on the train. Never again will I see the Rhine. The Rhine! The Rhine! Never again! This train is simply taking me along, carting me off to Przemysl, and there's Poland, hopeless hapless Poland, and I'll never see the Rhine, never smell it again, that exquisite tang of water and seaweed that coats and clings to every stone along the banks of the Rhine. Never again the avenues along the Rhine, the gardens behind the villas, and the boats, so bright and clean and gay, and the bridges, those splendid bridges, spare and elegant, leaping over the water like great slender animals.

"Pass me the bottle again," he said huskily. His companion handed it to him, and he drank long and deep of that fire, that liquid fire that burns out the bleak misery of the heart. Then he lit a cigarette, and he wished his friend would say something. But first he wanted to pray, just because he felt so miserable, that was why he wanted to pray. He said the same prayers as the evening before, but this time he prayed first for the eyes, so he wouldn't forget them. The eyes were always with him, but not always with the same clarity. Sometimes they submerged for months and were only there in the sense that his lips were there and his feet, which were always with him and of which he was only occasionally aware, only when they hurt; and sometimes, at irregular intervals, often after months, the eyes would surface like some new burning pain, and on days like that he prayed in the evening for the eyes; today he had to pray for the eyes in the morning. He also prayed again for the Jews of Cernauti, and for the Jews of Stanislav and Kolomyya; there were Jews all over Galicia, Galicia, the word was like a snake with tiny feet and shaped like a knife, a snake with glittering eyes gliding smoothly over the ground and slicing, slicing the ground in two. Galicia . . . a dark, beautiful word, filled with anguish, and in this country I am going to die.

There was a lot of blood in that word, blood made to flow by the knife. Bucovina, he thought, that's a good solid word, I shan't die there, I shall die in Galicia, in Eastern Galicia. I must have a look, when it gets light, and see where the province of Bucovina begins, I won't see it any more now; I'm getting closer and closer. Cernauti is already in Bucovina, I won't see that.

"Kolomyya," he asked his companion, "is that in Galicia?"

"Don't know. Poland, I think."

Every border has a terrible finality. There's a line, and that's it. And the train goes across it just as it would go across a dead body, or a live body. And hope is dead, the hope of being sent back once more to France and finding the eyes again and the lips belonging to the eyes, and the heart and the breast, a woman's breast that must belong to those eyes. That hope is quite dead, completely cut off. For ever and ever those eyes will only be eyes, they will never surround themselves again with body and clothes and hair, no hands, no human hands, no woman's hands that might one day caress you. That hope had always been there, for after all it was a human being, a living human being, to which those eyes belonged, a girl or a woman. But not now. Now there were only eyes, no lips now, never again a mouth, a heart, never again to feel a living heart under a soft skin beating against your hand, never again . . . never . . . never. Sunday morning between Lvov and Kolomyya. Cernauti was far away now, as far as Nikopol and Kishinev. That Soon had narrowed down even more, it was very narrow now. Two days, Lvov, Kolomyya. He knew he might get barely as far as Kolomyya, but certainly no farther. No heart, no mouth, only eyes, only the soul, that unhappy lovely soul that had no body; wedged between two elbows like a witch pinned to her stake before they burn her. . . .

The border had cut off a lot of things. Paul was finally gone too. Only memory, hope, and dream. "We live on hope," Paul had once said. As if one were to say: "We live on credit." We have no security . . . nothing . . . only eyes, and don't know whether three and a half years of prayer have coaxed those eyes over to the place we may hope to reach. . . .

Yes, later on he did limp up that hill, from the hospital in Amiens, and nothing was the same. The road was not gray as it ran up the hill, it was just an ordinary road. The hill carried the road on its back, and the wall had no intention of swaying and charging; the wall just stood there. And there was the house, which he hadn't recognized, only the wall, he had recognized that, a wall made of bricks with gaps in them where bricks had been left out to make a kind of pattern. A Frenchman was standing there, a real lower-middle-class type, his pipe between his teeth, his eyes full of that truly French derision—ponderous, bourgeois—and the man had known nothing. He knew only that they had all gone, fled, and that the Germans had looted everything although a banner had been strung right across the road saying: Looting punishable by death. No, no eyes, only the man's wife, an obese matron who kept her hand tucked in the top of her dress, a face rather like a rabbit's. No child, no daughter, no sister, no sister-in-law, nothing! Just poky rooms full of kitsch and stale air and the couple's derisive looks as they watched him searching helplessly, agonizingly.

That glass cabinet: the Germans had smashed it up. And burned holes in the carpet with their cigarette butts, and slept on the couch with their whores and messed it all up. He spat with contempt. But that had all happened later, not during the battle while Amiens was smoking, much later, after the pilot had crashed in the wheatfield over there where you could see the tail of the aircraft sticking in the earth. The pipe pointed out of the window ... yes, there it was, sticking in the earth, the tail with the emblem, and on the French steel helmet on the grave right next to it the sun was glinting; it was all real, as real as the smell from the kitchen of the roast in the oven, and the smashed glass cabinet and, down there in the valley, the cathedral in Amiens. "A fine example of French Gothic architecture. . . ."

No eyes. Nothing, nothing at all. . . .

"Maybe," said the man, "maybe it was a whore." But the man pitied him, it was a miracle that this bourgeois little man could feel pity, pity for a German soldier who belonged to the same army as the ones who had stolen his knives and forks and his clocks, and had slept on his couch with their whores, messing it all up, ruining it.

The pain was so overpowering that he just stood there in the doorway, looking at the spot on the road where he had passed out, the pain was so great that he didn't feel it. The man shook his head, perhaps he had never seen such unhappy eyes as those of this soldier leaning heavily on his cane.

"Peut-être," he said before Andreas left, "peut-être une folle, a madwoman from the asylum over there." He gestured toward the wall, where red-roofed buildings showed among fine tall trees. "A mental asylum. During the battle they all ran away, you see, and they all had to be rounded up again, a tough job. . . ."

"Thanks . . . thanks." On up the hill toward the asylum. The wall began close by, but there was no gate. It was a long, long walk up the hot hill until he reached a gate, and he knew in advance, he knew there would be no one left. A sentry in a steel helmet stood at the gate, and there were no more lunatics, only some sick and wounded and a V.D. treatment center.

"A big V.D. center," said the sentry, "did you pick up something too, bud?"

Andreas looked across to the big field where the aircraft's tail with the emblem was sticking in the earth and the steel helmet was glinting in the sun.

"It's so cheap here, that's the trouble," said the sentry, who was bored. "You can have it for fifty pfennigs," he laughed, "fifty pfennigs!"

"That's right," said Andreas . . . forty million, he thought, France has forty million inhabitants, that's too many. You can't search among all those, I must wait . . . I must look into every pair of eyes I meet. He didn't feel like walking on another three minutes and having a look at the field where he had been wounded. For it wasn't the same field, everything was different. It wasn't the same road, or the same wall, they had all forgotten; the road had forgotten too, just as people forget, and the wall had forgotten that once it had collapsed with fear and he with it. And the tail of the aircraft over there was a dream, a dream with a French emblem. Why go and look at the field? Why walk those extra three minutes and recall with hate and pain the patriotic poem that he had remembered against his will? Why torment his tired legs any further?

"Now," said the soldier who needed a shave, "now we're getting close to Przemysl." "Pass me the bottle again," said Andreas. He took another swig.

It was still cold, but dawn was softly breaking, and soon the horizon would be visible, that Polish horizon. Dark houses and a plain full of shadows, and the sky above it always threatening to collapse because there was nothing to hold it up. Perhaps this was already Galicia, perhaps this plain rising out of the dusk, drab and gray and full of sorrow and blood, perhaps this plain was already Galicia ... Galicia ... Eastern Galicia....

"You've had a good long sleep," said the soldier who needed a shave. "From seven to five. It's five o'clock already. Krakow to Tarnov ... all gone; I didn't sleep a wink. That's how long we've already been in Poland. Krakow to Tarnov, and now Przemysl...."

What a fantastic difference between Przemysl and the Rhine. I've slept for ten hours, and now I'm hungry again, and I've got forty-eight hours to live. Forty-eight hours have already gone by. For forty-eight hours this Soon has been suspended inside me: Soon I'm going to die. At first it was certain, but far off; certain, but unclear, and it's been getting steadily narrower and narrower, already it's narrowed down to a few miles of road and two days away, and every turn of these wheels brings me closer. Every turn of the wheels tears a piece off my life, off an unhappy life. These wheels are grinding away my life, whittling away my life with their stupid rhythm; they rattle across Polish soil as heedlessly as they rattled along by the Rhine, and they are the same wheels. Maybe Paul caught sight of the wheel that's under this door, this oily, dirt-encrusted train-wheel that's come all the way from Paris, maybe even from Le Havre. From Paris, the Gare Montparnasse ... soon they'll be sitting in wicker chairs under awnings and drinking wine in the autumn breeze, swallowing that sweet dust of Paris and sipping absinthe or Pernod, nonchalantly flicking their cigarette butts into the gutter that runs under that soft sky, that ever-mocking sky. There are only five million people in Paris, and many streets, many alleys, and many, many houses, and from not one of the windows do those eyes look out; even five million are too many....

All at once the soldier who needed a shave began speaking very rapidly. It was lighter now, and the first of the sleeping men began to stir, to turn over in their sleep, and it seemed as if he must speak before they were fully awake. He wanted to speak into the night, into a listening ear in the night. . . .

"The terrible part is that I shall never see her again, I know I won't," he said in a low voice, "and I don't know what'll become of her. It's three days now since I left, three days. What's she been doing in those three days? I don't believe that Russian is still with her—because she screamed like an animal, like an animal facing the muzzle of a hunter's gun. There's no one with her. She's waiting. God, I wouldn't want to be a woman. Always waiting . . . waiting . . . waiting . . . waiting."

The unshaven soldier screamed softly, but it was a scream all right, a terribly soft scream. "She's waiting. . . she can't live without me. There's no one with her, and no one will ever go to her now. She's waiting only for me, and I love her. Now she's as innocent as a girl that's never thought of kissing, and that innocence is all for me. That ghastly, terrible shock has completely cleansed her, I know it has . . . and no one, no one on earth can help her but me, no one, and here I am on a train heading for Przemysl . . . I'm going to Lvov . . . to Kolomyya . . . and never again will I cross the German border. That's something no one would ever be able to understand, why I don't take the next train back to her . . . why don't I? No one would ever be able to understand that. But I'm scared of that innocence . . . and I love her very much, and I'm going to die, and all she'll ever get from me now will be an official letter saying: Fallen for Greater Germany. . . ." He took a long, deep drink.

"How slowly the train's going, mate, don't you think? I want to get away, far away . . . and quickly, and I don't know why I don't change trains and go back, I've still got time . . . I wish the train would go faster, much faster. . . ."

Some of the men had woken and were blinking morosely into the false light rising from the plain. . . .

"I'm scared," whispered the unshaven soldier into Andreas' ear,

"I'm scared, that's what, scared of dying but even more scared of going back, going back to her ... that's why I'd rather die ... maybe I'll write to her. ..."

The men who had woken up were combing back their hair, lighting cigarettes, and looking contemptuously out of the windows, where dark huts stood among what seemed to be barren fields; there were no people in this country ... somewhere over there were some hills ... everything was gray ... Polish horizon. ...

The unshaven soldier was silent. There was hardly any life left in him. He had not been able to sleep all night; the spark in him had gone out, and his eyes were like blind mirrors, his cheeks yellow and cavernous, and what had been the need for a shave was now a beard, a reddish-black beard below the thick hair on his forehead.

"Those are precisely the advantages of the 37 antitank weapon," came a clipped voice, "those are precisely the advantages ... mobility ... mobility...." "And no louder than a knock at the door," laughed an equally clipped voice.

"Not really?" "Yes, he got the Knight's Cross for that ... and all we did was shit in our pants...."

"They ought to listen to the Führer, that's what I say. Get rid of the aristocrats. Von Kruseiten he was called. What a name. A damned know-it-all...." Lucky fellow, that one with the beard, asleep now when the nattering starts up and able to stay awake when everything's quiet. I must be grateful, I've still got two more nights, thought Andreas ... two long, long nights; I'd like to be alone then. If they knew I'd prayed for the Jews in Cernauti and Stanislav and Kolomyya, they'd arrest me on the spot or stick me in the madhouse.... 37 antitank weapon.

The blond fellow rubbed his narrow, hideously filmy eyes for a very long time. There was something scaly in the corners of them, something disgusting, but it didn't stop him offering Andreas bread, white bread and jam. And he still had some coffee in the flask. It felt good to eat; Andreas realized he was very hungry again. It was almost a craving, and he could no longer control his eyes as they embraced the great loaf of bread. That white bread was unbelievably good.

"Yes," sighed the blond fellow, "my mother baked it for me just before I left." Later on Andreas sat for a long time in the john, smoking. The john was the only place where you could be really alone. The only place in the whole world, in the whole of Hitler's great-and-glorious army. It was good to sit there and smoke, and he felt he had once again got the better of his depression. Depression was only a bogey that haunted you just after you woke up; here he was alone, and he had everything. When he wasn't alone he had nothing. Here he had everything, Paul and the eyes of the girl he loved . . . the blond fellow and the man who needed a shave, and the one who had said: Practically speaking, practically speaking we've already won the war, and the one who had just said: Those are precisely the advantages of the 37 antitank weapon—they were all there, and the prayers were alive too, very close and warm, and it felt good to be alone. When you were alone you didn't feel so lonely any more. This evening, he thought, I'll pray for a long time again, this evening in Lvov. Lvov is the springboard . . . between Lvov and Kolomyya . . . the train was getting closer and closer to the goal, and the wheels that had rumbled through Paris, the Gare Montparnasse, maybe through Le Havre or Abbeville, were going as far as Przemysl . . . till they got quite close to the springboard. . . .

It was full daylight now, but the sun didn't seem to be coming through today; somewhere in the thick gray mass of clouds hung a pale spot with a soft gray light streaming from it that lit up the forests, distant hills . . . villages and the dark-clad figures who shaded their eyes to follow the train out of sight. Galicia . . . Galicia. . . . He stayed in the john until the deafening thumping and swearing on the other side of the door drove him out.

The train arrived in Przemysl on time. It was almost pleasant there. They waited until everyone had left the train, then woke up the man with the beard. The platform was already empty. The sun had come through and was beating down on dusty piles of rock and sand. The man with the beard knew at once what to do.

"Yes," was all he said. Then he stood up and cut the wire so they could get out right there. Andreas had the least luggage, just his pack, which was very light now that the heavy air-raid sandwiches had all been eaten. He had only a shirt and a pair of socks and some writing paper and his flask, which was always empty, and his steel helmet, since he had left his rifle behind in Paul's clothes closet where it stood propped up behind the raincoat.

The blond fellow had a Luftwaffe rucksack and a suitcase, and the bearded soldier had two cartons and a knapsack; both men also had pistols. Stepping out into the sunshine, they saw for the first time that the bearded soldier was a sergeant. The dull braid showed up now against his gray collar. The platform was deserted, the place looked like a freight yard. To the right lay army huts, hut after hut, delousing huts, cookhouse huts, recreation huts, dormitory huts, and no doubt a brothel hut where everything was guaranteed fully sanitary. Huts wherever you looked, but they walked to the left, way over to the left where there was a dead, overgrown track and an overgrown loading ramp by a fir tree. There they lay down, and in the sunshine behind the army huts they could see the old towers of Przemysl on the River San.

The bearded soldier did not sit down. He merely set his baggage on the ground and said: "I'll go and pick up our rations and find out when the train leaves for Lvov, eh? You fellows try and get some sleep." He took their leave passes and disappeared very slowly down the platform. He ambled along at a terribly slow, maddeningly slow, pace, and they saw that his blue work pants were soiled, full of stains and torn places as if from barbed wire; he walked very slowly, with almost a rolling gait, and from a distance he might have been taken for a sailor.

It was noon, very hot, and the shade of the fir tree was already drenched with heat, a dry shade without gentleness. The blond fellow had spread out his blanket, and they lay with their heads on their packs, looking toward the city across the hot steaming roofs of all those army huts. At some point the bearded soldier vanished between two huts, walking as if he didn't care where he was going. . . .

Alongside another platform stood a train about to leave for Germany. The locomotive already had steam up, and bare-headed soldiers were looking out of the windows. Why don't I get on, thought Andreas, it's really very odd. Why don't I find a seat in that train and go back to the Rhine? Why don't I buy myself a leave pass in this country where you can buy anything, and go back to Paris, the Gare Montparnasse, and comb the streets, one by one, hunt through every house and look for one little tender gesture from the hands that must belong to those eyes? Five million, that's one eighth, why shouldn't she be among them . . . why don't I go to Amiens, to the house with the pierced brick wall, and put a bullet through my head at the spot where her gaze, very close and tender, true and deep, rested in my soul for a quarter of a second? But these thoughts were as leaden as his legs. It felt great to stretch your legs, your legs got longer and longer, and he felt as though he could stretch them all the way to Przemysl.

They lay there smoking, sluggish and weary as only men can be who have been sleeping and sitting in a cramped railway car.

The sun had made a wide arc by the time Andreas awoke. The bearded soldier still was not back. The blond fellow was awake and smoking.

The train for Germany had left, but already there was another train for Germany standing there, and from the large delousing hut on the other side emerged gray figures with their parcels and knapsacks, rifles slung around their necks, bound for Germany. One of them started running, then three ran, then ten, then they were all running, bumping into one another, knocking parcels out of hands . . . and the whole gray weary wretched column of men was running because one of them had begun to panic. . . .

"Where did you put the map?" asked the blond fellow. These were the first words spoken by either of them in a long while.

Andreas pulled the map out of his tunic pocket, unfolded it, and sat up, spreading it out on his knees. His eyes went to where Galicia was, but the blond fellow's finger was lying much farther to the south and east, it was a long, shapely finger, with fine hair on it, a finger that not even the dirt had deprived of any of its good breeding.

"There," he said, "that's where I'm heading. With any luck it'll take me another ten days." His finger with its flat, still glossy, blue-sheened nail filled the whole bay between Odessa and the Crimea. The edge of the nail lay beside Nikolayev.

"Nikolayev?" Andreas asked.

"No," the blond fellow winced, and his nail slid lower down, and Andreas noticed that he was staring at the map but seeing nothing and thinking of something else. "No," said the blond fellow. "Ochakov. I'm with the antiaircraft; before that we were in Anapa, in the Kuban, you know, but we got out of there. And now it's Ochakov."

Suddenly the two men looked at one another. For the first time in the forty-eight hours they had been cooped up together, they looked at one another. They had played cards together by the hour, drunk and eaten and slept leaning against each other, but now for the first time they looked at one another. A strangely repellent, whitish-gray, slimy film coated the blond fellow's eyes. To Andreas it looked as though the man's gaze were piercing the faint first scab that closes over a festering wound. Now all at once he realized what that repulsive aura was which emanated from this man who at one time, when his eyes were still clear, must have been handsome, fair and slender with well-bred hands. So that's it, thought Andreas.

"Yes," said the blond fellow very quietly, "that's it," as if he realized what Andreas was thinking. He went on speaking, his voice quiet, uncannily quiet. "That's it. He seduced me, that sergeant major. I'm totally corrupted now, rotten to the core, life holds no more pleasure for me, not even eating, it just looked as if I enjoyed that, I eat automatically, I drink automatically, I sleep automatically. It's not my fault, they corrupted me!" he cried, then his voice subsided again.

"For six weeks we lay in a gun emplacement, way up along the Sivash River ... not a house in sight ... not even a broken wall. Marshes, water ... willow shrubs ... and the Russians flew over it when they wanted to attack our planes flying from Odessa to the Crimea. For six weeks we lay there. Words can't describe it. We were just one cannon with six men and the sergeant major. Not a living soul for miles. Our food supplies were trucked in as far as the edge of the marsh, and we had to pick them up from there and carry them across log-walks to our emplacement; the rations were always for two weeks, no shortage of grub. Eating was the only break in the monotony, that and catching fish and chasing mosquitoes ... those fantastic swarms of mosquitoes, I don't know why we didn't go out of our minds. The sergeant major was like an animal. Filth poured from his mouth all day long, those first few days, and his eating habits were foul. Meat and fat, hardly any bread." A terrible sigh was wrenched from his breast: "Any man who doesn't eat bread is a hopeless case, I tell you. Yes. . . ." Terrible silence, while the sun stood golden and warm and fair over Przemysl.

"My God," he groaned, "so he seduced us, what else is there to say? We were all like that ... except one. He refused. He was an old fellow, married and with a family; in the evening he used often to show us snapshots of his kids, and weep ... that was before. He refused, he would hit out, threaten us ... he was stronger than the five of us put together; and one night when he was alone on sentry duty, the sergeant major shot him. He crept out and put a bullet through him—from behind. With the man's own pistol; then he yanked us out of our bunks and we had to help him throw the body into the marshes. Corpses are heavy ... I'm telling you, the bodies of dead men weigh a ton. Corpses are heavier than the whole world, the six of us could scarcely carry him; it was dark and raining, and I thought: This is what hell must be like. And the sergeant major sent in a report that the old fellow had mutinied and threatened him with his weapon, and he took along the old fellow's pistol as proof—there was one bullet missing from it, of course. And they sent his wife a letter saying he had fallen for Greater Germany in the Sivash marshes . . . yes; and a week later the first food truck arrived with a telegram for me saying our factory had been destroyed and I was to go on leave; and I didn't even go back to the emplacement, I just took off!" There was a fierce joy in his voice: "I just took off! He must have hit the roof! And they first interrogated me in the office about the old fellow, and I gave them exactly the same story as the sergeant major's. And then I was off . . . off! From the battery to the section in Ochakov, then Odessa and then I took off. . . ." Terrible silence, while the sun still shone, fair and warm and gentle; Andreas felt an appalling nausea. That's the worst, he thought, that's the worst. . . .

"After that I never enjoyed anything again, and I never will. I'm scared to look at a woman. The whole time I was home I just lay around in a kind of stupor, crying away like some idiot child, and my mother thought I had some awful disease. But how could I tell her about it, it was something you can't tell anyone. . . ."

How crazy for the sun to shine like that, Andreas thought, and a dreadful nausea lay like poison in his blood. He reached for the blond fellow's hand, but the man shrank back in horror. "No," he cried, "don't!" He threw himself onto his stomach, hid his head in his arms, and sobbed. It sounded as if the ground would burst open, and above his sobbing the sky was smiling, above the army huts, above all those huts and above the towers of Przemysl on the River San. . . .

"Let me die," he sobbed, "I just want to die, then it'll be all over. Let me die. . . ." His words were stifled by a choking sound, and now Andreas could hear him crying, crying real tears, wet tears.

Andreas saw no more. A torrent of blood and dirt and slime had poured over him; he prayed, prayed desperately, as a drowning man shouts who is struggling all alone out in the middle of a lake and can see no shore and no rescuer. . . .

That's wonderful, he thought, crying is wonderful, crying is good for you, crying, crying, what wretched creature has never cried? I should cry too, that's what I should do. The sergeant cried, and the blond fellow cried, and I haven't cried for three and a half years, not one tear since I walked back down that hill into Amiens and was too lazy to walk those extra three minutes as far as the field where I had been wounded.

The second train had left too, the station was empty now. Funny, thought Andreas, even if I wanted to I couldn't go back now. I could never leave these two fellows alone. Besides, I don't want to go back, I never want to go back. . . .

The station with all its various tracks was deserted now. A heat haze danced between the rails, and somewhere back there by the entrance a group of Poles were working, shoveling ballast onto the tracks, and coming along the platform was an odd figure wearing the pants of the unshaven soldier. From way off you could see it was no longer the bearded, fierce, desperate fellow who had been cooped up in the train and drinking to drown his sorrows. This was a different person, only the pants were still those of the unshaven soldier. His face was all smooth and pink, his cap at a slight angle, and in his eyes, as he came closer, could be seen something of the real sergeant, a mixture of indifference, mockery, cynicism, and militarism. Those eyes seemed to have done with dreaming, the unshaven soldier was now shaved and washed, his hair was combed, his hands were clean, and it was just as well to know that his name was Willi, for it was impossible to think of him any more as the unshaven soldier, you had to think of him as Willi. The blond fellow was still lying on his blanket, his face on his folded arms, and from his heavy breathing you couldn't tell whether he was sleeping, groaning, or crying.

"Is he asleep?" Willi asked.

"Yes." Willi unpacked the rations and arranged everything

neatly in two piles. "Three days' supply," he said. For each man there was a whole loaf of bread and a large sausage, its wrapping paper wet with the moisture oozing from it. For each man there was slightly less than half a pound of butter, eighteen cigarettes, and three rolls of fruit drops.

"Nothing for you?" Andreas asked.

Willi looked at him in surprise, almost offended. "But I've still got my ration cards for sixteen days!" Strange to think that all that hadn't been a dream, all those things Willi had talked about during the night. It had been the truth, it had been the same person as this man facing him now, smoothly shaven, the quiet eyes holding no more than a modicum of pain; the same person who was now standing in the shade of the fir tree and, very carefully, so as not to spoil the creases, pulling on the pants of his black Panzer uniform. Brand-new pants that suited him down to the ground. He now looked every inch a sergeant.

"There's some beer here too," said Willi. He unpacked three bottles of beer, and they set up Willi's carton between them as a table and began to eat. The blond fellow did not stir, he lay there on his face as many a dead man lies on the battlefield. Willi had some Polish bacon, white bread, and onions. The beer was excellent, it was even cool.

"These Polish barbers," said Willi, "they're tremendous. For six marks, everything included, they make a new man of you, they even shampoo your hair! Just tremendous, and can they ever cut hair!" He took off his peaked cap and pointed to the well-contoured back of his head. "That's what I call a haircut." Andreas was still looking at him in amazement. In Willi's eyes there was now something sentimental, some sergeant-like sentimentality. It was very pleasant eating like this as if at a proper table, well away from those army huts.

"You fellows," said Willi, chewing and clearly enjoying his beer, "you fellows should go and have a wash, or get yourselves washed, makes you feel like a new man. You get rid of everything, all that dirt. And then the shave! You could use one." He glanced at Andreas' chin. "You could certainly use one. I tell you, it's tremendous, you don't feel tired any more, you ... you—" he was groping for the right word—"all I can say is, you feel like a new man. You've still got time, our train doesn't leave for two hours. We'll be in Lvov this evening. From Lvov we take the civilian express, the courier train, the one that goes direct from Warsaw to Bucharest. It's a terrific train, I always take it, all you need is to get your pass stamped, and we'll see to that," he guffawed, "we'll see to that, but I'm not letting on how!"

But surely we won't need twenty-four hours to get from Lvov to that place where it's going to happen, thought Andreas. Something's wrong there. We won't be leaving Lvov as early as five tomorrow morning. The sandwiches tasted marvelous. He spread the butter thickly on the bread and ate it with chunks of the juicy sausage. That's really strange, he thought, this is Sunday's butter and maybe even part of Monday's, I'm eating butter I'm no longer entitled to. I'm not even entitled to Sunday's butter. Rations are calculated from noon to noon, and starting Sunday noon I'm not entitled to any more butter. Perhaps they'll court-martial me ... they'll lay my body on a desk before a tribunal and say: He ate Sunday's butter and even part of Monday's, he robbed the great-and-glorious German Wehrmacht. He knew he was going to die, but that didn't stop him from eating the butter and bread and sausage and candy and from smoking the cigarettes. We can't enter that anywhere, there's no place to enter rations for the dead. We're not heathens, after all, who place food in graves for their dead. We are positive Christians, and he has robbed the positive-Christian, glorious Greater German Wehrmacht. We must find him guilty....

"In Lvov," Willi laughed, "that's where I'll get that rubber stamp, in Lvov. You can get anything in Lvov, I know my way around there."

Andreas had only to say one word, only to ask, and he would have found out how and where one obtained the rubber stamp in

Lvov. Willi was just itching to tell him. But Andreas didn't care about finding out. It was fine with him if they got the stamp. The civilian express was fine with him. It was wonderful to travel by civilian train. They weren't for soldiers only, for men only. It was terrible to be always among men, men were so womanish. But in that train there would be women ... Polish women ... Rumanian women ... German women ... women spies ... diplomats' wives. It was nice to ride on a train with women ... as far as ... as ... where he was going to die. What would happen? Partisans? There were partisans all over the place, but why would partisans attack a train carrying civilians? There were plenty of leave-trains carrying whole regiments of soldiers with weapons, luggage, food, clothing, money, and ammunition.

Willi was disappointed that Andreas did not ask where he could get hold of the stamp in Lvov. He wanted so badly to talk about Lvov. "Lvov," he cried with a laugh. And since Andreas still did not ask, he launched out anyway: "In Lvov, you know, we always flogged the cars."

"Always?" Andreas was listening now. "You always flogged them?"

"I mean, when we had one to flog. We're a repair depot, see, and often there's a wreck left over, often it's a wreck that's not really a wreck at all. You just have to say it's scrap, that's all. And the superintendent has to close both eyes because he's been going to bed all the time with that Jewish girl from Cernauti. But it isn't scrap at all, that car, see? You can take two or three and make a terrific car out of them, the Russians are terrific at that. And in Lvov they'll give you forty thousand marks for it. Divided by four. Me and three men from my column. It's damn dangerous, of course, you're taking a hell of a risk." He sighed heavily. "You sweat blood, I can tell you. You never know whether the fellow you're dealing with mightn't be from the Gestapo, you can never tell, not till it's all over. For two whole weeks you sweat blood. If after two weeks there's been no report and none of the bunch have been arrested, that means you've come out on top again. Forty thousand marks." He took a drink of beer with obvious enjoyment.

"When I think of all that stuff lying in the mud around Nikopol. It's worth millions, I tell you, millions! And not a bloody soul gets a thing out of it, only the Russians. You know," he lit a cigarette, savoring it, "now and again we could flog something that wasn't so dangerous. One day a spare part, another day a motor or some tires. Clothing too. They're keen as hell to get hold of clothing. Coats, now . . . they'll fetch a thousand marks, a good coat will. Back home, you know, I've built myself a little house, a nice little house with a workshop . . . for . . . for . . . what did you say?" he asked abruptly. But Andreas had said nothing, he shot him a quick glance and saw that his eye had darkened, he was frowning, and that he hurriedly finished his beer. Even without the beard, the old face was there again . . . the sun was still shining golden above the towers of Przemysl on the River San, and the blond fellow was stirring. It was obvious he had only been pretending to be asleep. Now he was pretending to wake up. He stretched his limbs very deliberately, turned over, and opened his eyes, but he didn't know that the traces of tears in his grimy face were still plainly visible. There were proper furrows, furrows in the grime as on the face of a very little girl who has had her sandwich pinched on the playground. He didn't know this, maybe he had even forgotten that he had been crying. His eyes were red-rimmed and unsightly; he really did look as if he might have venereal disease. . . .

"Aaah," he yawned, "I'm glad there's some grub." His beer had got a bit tepid, but he gulped it down thirstily and began to eat while the other two smoked and very slowly, without the least hurry, drank vodka, crystal-clear, wonderful vodka unpacked by Willi.

"Yes," laughed Willi, but he broke off so abruptly that the other two looked at him in alarm; Willi blushed, looked at the ground, and took a big gulp of vodka.

"What was that?" Andreas asked quietly. "What were you going to say?"

Willi spoke in a very low voice. "I was going to say that I'm now drinking up our mortgage, literally our mortgage. You see, there was a mortgage on the house my wife owned when we got married, a small one of four thousand, and I had been meaning to pay it off now ... but come on, let's drink, prost!"

The blond fellow also didn't feel like going into town to some barber, or to a washroom in one of those army huts. They tucked towels and soap under their arms, and off they went.

"And make sure your boots are nice and clean too, boys!" Willi called after them. His own boots were indeed shining with fresh polish.

Somewhere down at the end of a track there was a big water pump for the locomotives. It dripped constantly, slowly; a steady trickle of water flowed from it, and the sand all around was one large puddle. It was true, it did feel good to have a wash. If only the soap would lather properly. Andreas took his shaving soap. I shan't be needing it any more, he thought. Although it's enough for three months, of course, and it was only "issued" to me a month ago, but I shan't be needing it any more, and the partisans can have what's left. The partisans need soap too, Poles love shaving. Shaving and shoeshining are their specialties. But just as they were about to start shaving, they saw Willi in the distance calling and waving, and his gestures were so emphatic, so dramatic you might say, that they packed up their things and dried themselves off as they ran back.

"Boys!" called Willi. "There's a leave-train for Kovel just come in, it's running late, we'll be in Lvov in four hours, you can get a shave in Lvov...." They slipped their tunics and coats back on again, put on their caps, and carried their luggage over to the platform where the delayed train for Kovel was standing. Not many got out at Przemysl, but Willi found a compartment from which a whole group of Panzer soldiers emerged, young fellows, boys in new uniforms that filled the air with the smell of army stores. A whole corridor became empty, and they quickly boarded the train before the ones who had stayed on it had a chance to spread themselves out with their luggage.

"Four o'clock!" cried Willi triumphantly. "That means we'll be in Lvov by ten at the very latest. That's great. Couldn't have made better time, this glorious delayed train! A whole night to ourselves, a whole night!"

They quickly installed themselves in such a way that they could at least sit back to back.

As he sat there Andreas finally managed to dry his wet ears properly; then he took everything out of his pack and neatly rearranged all the things he had hastily stuffed into it. Now there were a soiled shirt and soiled underpants and a pair of clean socks, the remains of the sausage, the remains of the butter in its container. Monday's sausage and half Monday's butter and Sunday's and Monday's candy, and cigarettes, to which he was even entitled, and even some bread left over from Sunday noon; and his prayer book, he had lugged his prayer book around all through the war and never used it. He always said his prayers just as they came to him, but he could never go on a trip without it. How strange, he thought, how strange it all is, and he lit a cigarette, one to which he was still entitled, a Saturday's cigarette, for the ration period from Friday noon to Saturday noon. . . .

The blond fellow was playing his mouth organ, and the two of them smoked in silence while the train got under way. The blond fellow was playing properly now, improvising, it seemed; soft, moving, amorphous forms that made you think of swampland.

That's it, thought Andreas, the Sivash marshes, I wonder what they're doing there now beside their cannon. He shuddered. Maybe they've killed each other off, maybe they've finished off the sergeant major, maybe they've been relieved. Let's hope they've been relieved. Tonight I'll say a prayer for the men beside the cannon in the Sivash marshes, and also for the man who fell for Greater Germany because he didn't want, because he didn't want ... to get that way; that's truly a hero's death. His bones are lying somewhere up there in a marsh in the Crimea, no one knows where his grave is, no one's going to dig him up and take him to a heroes' cemetery, no one's ever going to think of it again, and one day he'll rise again, way up there out of the Sivash marshes, the father of two kids with a wife living in Germany, and the local Nazi leader, with a terribly sad expression, took her the letter, in Bremen or in Cologne, or in Leverkusen, maybe his wife lives in Leverkusen. He will rise again, way up there out of the Sivash marshes, and it will be revealed that he did not fall for Greater Germany at all, nor because he mutinied and attacked the sergeant major, but because he didn't want to get that way.

They were both startled when the blond fellow abruptly broke off playing; they had been swathed, wreathed about, in those soft gentle misty melodies, and now the web was torn. "Look," said the blond fellow, pointing to the arm of a soldier standing by the window and smoking a pipe, "that's what we used to make back home. Funny thing, you see so few of them, yet we used to make thousands." They didn't know what he was talking about. The blond fellow looked confused, and he blushed as he faced their puzzled eyes. "Crimea badges," he said impatiently. "We used to make lots of Crimea badges. Now they're making Kuban badges, they'll soon be handing those out. We used to make the medals for blowing up tanks too, and years ago the Sudeten medals with the tiny shield showing Hradshin Castle. In 'thirty-eight." They continued to look at him as if he were talking Greek, their eyes were still puzzled, and he reddened still further.

"For God's sake," he almost shouted, "we had a factory back home!"

"Oh," said the two others.

"Yes, a patriotic-flag factory."

"A flag factory?" Willi asked.

"Yes, that's what they called it, of course we made flags too. Truckloads of flags, I'm telling you, years ago ... let's see ... in 'thirty-three, I think it was. Of course, that's when it must have been. But mostly we made medals and trophies and badges for clubs, you know the sort of thing, little shields saying: 'Club Champion 1934,' or some such thing. And badges for athletic clubs and swastika pins and those little enamel flags to pin on. Red-white-and-blue, or the French vertical blue-white-and-red. We exported a lot. But since the war we've only made for ourselves. Wound badges too, huge quantities of those. Black, silver, and gold. But black, huge quantities of black. We made a lot of money. And old medals from World War I, we made those too, and combat badges, and the little ribbons you wear with civilian dress. Yes ..." he sighed, broke off, glanced once more at the Crimea badge of the soldier who was leaning on the window and still smoking his pipe, and then he started to play again. Slowly, slowly the light bgean to fade ... and suddenly, without transition, twilight was there, welling up stronger and dark-er until evening swiftly came, and you could sense the cool night on the threshold. The blond fellow went on playing his swampy melodies that wafted dreamily into them like drugs ... Sivash, An-dreas thought, I must pray for the men beside the cannon in the Sivash marshes before I go to sleep. He realized he was begin-ning to doze off again, his last night but one. He prayed ... prayed ... but the words got mixed up, everything became blurred. ... Willie's wife in her red pajamas ... the eyes ... the smug little Frenchman ... the blond fellow, and the one who had said: Practically speaking, practically speaking we've already won the war.

This time he woke up because the train stopped for a long time. At a railway station it was different, you turned over with a yawn and could feel the impatience in the wheels, and you knew the train would soon be under way. But this time the train stopped for so long that the wheels seemed frozen to the rails. The train was at a standstill. Not at a station, not on a siding. Half-asleep, An-dreas groped his way to his feet and saw everyone crowding around the windows. He felt rather forlorn, all by himself like that in the dark corridor, especially since he couldn't spot Willi and the blond fellow right away. They must be up front by the windows. It was dark outside and cold, and he guessed it was at least one or two in the morning. He heard railroad cars rumbling past outside, and he heard soldiers singing in them ... their stale, stupid, fatuous songs that were so deeply buried in their guts that they had worn a groove like a tune in a record, and as soon as they opened their mouths they sang, sang those songs: Heidemarie and Jolly Huntsman .... He had sung them too sometimes, without knowing or wanting to, those songs that had been sunk into them, buried in them, drilled into them so as to kill their thoughts. These were the songs they were now shouting into the dark, somber, sorrowful Polish night, and it seemed to Andreas that far off, somewhere far away he would be able to hear an echo, beyond the somber invisible horizon, a mocking, diminutive, and very distinct echo ... Jolly Huntsman ... Jolly Huntsman ... Heidemarie. A lot of cars must have passed, then no more, and everyone left the windows and went back to their places. Including Willi and the blond fellow.

"The S.S.," said Willi. "They're being thrown in around Cherkassy. There's another pocket there or something. Pickpockets!"

"They'll manage it somehow," said a voice. . . .

Willi sat down beside Andreas and said it was two o'clock. "Shit, we'll miss the train at Lvov if we don't get moving right away. It's still another two hours. We'll have to leave Sunday morning. . . ."

"But we'll be starting up any minute," said the blond fellow, who was standing at the window again.

"Maybe," said Willi, "but then we won't have any time in Lvov. Half an hour is the craps for Lvov. Lvov!" He laughed.

"Me?" they suddenly heard the blond fellow call.

"Yes, you!" shouted a voice outside. "Get ready to take up your post." Grumbling, the blond fellow came back, and outside someone in a steel helmet stood on the step and stuck his face in through the train window. It was a heavy, thick skull, and they saw dark eyes and an official-looking forehead, the blond fellow having lit a match to find his belt and steel helmet.

"Any noncoms in there?" shouted the voice under the steel helmet. It was a voice that could only shout. No one spoke up. "Are there any noncoms in there, I said!"

No one spoke up. Willi gave Andreas a derisive nudge.

"Don't make me come and look for myself; if I find a noncom in there it's going to be tough for him!"

For a further second nobody spoke up, although Andreas could see that the place was swarming with noncoms. Suddenly someone quite near Andreas said: "Here!"

"Fast asleep, eh?" shouted the voice under the steel helmet.

"Yessir," said the voice, and Andreas now saw it was the man with the Crimea badge.

A few of the men laughed.

"What's your name?" shouted the voice under the steel helmet.

"Corporal Schneider."

"You'll be in charge for as long as we stop here, understand?"

"Yessir!"

"Good. You there—" he pointed to the blond fellow—"what's your name?"

"Private Siebental."

"Okay: Private Siebental will stand guard outside this car until four o'clock. If we're still here by then, have him relieved. Also, place a sentry outside the car on the other side and have him relieved too if necessary. There may be partisans in the area."

"Yessir!"

The face under the steel helmet vanished, muttering to itself: "Corporal Schneider."

Andreas was trembling. I hope to God I don't have to stand guard, he thought. I'm sitting right next to him, and he'll grab my sleeve and put me on duty. Corporal Schneider had switched on his flashlight and was shining it along the corridor. First he shone it on the collars of those who were lying down and pretending to be asleep, then he grabbed one of them by the collar, saying with a laugh: "Come on, take your gun and stand out there, and don't blame me!"

The one who had been picked swore as he got ready. I hope to God they don't find out I've no rifle, no weapon at all, that my rifle's standing propped up in Paul's closet behind his raincoat. What's Paul going to do with the rifle anyway? A chaplain with a rifle, the Gestapo'll just love that. He can't report it, because then he'd have to give my name and he would worry that they might write to my platoon. How awful that on top of everything else I had to leave my rifle behind at Paul's. . . .

"Come on, man, it's only till we get going again," said the corporal to the soldier who was cursing as he groped his way to the door and flung it open. It seemed strange that the train didn't move on; a quarter of an hour passed, they were too tense to sleep. Maybe there really were partisans in the area, and it was no joke being attacked in a train. Maybe it would be the same tomorrow night. Strange . . . strange. Maybe that's how it would be between Lvov and . . . no, not even Kolomyya. Twenty-four hours to go, twenty-four or at most twenty-six. It's already Saturday, it's actually Saturday. How utterly thoughtless I've been . . . I've known since Wednesday . . . and I've done nothing, I know it with absolute certainty, and I've hardly prayed any more than usual. I played cards. I drank. I ate and really enjoyed my food, and I slept. I slept too much, and time has leaped forward, time always leaps forward, and now here I am only twenty-four hours away from it. I've done nothing: after all, when you know you're going to die you have all kinds of things to settle, to regret, prayers to say, many prayers to say, and I've prayed hardly any more than I usually do. And yet I know for sure. I know for sure. Saturday morning. Sunday morning. Literally one more day. I must pray, pray. . . .

"Got a drink? It's lousy cold out here." The blond fellow stuck his head in through the window, and under the steel helmet his effete grayhound-head looked terrible. Willi held the bottle to the man's mouth and let him have a long drink. He also held the bottle out to Andreas.

"No," said Andreas.

"There's a train coming." It was the blond fellow's voice again. Everyone dashed to the window. It was half an hour behind the first train, and it was another of those, another troop-train, with more songs, more Jolly Huntsman ... Jolly Huntsman and Heidemarie in that dark sorrowful Polish night.... Jolly Huntsman. A train like that took a long time to pass ... with baggage car and cookhouse car and the cars for the soldiers, and all the time Jolly Huntsman and "Today it's Germany that's ours, tomorrow all the world ... all the world ... all the world...."

"More S. S. troops," said Willi, "and all going to Cherkassy. The crap there seems to be collapsing too." He said this in an undertone, since eager and optimistic voices next to him were saying they would manage it somehow.

Softly the Jolly Huntsman died away in the night, the song growing dim in the direction of Lvov, like a subdued, very soft whimpering, and once again there was the dark sorrowful Polish night....

"Let's hope there won't be another seventeen of these trains," muttered Willi. He offered Andreas the bottle again, but again Andreas refused. It's high time for me to say my prayers, he thought. This is the last night of my life but one, and I'm not going to spend it sleeping or napping. I'm not going to defile it with drink or waste it. I must say my prayers now, and above all repent. There's always so much to repent; even in an unhappy life like mine there are a lot of things to repent. That time in France when I drank a whole bottle of cherry brandy on a broiling hot day, like an animal; I keeled over like an animal, it nearly finished me. A whole bottle of cherry brandy when it was ninety in the shade, on a treeless street in some French hamlet. Because I was almost passing out with thirst and had nothing else to drink. It was ghastly, and it took me a week to get rid of my headache. And

I had a row with Paul, I always insulted him by calling him a bloody parson, I was always talking about bloody parsons. It's terrible, when you've got to die, to think you've insulted someone. I used to talk back to my teachers at school too, and I wrote Shit on the bust of Cicero; it was stupid, I was just a kid, but I knew it was wrong and silly, I did it anyway because I knew the other kids would laugh, that was the only reason I did it, because I wanted the others to laugh at a joke of mine. Out of vanity. Not because I really thought Cicero was shit; if I had done it for that reason it wouldn't have been as bad, but I did it for a joke. One should never do anything for a joke. And I used to make fun of Lieutenant Schreckmüller, of that sad, pale little fellow; the lieutenant's shoulder patches lay so heavily on his shoulders, so heavily, and you could tell he was marked for death. I used to make fun of him too, because I couldn't resist being known as a wit, as a sarcastic old trooper. That was worse than anything, maybe, and I don't know if God can forgive that. I made fun of him, of the way he looked like a Hitler Youth kid, and he was marked for death, I could tell from his face, and he was killed; he was shot down during the first attack in the Carpathians, and his body rolled down a slope, it was horrible the way it rolled down, and as the body rolled over it got covered with dirt; it was horrible, and to tell the truth it looked kind of ridiculous, that body rolling down, faster and faster, faster and faster, till it bounced onto the floor of the valley. . . .

And in Paris I abused a whore. In the middle of the night, that was awful. It was cold, and she accosted me . . . she practically assaulted me, and I could see from her fingers and the tip of her nose that she was chilled to the marrow, shivering with hunger. I felt quite sick when she said: "Come on, dearie," and I pushed her away, although she was shivering and ugly and all alone on that great wide street, and she might have been glad if I had lain beside her in her pitiful bed and just warmed her up a bit. And I actually pushed her away into the gutter and spat out abuse after her. If I only knew what became of her that night. Perhaps she drowned herself in the Seine because she was too ugly to get a nibble from anyone that night, and the terrible part is that I wouldn't have treated her so badly if she had been pretty.... If she had been pretty I might not have been so disgusted by her profession and she wouldn't have been pushed into the gutter and I might have been quite glad to warm up beside her and do some other things too. God knows what would have happened if she had been pretty. It's a terrible thing to maltreat a person because that person seems ugly to you. There are no ugly people. That poor soul. God forgive me twenty-four hours before my death for having pushed away that poor, ugly, shivering whore, at night, on that wide empty Paris street where there wasn't one single customer left for her, no one but me. God forgive me for everything, you can't undo what's done, nothing can ever be undone, and the pathetic whimpering of that poor girl will haunt that Paris street for ever and ever and accuse me, and the wretched doglike eyes of that Lieutenant Schreckmüller whose childish shoulders were not nearly strong enough for the weight of his shoulder patches....

If I could only cry. I can't even cry over all these things. I feel heartsick and contrite and terrible, but I can't cry over them. Everyone else can cry, even the blond fellow, everyone but me. God grant me the power to cry....

There must be a lot of other things I can't think of right now. That can't be all by a long way. There were the people I despised and loathed and mentally abused, for instance, like the man who said: Practically speaking, practically speaking we've already won the war; I hated that man too, but I forced myself to pray for him because he was such a fool. I still have to pray for the one who just said: They'll manage it somehow, and for all the ones who sang the Jolly Huntsman with such gusto.

I hated the lot of them, all those fellows who just went by in the train singing the Jolly Huntsman ... and Heidemarie ... and ... A Soldier's Life is a Splendid Life ... and ... Today it's Germany that's ours, tomorrow all the world. I hated the lot of them, the whole lot, all those fellows who lay squashed up against me in the train and in barracks. God, those barracks. . . .

"That's it!" shouted a voice outside. "Everyone back on the train!" The blond fellow got on and the man from the other side, and the train whistled and moved off. "Thank God for that," said Willi. But it was too late anyway. It was three-thirty, and it would take them at least another two hours to get to Lvov, and the courier train, the civilian express from Warsaw to Bucharest, left at five.

"So much the better," said Willi. "That gives us a whole day in Lvov." He laughed again. He wanted so badly to tell them some more about Lvov. You could hear it in his voice, but nobody reacted, nobody asked him to go on. They were tired, it was three-thirty and cold, and the dark Polish sky hung over them, and those two battalions or regiments that were being thrown into the Cherkassy pocket had set them thinking. No one spoke, although none of them were asleep. Only the rattle of the train lulled them to sleep, killed their thoughts, sucked the thinking out of their heads, that regular clickety-clack, clickety-clack, it put them to sleep. They were all poor, gray, hungry, misguided, and deluded children, and their cradle was the trains, the leave-trains that went clickety-clack and lulled them to sleep.

The blond fellow seemed to be genuinely asleep now. He had got very cold outside, and the fug here in the corridor must have actually seemed quite warm and put him to sleep. Only Willi was awake, Willi who had once been the soldier in need of a shave. From time to time he could be heard reaching for his bottle of vodka and gulping the stuff down, swearing at intervals under his breath, and from time to time he would strike a match and smoke, and then he would light up Andreas' face and see that he was wide awake. But he said nothing. And it was odd that he should say nothing. . . .

Andreas wanted to pray, he wanted desperately to pray; first, all the prayers he had always said, and then a few more of his own, and then he wanted to say over the names, to begin to say over the names, of all the people he had to pray for, but then he thought that was crazy, to say all those names. You would have to include everybody, the whole world. You would have to say two billion names ... forty million, he thought ... no, two billion names it would have to be. You'd simply have to say: Everyone. But that wasn't enough, he had at least to begin to say the names of the people he had to pray for. First the ones you had hurt, the ones you were indebted to. He began with his school, then with the labor service, then the barracks and the war and all the people whose names occurred to him along the way. His uncle, he had hated him too because he had always spoken so glowingly of the army, of the happiest days of his life. He thought about his parents, whom he had never known. Paul. Paul would be getting up soon and saying mass. It will be the third he's said since I left, thought Andreas, perhaps he understood when I called out: I'm going to die ... soon. Perhaps Paul understood and will say a mass for me Sunday morning, an hour before or after I've died. I hope Paul thinks about the others, about the soldiers who are like the blond fellow, and the ones who are like Willi, and the ones who say: Practically speaking, practically speaking we've already won the war, and the ones who day and night sing Jolly Huntsman and Heidemarie, and A Soldier's Life is a Splendid Life, and Oh, the Sun of Mexico. On this cold, miserable morning under the dark sorrowful Galician sky, he didn't think of the eyes at all. Now we must be in Galicia, he thought, quite close to Lvov, since Lvov is the capital of Galicia. Now I must be just about in the center of the net where I'm going to be caught. There's only one more province: Galicia, and I'm in Galicia. As long as I live I shall never see anything but Galicia. It has narrowed down very much, that Soon. To twenty-four hours and a few miles. Not many miles now to Lvov, maybe forty, and beyond Lvov at most another forty. My life's already been narrowed down to eighty miles in Galicia, in Galicia ... like a knife on invisible snake's feet, a knife creeping along, softly creeping along, a softly creeping knife. Galicia. How

will it happen, I wonder? Will I be shot or stabbed . . . or tram-
pled to death . . . or will I be simply crushed to death in a crushed
railway car? There are such an infinite number of ways to die. You
can also be shot by a sergeant major for refusing to do what the
blond fellow did; you can die any way you like, and the letter will
always say: He fell for Greater Germany. And I must be sure and
pray for the men with the cannon down there in the Sivash
marshes . . . must be sure . . . must be sure . . . clickety-clack . . .
must be sure . . . clickety-clack . . . must be sure men with cannon
. . . in the Sivash marshes . . . clickety-clack. . . .

It was terrible to find he had finally fallen asleep after all. And
now they were in Lvov. It was a big station, black iron girders and
grimy white signboards, and there it was, in black and white, between the platforms: Lvov. This was the springboard. It was almost incredible how quickly you could get from the Rhine to
Lvov. Lvov, there it was in black and white, irrevocably: Lvov.
Capital of Galicia. Another forty miles less. The net was quite
small now. Forty miles, maybe even less, maybe only five. Beyond
Lvov, between Lvov and Cernauti, that could mean a mile beyond
Lvov. Again this was as elastic as the Soon that he thought he had
managed to narrow down. . . .

"Boy, can you ever sleep!" said Willi, now cheerfully collecting
his belongings. "Can you ever sleep! I never saw anything like it.
The train stopped twice. You nearly had to do sentry duty, but I
told the corporal you were sick and he let you go on sleeping.
Time to get up!" The car was empty, and the blond fellow was already standing outside with his Luftwaffe rucksack and his suitcase.

It felt very odd to be walking along a platform in the main station of Lvov. . . .

It was eleven o'clock, almost midday, and Andreas felt famished.
But the thought of the sausage disgusted him. Butter and bread
and something hot! It's ages since I had a hot meal, I'd like some-

thing hot to eat. Funny, he thought, as he followed Willi and the blond fellow, my first thought in Lvov is that I'd like a hot meal. Fourteen or fifteen hours before your death you feel you've got to have a hot meal. He laughed, and this made the other two turn around and look at him in surprise, but he avoided their eyes and blushed. There was the barrier, there stood a sentry in a steel helmet, as at every station in Europe, and the sentry said to Andreas, because he was the last of the three: "Waiting-room to the left, for the use of enlisted men too."

Once past the barrier Willi became almost aggressive. There he stood, in the middle of the station, lighted a cigarette, and mimicked in a loud voice: "Waiting-room for the use of enlisted men to the left! That's what they'd like, to herd us cattle into the barn they've fixed up for us." They looked at him in alarm, but he laughed. "Just leave it to me, boys. Lvov's right up my alley. Waiting-room for the use of enlisted men! There are bars in this place, restaurants," he clicked his tongue, "as good as any in Europe," and he repeated sarcastically, "as any in Europe."

His face was already beginning to look somewhat unshaven again, he seemed to have a tremendously strong growth of beard. It was the same face as before, very sad and desperate.

Without a word he preceded the others through the exit, crossed, still without a word, a big crowded square, and very quickly they found themselves in a dark narrow side street; a car was standing at the corner, a ramshackle old taxi, and, as in a dream, it turned out Willi knew the driver. "Stani," he shouted, and again as in a dream a sleepy-eyed, grubby old Pole hoisted himself in the driver's seat and recognized Willi with a grin. Willi mentioned some Polish name, and the next moment they were sitting in the taxi with their luggage, driving through Lvov. The streets were the same as in any big city anywhere in the world. Wide, elegant streets, streets that had seen better days, sad streets with faded yellow façades and looking dead and deserted. People, people, and Stani drove very fast...as in a dream: all Lvov seemed to belong to Willi. They drove along a very wide avenue, an avenue like anywhere else in the world yet definitely a Polish avenue, and Stani came to a stop. He was given a bill, fifty marks as Andreas saw, and with a grin Stani helped them set their luggage on the sidewalk; it was all done in a few seconds, and in another few seconds they found themselves striding through a neglected front garden and entering a very long, musty hallway of a house whose façade seemed to be crumbling away. A house dating from the days of the old Hapsburg Empire. Andreas instantly recognized its aura of former Austrian Imperial grandeur; perhaps a high-ranking officer had lived here, long ago in the days of the waltz, or a senior civil servant. This was an old Austrian mansion, they could be found everywhere, all through the Balkans, in Hungary and Yugoslavia, and of course in Galicia too. All this flashed through his mind in the brief second it took to enter the long, dark, musty hallway.

But then with a happy smile Willi opened a soiled white door, very high and wide, and there was a restaurant with comfortable chairs, and attractively set tables with flowers on them, autumn flowers, thought Andreas, the kind you see on graves, and he thought: This will be my last meal before my execution. Willi led them over to an alcove that could be curtained off, and there were more comfortable chairs and an attractively set table, and it was all like a dream. Wasn't I standing a minute ago under a signboard with letters on it in black and white: Lvov?

Waiter! A smart Polish waiter wearing shiny shoes, shaved to perfection and grinning, only his jacket was a bit soiled. They all grin here, thought Andreas. The waiter's jacket was a bit soiled, but never mind, his shoes were like a grand duke's and he was shaved like a god . . . highly polished black shoes. . . .

"Georg," said Willi, "these gentlemen would like a wash and a shave." It sounded like an order. No, it was an order. Andreas had to laugh as he followed the grinning waiter. He felt as if he had been invited to the home of a genteel grandmother or a genteel uncle, and Uncle had said: Unshaven or unwashed children may not come to table. . . .

The washroom was spacious, clean. Georg brought hot water. "Perhaps the gentlemen would like some toilet soap, excellent quality, fifteen marks." "Bring it," said Andreas with a laugh, "Papa will pay for everything."

Georg brought the soap and repeated with a grin: "Papa will pay." The blond fellow had a wash too; they stripped to the waist, soaped themselves, dried themselves voluptuously, their arms and all over their yellowish-white, unaired soldiers' skin. It's lucky I brought along my socks, thought Andreas, I'll wash my feet too, and I can put on my clean socks.

Socks must be very expensive here, and why should I leave the socks in my pack? I'm sure the partisans have socks. He washed his feet and laughed at the blond fellow, who looked very astonished. The blond fellow really was in a daze.

It feels great to have a smooth chin again, as smooth as a Pole's, and I'm only sorry that tomorrow morning I'll have stubble on it again, thought Andreas. The blond fellow did not need to shave, he had only a trace of down on his upper lip. Andreas wondered for the first time how old the blond fellow might be, as he drew on his nice clean shirt, with a proper civilian collar so he could leave off that stupid army neckband; a blue shirt that had once been quite dark but was now sky-blue. He buttoned it up and drew on his tunic, his shabby gray tunic with the wound badge. Perhaps the badge was made in this fellow's patriotic-flag factory, he thought. Oh yes, he had meant to figure out the blond fellow's age. He has no beard, of course, but Paul had no beard either, and Paul is twenty-six. This fellow might be seventeen or he might be forty, he has a strange face, I expect he's twenty. Besides, he's already a private first class, he must have been serving for more than a year or almost two. Twenty—twenty-one, Andreas figured. All right. Tunic on, collar done up, it really felt great to be clean.

No thanks, they could find their way back to the alcove alone. By this time a few officers, whom they had to salute, were sitting in the restaurant. That was awful, having to salute, saluting was terrible, and it was a relief to be back in the shelter of the alcove.

"That's how I like to see you, boys," said Willi. Willi was drinking wine and smoking a cigar. The table had already been set with various plates, forks, knives, and spoons.

Georg waited on them silently. First came a soup. Bouillon, Andreas thought. He prayed softly, a long prayer; the others had already begun their soup, and he was still praying, and it was odd that they did not comment.

After the soup came some sort of potato salad, just a tiny portion. With it an aperitif. Like in France. Then came a series of meat dishes. First some meat patties . . . then something very peculiar-looking. "And what is this?" Willi asked majestically, but he laughed as he said it.

"That?" Georg grinned. "That's pork heart . . . very good pork heart. . . ." Then came a cutlet, a good juicy cutlet. A real "last meal," thought Andreas, just right for a condemned man, and he was shocked to find how good it all tasted. It's disgraceful, he thought. I ought to be praying, praying, spending the whole day somewhere on my knees, and here I am eating pork heart. . . . It's disgraceful. Next came vegetables, the first vegetables, peas. Then finally some potatoes. And then more meat, something resembling a goulash, a very tasty goulash. More vegetables, and a salad. Finally something green. And wine with everything; Willi poured, very majestically, laughing as he did so.

"We'll blow the whole mortgage today, long live the Lvov mortgage!" They drank a toast to the Lvov mortgage.

A whole series of desserts. Like in France, Andreas thought. First some creamy pudding, with real eggs in it. Then a piece of cake with hot vanilla sauce. With this they had more wine, poured by Willi, a very sweet wine. Then came something very small, a tiny object lying on a white plate. It was something with chocolate icing, puff pastry with chocolate icing and cream inside, real cream. Pity it's so small, thought Andreas. No one said a word, the blond fellow was still in a daze, it was frightening to see his face, he kept his mouth open and chewed and ate and drank. And finally there actually came some cheese. Why damn it all, exactly like in France, cheese and bread, and that was it. Cheese closes the stomach, thought Andreas; they drank white wine with it, white wine from France ... Sauternes. ...

My God, hadn't he drunk Sauternes in Le Treport on a terrace overlooking the sea, Sauternes, delicious as milk, fire, and honey, Sauternes in Le Treport on a terrace overlooking the sea on a summer evening, and hadn't those beloved eyes been with him that evening, almost as close as all those years ago in Amiens? Sauternes in Le Treport. It was the same wine. He had a good memory for tastes. Sauternes in Le Treport, and she had been close to him with mouth and hair and her eyes, the wine makes all this possible, and it's good to eat bread and cheese with white wine. ...

"Well, boys," said Willi, in the best of spirits, "did you enjoy your meal?" Yes, they had really enjoyed it, they felt very content.

They had not overeaten. You must drink wine with your meal, it's wonderful. Andreas prayed ... you must say grace after a meal, and he prayed for a long time—while the others leaned back in their chairs and smoked, Andreas propped his elbows on the table and prayed. ...

Life is beautiful, he thought, it was beautiful. Twelve hours before my death I have to find out that life is beautiful, and it's too late. I've been ungrateful, I've denied the existence of human happiness. And life was beautiful. He turned red with humiliation, red with fear, red with remorse. I really did deny the existence of human happiness, and life was beautiful. I've had an unhappy life ... a wasted life as they say, I've suffered every instant from this ghastly uniform, and they've nattered my ears off, and they made me shed blood on their battlefields, real blood it was, three times I was wounded on the field of so-called honor, outside Amiens, and down at Tiraspol, and then in Nikopol, and I've seen nothing but dirt and blood and shit and smelled nothing but filth ... and misery ... heard nothing but obscenities, and for a mere tenth of a second I was allowed to know true human love, the love of man and woman, which surely must be beautiful, for a mere tenth of a second, and twelve hours or eleven hours before my death I have to find out that life was beautiful. I drank Sauternes . . . on a terrace above Le Treport by the sea, and in Cayeux, in Cayeux I also drank Sauternes, also on a summer evening, and my beloved was with me . . . and in Paris I used to spend hours at those sidewalk cafés soaking up some other glorious golden wine. I know for sure my beloved was with me, and I didn't need to comb through forty million people to find happiness. I thought I had forgotten nothing, I had forgotten everything . . . everything . . . and this meal was wonderful. . . . And the pork heart and the cheese, and the wine that gave me the power to remember that life is beautiful . . . twelve hours, or eleven hours, to go. . . .

Last of all he thought once more about the Jews of Cernauti, then he remembered the Jews of Lvov, and the Jews of Stanislav and Kolomyya, the cannon down there in the Sivash marshes. And the man who had said: Those are precisely the advantages of the 37 antitank weapon. . . . And that poor ugly shivering whore in Paris whom he had pushed away in the night. . . .

"Come on, mate, have another drink!" said Willi roughly, and Andreas raised his head and drank. There was still some wine left, the bottle was standing in the ice bucket; he emptied his glass and Willi refilled it.

All this is happening in Lvov, everything I'm doing here, he thought, in a mansion of the old Hapsburg Empire, in an old dilapidated Imperial mansion, in one of the great rooms of this house where they used to entertain on a grand scale, give glamorous balls where they danced the waltz, at least—he counted under his breath—at least twenty-eight years ago, no, twenty-nine, twenty-nine years ago there was no war yet. Twenty-nine years ago all this was still Austria . . . then it was Poland . . . then it was Russia . . . and now, now it's all Greater Germany. They used to have balls . . . they danced the waltz, wonderful waltzes, and they would smile at one another and dance . . . and outdoors, in the big garden that must be behind the house, in that big garden they would kiss, the lieutenants and the girls . . . and maybe the majors and the wives, and the host, he must have been a colonel or a general and he pretended not to see what was going on ... or maybe he was a very senior civil servant or some such thing ... maybe. ...

"Come on, mate, have another drink!" Yes, he'd like some more wine ... time is running out, he thought, I wonder what time it is. It was eleven, or eleven-fifteen, when we left the station, by now it must be two or three o'clock ... twelve more hours, no, more than that. The train doesn't leave till five, and then I've got till ... soon. That Soon was all blurred again now. Forty miles beyond Lvov, it won't be more than that. Forty miles, that'll be an hour and a half by train, that would make it six-thirty, it'll be light by then. All of a sudden, just as he was raising his glass to his lips, he knew it would never be light again. Thirty miles ... an hour or three quarters of an hour before the first hint of dawn. No, it'll still be dark, there'll be no dawn! That's it! That's it exactly! Five forty-five, and tomorrow is already Sunday, and tomorrow Paul begins his new week, and all this week Paul has the six o'clock mass. I shall die as Paul is mounting the steps to the altar. That's absolutely certain, when he starts reciting the antiphons without an altar boy. He once told me that you can't count on altar boys nowadays. When Paul is reciting the antiphons between Lvov and ... he must look and see which place is thirty miles beyond Lvov. He must get hold of the map. He glanced up and saw that the blond fellow was still dozing in his chair; he was tired, he had had sentry duty. Willi was awake and smiling happily, Willi was drunk, and the map was in the other man's pocket. But there was plenty of time. More than twelve hours, fifteen hours to go ... in these fifteen hours he had to see to a lot of things. Say my prayers, say my prayers, no more sleep ... whatever happened, no more sleep, and I'm glad I'm so sure now. Willi also knows he's going to die, and the blond fellow is ready to die too, their lives are over; it will soon be full, the hourglass is nearly full, and death has only a few, a very few, more grains of sand to add.

"Well, boys," said Willi, "sorry, but it's time we were moving. Nice here, wasn't it?" He nudged the blond fellow, who woke up.

He was still dreaming, his face was all dreams, and his eyes no longer had that nasty slimy look; there was something childlike about them, and that might have been because he had had a real dream, had been genuinely happy. Happiness washes away many things, just as suffering washes away many things.

"Because now," said Willi, "now we have to go to the rubber-stamp place. But I'm not giving anything away yet!" He was rather hurt that nobody asked him; he beckoned to Georg and paid something over four hundred marks. The tip was a princely one. "And a taxi," said Willi. They picked up their luggage, buckled their belts, put on their caps, and went out past the officers, past the civilians, and past the ones in the brown uniforms. And there was much amazement in the eyes of the officers and of the ones in the brown uniforms. And it was just like in every bar in Europe, in French bars, Hungarian, Rumanian, Russian, and Yugoslav bars, and Czech and Dutch and Belgian and Norwegian and Italian and Luxembourg bars: the same buckling of belts and putting on of caps and saluting at the door, as if one were leaving a temple inhabited by very stern gods.

And they left the Imperial mansion, the Imperial driveway, and Andreas cast one more glance at that crumbling façade, the waltz façade, before they got into the taxi . . . and were off.

"Now," said Willi, "now we're going to the rubber-stamp place, they open at five."

"May I have another look at the map?" Andreas asked the blond fellow, but before the latter could pull the map out of his Luftwaffe pack they were stopping again. They had driven only a short distance along the wide brooding Imperial avenue. Beyond lay open country and a few villas, and the house they had stopped at was a Polish house. The roof was flattish, the façade a dirty yellow, and the narrow tall windows were closed with shutters reminiscent of France, shutters with very narrow slits, very flimsy-looking, painted gray. It was a Polish house, this rubber-stamp place, and something told Andreas immediately that it was a brothel. The whole ground floor was hidden by a thick beech hedge, and as they walked through the front garden he saw that the ground-floor windows were not shuttered. . . .

He saw russet-colored curtains, dirty russet-colored, almost dark brown with a touch of red. "You can get any stamp in the world here," said Willi with a laugh. "You just have to know the ropes and be firm." They stood with their luggage outside the front door after Willi had pulled the bell, and it was some time before they heard any sound in the silent, mysterious house. Andreas was sure they were being watched. They were watched for a long time, so long that Willi began to get uneasy. "Damn it all," he said peevishly, "they don't have to hide anything from me. They hide everything suspicious, see, when someone they don't know comes to the door." But at that moment the door opened, and an oldish woman came toward Willi with outstretched arms and a fulsome smile.

"I almost didn't recognize you," she said in welcoming tones. "Come in! And these," she said, indicating Andreas and the other man, "these are two young friends of yours," she shook her head disapprovingly, "two very, very young friends for our house."

All three men went inside and set down their luggage in an alcove in the hall.

"We need our passes stamped for the train tomorrow morning at five, the courier train, you know the one I mean."

The woman looked doubtfully at the two younger men. She was a bit nervous. Her graying hair was a wig, you could tell. Her narrow, sharp-featured face with the gray, indeterminate eyes was made up, very discreetly made up. She was wearing a smart dress patterned in red and black, closed at the neck so as not to show her skin, that faded neck-skin, like the skin of a fowl She ought to wear a high closed collar, Andreas thought, a general's collar.

"Very well," said the woman, with some hesitation, "and . . . anything else?"

"Maybe a drink, and I'd like a girl, how about you fellows?"

"No," said Andreas, "no girl."

The blond fellow flushed and was sweating with fear. It must be terrible for him, Andreas thought, maybe it would help him to have a girl.

Suddenly Andreas heard music. It was a snatch of music, the merest shred. Somewhere a door had been opened to a room where there must be a radio, and in the half-second that the door was open he heard a few snatches of music, like someone searching along a radio panel for the right station ... jazz ... marching songs ... a resounding voice and a bit of Schubert ... Schubert ... Schubert.... Now the door was shut again, but Andreas felt as if someone had thrust a knife into his heart and opened a secret floodgate: he turned pale, swayed, and leaned against the wall. Music ... a snatch of Schubert ... I'd give ten years of my life to hear a whole Schubert song again, but all I've got is twelve and three-quarter hours, it must be five o'clock by now.

"How about you," asked the oldish woman, whose mouth was horrible. He could see that now, it was a narrow, cramped slot of a mouth, a mouth that was only interested in money, a moneybox mouth. "How about you," asked the woman, alarmed, "don't you want anything?"

"Music," stammered Andreas, "do you sell music here too?" She looked at him in bewilderment, hesitated. No doubt there was nothing she had not sold. Rubber stamps and girls and pistols— that mouth was a mouth that dealt in everything, but she didn't know whether it was possible to sell music.

"I ..." she said, embarrassed, "music ... but of course." It's always a good idea to start with yes. You can always say no later. If you say no right off, your chances of doing business are nil.

Andreas had straightened up again. "Will you sell me some music?"

"Not without a girl," smiled the woman.

Andreas threw Willi an agonized look. He didn't know what it

would cost. Music *and* a girl, and strangely enough Willi understood that look at once. "Remember the mortgage, my lad," he
cried, "long live the Lvov mortgage! It's all ours!"

"All right," Andreas said to the woman, "I'll take some music
and a girl." The door was opened by three girls who stood laughing in the hall, they had been listening to the negotiations, two
were brunettes and one was a redhead. The redhead, who had recognized Willi and flung her arms around his neck, called out to
the oldish woman: "Why don't you sell him the 'opera singer'?"
The two brunettes laughed, and one of them appropriated the
blond fellow and laid a hand on his arm. He gave a sob at her
touch, buckled at the knees like a straw, and the brunette had to
grab him and hold on to him, whispering: "Don't be scared,
dearie, there's no need to be scared!"

Actually it was a good thing the blond fellow was sobbing; Andreas wanted to weep too, the waters behind the floodgate were
pressing forward to where the wall had been pierced. At last I'll be
able to cry, but I'm not going to cry in front of this slot of a
mouth that's only interested in money. Maybe I'll cry when I'm
with the "opera singer."

"That's right," said the remaining brunette pertly. "If he wants
music, send him the opera singer." She turned away, and Andreas,
still leaning against the wall, could hear the door being opened
again, and again his ear caught a snatch of music, but it wasn't
Schubert . . . it was something by Liszt . . . Liszt was beautiful
too . . . and Liszt could make me cry, he thought, I haven't cried
for three and a half years.

The blond fellow was leaning against his brunette like a child,
his head resting on her breast; he was weeping, and this weeping
was good. No more Sivash marshes in these tears, no more terror,
and yet much pain, much pain. And the redhead, who had a good-
natured face, said to Willi, whose arm was clasped around her
waist: "Buy him the opera singer, he's a sweetie, I think he's a real
sweetie with his music." She blew Andreas a kiss: "He's young and

a real sweetie, you old rascal, and you must buy him the opera singer and a piano...."

"The mortgage, the whole Lvov mortgage is ours!" Willi shouted.

The oldish woman led Andreas up the stairs and along a corridor, past many closed doors, into a room furnished with some easy chairs, a couch, and a piano.

"This is a little bar for special occasions," she said. "The price is six hundred a night, and the opera singer—that's a nickname, of course—the opera singer costs two hundred and fifty a night, not including refreshments."

Andreas staggered over to one of the armchairs, nodded, waved her away, and was glad to see the woman go. He heard her call out in the corridor: "Olina . . . Olina. . . ."

I ought to have rented just the piano, thought Andreas, just the piano, but then he shuddered at the idea of being in this house at all. In despair he dashed to the window and flung back the curtain. Outside it was still light. Why this artificial darkness, it's the last day I'll ever see, why draw the curtains over it? The sun was still above a hill and shining with gentle warmth into gardens lying behind handsome villas, shining on the roofs of the villas. It's time they harvested the apples, Andreas thought, it's the end of September, the apples must be ripe here too. And in Cherkassy another pocket has been closed, and the pickpockets will manage it somehow. Everything's being managed, everything's being managed, and here I sit by a window in a brothel, in the "rubber-stamp house," with only twelve more hours to live, twelve and a half hours, and I ought to be praying, praying, on my knees, but I'm powerless against this floodgate that's been opened, pierced open by the dagger that was thrust into me downstairs in the hall: music. And it's just as well I'm not going to spend the whole night alone with this piano. I'd go crazy, a piano especially. A piano. It's a good thing Olina is coming, the "opera singer." The map! I forgot the map, he thought. I forgot to ask the blond fellow for it; I just have to know what lies thirty miles beyond Lvov . . . I just have to . . . it can't be Stanislav, not even Stanislav, I won't even get as far as Stanislav. Between Lvov and Cernauti . . . how certain I was at first about Cernauti! At first I would have been ready to bet I'd get to see Cernauti, a suburb of Cernauti . . . only another thirty miles now . . . another twelve hours. . . .

He swung round in alarm at a very soft sound, as of a cat slipping into the room. The opera singer was standing by the door, which she had closed softly behind her. She was small and very slight, with fine, delicate features, and her golden, very beautiful hair was tied loosely back on the crown of her head. There were red slippers on her feet, and she wore a pale-green dress. As soon as their eyes met her hand went to her shoulder, as though to undo her dress then and there. . . .

"No!" cried Andreas, and instantly regretted letting fly at her like that. I've already bawled out one of them, he thought, and I'll never be able to wipe that out. The opera singer looked at him less offended than surprised. The strange note of anguish in his voice had caught her ear. "No," said Andreas more gently, "don't."

He moved toward her, stepped back, sat down, stood up again, and added: "Is it all right to call you by your first name?"

"Yes," she said, very low. "My name is Olina."

"I know," he said. "Mine's Andreas."

She sat down in the armchair he gestured toward and gave him a puzzled, almost apprehensive look. He walked to the door and turned the key in the lock. Sitting beside her he studied her profile. She had a finely drawn nose, neither round nor pointed, a Fragonard nose, he thought, and a Fragonard mouth too. She looked wanton in a way, but she could just as easily be innocent, as innocently wanton as those Fragonard shepherdesses, but she had a Polish face, the nape of her neck was Polish, supple, elemental.

He was glad he had brought cigarettes. But he was out of matches. She quickly got up, opened a closet that was crammed with bottles and boxes, and took out some matches. Before handing them to him she wrote something down on a sheet of paper lying in the closet. "I have to note down everything," she said, her voice still low, "even these."

They smoked and looked out into the golden countryside with the gardens of Lvov behind the villas.

"You used to be an opera singer?" asked Andreas.

"No," she said, "they just call me that because I studied music. They think if you've studied music you must be an opera singer."

"So you can't sing?"

"Oh yes I can, but I didn't study singing, I just sing ... like that, you know."

"And what did you study?"

"The piano," she said quietly, "I wanted to be a pianist."

How strange, thought Andreas, I wanted to be a pianist too. A stab of pain constricted his heart. I wanted to be a pianist, it was the dream of my life. I could play quite nicely, really, quite well, but school hung around my neck like a leaden weight. School prevented me. First I had to finish school. Everyone in Germany first has to finish school. You can't do a thing without a high-school diploma. First I had to finish school, and by the time I'd done that it was 1939, and I had to join the labor service, and by the time I was through with that the war had started; that was four and a half years ago and I haven't touched a piano since. I wanted to be a pianist. I dreamed about it, just as much as other people dream of becoming school principals. But I wanted to be a pianist, and I loved the piano more than anything else in the world, but nothing came of it. First school, then labor service, and by that time they'd started a war, the bastards. ... The pain was suffocating him, and he had never felt as wretched in his life. It'll do me good to suffer. Perhaps that'll help me to be forgiven for sitting here in a brothel in Lvov beside the opera singer who costs two hundred and fifty for a whole night without matches and without piano, the piano that costs six hundred. Perhaps I'll be forgiven for all that because this pain is numbing me, paralyzing me, because she said the words "pianist" and "piano." It's excruciating, this pain, it's like

an acrid poison in my throat and it's sliding farther and farther
down, through my gullet and into my stomach and spreading all
through my body. Half an hour ago I was still happy because I'd
drunk Sauternes, because I remembered the terrace above Le Treport where the eyes had been very close to me, and where I played
the piano to them, to those eyes, in my imagination, and now I'm
consumed with agony, sitting in this brothel beside this lovely girl
whom the entire great-and-glorious German Wehrmacht would
envy me. And I'm glad I'm suffering, I'm glad I'm almost passing
out with pain, I'm happy to be suffering, suffering so excruciat-
ingly, because then I may hope to be forgiven everything, forgiven
for not praying, praying, praying, not spending my last twelve
hours on my knees praying. But where could I kneel? Nowhere on
earth could I kneel in peace. I'll tell Olina to keep watch at the
door, and I'll get Willi to pay six hundred marks for the piano, and
two hundred and fifty marks for the beautiful opera singer without
matches, and I'll buy Olina a bottle of wine so she won't get
bored. . . .

"What's the matter?" Olina asked. There was surprise in her
gentle voice since he had cried no.

He looked at her, and it was wonderful to see her eyes. Gray,
very gentle, sad eyes. He must give her an answer.

"Nothing," he said; and then suddenly he asked, and it was a
tremendous effort to force the few words out of his mouth
through the poison of his pain: "Did you finish your music studies?"

"No," she said shortly, and he saw it would be cruel to question
her. She tossed her cigarette into the large metal ashtray that she
had placed on the floor between their two armchairs, and asked,
her voice low and gentle again: "Shall I tell you about it?"

"Yes," he said, not daring to look at her, for those gray eyes,
that were perfectly calm, scared him.

"All right." But she did not begin. She was looking at the floor;
he was aware when she raised her head, then she asked suddenly:
"How old are you?"

"In February I would be twenty-four," he said quietly.

"In February you would be twenty-four. Would be ... won't you be?"

He looked at her, astonished. What a sensitive ear she had! And all at once he knew he would tell her about it, her alone. She was the only person who was to know everything, that he was going to die, tomorrow morning, just before six, or just after six, in. . . .

"Oh well," he said, "it's just a manner of speaking. What's the place called," he asked suddenly, "that lies thirty miles beyond Lvov toward ... toward Cernauti?"

Her astonishment was growing. "Stryy," she said.

Stryy? What a strange name, Andreas thought, I must have overlooked it on the map. For God's sake, I must pray for the Jews of Stryy too. Let's hope there are still some Jews in Stryy ... Stryy ... so that's where it will be, he would die just this side of Stryy ... not even Stanislav, not even Kolomyya, and a long long way this side of Cernauti. Stryy! That was it! Maybe it wasn't even on that map of Willi's. . . .

"So you'll be twenty-four in February," said Olina. "Funny, so will I." He looked at her. She smiled. "So will I," she repeated. "I was born February 12, 1920."

They looked at each other for a long time, a very long time, and their eyes sank into one another's, and then Olina leaned toward him, and because the chairs were too far apart she rose, moved toward him, and made as if to put her arms around him, but he turned aside. "No," he said quietly, "not that, don't be angry with me, later ... I'll explain.... My ... my birthday's February 15."

She lit another cigarette, he was glad he hadn't offended her. She was smiling. She was thinking, after all he's hired the room and me for the whole night. And it's only six o'clock, not even quite six. . . .

"You were going to tell me about it," said Andreas.

"Yes," she said. "We're the same age, I like that. I'm three days older than you. I expect I'm your sister. . . ." She laughed. "Maybe I really am your sister."

"Please tell me about it."

"I am," she said, "I am telling you. In Warsaw I studied at the Conservatory of Music. You wanted to hear about my studies, didn't you?"

"Yes!"

"Do you know Warsaw?"

"No."

"Well then. Here we go. Warsaw is a big city, a beautiful city, and the Conservatory was in a house like this one. Only the garden was bigger, much bigger. During recess we could stroll in that lovely big garden and flirt. They told me I was very talented. I took piano. I would rather have played only the harpsichord at first, but no one taught that, so I had to take piano. For my entrance test I had to play a short, simple little Beethoven sonata. That was tricky. It's so easy to make a mess of those simple little things, or one plays them too emotionally. It's very difficult to play those simple things. It was Beethoven, you know, but a very early Beethoven, almost classical in style, almost like Haydn. A very subtle piece for an entrance test, d'you see?"

"Yes," said Andreas, and he could sense that soon he was going to cry.

"Good. I passed, with Very Good. I studied and played till . . . let's see . . . till the war started. That's right, it was the fall of 'thirty-nine, two years; I learned a lot and flirted a lot. I always did like kissing and all that, you know. I could play Liszt quite well by that time, and Tchaikovsky. But I could never really play Bach properly. I would have liked to play Bach. And I could play Chopin quite well too. Fine. Then came the war. . . . Oh yes, and there was a garden behind the Conservatory, a wonderful garden, with benches and arbors, and sometimes we had parties, and there would be music and dancing in the garden. Once we had a Mozart evening, a wonderful Mozart evening. . . . Mozart was another one I could already play quite well. Well, then came the war!"

She broke off abruptly, and Andreas turned questioning eyes on her. She looked angry. The hair seemed to bristle above that Fragonard forehead.

"For God's sake," she burst out, "do what the others all do with me. This is ridiculous!"

"No," said Andreas, "you have to tell me."

"That," she said frowning, "is something you can't pay for."

"Yes I can," he said, "I'll pay in the same coin. I'll tell you my story too. Everything. . . ."

But she was silent. She stared at the floor and was silent. He studied her out of the corner of his eye and thought: she does look like a tart after all. There's sex in every fiber of that pretty face, and she's not an innocent shepherdess, she's a very wanton shepherdess. It gave him a pang to find that she was a tart after all. The dream had been very lovely. She might be standing anywhere in the Gare Montparnasse. And it did him good to feel that pain again. For a time it had completely gone. He loved listening to her gentle voice telling him about the Conservatory. . . .

"It's boring," she said suddenly. She spoke with complete indifference.

"Let's have some wine," said Andreas.

She rose, walked briskly to the closet, and in a businesslike voice asked: "What would you like to drink?" She looked into the closet: "There's some red wine and some white, Moselle, I think."

"All right," he said, "let's have some Moselle."

She brought over the bottle, pushed a little table up to their chairs, handed him the corkscrew, and set out glasses while he opened the bottle. He watched her, then poured the wine, they raised their glasses, and he smiled into her angry eyes.

"Let's drink to the year of our birth," he said, "1920."

She smiled against her will. "All right, but I'm not going to tell you any more."

"Shall I tell you my story?"

"No," she said. "All you fellows can talk about is the war. I've been listening to that for two years now. Always the war. As soon as you've finished . . . you begin talking about the war. It's boring."

"What would you like to do then?"

"I'd like to seduce you, you're a virgin, aren't you?"

"Yes," said Andreas, and was taken aback at the way she promptly jumped up. "I knew it," she cried, "I knew it!" He saw her eager, flushed face, the eyes flashing at him, and thought: Funny, I've never seen any woman I've desired less than this one, and she's beautiful, and I could have her right now. Oh yes, sometimes a thrill has gone through me, without my trying or wanting it, and for that split second I've known that it must be truly wonderful to possess a woman. But there's never been one I desired as little as this one. I'll tell her about it, I'll tell her everything. . . .

"Olina," he said, pointing to the piano, "Olina, play the little Beethoven sonata."

"Promise you'll . . . promise you'll make love to me."

"No," he said quietly. "Come and sit here." He made her sit beside him in the armchair, and she looked at him without saying a word.

"Now listen," he said, "I'm going to tell you my story."

He looked out of the window and saw that the sun had gone down and that only a very little light remained over the gardens. Very soon there would be no more sunlight outside in the gardens, and never again, never again would the sun shine, never again would he see a single ray of sunshine. The last night was beginning, and the last day had passed like all the others, wasted and meaningless. He had prayed a bit and drunk some wine and now he was in a brothel. He waited until it was dark. He had no idea how long it took, he had forgotten the girl, forgotten the wine, the whole house, and all he saw was a last little bit of the forest whose treetops caught a few final glints from the setting sun, a few tiny glints from the sun. Some reddish gleams, exquisite, indescribably beautiful on those treetops. A tiny crown of light, the last light he would ever see. Now it was gone . . . no, there was still a bit, a tiny little bit on the tallest of the trees, the one that reached up the highest and could still catch something of the golden reflection that would remain for only half a second ... until it was all gone. It's still there, he thought, holding his breath ... still a particle of light up there on the treetop ... an absurd little shimmer of sunlight, and no one in the world but me is watching it. Still there ... still there, it was like a smile that faded very slowly ... still there, and now it was gone! The light has gone out, the lantern has vanished, and I shall never see it again. ...

"Olina," he said softly, and he felt he could speak now, and he knew he would win her because it was dark. A woman can only be won in the dark. Funny, he thought, I wonder if that's really true? He had the feeling that Olina belonged to him now, had surrendered to him. "Olina," he said softly, "tomorrow morning I must die. That's right," he said calmly, looking at her shocked face, "don't be scared! Tomorrow morning I must die. You're the first and only person I've told. I am certain. I must die. A moment ago the sun went down. Just this side of Stryy I shall die. ..."

She jumped to her feet and looked at him in horror. "You're mad," she whispered, white-faced.

"No," he said, "I'm not mad, that's how it is, you must believe me. You must believe that I'm not mad, that tomorrow morning I shall die, and now you must play me the little Beethoven sonata."

She stared at him, aghast, and murmured: "But ... but that's impossible."

"I'm absolutely certain and you have told me the last thing I needed to know, Stryy, that's it. What a terrible name, Stryy. What kind of a word is that? Stryy? Why must I die just this side of Stryy? Why did it have first to be between Lvov and Cernauti ... then Kolomyya ... then Stanislav ... then Stryy. The moment you said Stryy I knew that was the place. Wait!" he called, as she rushed to the door and stood staring at him with terrified eyes.

"You must stay with me," he said, "you must stay with me. I'm a human being, and I can't stand it alone. Stay with me, Olina. I'm not mad. Don't scream." He held his hand over her mouth. "My God, what can I do to prove to you I'm not mad? What can I do? Tell me what I can do to prove to you I'm not mad?"

But she was too frightened to hear what he was saying. She merely stared at him with her terrified eyes, and all at once he realized what a dreadful profession she had. If he were really mad, she would now be standing there helpless. They send her to a room, and two hundred and fifty marks are paid for her because she is the "opera singer," a very valuable little doll, and she has to go to that room like a soldier going to the front. She has to go, even though she is the opera singer, a very valuable little doll. A terrible life. They send her to a room and she has no idea who is inside. An old man, a young one, an ugly man or a handsome one, bestial or innocent. She has no idea and goes to the room, and now there she is, frightened, just frightened, too frightened to hear what he is saying. It is truly a sin to go to a brothel, he thought. They send girls to a room, just like that. . . . He gently stroked the hand he was restraining her by, and strangely enough the fear in her eyes began to recede. He went on stroking it, and felt as if he were stroking a child. I've never desired a woman as little as this one. A child . . . and suddenly he saw that poor grubby little girl in a suburb of Berlin, playing among prefabs where there were some scrawny gardens, and the other kids had taken her doll and thrown it into a puddle . . . and then run away. And he had bent down and pulled the doll out of the puddle; it was dripping with dirty water, a dangling, frayed, cheap ragdoll, and he had to stroke the child for a long time and try and console her for her poor doll having got wet . . . a child. . . .

"You're all right now, aren't you?" he said. She nodded, and there were tears in her eyes. He led her gently back to the chair. The dusk had become heavy and sad.

She sat down obediently, keeping her still somewhat nervous gaze on him. He poured her some wine. She drank. Then she sighed deeply. "God, how you scared me," she said, and thirstily gulped down the rest of her wine.

"Olina," he said, "you're twenty-three now. Just ask yourself whether you're going to be twenty-five, will you?" he urged her. "Say to yourself: I am twenty-five years old. That's February 1945,

Olina. Try, think hard." She closed her eyes, and he saw from her lips that she was saying something under her breath that in Polish must mean: February 1945.

"No," she said, as if waking up, and she shook her head. "There's nothing there, as if it didn't exist—how odd."

"You see?" he said. "And when I think: Sunday noon, tomorrow noon, that doesn't exist for me. That's the way it is. I'm not mad." He saw her close her eyes again and say something under her breath. . . .

"It's odd," she said softly, "but February 1944 doesn't exist either. . . ."

"Oh for heaven's sake," she broke out, "why won't you make love? Why won't you dance with me?" She moved swiftly to the piano and sat down. And then she played: "I'm dancing with you into heaven, the seventh heaven of love. . . ."

Andreas smiled. "Come on, play the Beethoven sonata . . . play a. . . ."

But again she was playing: I'm dancing with you into heaven, the seventh heaven of love. She played it very softly, as softly as dusk was now sinking into the room through the open curtains. She played the sentimental tune unsentimentally, which was strange. The notes sounded crisp, almost staccato, very soft, almost as if suddenly she were turning this brothel piano into a harpsichord. Harpsichord, thought Andreas, that's the right instrument for her, she ought to play the harpsichord. . . .

The popular tune she was now playing was no longer the same, yet it was the same. What a lovely tune it is, thought Andreas. It's fantastic, what she can make of it. Perhaps she studied composition too, and she's turning this trivial tune into a sonata hovering in the dusk. Now and again, at intervals, she would play the original melody again, pure and clear, unsentimentally: I'm dancing with you into heaven, the seventh heaven of love. Now and again, between the gentle, playful waves, she allowed the theme to rear up like a granite cliff.

It was almost dark now, it was getting chilly, but he didn't care; the music sounded so beautiful that he wasn't going to get up and close the window; even if subzero air were to come in through the window from the gardens of Lvov, he wasn't going to get up. . . . Maybe I'm dreaming it's 1943 and I'm sitting here in a Lvov brothel wearing the gray tunic of Hitler's army; maybe I'm dreaming, maybe I was born in the seventeenth century or the eighteenth, and I'm sitting in my mistress's drawing-room, and she's playing the harpsichord, just for me, all the music in the world just for me . . . in a chateau somewhere in France, or a little schloss in western Germany, and I'm listening to the harpsichord in an eighteenth-century drawing-room, played by someone who loves me, who is playing just for me, just for me. The whole world is mine, here in the dusk; very soon the candles will be lit, we won't call a servant . . . no, no servant . . . I shall light the candles with a paper spill, and I shall light the paper spill with my pay-book from the fire in the hearth. No, there's no fire burning in the hearth. I shall light the fire myself, the air from the garden, from the grounds of the chateau, is damp and cool; I shall kneel by the hearth, tenderly place the kindling in layers, crumple each page of my paybook, and light the fire with the matches she noted down. Those matches will be paid for with the Lvov mortgage. I shall kneel at her feet, for she will be waiting with tender impatience for the fire to be lit in the hearth. Her feet have grown cold at the harpsichord; she has sat at the open window in this damp, cool air for a long, long time, playing for me, my sister, she has been playing so beautifully that I wouldn't get up to close the window . . . and I shall make a lovely bright fire, and we won't need any servants, no indeed, no servants! Just as well the door is locked. . . .

1943. A terrible century; what awful clothes the men will be wearing; they will glorify war and wear dirt-colored clothes in the war, while we never glorified war, war was an honest craft at which now and again a man got cheated of his rightful wages; and we wore cheerful clothes when we worked at this craft, just as a doctor wears cheerful clothes and a mayor . . . and a prostitute; but those people will be wearing horrible clothes and will glorify

war and fight wars for their national honor: a terrible century;
1943. . . .

We have all night, all night. Dusk has only just fallen in the
garden, the door is locked, and nothing can disturb us; the whole
chateau is ours; wine and candles and a harpsichord! Eight
hundred and fifty marks without the matches; millions lying
around Nikopol! Nikopol! Nothing! . . . Kishinev? Nothing! . . .
Cernauti? Nothing! . . . Kolomyya? Nothing! . . . Stanislav? Nothing! Stryy . . . Stryy . . . that terrible name that is like a streak, a
bloody streak across my throat! In Stryy I'm going to be murdered.
Every death is a murder, every death in war is a murder for which
someone is responsible. In Stryy!

I'm dancing with you into heaven, the seventh heaven of love!

It was not a dream at all, a dream ending with the last note of
that melodic paraphrase, it merely tore the frail web that had been
cast over him, and now for the first time, by the open window, in
the cool of the dusk, he realized he had been crying. He had neither known it nor felt it, but his face was wet, and Olina's hands,
soft and very small, were drying his face; the rivulets had run
down his face and collected in the closed collar of his tunic; she
undid the hook and dried his neck with her handkerchief. She
dried his cheeks and around his eyes, and he was grateful that she
said nothing. . . .

A strangely sober joy filled him. The girl switched on the light,
closed the window with averted face, and it was possible she had
been crying too. This chaste happiness is something I have never
known, he thought, as she crossed to the closet. I've always only
desired, I've desired an unknown body, and I've desired that soul
too, but here I desire nothing. . . . How strange that I have to find
this out in a Lvov brothel, on the last evening of my life, on the
threshold of the last night of my earthly existence that is to come
to an end tomorrow morning in Stryy with a bloody streak. . . .

"Lie down," said Olina. She indicated the little sofa, and he noticed that she had switched on an electric kettle in that mysterious
closet.

"I'll make some coffee," she said, "and until it's ready I'll go on with my story."

He lay down, and she sat beside him. They smoked, the ashtray lying conveniently on a stool so they could both reach it. He barely needed to stretch out his hand.

"I needn't tell you," she began quietly, "that you musn't ever speak to anyone about it. Even if you ... if you were not to die— you would never betray my secret. I know that. I had to swear by God and all the saints and by our beloved Poland that I would never tell a soul, but if I tell you it's as if I were telling myself, and I can't keep anything from you any more than I can keep anything from myself!" She stood up and poured the bubbling water very slowly and tenderly into a small coffeepot. Each time she paused for a few seconds she would smile at him before continuing to pour, very slowly, and now he could see she had been crying too. Then she filled the cups that were standing beside the ashtray.

"The war broke out in 1939. In Warsaw my parents were buried under the ruins of our big house, and there I was all alone in the garden of the Conservatory, where I had been flirting, and the director was taken away because he was a Jew. Well, I just didn't feel like going on with the piano. The Germans had somehow or other raped us all, every single one of us." She drank some coffee, he took a sip too. She smiled at him.

"It's funny that you're a German and I don't hate you." She fell silent again, smiling, and he thought, it's remarkable how quickly she's surrendered. When she went to the piano she wanted to seduce me, and the first time she played I'm dancing with you into heaven, the seventh heaven of love, it was still far from clear. While she was playing she cried. . . .

"All Poland," she went on, "is a resistance movement. You people have no idea. No one suspects how big it is. There is hardly a single unpatriotic Pole. When one of you Germans sells his pistol anywhere in Warsaw or Krakow, he should realize that in doing so he's selling as many of his comrades' lives as there is ammunition in that pistol. When anywhere, anywhere at all," she went on passionately, "a general or a lance-corporal sleeps with a girl and so much as tells her they didn't get any rations near Kiev or Kishinev or some such place, or that they retreated only two miles, he never suspects that this is jotted down, and that this gladdens the girl's heart more than the twenty or two hundred and fifty zlotys she's been paid for her seeming surrender. It's so easy to be a spy among you people that I soon got disgusted with it. All one had to do was get on with it. I don't understand it."

She shook her head and gave him a look almost of contempt.

"I don't understand it. You're the most garrulous people in the world, and sentimental down to your fingertips. Which army are you with?"

He told her the number.

"No," she said, "he was from a different one. A general who used to come and see me here sometimes. He talked like a sentimental schoolboy who's had a bit too much to drink. 'My boys,' he would groan, 'my poor boys!' And a little later on the old lecher would be babbling away to me about all kinds of things that were vitally important. He's got a lot of his poor boys on his conscience . . . and he told me a lot of things. And then . . . then," she hesitated, "then I'd be like ice. . . ."

"And were there some you loved?" asked Andreas. Funny, he thought, that it should hurt to know there were some she might have loved.

"Yes," she said, "there were some I really loved, not many." She looked at him, and he saw she was crying again. He took her hand, sat up, and poured coffee with his free hand.

"Soldiers," she said softly. "Yes. There were some soldiers I loved . . . and I knew it made no difference that they were Germans whom actually I ought to have hated. You know, when I gave myself to them I felt I was no longer part of the terrible game we're all playing, the game I had an especially big part in. The game of sending others to their death, men one didn't know. You see," she whispered, "some fellow, a lance-corporal or a general, tells me something here, and I pass on the information—machinery is set in motion, and somewhere men die because I passed on that information, do you see what I mean?" She looked at him out of frantic eyes. "Do you see what I mean? Or take yourself: you tell some fellow at the station: Take that train, bud, rather than that one—and that's the very train the partisans attack, and your buddy dies because you told him: Take that train. That's why it was so wonderful just to give oneself to them, just abandon oneself, and forget everything else. I asked them nothing for our mosaic and told them nothing, I had to love them. And what's so terrible is that afterwards they're always sad. . . ."

"Mosaic," asked Andreas huskily, "what's that?"

"The whole espionage system is a mosaic. Everything's assembled and numbered, every smallest scrap we get hold of, until the picture's complete . . . it slowly fills out . . . and many of these mosaics make up the whole picture . . . of you people . . . of your war . . . your army. . . ."

"You know," she went on, looking at him very seriously, "the terrible part is that it's all so senseless. Everywhere it's only the innocent who are murdered. Everywhere. By us too. Somehow I've always known that—" she looked away from him—"but, you know what frightens me is that I didn't grasp it fully till I walked into this room and saw you. Your shoulders, the back of your neck, there in the golden sunshine." She pointed to the window where the two chairs were.

"I know that now. When they sent me here, when Madame told me: 'There's someone waiting for you in the bar, I don't think you'll get much out of him but at least he pays well'—as soon as she said that I thought: I'll get something out of him all right. Or it's someone I can love. Not one of the victims, because there are only victims and executioners. And when I saw you standing over there by the window, your shoulders, the back of your neck, your stooping young figure as if you were thousands of years old, it came to me for the first time that we also only murder the innocent . . . only the innocent. . . ."

The soundlessness of that crying was terrible. Andreas rose, stroked the nape of her neck in passing, and went to the piano. Her eyes followed him in astonishment. Her tears dried up at once, she watched him as he sat there, on the piano stool, staring at the keys, his hands spread apprehensively, and across his forehead there was a terrible furrow, an anguished furrow.

He's forgotten me, she thought, he's forgotten me, how awful it is that they always forget us at the very moment when they are really themselves. He's not thinking about me any more, he'll never think about me any more. Tomorrow morning he will die in Stryy . . . and he'll waste no more thoughts on me.

He is the first and only one I've loved. The first. He is absolutely alone now. He is unbelievably sad and alone. That furrow across his forehead, it cuts him in two, his face is pale with terror, and he has spread his hands as if he had to grasp some dreadful animal. . . . If he could only play, if he could only play, he would be with me again. The first note will give him back to me. To me, to me, he belongs to me . . . he is my brother, I am three days older than he is. If he could only play. There's some monstrous cramp inside him, spreading his hands, turning him deathly pale, making him fearfully unhappy. There's nothing left of all I wanted to give him with my playing . . . with my story, there's nothing of all that with him now. It's all gone, he's alone now with his pain.

And indeed, when all at once he attacked the keys with a fierce rage in his face, he raised his eyes, and his eyes went straight to her. He smiled at her, and she had never seen such a happy face as that face of his above the black surface of the piano in the soft yellow lamplight. Oh how I love him, she thought. How happy he is, he's mine, here in this room till morning. . . .

She had imagined he would play something crazy, some wild piece by Tchaikovsky or Liszt or one of those glorious lilting Chopin pieces, because he had attacked the keys like a madman.

No, he played a sonatina by Beethoven. A delicate little piece, very tricky, and for a second she was afraid he would "mess it up." But he played very beautifully, very carefully, perhaps a shade too carefully, as if he did not trust his own strength. How tenderly he played, and she had never seen such a happy face as that soldier's face above the polished surface of the piano. He played the sonatina a little uncertainly, but purely, more purely than she had ever heard it, very clear and clean.

She hoped he would go on playing. It was wonderful; she had lain down on the sofa, where he had been lying, and she saw the cigarette gradually burning away in the ashtray: she longed to draw on it but dared not move; the slightest movement might destroy that music; and the best part of all was that very happy soldier's face above the black, shining surface of the piano. . . .

"No," he said with a laugh as he got to his feet. "There's not much left. It's no use. The fact is, you have to have studied, and I never did." He bent over her and dried her tears, and he was glad she had cried. "No," he said softly, "stay where you are. I was going to tell you my story too, remember?"

"Yes," she whispered. "Tell me, and give me some wine."

This is happiness, he thought, as he went to the closet. This is bliss, although I've just discovered that I'm no good at the piano. There's been no miracle. I haven't suddenly become a pianist. It's done with now, and yet I'm happy. He looked into the closet and asked over his shoulder: "Which would you like?"

"Red," she said with a smile, "a red one now."

He took a less slender bottle out of the closet, then he saw the sheet of paper and the pencil and studied the paper. At the top was something in Polish: that would be the matches; then came "Mosel" in German, and in front of that a Polish word no doubt meaning bottle. What charming handwriting she has, he thought, pretty, feminine handwriting, and under "Mosel" he wrote "Bordeaux," and below the Polish word for bottle he made two dots. "Did you really put it down?" she asked, smiling, as he poured the wine.

"Yes."

"You wouldn't even cheat a madame."

"Yes I would," he said, and he suddenly remembered Dresden

station, and the taste of Dresden station, painfully distinct, was in his mouth, and he saw the fat, red-faced lieutenant. "Yes I would, I once tricked a lieutenant." He told her the story. She laughed. "But that isn't so bad."

"Yes it is," he said, "it's very bad. I shouldn't have done that, I should have called out after him: I'm not deaf. I said nothing, because I have to die soon and because he yelled at me like that ... because I was full of pain. Besides, I was too lazy. Yes," he said softly, "I actually was too lazy to do it because it was so wonderful to have the taste of life in my mouth. I wanted to get it clear, I remember exactly, I thought: You must never let someone feel humiliated on your account, even if it's a brand-new lieutenant, not even if he has brand-new medals on his chest. You must never let that happen, I thought, and I can still see him walking off, embarrassed and smarting, crimson in the face, followed by his grinning flock of subordinates. I can see his fat arms and his pathetic shoulders. When I think of those pathetic, stupid shoulders of his I almost have to weep. But I was too lazy, just too lazy, to open my mouth. It wasn't even fear, just plain laziness. God, I thought, how beautiful life is after all, all these people milling about on the platform. One's going to his wife, the other to his girl, and that woman's going to her son, and it's autumn, how wonderful, and that couple over there going toward the barrier, this evening or tonight they'll be kissing under the soft trees down by the Elbe." He sighed. "I'll tell you all the people I've cheated!"

"Oh no," she said, "don't. Tell me something nice ... and pour me some more!" She laughed. "Who could you ever have cheated?"

"I'll tell you the truth. Everything I've stolen and all the people I've cheated. . . ." He poured more wine, they raised their glasses, and in that second while they looked at each other, smiling, over the rims of their glasses, he drew her lovely face deep within himself. I mustn't lose it, he thought, I must never lose it, she is mine.

I love him, she thought, I love him. . . .

"My father," he said quietly, "my father died from the effects of a serious wound that plagued him for three years after the war. I was a year old when he died. And my mother soon followed him. That's all I know about it. I learned about all this one day when I had to be told that the woman I had always thought of as my mother wasn't my mother at all. I grew up with an aunt, a sister of my mother's who had married an attorney. He made good money, but we were always terribly poor. He drank. I took it so much for granted that a man should come to the breakfast table with a thick head and in a foul temper that later on, when I got to know other men, fathers of my friends, it seemed to me they weren't men at all. That there were men who weren't stewed every evening, and who didn't make hysterical scenes every morning at breakfast, was something I couldn't conceive. A 'thing which is not,' as Swift's Houyhnhnms say. I thought we were born to be yelled at, that women were born to be yelled at, to grapple with bailiffs, to fight terrible pitched battles with shopkeepers and go off and open a new account somewhere else. My aunt was a genius. She was a genius at opening new accounts. When things were at their blackest she would become very quiet, take an aspirin, and dash off, and by the time she came back she had money. And I thought she was my mother; and I thought that fat bloated monster with burst blood vessels all over his cheeks was my respected begetter. His eyes had a yellowish tinge, and his breath reeked of beer, he stank like stale yeast. I thought he was my father. We lived in a very grand villa, with a maid and all that, and often my aunt didn't even have small change for a short streetcar ride. And my uncle was a famous attorney. Isn't that boring?" he asked abruptly, getting up to refill the glasses.

"No," she whispered, "no, go on." It took him only two seconds carefully to refill the slender glasses that stood on the coffee table, yet she took in his hands and the pale narrow face and thought, I wonder what he looked like all those years ago, when he was five or six years old or thirteen, sitting at that breakfast table. She had no trouble picturing that fat, drunken fellow grumbling about the jam because all he really wanted was some sausage. When they have a hangover, all they ever want is sausage. And the woman, frail perhaps, and that pale little fellow sitting there, very timid, almost too scared to eat or cough although the heavy cigar smoke caught at his throat; he would have liked to cough and didn't dare because that drunken fat monster would fly into a rage, because that famous attorney would lose control of himself at the sound of that child's cough. . . .

"Your aunt," she said, "what did she look like? Tell me exactly what your aunt looked like!"

"My aunt was very small and frail."

"Was she like your mother?"

"Yes, she was very much like my mother, to judge by the photographs. Later on, when I was older and knew about a lot of things, I used to think: How terrible it must be when he . . . when he embraces her, that hulking great fellow with his breath and the burst blood vessels all over his distended cheeks and his nose; she's forced to see them right up close, and those great yellow bleary eyes and everything. That picture haunted me for months, once I had thought of it. And all the time I thought it was my father, and I would torment myself all night long with the question: Why do they marry men like that? And. . . ."

"And you cheated her too, your aunt, didn't you?"

"Yes," he said. He was silent for a moment and looked past her eyes. "That was terrible. You know, when he was seriously ill at one time—liver, kidneys, heart, his insides were all shot, of course —he was in hospital, and we took a taxi there one Sunday morning because he was to have an operation. It was a glorious sunny day, and I was absolutely miserable. And my aunt cried terribly, and she kept whispering to me, begging me to pray for him to get well. She kept whispering this to me, and I had to promise her. And I didn't do it. I was nine, and by that time I knew he wasn't my father, and I didn't pray for him to get well. I just couldn't. I didn't pray for him not to get well. No, I stopped short at that idea. But as to praying for him to get well: no, that I didn't do. I

couldn't help thinking all the time how wonderful it would be if
... yes, I did think that. The house all to ourselves, and no more
scenes or anything ... and yet I had promised my aunt to pray for
him. I couldn't do it. The only thing I could think was: Why on
earth do they marry men like that?"

"Because they love them," Olina interrupted.

"Yes," he said in surprise, "you know, don't you? She did love
him, she had loved him, and she still loved him. At the time, of
course, as a young attorney, he had looked different; there was a
photo of him taken just after he passed his finals. Wearing one of
those godawful student's caps, remember? 1907. He looked different then, but only on the outside."

"How do you mean?"

"Just that—only on the outside. To me his eyes looked exactly
the same. Only his stomach wasn't that fat yet. But to me he
looked dreadful even as a young man in that photo. I would have
seen him the way he was going to look at forty-five, I wouldn't
have married him. And she still loved him, although he was a
wreck, although he tormented her, wasn't even faithful to her. She
loved him absolutely and unconditionally. I can't understand
it. . . ."

"You can't understand it?" He looked at her again in surprise.
She was sitting up now, had swung her legs down, her face was
close to his.

"You can't understand it?" she asked passionately.

"No," he said, astonished.

"Then you don't know what love is. Yes," she looked at him,
and suddenly he was afraid of that solemn, wholly altered face.
"Yes," she repeated. "Unconditionally! Love is always uncondi-
tional, you see. Haven't you," she murmured, "haven't you ever
loved a woman?"

He quickly closed his eyes. Again that deep, thrusting stab of
pain. That too, he thought, I have to tell her about that too.
There must be no secrets between us, and I had been hoping I
could keep that, that memory of an unknown face, hoping I could

keep that gift to myself and take it with me. His eyes remained closed, and there was silence. He was trembling in his anguish. No, he thought, let me keep it. That's my own most private possession, and for three and a half years it's been all I've had to live on . . . just that tenth of a second on the hill outside Amiens. Why did she have to thrust so deeply and unerringly into me? Why did she have to open up that carefully protected scar with one word, a word that pierces me like a probe, the probe of an unerring surgeon. . . .

So that's it, she thought. He loves someone else. He's trembling, he's spreading his hands and closing his eyes, and I've hurt him. The ones you love are the ones you're bound to hurt the most, that's the law of love. His pain is too great for tears. Some pain is so great that tears are powerless, she thought. Ah, why aren't I that other woman he loves? Why can't I transpose this soul and this body? There's nothing, nothing of myself that I want to keep, I would surrender my whole self to have only . . . only the eyes of that other woman. This last night before his death, the last night for me too because when he's gone I shall have ceased to care about anything . . . ah, if only I could have her eyelashes, give my whole self in exchange for her eyelashes. . . .

"Yes," he said softly. His voice was without emotion, the voice of someone on the brink of death. "Yes, I loved her so much I would have sold my soul to feel her mouth for just one second. I've only just realized this—now that you ask me. And perhaps that's why I was never to know her. I would have committed murder just to see the hem of her dress as she turned a corner. Just something, something real. And I prayed, I prayed for her every day. All lies and all self-deception, because I believed I loved only her soul. Only her soul! And I would have sold all those thousands of prayers for one single kiss from her lips. I've only just realized this." He rose suddenly to his feet, and she was glad his voice was human again, a human voice that suffered and lived. Again the thought came to her that he was alone now, that he was no longer thinking of her, he was alone again.

"Yes," he said into the room, "I believed it was only her soul that I loved. But what is a soul without a body, what is a human soul without a body? I couldn't desire her soul so passionately, with all the insane passion I was capable of, without longing for her just to smile at me at least once, once. God," he slashed the air with his hand, "always the hope, and nothing but the hope, that that soul might become flesh," he cried, "only the insane burden of hope! What's the time?" He turned on her and, although he spoke roughly and brusquely as if she were a servant girl, she was glad to see that at least he had not forgotten her presence. "Forgive me," he added swiftly, grasping her hand, but she had already forgiven him, she had forgiven him before it happened. She glanced at the clock and smiled. "Eleven." And she was filled with a great happiness, only eleven. Not yet midnight, not even midnight, how glorious, how lovely, how wonderful. She was as gay as a carefree child, jumped up and danced across the room: I'm dancing with you into heaven, the seventh heaven of love. . . .

He watched her, thinking: it's strange, really, that I can't be angry with her. Here I am, half-dead with pain, deathly sick, and she's dancing, although she has shared my pain, and I can't be angry, I can't. . . .

"You know what?" she asked, suddenly pausing. "We must have something to eat, that's what we need."

"No," he said, appalled. "No."

"Why not?"

"Because then you'd have to leave me. No, no," he cried out in anguish, "you mustn't leave me for a single second. Without you . . . without you . . . without you I can't go on living!"

"What?" she asked, without knowing which word her lips were forming, for a delirious hope had sprung up within her.

"That's right," he said softly, "you mustn't go away."

No, she thought, that's not it after all. I'm not the one he loves. And aloud she said: "I don't have to go away! There's food too in the closet."

How miraculous, that somewhere in a drawer of that closet

there should be cookies, and cheese wrapped in silver foil. What a glorious meal, cookies and cheese and wine. He didn't like his cigarette. The tobacco was dry, and it had a kind of foul army taste.

"Give me a cigar," he said, and needless to say there was a cigar there too. A whole box of cigars good enough for a major, all for the Lvov mortgage. It felt good to stand there on the soft carpet, watching Olina arrange the little snack on the coffee table with gentle, loving hands. When she had finished, she suddenly turned to him and looked at him with a smile: "You couldn't go on living without me?"

"No," he said, and his heart was so heavy he couldn't laugh, and he thought: I ought to add now: because I love you, and that would be true and it would not be true. If I said it I would have to kiss her, and that would be a lie, everything would be a lie, and yet I could say with a clear conscience: I love you, but I would have to give a long, long explanation, an explanation that I don't know myself yet. Always those eyes of hers, very gentle and loving and happy, the opposite of the eyes I desired... still desire... and he repeated, looking straight into her eyes: "I couldn't go on living without you," and now he was smiling. ...

At the very moment when they were raising their glasses to drink a toast to their birthdays or their wasted lives, at that very moment their hands began to tremble violently; they put down their glasses and looked at one another in dismay: there had been a knock at the door. ...

Andreas held back Olina's arm and slowly stood up. He strode to the door, taking only three seconds to reach it. So this is the end, he thought. They're taking her away from me, they don't want her to stay with me till morning. Time is still alive, and the world is turning. Willi and the blond fellow are each in bed with a girl somewhere in this house, that old woman is downstairs lying in wait for her money, the slot of her mouth always open, slightly open. What shall I do when I'm alone? I shan't even be able to pray, to go down on my knees. I can't live without her, because I do love her. They mustn't do that. ...

"Yes," he asked softly.

"Olina," came the madame's voice. "I have to speak to O-lina."

Andreas looked around, pale, aghast. I'll give up the five hours if only I can spend just one more half-hour with her. They can have her then. But I want to spend one more half-hour with her, and look at her, just look at her, maybe she'll play the piano again. Even if it's only, I'm dancing with you into heaven. . . .

Olina smiled at him, and he knew from that smile that she would stay with him whatever happened. And yet he was scared, and he knew now, as Olina quietly unlocked the door, that he did not want to part with this fear for her. That he loved this fear too. "Leave your hand in mine, at least," he whispered as she was going out, and she left her hand in his, and he heard her outside beginning to talk to the madame in hurried, heated Polish. The two women were locked in combat. The moneybox was doing battle with Olina. He anxiously scanned her eyes when she came back without closing the door. He did not let go of her hand. She had turned pale too, and he could see that her confidence was no longer very great. . . .

"The general's turned up. He's offering two thousand. He's furious. He must be raising the roof down there. D'you have any money left? We have to make up the difference, otherwise. . . ."

"Yes," he said; he hastily turned out his pockets, which still contained money he had won from Willi at cards. Olina twittered something in Polish through the door. "Hurry," she whispered. She counted the bills. "Three hundred, right? I haven't a thing! Not a thing!" she said frantically. "Yes I have, here's a ring, that's five hundred. It's not worth more than that. Eight hundred."

"My coat," said Andreas, "here it is."

Olina went to the door with the three hundred, the ring, and the coat. She was even less confident on her return.

"She reckons the coat's worth four, only four—no more. And the ring six, thank God for that, six. Thirteen hundred. Don't you have anything else? Hurry!" she whispered. "If he gets impatient and comes upstairs, we're sunk."

"My paybook," he said.

"Yes, let me have it. A genuine paybook is worth a lot."

"And my watch."

"Yes," she laughed nervously, "the watch. You still have a watch. Is it running?"

"No," he said.

Olina went to the door with the paybook and the watch. More excited Polish whispering. Andreas ran after her. "Here's a sweater," he called through the door, "a hand, a leg. Can't you use a human leg, a wonderful, superb human leg . . . a leg from an almost-innocent? Can't you use that? To make up the difference. Are you still short?" His voice was quite matter-of-fact, not excited, and he kept Olina's hand in his.

"No," came the madame's voice from outside. "But your boots. Your boots would make up the difference."

It's hard work, taking off one's boots. But he managed, just as he had managed to pull them on quickly when the Russians came roaring up to the position. He took off his boots and passed them out by way of Olina's small hand.

And the door was shut again. Olina stood before him, her face quivering. "I have nothing," she wept, "my clothes belong to the old woman. So does my body, and my soul—she doesn't want my soul. Only the Devil wants souls, and humans are worse than the Devil. Forgive me," she wept, "I have nothing."

Andreas drew her towards him and softly stroked her face. "Come," he whispered, "come, I'll make love to you. . . ." But she raised her face and smiled. "No," she whispered, "no, never mind, it's not important."

Again footsteps approached along the corridor, those confident, unswerving footsteps, but strangely enough they were no longer afraid. They exchanged smiles.

"Olina," the voice called outside the door.

More Polish twittering. Olina smiled at him over her shoulder: "When do you have to leave?"

"At four."

She closed the door, without locking it, came back, and said: "At four the general's car is coming to pick me up."

Her trembling hands had spilled wine over the cheese, so she cleared it away, gathered up the soiled tablecloth, and rearranged the things. The cigar had not gone out, thought Andreas, who was watching her. The world had nearly come to an end, but the cigar had not gone out, and her hands were quieter than ever. "Coming?"

Yes, he sat down opposite her, laid aside the cigar, and for a few minutes they looked past one another, in silence and almost blushing, because they were both terribly ashamed at the knowledge that they were praying, that they were both praying, here in this brothel, on this couch. . . .

"It's midnight now," she said as they began eating. It's Sunday now, thought Andreas, Sunday, and he abruptly set down his glass and the cookie he had just begun; a frightful cramp paralyzed his jaws and hands and seemed even to blind his eyes; I don't want to die, he thought and, without realizing it, he stammered, like a weeping child: "I . . . I don't want to die."

I must be mad to think I can smell paint so vividly . . . I was barely seven at the time they painted the garden fence: it was the first day of school holidays, and Uncle Hans was away, it had rained in the night, and now the sun was shining in that moist garden . . . it was so wonderful . . . so beautiful, and as I lay in bed I could distinctly smell the garden and the paint, for the painters had already started painting the fence green . . . and I was allowed to stay in bed a while . . . because school was out, Uncle Hans was away, and I was to get hot chocolate for breakfast, Aunt Marianne had promised me the night before because she had just opened a new account . . . whenever we opened a new account, a brand-new one, we began by buying something special. And that paint, I can smell it as plainly as anything, but I must be mad . . . there can't possibly be a smell of green paint here. That pale face across from me, that's Olina, a Polish prostitute and spy . . . nothing here in this room can smell so cruelly of paint and conjure up that day in my childhood so vividly. "I don't want to die," stammered his mouth. "I don't want to leave all this behind ... no one can force me to get onto that train going to ... Stryy, no one on earth. My God, maybe it would be a mercy if I did lose my mind. But don't let me lose it! No, no! Even though it hurts like hell to smell that green paint now, let me rather savor this pain than go mad ... and Aunt Marianne's voice telling me I can stay in bed a while ... since Uncle Hans is away. ..."

"What's that?" he asked, startled. Olina had risen, without his noticing it; she was sitting at the piano, and her lips were quivering in her pale face.

"Rain," she said softly, and it seemed to cost her an unspeakable effort to open her mouth, she hardly had the strength to nod toward the window.

Yes, that soft rushing sound that roused him with the power of a sudden burst of organ music ... that was rain ... it was raining in the brothel garden ... and on the treetops where he had seen the sun for the last time. "No!" he cried as Olina touched the keys, "no," but then he felt the tears, and he knew he had never cried before in his life ... these tears were life, a raging torrent formed from countless streams ... all flowing together and welling up into one agonizing outburst ... the green paint that smelled of holidays ... and the terrible corpse of Uncle Hans laid out in its coffin in the study, shrouded in the heavy air of candles ... many, many evenings with Paul and the hours of exquisite torment spent trying to play the piano ... school and war, war ... war, and the unknown face he had desired, had ... and in that blinding wet torrent there floated, like a quivering disk, pale and agonizing, the sole reality: Olina's face.

All this because of a few bars of Schubert, making it possible for me to cry as I have never cried in my life, to cry as maybe I only cried when I was born, when that dazzling light threatened to cut me in two. .... Suddenly a chord struck his ear, a chord that shook him to the depths of his being, it was Bach, yet she had never been able to play Bach. ...

It was like a tower that was spiraling upward from within, piling level upon level. The tower grew and pulled him with it, as if it had been hurled up from the bowels of the earth by a gushing spring that was fiercely shooting its way past the gloom of centuries into the light, into the light. An aching happiness filled him as, against his will yet knowingly and consciously, he was borne upward on level after level of that pure, upthrusting tower; as if borne on a cloud of fantasy, wreathed in what seemed a weightless, poignant felicity, he was yet made to experience all the effort and all the pain of the climber; this was spirit, this was clarity, little remained of human aberration; a fantastically clean, clear playing of compelling force. It was Bach, yet she had never been able to play Bach ... perhaps she wasn't playing at all ... perhaps it was the angels ... the angels of clarity, singing in towers each more ethereal and radiant than the last ... light, light, O God ... that light. ...

"Stop!" he cried out, and Olina's hands recoiled from the keys as if his voice had torn them away. ...

He rubbed his aching forehead, and he saw that the girl sitting there in the soft lamplight was not only startled by his voice: she was exhausted, she was weary, infinitely weary, the towers she had had to climb with her frail hands had been unimaginably high. She was just tired, the corners of her mouth twitched like those of a child that is too tired even to cry; her hair had loosened ... she was pale, and deep shadows encircled her eyes.

Andreas moved toward her, took her in his arms, and laid her on the sofa; she closed her eyes and sighed; gently, very gently she shook her head as if to say: just let me rest ... all I want is to rest a little. ... Peace, and it was good to see her fall asleep; her face sank to one side.

Andreas rested his head in his hands on the little table and was also aware of an infinite weariness. It's Sunday, he thought, one o'clock in the morning, three more hours to go, and I must not sleep, I will not sleep, I shall not sleep; and he looked at her ardently and tenderly. That pure, gentle, small, wan girlish face, now faintly smiling in the bliss of sleep. I must not sleep, thought Andreas, yet he could feel his weariness bearing relentlessly down on him. I must not sleep. God, don't let me fall asleep, let me look at her face.... I needed to come to this brothel in Lvov, I needed to come here to find out that there is such a thing as love without desire, the way I love Olina ... I must not fall asleep, I must look at that mouth ... that forehead and those exhausted, golden, delicate wisps of hair over her face and the dark shadows of indescribable exhaustion around her eyes. She played Bach, to the very limits of human capacity. I must not fall asleep ... it's cold ... the cruel hostility of the morning is already waiting behind the dark curtains of the night. It's cold, and I have nothing to cover her with ... I've flogged my coat, and we made a mess of the tablecloth ... it's lying around somewhere stained with wine. My tunic, I could put my tunic over her ... I could cover the open neck of her dress with my tunic, but even as he thought this he simply felt too tired to get up and take off his tunic ... I can't even lift my arm, and I must not fall asleep; I've still got so many things to do, so many things to do. Just let me rest here a bit with my arms on the table, then I'll get up and put my tunic over her, and I'll pray, pray, kneel by this couch that has seen so many sins, kneel by that pure face from which I had to learn that there is such a thing as love without desire ... I must not fall asleep ... no, no, I must not fall asleep. ...

His awakening gaze was like a bird that suddenly dies high up in the air in flight and plunges, plunges into the infinity of despair; but Olina's smiling eyes caught him as he fell. He had been desperately afraid that it was too late ... too late to hurry to the appointed place. Too late to hurry to the only rendezvous that mattered. Her smiling gaze caught him, and she answered the unspoken yet anguished question, saying softly:

"It's three-thirty ... don't worry!" And only now did he feel her light hand resting on his head.

Her face lay on the same level as his, and he hardly needed to move his head to kiss her. It's a pity, he thought, that I don't desire her, a pity that it's no sacrifice for me not to desire her, no sacrifice not to kiss her and not to long to sink down into that seemingly sullied womb. . . .

And he touched her lips with his, and there was nothing. They exchanged smiles of amazement. There was nothing. It was like an ineffectual bullet bouncing off armor of which they themselves were not aware.

"Come on," she said softly, "I'd better see you get something for your feet, hadn't I?"

"No," said Andreas, "don't leave me, you mustn't leave me for a single second. Never mind the shoes. I can just as well die in my socks, lots of men have died in their socks. Fled in panic when they were suddenly confronted by the Russians, and died wounded in the back, facing Germany, wounded in the back, the worst disgrace that could befall the Spartans. Many died like that, never mind the shoes, I'm so tired. . . ."

"No," she said, glancing at her watch. "I could have given up my watch, and you would have kept your boots. One always thinks one has no more to give, and I honestly had forgotten my watch. I'll trade my watch for your boots, we won't be needing it any more . . . or anything else."

"Or anything else," he repeated under his breath, and he raised his eyes and looked around the room, and for the first time he saw how pitiful it was, the ancient wallpaper and meager furniture: old armchairs over there by the window, and a dingy couch.

"Yes," Olina murmured, "I'm going to get you away. Don't look so scared!" She smiled, her eyes close to his white, tired face. "That car of the general's is a gift from heaven. Just trust me and believe me: no matter where I take you, it will be life. Do you believe me?" Andreas nodded in bewilderment, and she repeated, her face close to his as if in solemn entreaty: "No matter where I take you, it will be life. Trust me!" She clasped his head. "There are tiny little places in the Carpathians where no one will ever find us. A few houses, a little chapel, no partisans even. I used to go to one, I would try to say a few prayers and play on the priest's old baby grand. D'you hear?" She sought his eyes, but his gaze was still roaming the soiled wallpaper against which bottles had been smashed and sticky fingers had been wiped. "We'll have music, d'you hear?"

"Yes," he groaned. "But the others, those other two. I can't leave them now. It's impossible."

"That's out!"

"And the driver," he asked, "what did you intend doing with the driver?" They stood face to face, and there was something like hostility between their eyes. Olina tried to smile. "Starting today," she said softly, "starting today I'm not going to hand over any more innocent men to the executioner. You must trust me! It wouldn't have been too difficult just with you. Simply have the driver stop somewhere, and then we'd run away ... disappear! Free, just disappear! But with your two friends it won't work."

"All right, then you'll have to leave me. No," he raised his arm to silence her. "I'm simply telling you there's to be no bargaining. It's either—or. You must understand, you must," he said, looking deep into her serious eyes, "because you loved them, some of them, didn't you? You must understand."

Slowly, heavily, Olina's head drooped. Andreas did not realize this was a nod until she said: "All right, I'll try...."

While Olina, her hand on the door, waited for him, he cast one more look around that dirty little Polish bar, then followed her out into the ill-lit corridor. But the room, the bar, was palatial compared with that corridor in the early morning. That mocking, chill, dingy half-light in a brothel corridor at four in the morning. Those doors, like doors in a barracks, all alike. All equally shabby. And that dreary, dreary squalor.

"In here," said Olina. She pushed open one of the doors and there was her room: scantily furnished with the necessities of her trade; a bed, a small table and two chairs, and a washbasin on a spindly, three-legged stand, next to the stand a pitcher, and a small closet against the wall. Only the bare necessities, like in a barracks....

It was all so unreal, sitting on the bed and watching Olina wash her hands, take her shoes out of the closet, remove her red slippers, and put on her shoes. Oh yes, there was a mirror too, for her to refurbish her beauty. Those traces of tears must be wiped away and fresh powder put on, there being nothing ghastlier than a red-eyed whore. Lipstick and eyebrow pencil had to be reapplied, nails cleaned, and all this was carried out as deftly as a soldier preparing for the alert.

"You must trust me," she said in a chatty, matter-of-fact tone. "I'm going to get you away, d'you hear? It won't be easy if you insist on taking along the other two, but it can be done. A lot can be done. . . ."

Don't let me go out of my mind, Andreas prayed, don't let me go out of my mind in this brutal attempt to grasp reality. The whole thing is impossible, this room in a brothel, shabby and faded in the gray dawn, full of revolting smells, and that girl over there by the mirror, crooning softly, crooning to me, while her fingers skillfully touch up the red on her lips. This is impossible, and this tired heart of mine that wishes for nothing, and these limp senses of mine that desire nothing, neither to smoke nor eat nor drink, and my soul that is deprived of all longing and wants only to sleep, to sleep. . . .

Maybe I'm already dead. Who can grasp all this, these bed-clothes I automatically pushed aside, the way one always does if one has to sit down on a bed, these sheets that are not dirty and yet not clean, these horribly mysterious sheets, not dirty and not clean. . . and that girl over there by the mirror, busy coloring her eyebrows, black, fine-drawn eyebrows on a pale forehead.

"A-hunting and fishing we will go, like in the good old days! D'you know that one?" asked Olina with a smile. "It's a German poem. 'Archibald Douglas.' It's about a man who was exiled from his native land. And we Poles, we have been exiled *into* our native land, into the midst of one's native land; no one knows what that means. Born 1920. A-hunting and fishing we will go, like in the good old days. Listen!" She was actually crooning that old ballad, and it seemed to Andreas that now the limit had been reached, a gray cold morning in a Polish brothel, and a ballad, set to music by Löwe, being crooned for his benefit. . . .

"Olina!" came that level voice again outside the door.

"Yes?"

"The bill. Hand it out to me, please. And get ready to leave, the car's at the door. . . ."

So this is the reality, the girl handing out the bill through the door, with tapering fingers, a bill on which everything had been written down, beginning with the matches, which he still had in his pocket, those matches he had been given yesterday evening at six. That's how fantastically fast time goes, this time we cannot grasp, and I've done nothing, nothing, in that time, and there's nothing I can do but follow this refurbished beauty, down the stairs to settle the account. . . .

"These Polish tarts," said Willi, "simply terrific! That's what I call passion, eh?"

"Yes."

The room downstairs was just as meagerly furnished. A few rickety chairs, a bench, a threadbare carpet that looked like frayed paper, and Willi was smoking. He was completely unshaven and was searching his luggage for more cigarettes.

"You were certainly the most expensive, my lad. My bill wasn't much less either. But this young friend of ours, he cost almost nothing. Hey there!" He dug the blond fellow, who was still asleep, in the ribs. "A hundred and forty-six marks." He snorted with laughter. "It seems he actually did sleep with the girl, literally slept. There were two hundred marks left over, so I slid them under the door of his girl's room, as a tip, see? Because she made him happy so cheaply. D'you happen to have a cigarette left?"

"Yes."

"Thanks."

What an incredibly long time Olina was taking to settle the account, over there in the madame's office, at four in the morning.

That was an hour when the whole world slept. Even in the girls' rooms all was quiet, and downstairs in the big reception room it was quite dark. The door from which the music had come was dark, and one could see and smell that dark room. The only sound was the discreet engine purring away outside. Olina was behind that reddish door, and it was all reality. It had to be reality. . . .

"So you think this general's whore-car will take us too?"

"Yes!"

"Hm. A Maybach, I can tell by the engine. Nifty job. Mind if I go ahead and speak to the driver? He's sure to be a noncom."

Willi shouldered his luggage and opened the door, and there it really was, the night, the gray-veiled night and the dim headlamps of a waiting car out there by the entrance. As coldly and inescapably real as all war-nights, full of cold menace, full of horrible mockery; out there in the dirty holes . . . in the cellars . . . in the many, many towns cowering in fear . . . summoned up, those appalling nights that at four in the morning have achieved their most deadly power, those ghastly, indescribably terrible war-nights. One of these was there outside the door, a night full of terror, a night with no home, not even the smallest, smallest warm corner to hide in . . . those nights that had been summoned up by the resounding voices. . . .

So she really believes she can rescue me. Andreas smiled. She believes it is possible to slip through the fine mesh of this net. This child believes there is such a thing as escape . . . she believes she will find ways to avoid Stryy. That word has been cradled within me since my birth. It has lain deep, deep down, unacknowledged and unawakened; it was with me when I was still a child, and maybe a dark shudder rippled through me, many years ago in school, when we learned about the foothills of the Carpathians and I read the words Galicia and Lvov and Stryy on the map, in the middle of that yellow-white patch. And I've forgotten that shudder. Maybe, often and often, the barb of death and summons was cast into me without ever catching in anything down there, and only that tiny little word had been set up and saved up for it, and finally the barb caught. . . .

Stryy . . . that tiny little word, terrible and bloody, has surfaced and expanded into an ominous cloud that now overshadows everything. And she believes she will find ways of avoiding Stryy. . . .

Besides, her promise doesn't attract me. I'm not attracted by that little village in the Carpathians where she proposes to play on the priest's piano. I'm not attracted by that seeming security . . . all we have is promises and pledges and a dark uncertain horizon over which we have to plunge to find security. . . .

At last the door opened, and Andreas was surprised by the rigid pallor of Olina's face. She had put on a fur coat, a charming little cap was perched on her beautiful loose hair, and there was no watch on her wrist, for he was wearing his boots again. The account had been settled. The old woman was smiling so mysteriously. Her hands were folded across her desiccated body, and after the soldiers had picked up their luggage and Andreas was opening the door she smiled and uttered a single word: "Stryy," she said. Olina did not hear it, she was already outside.

"I too," said Olina in a low voice as they sat side by side in the car, "I too am condemned. I too have betrayed my country because I spent all last night with you instead of sounding out the general." She took his hand and smiled at him: "But don't forget what I told you: no matter where I take you, it will be life. Right?"

"Right," said Andreas. The whole night ran through his memory like a smooth thread being reeled off, yet there was one knot that left him no peace. Stryy, the old woman had said, and how can she know that Stryy . . . he hadn't said anything about it to her, and still less would Olina have mentioned that word. . . .

So this is supposed to be reality: a discreetly purring car with its subdued headlamps lighting up the nameless road. Trees, and now and again houses, all saturated with gray darkness. In front of him those two necks, encircled by sergeants' braid almost identical, solid German necks, and the cigarette smoke drifting back from the driver's seat. Beside him the blond fellow, sleeping like a child worn out by playing, and on the right the steady gentle contact with Olina's fur coat and the smooth thread of the memory of that lovely night sliding by, faster and faster, and always stopping short at that strange knot, at the place where the old woman had said: Stryy....

Andreas leaned forward to look at the softly lit clock on the dashboard, and he saw it was six o'clock, just on six. An icy shock ran through him, and he thought: God, God, what have I done with my time, I've done nothing, I've never done anything, I must pray, pray for them all, and at this very moment Paul is walking up the altar steps at home and beginning to recite: Introibo. And on his own lips too the word began to form: Introibo.

But now an invisible giant hand passed over the softly gliding car, a terrible, silent stirring of the air, and into this silence came Willi's dry voice, asking: "Where are you taking us, bud?" "To Stryy!" said a disembodied voice.

And then the car was slashed by two raging knives that rasped with savage hatred, one from the front, the other from behind, tearing into that metal body which reared and turned, filled with the shriek of fear of its occupants. . . .

In the silence that followed there was no sound but the passionate devouring of the flames.

My God, thought Andreas, are they all dead? . . . and my legs . . . my arms, is only my head left? . . . is no one there? . . . I'm lying on this bare road, on my breast lies the weight of the world, so heavily that I can find no words to pray. . . .

Am I crying? he thought suddenly, for he could feel something moist running down his cheeks: no, something was dripping onto his cheeks; and in that ashen morning light, which was still without the yellow mildness of the sun, he saw that Olina's hand was hanging down over his head from a fragment of the car, and that blood was dripping onto his face from her hands, and he was past knowing that now he was really beginning to cry. . . .

Catalog

If you are interested in a list of fine Paperback
books, covering a wide range of subjects
and interests, send your name and address,
requesting your free catalog, to:

McGraw-Hill Paperbacks
1221 Avenue of Americas
New York, N.Y. 10020